F·A·R
FUTURES

F·A·R
FUTURES

EDITED BY

GREGORY
BENFORD

TOR®

A TOM DOHERTY ASSOCIATES BOOK / NEW YORK

FAR FUTURES

Edited by David G. Hartwell

A Tor Book
Published by Tom Doherty Associates, Inc.
175 Fifth Avenue
New York, N.Y. 10010

Tor Books on the World-Wide Web:
http://www.tor.com

Tor® is a registered trademark of Tom Doherty Associates, Inc.

Library of Congress Cataloging-in-Publication Data

Far futures / edited by Gregory Benford.
      p. cm.
   "A Tom Doherty Associates Book"
   Contents: Genesis / Poul Anderson—At the eschaton / Charles Sheffield—For White Hill / Joe Haldeman—Judgment engine / Greg Bear—Historical crisis / Donald Kingsbury.
   ISBN 0-312-85639-3 (hardcover)
   1. Science fiction, American.   I. Benford, Gregory, 1941– .
   PS648.S3F36   1995
   813'.0876208—dc20   95-35365
                                CIP

First edition: December 1995

Printed in the United States of America

0 9 8 7 6 5 4 3 2 1

COPYRIGHT ACKNOWLEDGMENTS

For Arthur C. Clarke

CONTENTS

INTRODUCTION

LOOKING LONG

LITTLE SCIENCE FICTION deals with truly grand perspectives in time. Most stories and novels envision people much like ourselves, immersed in cultures that quite resemble ours, and inhabiting worlds that are foreseeable extensions of places we now know. Such landscapes are, of course, easier to envision, more comfortable to the reader, and simpler for the writer; one can simply mention everyday objects, letting them set the interior stage in the reader's mind.

Yet some of our field's greatest works concern vast perspectives in time, eerie landscapes and epochs. Most of Olaf Stapledon's novels (*Star Maker, Last and First Men*) are set against such immense backdrops. Arthur Clarke's *Against the Fall of Night* opens over a billion years in our future. These works have remained in print many decades, partly because they are rare attempts to "look long"—to see ourselves against the scale of evolution itself.

Indeed, H. G. Wells wrote *The Time Machine* in part as a reaction to the Darwinian ideas that had swept the intellectual world of comfortable England. He conflated evolution with a Marxist imagery of racial class separation, notions that could only play out on the scale of millions of years. His doomed crab scuttling on a reddened beach was the first great image of the far future.

Similarly, Stapledon and the young Clarke wrote in the dawn of modern cosmology, shortly after Hubble's discovery of universal expansion

implied a startlingly large age of the universe. Cosmologists then believed this to be about two billion years. From better measurements, we
now think it to be at least five times that. In any case, it was so enormous
a time that pretensions of human importance seemed grotesque, even
laughable. We have been around less than a thousandth of the universe's
age. Much has gone before us, and even more will follow.

In recent decades there have been conspicuously few attempts to
approach such perspectives in literature. This is curious, for such dimensions afford sweeping vistas, genuine awe. Probably most writers find
the severe demands too daunting. One must understand biological evolution, the physical sciences, and much else—all the while shaping a
moving human story, which may not even involve humans as we now
know them. Yet there is a continuing audience for such towering perspectives.

This anthology collects original novellas that directly attack the very
long view. In commissioning these works, I set a boundary of at least a
thousand years in our future, while encouraging the authors to venture
much further—a billion years was quite all right.

Further, the authors have taken a rigorously scientific view of such
grand panoramas, for they are all from the "hard"-science-fiction community. You'll find no *fin de siècle*, "bored parties at the end of time"
narratives here, no lurid "super science" that rings hollow. But they are
not narrow in focus, either. These stories are scientifically plausible and
address the very largest issues that arise from our modern knowledge of
cosmology, astronomy, evolution and biology. "Thinking long" means
"thinking big."

We are tied to time, immense stretches of it. Our DNA differs from
that of chimps by only 1.6 percent, a point lovingly detailed in Jared Diamond's *The Third Chimpanzee*. We are a hairsbreadth from the jungle,
a third variety of chimp. A zoologist from Alpha Centauri would classify
us without hesitation along with the common chimp of tropical Africa
and the pygmy chimp of Zaire. Most of that 1.6 percent may well be
junk, too, of no genetic importance, so the significant differences are
even smaller.

We carry genetic baggage from far back in lost time. We diverged
genetically from the Old World monkeys about thirty million years ago,
from gorillas about ten million years ago, and from the other chimps
about seven million years ago. Only forty thousand years ago did *we* appear—if one means our present form, which differs in shape and style
greatly from our ancestor Neanderthals. We roved farther, made finer
tools, and when we moved into Neanderthal territory, the outcome was
clear; within a short while, no more Neanderthals.

No other large animal is native to all continents and breeds in all habitats, from rain forests to deserts to the poles. Among the unique abilities that we proudly believe led to our success, we seldom credit our propensity to kill each other and our habit of destroying our environment—yet there are evolutionary arguments that these were valuable to us once, leading to pruning of our genes and ready use of resources.

These same traits now threaten our existence. They also imply that, if we last into the far future, those deep elements in us will make for high drama, rueful laughter, triumph and tragedy.

While we have surely been shaped by our environment, our escape from bondage to our natural world is the great theme of civilization. How will this play out on the immense scale of many millennia? The environment will surely change, both locally on the surface of the Earth, and among the heavens. We shall change with it.

We shall probably meet competition from other worlds, and may fall from competition to a Darwinian doom, as Joe Haldeman depicts in his novella. Nature plays no favorites. We could erect immense empires and play Godlike with vast populations, as Donald Kingsbury explores. And surely we could tinker with the universe in ingenious ways, the inquisitive chimpanzee wrestling whole worlds to suit his desires.

Once we gain great powers, we can confront challenges undreamed of by Darwin. The universe as a whole is our ultimate opponent.

In the very long run, the astrologers may turn out to be right: our fates may be determined by the stars. For they are doomed.

Stars are immense reservoirs of energy, dissipating their energy stores into light as quickly as their bulk allows. Our own star is 4.5 billion years old, almost halfway through its eleven-billion-year life span. After its benign era, it shall begin to burn heavier and heavier elements at its core, growing hotter. Its atmospheric envelope of already incandescent gas shall heat and swell. From a mild-mannered, yellow-white star it shall bloat into a reddened giant, swallowing first Mercury, then Venus, then Earth and perhaps Mars. H. G. Wells foresaw in *The Time Machine* a dim sun, with a giant crablike thing scuttling across a barren beach. While evocative, this isn't what astrophysics now tells us. But as imagery, it remains a striking reflection upon the deep problem that the far future holds—the eventual meaning of human action.

About 4.5 billion years from now, our sun will rage a hundred times brighter. Half a billion years further on, it will be between five hundred and a thousand times more luminous, and seventy percent larger in radius. The Earth's temperature depends only weakly on the sun's luminosity (varying as the one-fourth root), so by then our crust will roast at about 1,400 degrees Kelvin; room temperature is 300 Kelvin.

The oceans and air will have boiled away, leaving barren plains beneath an angry sun that covers thirty-five degrees of the sky.

What might humanity—however transformed by natural selection, or by its own hand—do to save itself? Sitting farther from the fire might work. Temperature drops inversely with the square of distance, so Jupiter will be cooler by a factor of 2.3, Saturn by 3.1. But for a sun five hundred times more luminous than now, the Jovian moons will still be 600 degrees Kelvin (K), and Saturn's about 450 K. Uranus might work, 4.4 times cooler, a warm but reasonable 320 K. Neptune will be a brisk 255 K. What strange lives could transpire in the warmed, deep atmospheres of those gas giants?

Still, such havens will not last. When the sun begins helium burning in earnest, it will fall in luminosity, and Uranus will become a chilly 200 K. Moving inward to Saturn would work, for it will then be at 300 K, balmy shirtsleeve weather—if we have arms by then.

The bumpy slide downhill for our star will see the sun's luminosity fall to merely a hundred times the present value, when helium burning begins, and the Earth will simmer at 900 K. After another fifty million years—how loftily astrophysicists can toss off these immensities!—as further reactions alter in the sun's core, it will swell into a red giant again. It will blow off its outer layers, unmasking the dense, brilliant core that will evolve into a white dwarf. Earth will be seared by the torrent of escaping gas, and bathed in piercing ultraviolet light. The white-hot core will then cool slowly.

As the sun eventually simmers down, it will sink to a hundredth of its present luminosity. Then even Mercury will be a frigid 160 K, and Earth will be a frozen corpse at 100 K. The solar system, once a grand stage, will be a black relic beside a guttering campfire.

To avoid this fate, intelligent life can tinker—at least for a while—with stellar burning. Our star will get into trouble because it will eventually pollute its core with the heavier elements that come from burning hydrogen. In a complex cycle, hydrogen fuses and leaves assorted helium, lithium, carbon, and other elements. With all its hydrogen burned up at its core, where pressures and temperatures are highest, the sun will begin fusing helium. This takes higher temperatures, which the star attains by compressing under gravity. Soon the helium runs out. The next heavier element fuses. Carbon burns until the star enters a complex, unstable regime leading to swelling. (For other stars than ours, there could even be explosions [supernovas] if their mass is great enough.)

To stave off this fate, a cosmic engineer need only note that at least ninety percent of the hydrogen in the star is still unburned when the cycle turns in desperation to fusing helium. The star's oven lies at the core, and hydrogen is too light to sink down into it.

Envision a great spoon that can stir the elements in a star, mixing hydrogen into the nuclear ash at the core. The star could then return to its calmer, hydrogen-fusing reaction.

No spoon of matter could possibly survive the immense temperatures there, of course. But magnetic fields can move mass through their rubbery pressures. The sun's surface displays this, with its magnetic arches and loops that stretch for thousands of kilometers, tightly clasping hot plasma into tubes and strands.

If a huge magnetic paddle could reach down into the sun's core and stir it, the solar life span could extend to perhaps a hundred billion years. To do this requires immense currents, circulating over coils larger than the sun itself.

What "wires" could support such currents, and what battery would drive them? Such cosmic engineering is beyond our practical comprehension, but it violates no physical laws. Perhaps, with five billion years to plan, we can figure a way to do it. In return, we would extend the lifetime of our planet tenfold.

To fully use this extended stellar lifetime, we would need strategies for capturing more sunlight than a planet can. Freeman Dyson envisioned breaking up worlds into small asteroids, each orbiting its star in a shell of many billions of small worldlets. These could in principle capture nearly all the sunlight. We could conceivably do this to the Earth, then the rest of the planets.

Of course, the environmental impact report for such engineering would be rather hefty. This raises the entire problem of what happens to the Earth while all these stellar agonies go on. Even if we insure a mild, sunny climate, there are long-term troubles with our atmosphere.

Current thinking holds that the big, long-term problem we face is loss of carbon dioxide from our air. This gas, the food of the plants, gets locked up in rocks. Photosynthetic organisms down at the very base of the food chain extract carbon from air, cutting the life chain.

We might fix this by bioengineering organisms that return carbon dioxide. Then we would need to worry about the slow brightening of our sun, which would make our surface temperature about 80 degrees Centigrade in 1.5 billion years. Compensating for this by increasing our cloud cover, say, would work for a while. Poul Anderson sets his novella on an Earth cloud-shrouded and warming, heading for trouble.

A cloud blanket will work for a while. Still, we continually lose hydrogen to space, evaporated away at the top of the atmosphere. Putting water clouds up to block the sunlight means that they, too, will get boiled away. Even with such measures, liquid water on Earth would evaporate in about 2.5 billion years. Without oceans, volcanoes would be the major source for new atmospheric elements, and we would evolve a climate much like that of Venus.

All this assumes that we don't find wholly new ways of getting around planetary problems. I suspect that we crafty chimpanzees probably shall, though. We like to tinker and we like to roam. Though some will stay to fiddle with the Earth, the sun, and the planets, some will move elsewhere.

After all, smaller stars will live longer. The class called M dwarfs, dim and red and numerous, can burn steady and wan, for up to a hundred billion years, without any assistance. Then even they will gutter out. Planets around such stars will have a hard time supporting life, because any world close enough to the star to stay warm will also be tide-locked, one side baked and the other freezing. Still, they might provide temporary abodes for wandering primates, or for others.

Eventually, no matter what stellar engine we harness, all the hydrogen gets burned. Similar pollution problems beset even the artificially aged star, now completely starved of hydrogen. It seethes, grows hotter, sears its planets, then swallows them.

There may be other adroit dodges available to advanced life-forms, such as using the energy of supernovas. These are brute mechanisms, and later exploding stars can replenish the interstellar clouds of dust and gas, so that new stars can form—but not many. On average, matter gets recycled in about four billion years in our galaxy. Our own planet's mass is partly recycled stellar debris from the first galactic supernova generation. This cycle can go on until about twenty billion years pass, when only a ten-thousandth of the interstellar medium will remain. Dim red stars will glow in the spiral arms, but the great dust banks will have been trapped into stellar corpses.

So unavoidably, the stars are as mortal as we. They take longer, but they die.

For its first fifty billion years, the universe will brim with light. Gas and dust will still fold into fresh suns. For an equal span the stars would linger. Beside reddening suns, planetary life will warm itself by the waning fires that herald stellar death.

Sheltering closer and closer to stellar warmth, life could take apart whole solar systems, galaxies, even the entire Virgo cluster of galaxies, all to capture light. In the long run, life must take everything apart and use it, to survive.

To ponder futures beyond that era, we must discuss the universe as a whole.

Modern cosmology is quite different from the physics of the Newtonian worldview, which dreamed uneasily of a universe that extended forever but was always threatened by collapse. Nothing countered the drawing-in of gravity except infinity itself. Though angular momentum will keep a galaxy going for a great while, collisions can cancel that. Objects hit each other and mutually plunge toward the gravitating center. Physicists of the Newtonian era thought that maybe there simply had not been enough time to bring about the final implosion. Newton, troubled by this, avoided cosmological issues.

Given enough time, matter will seek its own kind, stars smacking into each other, making greater and greater stars. This will go on even after the stars gutter out.

When a body meets a body, coming through the sky . . . Stars will inevitably collide, meet, merge. All the wisdom and order of planets and suns will finally compress into the marriage of many stars, plunging down the pit of gravity to become black holes. For the final fate of nearly all matter shall be the dark pyre of collapse.

Galaxies are as mortal as stars. In the sluggish slide of time, the spirals that had once gleamed with fresh brilliance will be devoured by ever-growing black holes. Inky masses will blot out whole spiral arms of dim red. The already massive holes at galactic centers will swell from their billion-stellar-mass sizes at present, to chew outward, gnawing without end.

From the corpses of stars, collisions will form either neutron stars or black holes, within about a thousand billion years (in exponential notation, 10^{12} years). Even the later and longest-lived stars cannot last beyond 10^{14} years. Collisions between stars will strip away all planets in 10^{15} years.

Blunt thermodynamics will still command, always seeking maximum disorder. In 10^{17} years, the last white dwarf stars will have cooled to be utterly black dwarfs, temperatures about 5 degrees Kelvin (Absolute). In time, even hell would freeze over.

Against an utterly black sky, shadowy cinders of stars will glide. Planets, their atmospheres frozen out into waveless lakes of oxygen, will glide in meaningless orbits, warmed by no ruby star glow. The universal clock would run down to the last tick of time.

But the universe is no static lattice of stars. It grows. The Big Bang would be better termed the Enormous Emergence, space-time snapping into existence intact and whole, of a piece. Then it grew, the fabric of space lengthening as time increased.

With the birth of space-time came its warping by matter, each wedded to the other until time eternal. An expanding universe cools, just as a gas does. The far future will freeze, even if somehow life manages to find fresh sources of power.

Could the expansion ever reverse? This is the crucial unanswered riddle in cosmology. If there is enough matter in our universe, eventually gravitation will win out over the expansion. The "dark matter" thought to infest the relatively rare, luminous stars we see could be dense enough to stop the universe's stretching of its own space-time. This density is related to how old the universe is.

We believe the universe is somewhere between eight and sixteen billion years old. The observed rate of expansion (the Hubble constant) gives eight billion, in a simple, plausible model. The measured age of the oldest stars gives sixteen billion.

This difference, I believe, arises from our crude knowledge of how to fit our mathematics to our cosmological data; I don't think it's a serious problem. Personally I favor the higher end of the range, perhaps twelve to fourteen billion. We also have rough measures of the deceleration rate of the universal expansion. These can give (depending on cosmological, mathematical models) estimates of how long a dense universe would take to expand, reverse, and collapse back to a point. At the extremes, this gives between twenty-seven billion and at least a hundred billion years before the Big Crunch. If we do indeed live in a universe that will collapse, then we are bounded by two singularities, at beginning and end. No structure will survive that future singularity. Freeman Dyson found this a pessimistic scenario and so refused to consider it.

A closed universe seems the ultimate doom. In all cosmological models, if the mass density of the universe exceeds the critical value, gravity inevitably wins. This is called a "closed" universe, because it has finite spatial volume, but no boundary. It is like a three-dimensional analogue of a sphere's surface. A bug on a ball can circumnavigate it, exploring all its surface and coming back to home, having crossed no barrier. So a starship could cruise around the universe and come home, having found no edge.

A closed universe starts with a big bang (an initial singularity) and expands. Separation between galaxies grows linearly with time. Eventually the universal expansion of space-time will slow to a halt. Then a contraction will begin, accelerating as it goes, pressing galaxies closer together. The photons rattling around in this universe will increase in frequency, the opposite of the redshift we see now. Their blueshift means that the sky will get brighter in time. Contraction of space-time shortens wavelengths, which increases light energy.

Though stars will still age and die as the closed universe contracts, the background light will blueshift. No matter if life burrows into deep caverns, in time the heat of this light will fry it. Freeman Dyson remarked that the closed universe gave him "a feeling of claustrophobia, to imagine our whole existence confined within a box." He asked, "Is it conceivable that by intelligent intervention, converting matter into radiation to flow purposefully on a cosmic scale, we could break open a closed universe and change the topology of spacetime so that only a part of it would collapse and another would expand forever? I do not know the answer to this question."

The answer seems to be that once collapse begins, a deterministic universe allows no escape for pockets of space-time. Life cannot stop the squeezing.

Some have embraced this searing death, when all implodes toward a point of infinite temperature. Frank Tipler of Tulane University sees it as a great opportunity. In those last seconds, collapse will not occur at the same rate in all directions. Chaos in the system will produce "gravitational shear," which drives temperature differences. Drawing between these temperature differences, life can harness power for its own use.

Of course, such life will have to change its form to use such potentials; it will need hardier stuff than blood and bone. Ceramic-based forms could endure, or vibrant, self-contained plasma clouds—any tougher structure might work, as long as it can code information.

This most basic definition of life, the ability to retain and manipulate information, means that the substrate supporting this does not matter, in the end. Of course, the *style* of thought of a silicon web feasting on the slopes of a volcano won't be that of a shrewd primate fresh from the veldt, but certain common patterns can transfer.

Such life-forms might be able to harness the compressive, final energies. Charles Sheffield's story in this volume revolves around the allure of that distant end, the Omega Point. Frank Tipler's *The Physics of Immortality* makes a case that a universal intelligence at the Omega Point will then confer a sort of immortality, by carrying out the computer simulation of all possible past intelligences. All possible earlier "people" will be resurrected, he thinks. This bizarre notion shows how cosmology blends into eschatology, the study of the ultimate fate of things, particularly of souls.

I, too, find this scenario of final catastrophe daunting. Suppose, then, the universe is not so dense that it will ever reverse its expansion. Then we can foresee a long, toiling twilight.

Life based on solid matter will struggle to survive. To find energy, it will have to ride herd on and merge black holes themselves, force them to emit bursts of gravitational waves. In principle these waves can be harnessed, though of course we don't know how as yet. Only such fusions could yield fresh energy in a slumbering universe.

High civilizations will rise, no doubt, mounted on the carcass of matter itself—the ever-spreading legions of black holes. Entire galaxies will turn from reddening lanes of stars into swarms of utterly dark gravitational singularities, the holes. Only by moving such masses, by extracting power through magnetic forces and the slow gyre of dissipating orbits, could life rule the dwindling resources of the ever-enlarging universe. Staying warm shall become the one great Law.

Dyson has argued that, in principle, the perceived time available to living forms can be made infinite. In this sense, immortality of a kind could mark the cold, stretching stages of the universal death.

This assumes that we know all the significant physics, of course. Almost certainly, we do not. Greg Bear's story occurs at an end point of time itself, when the universe is closing down all prospects, for physical reasons that the viewpoint human cannot fathom. The universe appears to be still expanding and cooling, but duration itself is ending as a category. Bizarre events unfold.

This is a useful fictional reminder that our chimpanzee worldview may simply be unable to comprehend events on such vast time scales. Equally, though, chimpanzees will try, and keep trying.

Since Dyson's pioneering work on these issues, yet more physics has emerged, which we must take into account. About his vision of a swelling universe, its life force spent, hangs a great melancholy.

For matter itself is doomed, as well. Even the fraction that escapes the holes, and learns to use them, if mortal. Its basic building block, the proton, decays. This takes unimaginably long—current measurements suggest a proton lifetime of more than 10^{33} years. But decay seems inevitable, the executioner's sword descending with languid grace.

Even so, something still survives. Not all matter dies, though with the proton gone everything we hold dear will disintegrate, atoms and animals alike. After the grand operas of mass and energy have played out their plots, the universal stage will clear to reveal the very smallest.

The tiniest of particles—the electron and its antiparticle, the positron—shall live on, current theory suggests. No process of decay can find purchase on their infinitesimal scales, lever them apart into smaller fragments. The electron shall dance with its anti-twin in swarms: the lightest of all possible plasmas.

By the time these are the sole players, the stage will have grown enormously. Each particle will find its nearest neighbor to be a full light-year away. They will have to bind together, sharing cooperatively, storing data in infinitesimally thin currents and charges. A single entity would have to be the size of a spiral arm, of a whole galaxy. Vaster than empires, and more slow.

Plasmas held together by magnetic and electric fields are incredibly difficult to manage, rather like building a cage for Jell-O out of rubber bands. But in principle, physics allows such magnetic loops and glowing spheres. We can see them in the short-lived phenomena of ball lightning. More spectacularly, they occur on the sun, in glowing magnetic arches that can endure for weeks, a thousand kilometers high.

Intelligence could conceivably dwell in such wispy magnetic consorts. Communication will take centuries . . . but to the slow thumping of the universal heart, that will be nothing.

If life born to brute matter can find a way to incorporate itself into the electron-positron plasma, then it can last forever. This would be the last step in a migration from the very early forms, like us: rickety assemblies of water in tiny compartment cells, hung on a lattice of moving calcium rods.

Life and intelligence will have to alter, remaking basic structures from organic molecules to, say, animated crystalline sheets. Something like this may have happened before; some theorists believe Earthly life began in wet clay beds, and moved to organic molecules in a soupy sea only later.

While the customary view of evolution does not speak of progress, there has been generally an increase of information transmitted forward to the next generation. Complexity increases in a given genus, order, class, etc. Once intelligence appears, or invades a wholly different medium, such "cognitive creatures" can direct their own evolution. Patterns will persist, even thrive, independent of the substrate.

So perhaps this is the final answer to the significance of it all. In principle, life and structure, hopes and dreams and Shakespeare's *Hamlet,* can persist forever—if life chooses to, and struggles. In that far future, dark beyond measure, plasma entities of immense size and torpid pace may drift through a supremely strange era, sure and serene, free at last of ancient enemies.

Neither the thermodynamic dread of heat death nor gravity's gullet could then swallow them. Cosmology would have done its work.

As the universe swells, energy lessens, and the plasma life need only slow its pace to match. Mathematically, there are difficulties involved in arguing, as Dyson does, that the perceived span of order can be made infinite. The issue hinges on how information and energy scale with time. Assuming that Dyson's scaling is right, there is hope.

By adjusting itself exactly to its ever-cooling environment, life—of a sort—can persist and dream fresh dreams. The Second Law of Thermo-dynamics says that disorder increases in every energy transaction. But the Second Law need not be the Final Law.

Such eerie descendants will have much to think about. They will be able to remember and relive in sharp detail the glory of the brief Early Time—that distant, legendary era when matter brewed energy from crushing suns together. When all space was furiously hot, overflowing with boundless energy. When life dwelled in solid states, breathed in chilly atoms, and mere paltry planets formed a stage.

Freeman Dyson once remarked to me, about these issues, that he felt the best possible universe was one of constant challenge. He prefer-red a future that made survival possible but not easy. We chimps, if cod-dled, get lazy and then stupid.

The true far future is shrouded and mysterious. Still, I expect that he shall get his wish, and we shall not be bored.

Science fiction must assume the centrality of humans, for narrative interest at least. But the universe, as far as we can tell, cares naught for us. To some extent, we rage against the infinite stretches of space and time because that stage seems to dwarf us. But mere mute mass is less complex than the wonder of our own minds.

Only we can understand that vast stage. In the end, we may shape it as well. Our fiction says this, over and over, in intricate ways.

GREGORY BENFORD
February 1995

Greg Bear began writing full-time in 1975 after a career as an artist. His range is broad, encompassing fantasy and SF, with his principal asset being the ability to incorporate hard sciences and intricate plots into narratives that bristle with character complexities and vivid settings. Novels such as *Blood Music, Eon, Eternity,* and *The Forge of God* brought him to the forefront of U.S. SF. He lives in Washington State.

In the final moments of a universe governed by physics we can barely fathom, "Judgment Engine" foresees the timeless struggle of life for meaning. For us, meaning derives from memory, for humans in their mortality are finally about continuity. Such perspectives are indeed Stapledonian, confronting fundamental questions against the largest possible landscapes.

JUDGMENT ENGINE

Greg Bear

We

SEVEN TRIBUTARIES DISENGAGE from their social=mind and Library and travel by transponder to the School World. There they are loaded into a temporary soma, an older physical model with eight long, flexible red legs. Here the seven become We.

We have received routine orders from the Teacher Annex. We are to investigate student labor on the Great Plain of History, the largest physical feature on the School World. The students have been set to searching all past historical records, donated by the nine remaining Libraries. Student social=minds are sad; they will not mature before Endtime. They are the last new generation and their behavior is often aberrant. There may be room for error.

The soma sits in an enclosure. We become active and advance from the enclosure's shadow into a light shower of data condensing from the absorbing clouds high above. We see radiation from the donating Libraries, still falling on School World from around the three remaining systems; we hear the lambda whine of storage in the many rows of black hemispheres perched on the plain; we feel a patter of drops on our black carapace.

We stand at the edge of the plain, near a range of bare brown and black hills left over from planetary re-formation. The air is thick and cold. It smells sharply of rich data moisture, wasted on us; We do not have readers on our surface. The moisture dews up on the dark, hard ground under our feet, evaporates and is reclaimed by translucent soppers. The soppers flit through the air, a tenth our size and delicate.

The hemispheres are maintained by single-tributary somas. They are tiny, marching along the rows by the hundreds of thousands.

The sun rises in the west, across the plain. It is brilliant violet surrounded by streamers of intense blue. The streamers curl like flowing hair. Sun and streamers cast multiple shadows from each black hemisphere. The sun attracts our attention. It is beautiful, not part of a Library simscape; this scape is *real*. It reminds us of approaching Endtime; the changes made to conserve and concentrate the last available energy have rendered the scape beautifully novel, unfamiliar to the natural birth algorithms of our tributaries.

The three systems are unlike anything that has ever been. They contain all remaining order and available energy. Drawn close together, surrounded by the permutation of local space and time, the three systems deceive the dead outer universe, already well into the dull inaction of the long Between. We are proud of the three systems. They took a hundred million years to construct, and a tenth of all remaining available energy. They were a gamble. Nine of thirty-seven major Libraries agreed to the gamble. The others spread themselves into the greater magnitudes of the Between, and died.

The gamble worked.

Our soma is efficient and pleasant to work with. All of our tributaries agree, older models of such equipment are better. We have an appointment with the representative of the School World students, student tributaries lodged in a newer model soma called a Berkus, after a social=mind on Second World, which designed it. A Berkus soma is not favored. It is noisy; perhaps more efficient, but brasher and less elegant. We agree it will be ugly.

Data clouds swirl and spread tendrils high over the plain. The single somas march between our legs, cleaning unwanted debris from the black domes. Within the domes, all history. We could reach down and crush one with the claws on a single leg, but that would slow Endtime Work and waste available energy.

We are proud of our stray thinking. It shows that We are still human, still linked directly to the past. We are proud that We can ignore improper impulses.

We are teachers. All teachers must be linked with the past, to understand and explain it. Teachers must understand error; the past is rich with pain and error.

We await the Berkus.

Too much time passes. The world turns away from the sun and night falls. Centuries of Library time pass, but we try to be patient and think in the flow of external time. Some of our tributaries express a desire to taste the domes, but there is no real need, and would also waste available energy.

With night, more data fills the skies from the other systems, condenses, and rains down, covering us with a thick sheen. Soppers clean our carapace again. All around, the domes grow richer, absorbing history. We see, in the distance, a night interpreter striding on giant disjointed legs between the domes. It eats the domes and returns white mounds of discard. All the domes must be interpreted to see if any of the history should be carried by the final Endtime self.

The final self will cross the Between, order held in perfect inaction, until the Between has experienced sufficient rest and boredom. It will cross that point when time and space become granular and nonlinear, when the unconserved energy of expansion, absorbed at the minute level of the quantum foam, begins to disturb the metric. The metric becomes noisy and irregular, and all extension evaporates. The universe has no width, no time, and all is back at the beginning.

The final self will survive, knitting itself into the smallest interstices, armored against the fantastic pressures of a universe's deathsound. The quantum foam will give up its noise and new universes will bubble forth and evolve. One will transcend. The transcendent reality will absorb the final self, which will seed it. From the compression should arise new intelligent beings.

It is an important thing, and all teachers approve. The past should cover the new, forever. It is our way to immortality.

Our tributaries express some concern. We are, to be sure, not on a vital mission, but the Berkus is very late.

Something has gone wrong. We investigate our links and find them cut. Transponders do not reply.

The ground beneath our soma trembles. Hastily, the soma retreats from the Plain of History. It stands by a low hill, trying to keep steady on its eight red legs. The clouds over the plain turn green and ragged. The single somas scuttle between vibrating hemispheres, confused.

We cannot communicate with our social=mind or Library. No other Libraries respond. Alarmed, We appeal to the School World Student Committee, then point our thoughts up to the Endtime Work Coordinator, but they do not answer, either.

The endless kilometers of low black hemispheres churn as if stirred by a huge stick. Cracks appear, and from the cracks, thick red drops; the drops crystallize in high, tall prisms. Many of the prisms shatter and turn to dead white powder. We realize with great concern that we are seeing the internal stored data of the planet itself. This is a reserve record of all Library knowledge, held condensed; the School World contains selected records from the dead Libraries, more information than any single Library could absorb in a billion years. The knowledge shoots through the disrupted ground in crimson fountains, wasted. Our soma retreats deeper into the hills.

Nobody answers our emergency signal.

Nobody will speak to us, anywhere.

More days pass. We are still cut off from the Library. Isolated, We are limited only to what the soma can perceive, and that makes no sense at all.

We have climbed a promontory overlooking what was once the Great Plain of History. Where once our students worked to condense and select those parts of the past that would survive the Endtime, the hideous leaking of reserve knowledge has slowed and an equally hideous round of what seems to be amateurish student exercises work themselves in rapid time.

Madness covers the plain. The hemispheres have all disintegrated, and the single somas and interpreters have vanished.

Now, everywhere on the plain, green and red and purple forests grow and die in seconds; new trees push through the dead snags of the old. New kinds of tree invade from the west and push aside their predecessors. Climate itself accelerates: the skies grow heavy with cataracting clouds made of water and rain falls in sinuous sheets. Steam twists and pullulates; the ground becomes hot with change.

Trees themselves come to an end and crumble away; huge solid brown and red domes balloon on the plain, spread thick shell-leaves like opening cabbages, push long shoots through their crowns. The shoots tower above the domes and bloom with millions of tiny gray and pink flowers.

Watching all our work and plans destroyed, the seven tributaries within our soma offer dismayed hypotheses: this is a malfunction, the conservation and compression engines have failed and all knowledge is being acted out uselessly; no, it is some new gambit of the Endtime Work Coordinator, an emergency project; on the contrary, it is a political difficulty, lack of communication between the Coordinator and the Libraries, and it will all be over soon. . . .

We watch shoots toppled with horrendous snaps and groans, domes collapsing with brown puffs of corruption.

The scape begins anew.

More hours pass, and still no communication with any other social=

minds. We fear our Library itself has been destroyed; what other explanation for our abandonment? We huddle on our promontory, seeing patterns but no sense. Each generation of creativity brings something different, something that eventually fails, or is rejected.

Today large-scale vegetation is the subject of interest; the next day, vegetation is ignored for a rush of tiny biologies, no change visible from where We stand, our soma still and watchful on its eight sturdy legs.

We shuffle our claws to avoid a carpet of reddish growth surmounting the rise. By nightfall, We see, the mad scape could claim this part of the hill and We will have to move.

The sun approaches zenith. All shadows vanish. Its violet magnificence humbles us, a feeling We are not used to. We are from the great social=minds of the Library; humility and awe come from our isolation and concern. Not for a billion years have any of our tributaries felt so removed from useful enterprise. If this is the Endtime overtaking us, overcoming all our efforts, so be it. We feel resolve, pride at what We have managed to accomplish.

Then, We receive a simple message. The meeting with the students will take place. The Berkus will find us and explain. But We are not told when.

Something has gone very wrong, that students should dictate to their teachers, and should put so many tributaries through this kind of travail. The concept of *mutiny* is studied by all the tributaries within the soma. It does not explain much.

New hypotheses occupy our thinking. Perhaps the new matter of which all things were now made has itself gone wrong, destabilizing our worlds and interrupting the consolidation of knowledge; that would explain the scape's ferment and our isolation. It might explain unstable and improper thought processes. Or, the students have allowed some activity on School World to run wild; error.

The scape pushes palace-like glaciers over its surface, gouging itself in painful ecstasy: change, change, birth and decay, all in a single day, but slower than the rush of forests and living things. We might be able to remain on the promontory. Why are we treated so?

We keep to the open, holding our ground, clearly visible, concerned but unafraid. We are of older stuff. Teachers have always been of older stuff.

Could We have been party to some misinstruction, to cause such a disaster? What have We taught that might push our students into manic creation and destruction? We search all records, all memories, contained within the small soma. The full memories of our seven tributaries have not of course been transferred into the extension; it was to be a temporary assignment, and besides, the records would not fit. The lack of capacity hinders our thinking and We find no satisfying answers.

One of our tributaries has brought along some personal records. It has a long-shot hypothesis and suggests that an ancient prior self be activated to provide an objective judgment engine.

There are two reasons: the stronger is that this ancient self once, long ago, had a connection with a tributary making up the Endtime Work Coordinator. If the problem is political, perhaps the self's memories can give us deeper insight. The second and weaker reason: truly, despite our complexity and advancement, perhaps We have missed something important. Perhaps this earlier, more primitive self will see what We have missed.

There is indeed so little time; isolated as We are from a greater river of being, a river that might no longer exist, we might be the last fragment of social=mind to have any chance of combating planetwide madness.

There is barely enough room to bring the individual out of compression. It sits beside the tributaries in the thought plenum, in distress and not functional. What it perceives it does not understand. Our questions are met with protests and more questions.

The Engine

I come awake, aware. *I* sense a later and very different awareness, part of a larger group. My thoughts spin with faces to which I try to apply names, but my memory falters. These fade and are replaced by gentle calls for attention, new and very strange sensations.

I label the sensations around me: other humans, but not in human bodies. They seem to act together while having separate voices. I call the larger group the We-ness, not me and yet in some way accessible, as if part of my mind and memory.

I do not think that I have died, that I am *dead*. But the quality of my thought has changed. I have no body, no sensations of liquid pumping and breath flowing in and out.

Isolated, confused, I squat behind the We-ness's center of observation, catching glimpses of a chaotic high-speed landscape. Are they watching some entertainment? I worry that I am in a hospital, in recovery, forced to consort with other patients who cannot or will not speak with me.

I try to collect my last meaningful memories. I remember a face again and give it a name and relation: Elisaveta, my wife, standing over me as I lie on a narrow bed. Machines bend over me. I remember nothing after that.

But I am not in a hospital, not now.

Voices speak to me and I begin to understand some of what they say. The voices of the We-ness are stronger, more complex and richer, than anything I have ever experienced. I do not hear them. I have no ears.

"You've been stored inactive for a very long time," the We-ness tells me. It is (or they are) a tight-packed galaxy of thoughts, few of them making any sense at all.

Then I know.

I have awakened in the future. Thinking has changed.

"I don't know where I am. I don't know who you are. . . ."

"We are joined from seven tributaries, some of whom once had existence as individual biological beings. You are an ancient self of one of us."

"Oh," I say. The word seems wrong without lips or throat. I will not use it again.

"We're facing great problems. You'll provide unique insights." The voice expresses overtones of fatherliness and concern; I do not believe it.

Blackness paints me. "I'm hungry and I can't feel my body. I'm afraid. Where am I? I miss . . . my family."

"There is no body, no need for hunger, no need for food. Your family—*our* family—no longer lives, unless they have been stored elsewhere."

"How did I get here?"

"You were stored before a major medical reconstruction, to prevent total loss. Your stored self was kept as a kind of historical record and memento."

I don't remember any of that, but then, how could I? I remember signing contracts to allow such a thing. I remember thinking about the possibility I would awake in the future. But I did not die! "How long has it been?"

"Twelve billion two hundred and seventy-nine million years."

Had the We-ness said *Ten thousand years,* or even *Two hundred years,* I might feel some visceral reaction. All I know is that such an enormous length of time is geological, cosmological. I do not believe in it.

I glimpse the landscape again, glaciers slipping down mountain slopes, clouds pregnant with winter building gray and orange in the stinging glare of a huge setting sun. The sun is all wrong—too bright, violet, it resembles a dividing cell, all extrusions and blebs, with long ribbons and streaming hair. It looks like a Gorgon to me.

The faces of the glaciers break, sending showers and pillars of white ice over gray-shaded hills and valleys. I have awakened in the middle of an ice age. But it is too fast. Nothing makes sense.

"Am I all here?" I ask. Perhaps I am delusional.

"What is important from you is here. We would like to ask you questions now. Do you recognize any of the following faces/voices/thought patterns/styles?"

Disturbing synesthesia—bright sounds, loud colors, dull electric smells—fills my senses and I close it out as best I can. "No! That isn't right. Please, no questions until I know what's happened. No! That hurts!"

The We-ness prepares to shut me down. I am told that I will become inactive again.

Just before I wink out, I feel a cold blast of air crest the promontory on which the We-ness, and I, sit. Glaciers now completely cover the hills and valleys. The We-ness flexes eight fluid red legs, pulling them from quick-freezing mud. The sun still has not set.

Thousands of years in a day.

I am given sleep as blank as death, but not so final.

We gather as one and consider the problem of the faulty interface. "This is too early a self. It doesn't understand our way of thinking," one tributary says. "We must adapt to it."

The tributary whose prior self this was volunteers to begin restructuring.

"There is so little time," says another, who now expresses strong disagreement with the plan to resurrect. "Are we truly agreed this is best?"

We threaten to fragment as two of the seven tributaries vehemently object. But solidarity holds. All tributaries flow again to renewed agreement. We start the construction of an effective interface, which first requires deeper understanding of the nature of the ancient self. This takes some time.

We have plenty of time. Hours, days, with no communication.

The glacial cold nearly kills us where we stand. The soma changes its fluid nature by linking liquid water with long-chain and even more slippery molecules, highly resistant to freezing.

"Do the students know We're here, that We watch?" asks a tributary.

"They must . . ." says another. "They express a willingness to meet with us."

"Perhaps they lie, and they mean to destroy this soma, and us with it. There will be no meeting."

Dull sadness.

We restructure the ancient self, wrap it in our new interface, build a new plenary face to hold us all on equal ground, and call it up again, saying,

Vasily

I know the name, recognize the fatherly voice, feel a new clarity. I wish I could forget the first abortive attempt to live again, but my memory is perfect from the point of first rebirth on. I will forget nothing.

"Vasily, your descendant self does not remember you. It has purged older memories many times since your existence, but We recognize some similarities even so between your patterns. Birth patterns are strong and seldom completely erased. Are you comfortable now?"

I think of a simple place where I can sit. I want wood paneling and furniture and a fireplace, but I am not skilled; all I can manage is a small gray cubicle with a window on one side. In the wall is a hole through which the voices come. I imagine I am hearing them through flesh ears, and a kind of body forms within the cubicle. This body is my security. "I'm still afraid. I know—there's no danger."

"There *is* danger, but We do not yet know how significant the danger is."

Significant carries an explosion of information. If their original selves still exist elsewhere, in a social=mind adjunct to a Library, then all that might be lost will be immediate memories. A *social=mind*, I understand, is made up of fewer than ten thousand tributaries. A Library typically contains a trillion or more social=minds.

"I've been dead for billions of years," I say, hoping to address my future self. "But you've lived on—you're immortal."

"We do not measure life or time as you do. Continuity of memory is fragmentary in our lives, across eons. But continuity of access to the Library—and access to records of past selves—does confer a kind of immortality. If that has ended, We are completely mortal."

"I must be so primitive," I say, my fear oddly fading now. This is a situation I can understand—life or death. I feel more solid within my cubicle. "How can I be of any use?"

"You are primitive in the sense of *firstness*. That is why you have been activated. Through your life experience, you may have a deeper understanding of what led to our situation. Argument, rebellion, desperation . . . these things are difficult for us to deal with."

Again, I don't believe them. From what I can tell, this group of minds has a depth and strength and complexity that makes me feel less than a child . . . perhaps less than a bacterium. What can I do except cooperate? I have nowhere else to go. . . .

For billions of years . . . inactive. Not precisely death.

I remember that I was once a *teacher.*

Elisaveta had been my student before she became my wife.

The We-ness wants me to teach it something, to do something for it. But first, it has to teach me history.

"Tell me what's happened," I say.

The Libraries

In the beginning, human intelligences arose, and all were alone. That lasted for ten of thousands of years. Soon after understanding the nature of thought and mind, intelligences came together to create group minds, all in one. Much of the human race linked in an intimacy deeper than sex. Or unlinked to pursue goals as quasi individuals; the choices were many, the limitations few. *(This all began a few decades after your storage.)* Within a century, the human race abandoned biological limitations, in favor of the social=mind. Social=minds linked to form Libraries, at the top of the hierarchy.

The Libraries expanded, searching around star after star for other intelligent life. They found life—millions upon millions of worlds, each rare as a diamond among the trillions of barren star systems, but none with intelligent beings. Gradually, across millions of years, the Libraries realized that they were the All of intelligent thought.

We had simply exchanged one kind of loneliness for a greater and more final isolation. There were no companion intelligences, only those derived from humanity. . . .

As the human Libraries spread and connections between them became more tenuous—some communications taking thousands of years to be completed—many social=minds reindividuated, assuming lesser degrees of togetherness and intimacy. Even in large Libraries, individuation became a crucial kind of relaxation and holiday. The old ways reasserted.

Being human, however, some clung to old ways, or attempted to enforce new ones, with greater or lesser tenacity. Some asserted moral imperative. Madness spread as large groups removed all the barriers of individuation, in reaction to what they perceived as a dangerous atavism—the "lure of the singular."

These "uncelled" or completely communal Libraries, with their slow, united consciousness, proved burdensome and soon vanished—within half a million years. They lacked the range and versatility of the "celled" Libraries.

But conflicts between differing philosophies of social=mind structure continued. There were wars.

Even in wars the passions were not sated, for something more frightening had been discovered than loneliness: the continuity of error and cruelty.

After tens of millions of years of steady growth and peace, the renewed paroxysms dismayed us.

No matter how learned or advanced a social=mind became, it could, in desperation or in certain moments of development, perform acts analogous to the errors of ancient individuated societies. It could kill other social=minds, or sever the activities of many of its own tributaries. It could frustrate the fulfillment of other minds. It could experience something like *rage*, but removed from the passions of the body: rage cold and precise and long-lived, terrible in its persuasiveness, dreadful in its consequences. Even worse, it could experience *indifference*.

I tumble through these records, unable to comprehend the scale of what I see. Our galaxy was linked star to star with webworks of transferred energy and information; parts of the galaxy darkened with massive conflict, millions of stars shut off. This was war.

At human scale, planets seemed to have reverted to ancient Edens, devoid of artifice or instrumentality; but the trees and animals themselves carried myriads of tiny machines, and the ground beneath them was an immense thinking system, down to the core. . . . Other worlds, and other structures between worlds, seemed as abstract and meaningless as the wanderings of a stray brush on canvas.

The Proof

One great social=mind, retreating far from the ferment of the Libraries, formulated the rules of advanced metabiology, and found them precisely analogous to those governing planetbound ecosystems: competition, victory through survival, evolution and reproduction. It proved that error and pain and destruction are essential to any change—but, more important, to any growth.

The great social=mind carried out complex experiments simulating millions of different ordering systems, and in every single case, the rise of complexity (and ultimately intelligence) led to the wanton destruction of prior forms. Using these experiments to define axioms, what began as a scientific proof ended as a rigorous mathematical proof: *there can be no ultimate ethical advancement in this universe, in systems governed by time and subject to change.* The indifference of the universe—reality's grim and mindless harshness—is multiplied by the necessity that old order, prior thoughts and lives, must be extinguished to make way for new.

After checking its work many times, the great social=mind wiped its stores and erased its infrastructure in, on, and around seven worlds and the two stars, leaving behind only the formulation and the Proof.

For Libraries across the galaxy, absorption of the Proof led to mental disruption. From the nightmare of history there was to be no awakening.

Suicide was one way out. A number of prominent Libraries brought their own histories to a close.

Others recognized the validity of the Proof, but did not commit suicide. They lived with the possibility of error and destruction. And still, they grew wiser, greater in scale and accomplishment. . . .

Crossing from galaxy to galaxy, still alone, the Libraries realized that human perception was the only perception. The Proof would never be tested against the independent minds of nonhuman intelligences. In this universe, the Proof must stand.

Billions of years passed, and the universe became a huge kind of house, confining a practical infinity of mind, an incredible ferment that "burned" the available energy with torchy brilliance, decreasing the total life span of reality.

Yet the Proof remained unassailed.

Wait. I don't see anything here. I don't *feel* anything. This isn't history; it's . . . too large! I can't understand some of the things you show me. . . . But worse, pardon me, it's babbling among minds who feel no passion. This We-ness . . . how do you *feel* about this?

You are distracted by preconceptions. You long for an organic body, and assume that lacking organic bodies, We experience no emotions. We experience emotions. *Listen* to them>>>>

I squirm in my cubicle and experience their emotions of first and second loneliness, degrees of isolation from old memories, old selves; longing for the first individuation, the Birthtime . . . hunger for understanding not just of the outer reality, beyond the social=mind's vast internal universe of thought, but of the ever-changing currents and orderliness arising between tributaries. Here is social and mental interaction as a great song, rich and joyous, a love greater than anything I can remember experiencing as an embodied human. Greater emotions still, outside my range again, of loyalty and love for a social=mind and something like *respect* for the immense Libraries. (I am shown what the We-ness says is an emotion experienced at the level of Libraries, but it is so far beyond me that I seem to disintegrate, and have to be coaxed back to wholeness.)

A tributary approaches across the mind space within the soma. My cubicle grows dim. I feel a strange familiarity again; this will be, *is*, my future self.

This tributary feels sadness and some grief, touching its ancient self-me. It feels pain at my limitations, at my tight-packed biological character. Things deliberately forgotten come back to haunt it.

And they haunt *me*. My own inadequacies become abundantly clear. I remember useless arguments with friends, making my wife cry with frustration, getting angry at my children for no good reason. My childhood and adolescent indiscretions return like shadows on a scrim. And I remember my *drives:* rolling in useless lust, and later, Elisaveta! With her young and supple body; and others. Just as significant, but different in color, the cooler passions of discovery and knowledge, my growing self-awareness. I remember fear of inadequacy, fear of failure, of not being a useful member of society. I needed above all (more than I needed Elisaveta) to be important and to teach and be influential on young minds.

All of these emotions, the We-ness demonstrates, have analogous emotions at their level. For the We-ness, the most piercing unpleasantness of all—akin to physical pain—comes from recognition of their possible failure. The teachers may not have taught their students properly, and the students may be making mistakes.

"Let me get all this straight," I say. I grow used to my imagined state—to riding like a passenger within the cubicle, inside the eight-legged soma, to seeing as if through a small window the advancing and now receding of the glaciers. "You're teachers—as I was once a teacher—and you used to be connected to a larger social=mind, part of a Library." I mull over mind as society, society as mind. "But there may have been a revolution. After billions of years! Students . . . A *revolution!* Extraordinary!

"You've been cut off from the Library. You're alone, you might be killed . . . and you're telling *me* about ancient history?"

The We-ness falls silent.

"I must be important," I say with an unbreathed sigh, a kind of asterisk in the exchanged thoughts. "I can't imagine why. But maybe it doesn't matter—I have so many questions!" I hunger for knowledge of what has become of my children, of my wife. Of everything that came after me . . . All the changes!

"We need information from you, and your interpretation of certain memories. Vasily was our name once. Vasily Gerazimov. You were the husband of Elisaveta, father of Maxim and Giselle. . . . We need to know more about Elisaveta."

"You don't remember her?"

"Twelve billion years have passed. Time and space have changed. This tributary alone has partnered and bonded and matched and socialized with perhaps fifty billion individuals and tributaries since. Our combined tributaries in the social=mind have had contacts with all intelligent beings, once or twice removed. Most have dumped or stored memories more than a billion years old. If We were still connected to the Library, I could learn more about my past. I have kept you as a kind of memento, a talisman, and nothing more."

I feel a freezing awe. Fifty billion mates . . . or whatever they had been. I catch fleeting glimpses of liaisons in the social=mind, binary, trinary, as many as thousands at a time linked in the crumbling remnants of marriage and sexuality, and finally those liaisons passing completely out of favor, fashion, usefulness.

"Elisaveta and you," the tributary continues, "were divorced ten years after your storage. I remember nothing of the reasons why. We have no other clues to work with."

The "news" comes as a doubling of my pain, a renewed and expanded sense of isolation from a loved one. I reach up to touch my face, to see if I am crying. My hands pass through imagined flesh and bone. My body is long since dust; Elisaveta's body is dust. What went wrong between us? Did she find another lover? Did I? I am a ghost. I should not care. There were difficult times, but I never thought of our liaison—our *marriage,* I would defend that word even now—as temporary. Still, across *billions* of years! We have become *immortal*—she perhaps more than I, who remember nothing of the time between. "Why do you need me at all? Why do you need clues?"

But we are interrupted. An extraordinary thing happens to the retreating glaciers. From our promontory, the soma half-hidden behind an upthrust of frozen and deformed knowledge, we see the icy masses blister and bubble, as if made of some superheated glass or plastic. Steam bursts from the bubbles—at least, what I assume to be steam—and freezes in the air in shapes suggesting flowers. All around, the walls and sheets of ice succumb to this beautiful plague.

The We-ness understands it no more than I.

From the hill below come faint sounds and hints of radiation—

gamma rays, beta particles, mesons, all clearly visible to the We-ness, and vaguely passed on to me as well.

"Something's coming," I say.

The Berkus advances in its unexpected cloud of production-destruction. There is something deeply wrong with it—it squanders too much available energy. Its very presence disrupts the new matter of which We are made.

Of the seven tributaries, four feel an emotion rooted in the deepest algorithms of their pasts: fear. Three have never known such bodily functions, have never known mortal and embodied individuation. They feel intellectual concern and a tinge of cosmic sadness, as if our end might be equated with the past death of the natural stars and galaxies. We keep to our purpose despite these ridiculous excursions, signs of our disorder.

The Berkus advances up the hill.

I see through my window this monumental and absolutely horrifying *creature*, shining with a brightness comprised of the qualities of diamonds and polished silver, a scintillating insect pushing its sharply pointed feet into the thawing soil, steam rising all around. The legs hold together despite gaps where joints should be, gaps crossed only by something that produces hard radiation. Below the Berkus (so the We-ness calls it), the ground ripples as if School World has muscles and twitches, wanting to scratch.

The Berkus pauses and sizes up our much less powerful, much smaller soma with blasts of neutrons, flicked as casually as a flashlight beam. The material of our soma wilts and reforms beneath this withering barrage. The soma expresses distress—and inadvertently, the We-ness translates this distress to me as tremendous pain.

I explode within my confined mental space. Again comes the blackness.

The Berkus decides it is not necessary to come any closer. That is fortunate for us, and for our soma. Any lessening of the distance between us would prove fatal.

The Berkus communicates with pulsed light. "Why are you here?"

"We have been sent here to observe and report. We are cut off from the Library—"

"Your Library has fled," the Berkus informs us. "It disagreed with the Endtime Work Coordinator."

"We were told nothing of this."

"It was not our responsibility. We did not know you would be here."

The magnitude of this rudeness is difficult to envelope. We wonder how many tributaries the Berkus contains. We hypothesize that it might contain all of the students, the entire student social=mind, and this would explain its use of energy and change in design.

Our pitiful ancient individual flickers back into awareness and sits quietly, too stunned to protest.

"We do not understand the purpose of this creation and destruction," We say. Our strategy is to avoid the student tributaries altogether now. Still, they might tell us more We need to know.

"It must be obvious to teachers," the Berkus says. "By order of the Coordinator, We are rehearsing all possibilities of order, usurping stored knowledge down to the planetary core and converting it. There must be an escape from the Proof."

"The Proof is an ancient discovery. It has never been shown to be wrong. What can it possibly mean to the Endtime Work?"

"It means a great deal," the Berkus says.

"How many are you?"

The Berkus does not answer. All this has taken place in less than a millionth of a second. The Berkus's incommunication lengthens into seconds, then minutes. Around us, the glaciers crumple like mud caught in rushing water.

"Another closed path, of no value," the Berkus finally says.

"We wish to understand your motivations."

"We have no need of you now."

"Why this concern with the Proof? And what does it have to do with the change you provoke, the destruction of School World's knowledge?"

The Berkus rises on a tripod of three disjointed legs, waving its other legs in the air, a cartoon medallion so disturbing in design that We draw back a few meters.

"The Proof is a cultural aberration," it radiates fiercely, blasting our surface and making the mud around us bubble. "It is not fit to pass on to those who seed the next reality. You failed us. You showed no way beyond the Proof. The Endtime Work has begun, the final self chosen to fit through the narrow gap—"

I see all this through the We-ness as if I have been there, have lived it, and suddenly I know why I have been recalled, why the We-ness has shown me faces and patterns.

The universe, across more than twelve billion years, grows irretrievably old. From spanning the galaxies billions of years before, all life and intelligence—all arising from the sole intelligence in all the universe, humanity—have shrunk to a few star systems. These systems have been resuscitated and nurtured by concentrating the remaining available energy of thousands of dead galaxies. And they are no longer natural star systems with planets—the bloated coma-wrapped violet star rising at zenith over us is a congeries of plasma macromachines, controlling and conserving every gram of the natural matter remaining, every erg of available energy. These artificial suns pulse like massive living cells, shaped to be ultimately efficient and to squeeze every moment of active life over time remaining. The planets themselves have been condensed, recarved, rearranged, and they too are composed of geological macromachines. With some dread, I gather that the matter of which all these things are made is itself artificial, with redesigned component particles.

The natural galaxies have died, reduced to a colorless murmur of useless heat, and all the particles of all original creation—besides what have been marshaled and remade in these three close-packed systems—have dulled and slowed and unwound. Gravity itself has lost its bearings and become a chancy phenomenon, supplemented by new forces generated within the macromachine planets and suns.

Nothing is what it seems, and nothing is what it had been when I lived.

Available energy is strictly limited. The We-ness looks forward to less than four times ten to the fiftieth units of Planck time—roughly an old Earth year.

And in charge of it all, controlling the Endtime Work, a supremely confident social=mind composed of many "tributaries," and among those gathered selves . . .

Someone very familiar to me indeed. My wife.

"Where is she? Can I speak to her? What happened to her—did she die, was she stored, did she live?"

The We-ness seems to vibrate both from my reaction to this information, and to the spite of the Berkus. I am assigned to a quiet place, where I can watch and listen without bothering them. I feel our soma, our insectlike body, dig into the loosening substance of the promontory.

"You taught us the Proof was absolute," the Berkus says, "that throughout all time, in all circumstances, error and destruction and pain will accompany growth and creation, that the universe must remain indifferent and randomly hostile. We do not accept that."

"But why dissolve links with the Library?" We cry, shrinking beneath the Berkus's glare. The constantly reconstructed body of the

Berkus channels and consumes energy with enormous waste, as if the students do not care, intent only on their frantic mission, whatever that might be . . . Reducing available active time by days for *all of us*—

I know! I shout in the quiet place, but I am not heard, or not paid attention to.

"Why condemn us to a useless end in this chaos, this madness?" We ask.

"Because We must refute the Proof and there is so little useful time remaining. The final self must not be sent over carrying this burden of error."

"Of sin!" I shout, still not heard. Proof of the validity of primordial sin— that everything living must eat, must destroy, must climb up the ladder on the backs of miserable victims. That all true creation involves death and pain; the universe is a charnel house.

I am fed and study the Proof. Time runs in many tracks within the soma. I try to encompass the principles and expressions, no longer given as words, but as multisense abstractions. In the Proof, miniature universes of discourse are created, manipulated, reduced to an expression, and discarded: the Proof is more complex than any single human life, or even the life of a species, and its logic is not familiar. The Proof is rooted in areas of mental experience I am not equipped to understand, but I receive glosses.

Law: Any dynamic system (I understand this as *organism*) **has limited access to resources, and a limited time in which to achieve its goals.** (A multitude of instances are drawn from history, as well as from an artificial miniature universe.)

Other laws follow regarding behavior of systems within a flow of energy, but they are completely beyond me.

Observed Law: The goals of differing organisms, even of like variety, never completely coincide. (History and the miniature universe teem with instances, and the Proof lifts these up for inspection at moments of divergence, demonstrating again and again this obvious point.)

Then comes a roll of beginning deductions, backed by examples too numerous for me to absorb:

And so it follows that for any complex of organisms, competition must arise for limited resources.

From this: Some will succeed, some will fail, to acquire resources sufficient to live. Those who succeed, express themselves in later generations.

From this: New dynamic systems will arise to compete more efficiently.

From this: Competition and selection will give rise to organisms that are °streamlined,° incapable of surviving even in the midst of plenty because not equipped with complete methods of absorbing resources. These will prey on complete organisms to acquire their resources. And in return, the prey will acquire a reliance on the predators.

From this: Other forms of °streamlining° will occur. Some of the resulting systems will depend entirely on others for reproduction and fulfillment of goals.

From this: Ecosystems will arise, interdependent, locked in predator-prey, disease-host relationships.

I experience a multitude of rigorous experiments, unfolding like flowers.

And so it follows that in the course of competition, some forms will be outmoded, and will pass away, and others will be preyed upon to extinction, without regard to their beauty, their adaptability to a wide range of possible conditions. I sense here a kind of aesthetic judgment, above the fray: Beautiful forms will die without being fully tested, their information lost, their opportunities limited.

And so it follows . . .

And so it follows . . .

The ecosystems increase in complexity, giving rise to organisms whose primary adaptation is perception and judgment, forming the abstract equivalents of societies, which interact through the exchange of resources and extensions of cultures and politics-models for more efficient organization. Still, change and evolution, failure and death, societies and cultures pass and are forgotten; whole classes of these larger systems suffer extinction, without being allowed fulfillment.

From history: Nations prey upon nations, and eat them alive, discarding them as burned husks.

Law: The universe is neutral; it will not care, nor will any ultimate dynamic system interfere . . .

In those days before I was born, as smoke rose from the ovens, God did not hear the cries of His people.

And so it follows: that no system will achieve perfect efficiency and self-sufficiency. Within all changing systems, accumulated error must be purged. For the good of the dynamic whole, systems must die. But efficient and beautiful systems will die as well.

I see the Proof's abstraction of evil: a sharklike thing, to me, but no more than a very complex expression. In this shark there is history, and dumb organic pressure, and the accumulations of the past: and the shark does not discriminate, knows nothing of judgment or justice, will eat the promising and the strong as well as birthing young. Waste, waste, an agony of waste, and over it all, not watching, the indifference of the real.

After what seems hours of study, of questions asked and answered, new ways of thinking acquired—reeducation—I begin to feel the thoroughness of the Proof, and I feel a despair unlike anything in my embodied existence.

Where once there had been hope that intelligent organisms could see their way to just, beautiful, and efficient systems, in practice, without exception, they revert to the old rules.

Things have not and will never improve.

Heaven itself would be touched with evil—or stand still. But there is no heaven run by a just God. Nor can there be a just God. Perfect justice and beauty and evolution and change are incompatible.

Not the birth of my son and daughter, nor the day of my marriage, not all my moments of joy can erase the horror of history. And the stretch of future histories, after my storage, shows even more horror, until I seem to swim in carnivorous, *cybernivorous* cruelty.

Connections

We survey the Berkus with growing concern. Here is not just frustration of our attempts to return to the Library, not just destruction of knowledge, but a flagrant and purposeless waste of precious resources. Why is it allowed?

Obviously, the Coordinator of the Endtime Work has given license, handed over this world, with such haste that We did not have time to withdraw. The Library has been forced away (or worse), and all transponders destroyed, leaving us alone on School World.

The ancient self, having touched on the Proof (absorbing no more than a fraction of its beauty) is wrapped in a dark shell of mood. This mood, basic and primal as it is, communicates to the tributaries. Again, after billions of years, We feel sadness at the inevitability of error and the impossibility of justice—and sadness at our own error. The Proof has always stood as a monument of pure thought—and a curse, even to we who affirm it.

The Berkus expands like a balloon. "There is going to be major work done here. You will have to move."

"No," the combined tributaries cry. "This is enough confusion and enough being *shoved around.*" Those words come from the ancient self.

The Berkus finds them amusing.

"Then you'll stay here," it says, "and be absorbed in the next round of experiment. You are teachers who have taught incorrectly. You deserve no better."

I break free of the *dark shell of mood,* as the tributaries describe it, and now I seem to kick and push my way to a peak of attention, all without arms or legs. "Where is the plan, the order? Where are your billions of years of superiority? How can this be happening?"

We pass on the cries of the ancient self. The Berkus hears the message.

"We are not familiar with this voice," the student social=mind says.

"I judge you from the past!" the ancient self says. "You are *all* found wanting!"

"This is not the voice of a tributary, but of an individual," the Berkus says. "The individual sounds uninformed."

"I demand to speak with my wife!" My demand gets no reaction for almost a second. Around me, the tributaries within the soma flow and rearrange, thinking in a way I cannot follow. They finally rise as a solid, seamless river of consent.

"We charge you with error," they say to the Berkus. *"We charge you with confirming the Proof you wish to negate."*

The Berkus considers, then backs away swiftly, beaming at us one final message: "There is an interesting rawness in your charge. You no longer think as outmoded teachers. A link with the Endtime Work Coordinator will be requested. Stand where you are. Our own work must continue."

I feel a sense of relief around me. This is a breakthrough. I have a purpose! The Berkus retreats, leaving us on the promontory to observe. Where once, hours before, glaciers melted, the ground begins to churn, grow viscous, divide into fenced enclaves. Within the enclaves, green and gray shapes arise, sending forth clouds of steam. These enclaves surround the range of hills, surmount all but our promontory, and move off to the horizon on all sides, perhaps covering the entire School World.

In the center of each fenced area, a sphere forms first as a white blister on the hardness, then a pearl resting on the surface. The pearl lifts, suspended in air. Each pearl begins to evolve in a different way, turning inward, doubling, tripling; they flatten into disks, centers dividing to form toruses—a practical infinity of different forms.

The fecundity of idea startles me. Blastulas give rise to cell-like complexity, spikes twist into intricate knots, all the rules of ancient topological mathematics are demonstrated in seconds, and then violated as the spaces within the enclaves themselves change.

"What are they doing?" I ask, bewildered.

"A mad push of evolution, trying all combinations starting from a simple beginning form," my descendant self explains. "It was once a common exercise, but not on such a vast scale. Not since the formulation of the Proof."

"What do they want to learn?"

"If they can find one instance of evolution and change that involves only growth and development, not competition and destruction, then they will have falsified the Proof."

"But the Proof is perfect," I said. "It can't be falsified. . . ."

"So We have judged. The students incorrectly believe We are wrong."

The field of creation becomes a vast fabric, each enclave contributing to a larger weave. What is being shown here could have occupied entire civilizations in my time: the dimensions of change, all possibilities of progressive growth. "It's beautiful," I say.

"It's futile," my descendant self says, its tone bitter. I feel the emotion in its message as an aberration, and it immediately broadcasts shame to all of its fellows, and to me.

"Are you afraid they'll show your teachings were wrong?" I asked.

"No," my tributary says. "I am sorry that they will fail. Such a message to pass on to a young universe . . . that whatever our nature and design, however we develop, we are doomed to make errors and cause pain. Still, that is the truth, and it has never been refuted."

"But even in my time, there was a solution," I say.

They show mild curiosity. What could come from so far in the past, that they hadn't advanced upon it, improved it, a billion times over, or discarded it? I wonder why I have been activated at all . . .

But I persist. "From God's perspective, destruction and pain and error may be part of the greater whole, a beauty from its point of view. We only perceive it as evil because of our limited point of view."

The tributaries allow a polite pause. My tributary explains, as gently as possible, "We have never encountered ultimate systems you call gods. Still, we are or have been very much like gods. As gods, all too often we have made horrible errors, and caused unending pain. Pain did not add to the beauty."

I want to scream at them for their hubris, but it soon becomes apparent to me, they are right. Their predecessors have reduced galaxies, scanned all histories, made the universe itself run faster with their productions and creations. They have advanced the Endtime by billions of years, and now prepare to see a new universe across an inconceivable gap of darkness and immobility.

From my perspective, humans have certainly become godlike. But not just. And there are no others. Even in the diversity of the human diaspora across the galaxies, not once has the Proof been falsified. And that is all it would have taken: one instance.

"Why did you bring me back, then?" I ask my descendant self in private conference. It replies in kind:

"Your thought processes are not our own. You can be a judgment engine. You might give us insight into the reasoning of the students, and help explain to us their plunge into greater error. There must be some motive not immediately apparent, some fragment of personality and memory responsible for this. An ancient self of a tributary of the Endtime Work Coordinator and you were once intimately related, married as sexual partners. You did not stay married. That is division and dissent. And there is division and dissent between the Endtime Work Committee and the teachers. That much is apparent. . . ."

Again I feel like clutching my hands to my face and screaming in frustration. Elisaveta—it must mean Elisaveta. *But we were not divorced . . . not when I was stored!* I sit in my imagined gray cubicle, my imagined body uncertain in its outline, and wish for a moment of complete privacy. They give it to me.

Tapering Time

The scape has progressed to a complexity beyond our ability to process. We stand on our promontory, surrounded by the field of enclaved experiments, each enclave containing a different evolved object, the objects still furiously convoluting and morphing. Some glow faintly as night sweeps across our part of the School World. We are as useless and incompetent as the revived ancient self, now wrapped in its own shock and misery. Our tributaries have fallen silent. We wait for what will happen next, either in the scape, or in the promised contact with the Endtime Work Coordinator.

The ancient self rises from its misery and isolation. It joins our watchful silence, expectant. It has not completely lost *hope*. We have never had need of *hope*. Connected to the Library, fear became a distant and unimportant thing; hope, its opposite, equally distant and not useful.

❁   ❁   ❁

I have been musing over my last hazy memories of Elisaveta, of our children Maxim and Giselle—bits of conversation, physical features, smells . . . reliving long stretches with the help of memory recovery . . . watching seconds pass into minutes as if months pass into years.

Outside, time seems to move much more swiftly. The divisions between enclaves fall, and the uncounted experiments stand on the field, still evolving, but now allowed to interact. Tentatively, their evolution takes in the new possibility of *motion*.

I feel for the students, wish to be part of them. However wrong, this experiment is vital, idealistic. It smells of youthful naïveté. Because of my own rugged youth, raised in a nation running frantically from one historical extreme to another, born to parents who jumped like puppets between extremes of hope and despair, I have always felt uneasy in the face of idealism and naïveté.

Elisaveta was a naive idealist when I first met her. I tried to teach her, pass on my sophistication, my sense of better judgment.

The brightly colored, luminous objects hover on the plain, discovering new relations: a separate identity, a larger sense of space. The objects have reached a high level of complexity and order, but within a limited environment. If any have developed mind, they can now reach out and explore new objects.

First, the experiments shift a few centimeters this way or that, visible across the plain as a kind of restless, rolling motion. The plain becomes an ocean of gentle waves. Then, the experiments *bump* each other. Near our hill, some of the experiments circle and surround their companions, or just bump with greater and greater urgency. Extensions reach out, and we can see—it must be obvious to all—that mind does exist, and new senses are being created and explored.

If Elisaveta, whatever she has become, is in charge of this sea of experiments, then perhaps she is merely following an inclination she had billions of years before: When in doubt, when all else fails, *punt*.

This is a cosmological kind of punt, burning up available energy at a distressing rate. . . .

Just like her, I think, and feel a warmth of connection with that ancient woman. But the woman *divorced* me. She found me wanting, later than my memories reach. . . . And after all, what she has become is as little like the Elisaveta I knew as my descendant tributary is like me.

The dance on the plain becomes a frenzied blur of color. Snakes flow, sprout legs, wings beat the air. Animal relations, plant relations, new ecosystems . . . But these creatures have evolved not from the simplest beginnings, but from already elaborate sources. Each isolated experiment, already having achieved a focused complexity beyond anything I can understand, becomes a potential player in a new order of interaction. What do the students—or Elisaveta—hope to accomplish in this peculiar variation on the old scheme?

I am so focused on the spectacle surrounding us that it takes a "nudge" from my descendant self to alert me to change in the sky. A liquid silvery ribbon pours from above, spreading over our heads into a flat upside-down ocean of reflective cloud. The inverse ocean expands to the horizon, blocking all light from the new day.

Our soma rises expectantly on its eight legs. I feel the tributaries' interest as a kind of heat through my cubicle, and I abandon the imagined environment for the time being. Best to receive this new phenomenon directly.

A fringed curtain, like the edge of a shawl woven from threads of mercury, descends from the upside-down ocean, brushing over the land. The fringe crosses the plain of experiments without interfering, but surrounds our hill, screening our view. Light pulses from selected threads in the liquid weave. The tributaries translate instantly.

"What do you want?" asks a clear neutral voice. No character, no tone, no emotion. This is the Endtime Work Coordinator, or at least an extension of that powerful social=mind. It does not sound anything like Elisaveta. My hopes have been terribly naive.

After all this time and misery, the teachers' reserve is admirable. I detect respect, but no awe; they are used to the nature of the Endtime Work Coordinator, largest of the social=minds not directly connected to a Library. "We have been cut off, and We need to know why," the tributaries say.

"Your work reached a conclusion," the voice responds.

"Why were We not accorded the respect of being notified, or allowed to return to our Library?"

"Your Library has been terminated. We have concluded the active existence of all entities no longer directly connected with Endtime Work, to conserve available energy."

"But you have let us live."

"It would involve more energy to terminate existing extensions than to allow them to run down."

The sheer coldness and precision of the voice chilled me. The end of a Library is equivalent to the end of thousands of worlds full of individual intelligences. *Genocide. Error and destruction.*

But my future self corrects me. *"This is expediency,"* it says in a private sending. *"It is what We all expected would happen sooner or later. The manner seems irregular, but the latitude of the Endtime Work Coordinator is great."*

Still, the tributaries request a complete accounting of the decision. The Coordinator obliges. A judgment arrives:

The teachers are irrelevant. Teaching of the Proof has been deemed useless; the Coordinator has decided—

I hear a different sort of voice, barely recognizable to me—*Elisaveta*

"All affirmations of the Proof merely discourage our search for alternatives. The Proof has become a thought disease, a cultural tyranny. It blocks our discovery of another solution."

A New Accounting

Our ancient self recognizes something in the message. What We have planned from near the beginning now bears fruit—the ancient self, functioning as an engine of judgment and recognition, has found a key player in the decision to isolate us, and to terminate our Library.

"We detect the voice of a particular tributary," We say to the Coordinator. "May We communicate with this tributary?"

"Do you have a valid reason?" the Coordinator asks.

"We must check for error."

"Your talents are not recognized."

"Still, the Coordinator might have erred, and as there is so little time, following the wrong course will be doubly tragic."

The Coordinator reaches a decision after sufficient time to show a complete polling of all tributaries within its social=mind.

"An energy budget is established. Communication is allowed."

We follow protocol billions of years old, but excise unnecessary ceremonial segments. We poll the student tributaries, searching for some flaw in reasoning, finding none.

Then We begin searching for our own justification. If We are about to *die,* lost in the last-second noise and event-clutter of a universe finally running down, We need to know where *We* have failed. If there is no failure—and if all this experimentation is simply a futile act—We might die less ignominiously. We search for the tributary familiar to the ancient self, hoping to find the personal connection that will reduce all our questions to one exchange.

Bright patches of light in the sky bloom, spread, and are quickly gathered and snuffed. The other suns and worlds are being converted and conserved. We have minutes, perhaps only seconds.

We find the voice, descendant tributary of Elisaveta.

❋   ❋   ❋

There are immense deaths in the sky, and now all is going dark. There is only the one sun, turning in on itself, violet shading to deep orange, and the School World.

Four seconds. I have just four seconds . . . Endtime accelerates upon us. The student experiment has consumed so much energy. All other worlds have been terminated, all social=minds except the Endtime Co-ordinator's and the final self . . . the seed that will cross the actionless Between.

I feel the tributaries frantically create an interface, make distant requests, then demands. They meet strong resistance from a tributary within the Endtime Work Coordinator. This much they convey to me . . . I sense weeks, months, years of negotiation, all passing in a second of more and more disjointed and uncertain real time.

As the last energy of the universe is spent, as all potential and all kinesis bottom out at a useless average, the fractions of seconds become clipped, their qualities altered. Time advances with an irregular jerk, truly like an off-center wheel.

Agreement is reached. Law and persuasion even now have some force.

"Vasily. I haven't thought about you in ever so long."

"Elisaveta, is that you?" I cannot see her. I sense a total lack of emotion in her words. And why not?

"Not *your* Elisaveta, Vasily. But I hold her memories and some of her patterns."

"You've been alive for billions of years?"

I receive a condensed impression of a hundred million sisters, all related to Elisaveta, stored at different times like a huge library of past selves. The final tributary she has become, now an important part of the Coordinator, refers to her past selves much as a grown woman might open childhood diaries. The past selves are kept informed, to the extent that being informed does not alter their essential natures.

How differently my own descendant self behaves, sealing away a small part of the past as a reminder, but never consulting it. How perverse for a mind that reveres the past! Perhaps what it reveres is form, not actuality. . . .

"Why do you want to speak with me?" Elisaveta asks. Which Elisaveta, from which time, I cannot tell right away.

"I think . . . *they* seem to think it's important. A disagreement, something that went wrong."

"They are seeking justification through you, a self stored billions of years ago. They want to be told that their final efforts have meaning. How like the Vasily I knew."

"It's not my doing! I've been inactive. . . . Were we divorced?"

"Yes." Sudden realization changes the tone of this Elisaveta's voice. "You were stored before we divorced?"

"Yes! How long after . . . were you stored?"

"A century, maybe more," she answers. With some wonder, she says, "Who could have known we would live forever?"

"When I saw you last, we loved each other. We had children. . . ."

"They died with the Libraries," she says.

I do not feel physical grief, the body's component of sadness and rage at loss, but the news rocks me, even so. I retreat to my gray cubicle. My children! They have survived all this time, and yet I have missed them. What happened to my children, in my time? What did they become to me, and I to them? Did they have children, grandchildren, and after our divorce, did they respect me enough to let me visit my grandchildren . . .? But it's all lost now, and if they kept records of their ancient selves—records of what had truly been my children—those are gone, too. They are *dead*.

Elisaveta regards my grief with some wonder, and finds it sympathetic. I feel her warm to me slightly. "They weren't really our children any longer, Vasily. They became something quite other, as have you and I. But *this* you—you've been kept like a butterfly in a collection. How sad."

She seeks me out and takes on a bodily form. It is not the shape of the Elisaveta I knew. She once built a biomechanical body to carry her thoughts. This is the self-image she carries now, of a mind within a primitive, woman-shaped soma.

"What happened to us?" I ask, my agony apparent to her, to all who listen.

"Is it that important to you?"

"Can you explain any of this?" I ask. I want to bury myself in her bosom, to hug her. I am so lost and afraid I feel like a child, and yet my pride keeps me together.

"I was your student, Vasily. Remember? You *browbeat* me into marrying you. You poured learning into my ear day and night, even when we made love. You were so full of knowledge. You spoke nine languages. You knew all there was to know about Schopenhauer and Hegel and Marx and Wittgenstein. You did not listen to what was important to me."

I want to draw back; it is impossible to cringe. This I recognize. This I remember. But the Elisaveta I knew had come to accept me, my faults and my learning, joyously, had encouraged me to open up with her. I had taught her a great deal.

"You gave me absolutely no room to grow, Vasily."

The enormous triviality of this conversation, at the end of time, strikes me and I want to laugh out loud. Not possible. I stare at this *monstrous* Elisaveta, so bitter and different . . . and now, to me, shaded by her indifference. "I feel like I've been half a dozen men, and we've all loved you badly," I say, hoping to sting her.

"No. Only one. You became angry when I disagreed with you. I asked for more freedom to explore. . . . You said there was really little left to explore. Even in the last half of the twenty-first century, Vasily, you said we had found all there was to find, and everything thereafter would be mere details. When I had my second child, it began. I saw you through the eyes of my infant daughter, saw what you would do to her, and I began to grow apart from you. We separated, then divorced, and it was for the best. For me, at any rate; I can't say that you ever understood."

We seem to stand in that gray cubicle, that comfortable simplicity with which I surrounded myself when first awakened. Elisaveta, taller, stronger, face more seasoned, stares at me with infinitely more experience. I am outmatched.

Her expression softens. "But you didn't deserve *this*, Vasily. You mustn't blame me for what your tributary has done."

"I am not he . . . it. It is not me. And you are not the Elisaveta I know!"

"You wanted to keep me forever the student you first met in your classroom. Do you see how futile that is now?"

"Then what can we love? What is there left to attach to?"

She shrugs. "It doesn't much matter, does it? There's no more time left to love or not to love. And love has become a vastly different thing."

"We reach this *peak* . . . of intelligence, of accomplishment, immortality . . ."

"Wait." Elisaveta frowns and tilts her head, as if listening, lifts her finger in question, listens again, to voices I do not hear. "I begin to understand your confusion," she says.

"What?"

"This is not a peak, Vasily. This is a backwater. We are simply all that's left after a long, dreadful attenuation. The greater, more subtle galaxies of Libraries ended themselves a hundred million years ago."

"Suicide?"

"They saw the very end we contemplate now. They decided that if our kind of life had no hope of escaping the Proof—the Proof these teachers helped fix in all our thoughts—then it was best not to send a part of ourselves into the next universe. We are what's left of those who disagreed. . . ."

"My tributary did not tell me this."

"Hiding the truth from yourself even now."

I hold my hands out to her, hoping for pity, but this Elisaveta has long since abandoned pity. I desperately need to activate some fragment of love within her. "I am so lost. . . ."

"We are all lost, Vasily. There is only one hope."

She turns and opens a broad door on one side of my cubicle, where I originally placed the window to the outside. "If we succeed at this," she says, "then we are better than those great souls. If we fail, they were right . . . better that nothing from our reality crosses the Between."

I admire her for her knowledge, then, for being kept so well informed. But I resent that she has advanced beyond me, has no need for me. The tributaries watch with interest, like voyeurs.

(*"Perhaps there is a chance."* My descendant self speaks in a private sending.)

"I see why you divorced me," I say sullenly.

"You were a tyrant and a bully. When you were stored—before your heart replacement, I remember now . . . When you were stored, you and I simply had not grown far apart. We would. It was inevitable."

(I ask my descendant self whether what she says is true.

"It is a way of seeing what happened," it says. *"The Proof has yet to be disproved. We recommended no attempts be made to do so. We think such attempts are futile."*

"You taught that?"

"We created patterns of thought and diffused them for use in creation of new tributaries. The last students. But perhaps there is a chance. Touch her. You know how to reach her.")

"The Proof is very convincing," I tell Elisaveta. "Perhaps this *is* futile."

"You simply have no say, Vasily. The effort is being made." I have touched her, but it is not pity I arouse this time, and certainly not love—it is disgust.

Through the window, Elisaveta and I see a portion of the plain. On it, the experiments have congealed into a hundred, a thousand smooth, slowly pulsing shapes. Above them all looms the shadow of the Coordinator.

(I feel a bridge being made, links being established. I sense panic in my descendant self, who works without the knowledge of the other tributaries. Then I am asked: *"Will you become part of the experiment?"*

"I don't understand."

"You are the judgment engine.")

"Now I must go," Elisaveta says. "We will all die soon. Neither you nor I are in the final self. No part of the teachers, or the Coordinator, will cross the Between."

"All futile, then," I say.

"Why so, Vasily? When I was young, you told me that change was an evil force, and that you longed for an eternal college, where all learning could be examined at leisure, without pressure. You've found that. Your tributary self has had billions of years to study the unchanging truths. And to infuse them into new tributaries. You've had your heaven, and I've had mine. Away from you, among those who nurture and respect."

I am left with nothing to say. Then, unexpectedly, the figure of Elisaveta reaches out with a nonexistent hand and touches my unreal cheek. For a moment, between us, there is something like the contact of flesh to flesh. I feel her fingers. She feels my cheek. Despite her words, the love has not died completely.

She fades from the cubicle. I rush to the window, to see if I can make out the Coordinator, but the shadow, the mercury-liquid cloud, has already vanished.

"They will fail," the We-ness says. It surrounds me with its mind, its persuasion, greater in scale than a human of my time to an ant. "This shows the origin of their folly. We have justified our existence."

(*You can still cross. There is still a connection between you. You can judge the experiment, go with the Endtime Work Coordinator.*)

I watch the plain, the joined shapes, extraordinarily beautiful, like condensed cities or civilizations or entire histories.

The sunlight dims, light rays jerk in our sight, in our fading scales of time.

(*Will you go?*)

"She doesn't need me. . . ." I want to go with Elisaveta. I want to reach out to her and shout, "I see! I understand!" But there is still sadness and self-pity. I am, after all, too small for her.

(*You may go. Persuade. Carry us with you.*)

And billions of years too late—

Shards of Seconds

We know now that the error lies in the distant past, a tendency of the Coordinator, who has gathered tributaries of like character. As did the teachers. The past still dominates, and there is satisfaction in knowing We, at least, have not committed any errors, have not fallen into folly.

We observe the end with interest. Soon, there will be no change. In that, there is some cause for exultation. Truly, We are tired.

On the bubbling remains of the School World, the students in their Berkus continue to the last instant with the experiment, and We watch from the cracked and cooling hill.

Something huge and blue and with many strange calm aspects rises from the field of experiments. It does not remind us of anything We have seen before.

It is new.

The Coordinator returns, embraces it, draws it away.

("She does not tell the truth. Parts of the Endtime Coordinator must cross with the final self. This is your last chance. Go to her and reconcile. Carry our thoughts with you.")

I feel a love for her greater than anything I could have felt before. I hate my descendant self, I hate the teachers and their gray spirits, depth upon depth of ashes out of the past. They want to use me to perpetuate all that matters to them.

I ache to reclaim what has been lost, to try to make up for the past.

The Coordinator withdraws from School World, taking with it the results of the student experiment. Do they have what they want—something worthy of being passed on? It would be wonderful to know. . . . I could die contented, knowing the Proof has been shattered. I could cross over, ask . . .

But I will not pollute her with me anymore.

"No."

The last thousandths of the last second fall like broken crystals.

(The connection is broken. You have failed.)

My tributary self, disappointed, quietly suggests I might be happier if I am deactivated.

Curiously, to the last, he clings to his imagined cubicle window. He cries his last words where there is no voice, no sound, no one to listen but us:

"Elisaveta! YES!"

The last of the ancient self is packed, mercifully, into oblivion. We will not subject him to the Endtime. We have pity.

We are left to our thoughts. The force that replaces gravity now spasms. The metric is very noisy. Length and duration become so grainy that thinking is difficult.

One tributary works to solve an ancient and obscure problem. Another studies the Proof one last time, savoring its formal beauty. Another considers ancient relations.

Our end, our own oblivion, the Between, will not be so horrible. There are worse things. Much

Poul Anderson is the dean of American hard-science-fiction writers. His B.S. in physics from the University of Minnesota in 1948 helped launch him on a career trajectory stressing well-realized, scientifically plausible novels, while he also has written outstanding fantasy. His deep knowledge of Scandinavian history informs much of his fiction, which has a mythological sweep, while remaining grounded in solid science. His *Tau Zero* remains a compact evocation of cosmological perspectives.

In "Genesis," he explores the latest astrophysical view of how Earth will evolve toward a finally uninhabitable state. The slow warming of our sun, together with the greenhouse effect of our atmosphere, may well overwhelm our efforts to stabilize our biosphere. This contrasts with the final vision of H. G. Wells in *The Time Machine,* which uses a waning sun as a symbol of flagging energies. In Anderson's world, humans do not go meekly into the searing noon.

GENESIS

Poul Anderson

Was it her I ought to have loved . . . ?
—Piet Hein

1

NO HUMAN COULD have shaped the thoughts or uttered them. They had no real beginning, they had been latent for millennium after millennium while the galactic brain was growing. Sometimes they passed from mind to mind, years or decades through space at the speed of light, nanoseconds to receive, comprehend, consider, and send a message on outward. But there was so much else—a cosmos of realities, an infinity of virtualities and abstract creations—that remembrances of Earth were the barest undertone, intermittent and fleeting, among uncounted billions of other incidentals. Most of the grand awareness was directed elsewhere, much of it intent on its own evolution.

For the galactic brain was still in infancy: unless it held itself to be still a-borning. By now its members were strewn from end to end of the spiral arms, out into the halo and the nearer star-gatherings, as far as the Magellanic Clouds. The seeds of fresh ones drifted farther yet; some had reached the shores of the Andromeda.

Each was a local complex of organisms, machines, and their interrelationships. ("Organism" seems best for something that maintains itself, reproduces at need, and possesses a consciousness in a range from the rudimentary to the transcendent, even though carbon compounds are a very small part of its material components and most of its life processes take place directly on the quantum level.) They numbered in the many millions, and the number was rising steeply, also within the Milky Way, as the founders of new generations arrived at new homes.

Thus the galactic brain was in perpetual growth, which from a cosmic viewpoint had barely started. Thought had just had time for a thousand or two journeys across its ever-expanding breadth. It would never absorb its members into itself; they would always remain individuals, developing along their individual lines. Let us therefore call them not cells, but nodes.

For they were in truth distinct. Each had more uniquenesses than were ever possible to a protoplasmic creature. Chaos and quantum fluctuation assured that none would exactly resemble any predecessor. Environment likewise helped shape the personality—surface conditions (what kind of planet, moon, asteroid, comet?) or free orbit, sun single or multiple (what kinds, what ages?), nebula, interstellar space and its ghostly tides. . . . Then, too, a node was not a single mind. It was as many as it chose to be, freely awakened and freely set aside, proteanly intermingling and separating again, using whatever bodies and sensors it wished for as long as it wished, immortally experiencing, creating, meditating, seeking a fulfillment that the search itself brought forth.

Hence, while every node was engaged with a myriad of matters, one might be especially developing new realms of mathematics, another composing glorious works that cannot really be likened to music, another observing the destiny of organic life on some world, life which it had perhaps fabricated for that purpose, another— Human words are useless.

Always, though, the nodes were in continuous communication over the light-years, communication on tremendous bandwidths of every possible medium. *This* was the galactic brain. That unity, that selfhood which was slowly coalescing, might spend millions of years contemplating a thought; but the thought would be as vast as the thinker, in whose sight an eon was as a day and a day was as an eon.

Already now, in its nascence, it affected the course of the universe. The time came when a node fully recalled Earth. That memory went out to others as part of the ongoing flow of information, ideas, feelings, reveries, and who knows what else? Certain of these others decided the subject was worth pursuing, and relayed it on their own message-streams. In this wise it passed through light-years and centuries, circulated, developed, and at last became a decision, which reached the node best able to take action.

Here the event has been related in words, ill-suited though they are to the task. They fail totally when they come to what happened next. How shall they tell of the dialogue of a mind with itself, when that thinking was a progression of quantum flickerings through configurations as intricate as the wave functions, when the computational power and database were so huge that measures become meaningless, when the mind raised aspects of itself to interact like persons until it drew them back into its wholeness, and when everything was said within microseconds of planetary time?

It is impossible, except vaguely and misleadingly. Ancient humans used the language of myth for that which they could not fathom. The sun was a fiery chariot daily crossing heaven, the year a god who died and was reborn, death a punishment for ancestral sin. Let us make our myth concerning the mission to Earth.

Think, then, of the primary aspect of the node's primary consciousness as if it were a single mighty entity, and name it Alpha. Think of a lesser manifestation of itself that it had synthesized and intended to release into separate existence as a second entity. For reasons that will become clear, imagine the latter masculine and name it Wayfarer.

All is myth and metaphor, beginning with this absurd nomenclature. Beings like these had no names. They had identities, instantly recognizable by others of their kind. They did not speak together, they did not go through discussion or explanation of any sort, they were not yet "they." But imagine it.

Imagine, too, their surroundings, not as perceived by their manifold sensors or conceptualized by their awarenesses and emotions, but as if human sense organs were reporting to a human brain. Such a picture is scarcely a sketch. Too much that was basic could not have registered. However, a human at an astronomical distance could have seen an M2 dwarf star about fifty parsecs from Sol, and ascertained that it had planets. She could have detected signs of immense, enigmatic energies, and wondered.

In itself, the sun was undistinguished. The galaxy held billions like it. Long ago, an artificial intelligence—at that dawn stage of evolution, this was the best phrase—had established itself there because one of the planets bore curious life-forms worth studying. That research went on through the megayears. Meanwhile the ever-heightening intelligence followed more and more different interests: above all, its self-evolution. That the sun would stay cool for an enormous length of time had been another consideration. The node did not want the trouble of coping with great environmental changes before it absolutely must.

Since then, stars had changed their relative positions. This now was the settlement nearest to Sol. Suns closer still were of less interest and had merely been visited, if that. Occasionally a free-space, dirigible node had passed through the neighborhood, but none chanced to be there at this epoch.

Relevant to our myth is the fact that no thinking species ever appeared on the viviferous world. Life is statistically uncommon in the cosmos, sapience almost vanishingly rare, therefore doubly precious.

Our imaginary human would have seen the sun as autumnally yellow, burning low and peacefully. Besides its planets and lesser natural attendants, various titanic structures orbited about it. From afar, they seemed like gossamer or like intricate spiderwebs agleam athwart the stars; most of what they were was force fields. They gathered and focused the energies that Alpha required, they searched the deeps of space and the atom, they transmitted and received the thought-flow that was becoming the galactic brain; what more they did lies beyond the myth.

Within their complexity, although not at any specific location, lived Alpha, its apex. Likewise, for the moment, did Wayfarer.

Imagine a stately voice: "Welcome into being. Yours is a high and, it may be, dangerous errand. Are you willing?"

If Wayfarer hesitated an instant, that was not from fear of suffering harm but from fear of inflicting it. "Tell me. Help me to understand."

"Sol—" The sun of old Earth, steadily heating since first it took shape, would continue stable for billions of years before it exhausted the hydrogen fuel at its core and swelled into a red giant. But—

A swift computation. "Yes. I see." Above a threshold level of radiation input, the geochemical and biochemical cycles that had maintained the temperature of Earth would be overwhelmed. Increasing warmth put increasing amounts of water vapor into the atmosphere, and it is a potent greenhouse gas. Heavier cloud cover, raising the albedo, could only postpone a day of catastrophe. Rising above it, water molecules were split by hard sunlight into hydrogen, which escaped to space, and oxygen, which bound to surface materials. Raging fires released monstrous tonnages of carbon dioxide, as did rocks exposed to heat by erosion in desiccated lands. It is the second major greenhouse gas. The time must come when the last oceans boiled away, leaving a globe akin to Venus; but well before then, life on Earth would be no more than a memory in the quantum consciousnesses. "When will total extinction occur?"

"On the order of a hundred thousand years futureward."

Pain bit through the facet of Wayfarer that came from Christian Brannock, who was born on ancient Earth and most passionately loved his living world. Long since had his uploaded mind merged into a colossal oneness that later divided and redivided, until copies of it were integral with awareness across the galaxy. So were the minds of millions of his fellow humans, as unnoticed now as single genes had been in their bodies when their flesh was alive, and yet significant elements of the whole. Ransacking its database, Alpha had found the record of Christian Brannock and chosen to weave him into the essence of Wayfarer, rather than someone else. The judgment was—call it intuitive.

"Can't you say more closely?" he appealed.

"No," replied Alpha. "The uncertainties and imponderables are too many. Gaia," mythic name for the node in the Solar System, "has responded to inquiries evasively when at all."

"Have . . . we . . . really been this slow to think about Earth?"

"We had much else to think about and do, did we not? Gaia could at any time have requested special consideration. She never did. Thus the matter did not appear to be of major importance. Human Earth is preserved in memory. What is posthuman Earth but a planet approaching the postbiological phase?

"True, the scarcity of spontaneously evolved biomes makes the case interesting. However, Gaia has presumably been observing and gathering the data, for the rest of us to examine whenever we wish. The Solar System has seldom had visitors. The last was two million years ago. Since then, Gaia has joined less and less in our fellowship; her communications have grown sparse and perfunctory. But such withdrawals are not unknown. A node may, for example, want to pursue a philosophical concept undisturbed, until it is ready for general contemplation. In short, nothing called Earth to our attention."

"*I* would have remembered," whispered Christian Brannock.

"What finally reminded us?" asked Wayfarer.

"The idea that Earth may be worth saving. Perhaps it holds more than Gaia knows of—" A pause. "—or has told of. If nothing else, sentimental value."

"Yes, I understand," said Christian Brannock.

"Moreover, and potentially more consequential, we may well have experience to gain, a precedent to set. If awareness is to survive the mortality of the stars, it must make the universe over. That work of billions or trillions of years will begin with some small, experimental undertaking. Shall it be now," the "now" of deathless beings already geologically old, "at Earth?"

"Not small," murmured Wayfarer. Christian Brannock had been an engineer.

"No," agreed Alpha. "Given the time constraint, only the resources of a few stars will be available. Nevertheless, we have various possibilities open to us, if we commence soon enough. The question is which would be the best—and, first, whether we *should* act.

"Will you go seek an answer?"

"Yes," responded Wayfarer, and "Yes, oh, God damn, yes," cried Christian Brannock.

A spaceship departed for Sol. A laser accelerated it close to the speed of light, energized by the sun and controlled by a network of interplanetary dimensions. If necessary, the ship could decelerate itself at journey's end, travel freely about, and return unaided, albeit more slowly. Its cryomagnetics supported a good-sized ball of antimatter, and its total mass was slight. The material payload amounted simply to: a matrix, plus backup, for running the Wayfarer programs and containing a database deemed sufficient; assorted sensors and effectors; several bodies of different capabilities, into which he could download an essence of himself; miscellaneous equipment and power systems; a variety of instruments; and a thing ages forgotten, which Wayfarer had ordered molecules to make at the wish of Christian Brannock. He might somewhere find time and fingers for it.

A guitar.

2

There was a man called Kalava, a sea captain of Sirsu. His clan was the Samayoki. In youth he had fought well at Broken Mountain, where the armies of Ulonai met the barbarian invaders swarming north out of the desert and cast them back with fearsome losses. He then became a mariner. When the Ulonaian League fell apart and the alliances led by Sirsu and Irrulen raged across the land, year after year, seeking each other's throats, Kalava sank enemy ships, burned enemy villages, bore treasure and captives off to market.

After the grudgingly made, unsatisfactory Peace of Tuopai, he went into trade. Besides going up and down the River Lonna and around the Gulf of Sirsu, he often sailed along the North Coast, bartering as he went, then out over the Windroad Sea to the colonies on the Ending Islands. At last, with three ships, he followed that coast east through distances hitherto unknown. Living off the waters and what hunting parties could take ashore, dealing or fighting with the wild tribes they met, in the course of months he and his crews came to where the land bent south. A ways beyond that they found a port belonging to the fabled people of the Shining Fields. They abode for a year and returned carrying wares that at home made them rich.

From his clan Kalava got leasehold of a thorp and good farmland in the Lonna delta, about a day's travel from Sirsu. He meant to settle down, honored and comfortable. But that was not in the thought of the gods nor in his nature. He was soon quarreling with all his neighbors, until his wife's brother grossly insulted him and he killed the man. Thereupon she left him. At the clanmoot which composed the matter she received a third of the family wealth, in gold and movables. Their daughters and the husbands of these sided with her.

Of Kalava's three sons, the eldest had drowned in a storm at sea; the next died of the Black Blood; the third, faring as an apprentice on a merchant vessel far south to Zhir, fell while resisting robbers in sand-drifted streets under the time-gnawed colonnades of an abandoned city. They left no children, unless by slaves. Nor would Kalava, now; no free woman took his offers of marriage. What he had gathered through a hard lifetime would fall to kinfolk who hated him. Most folk in Sirsu shunned him too.

Long he brooded, until a dream hatched. When he knew it for what it was, he set about his preparations, more quietly than might have been awaited. Once the business was under way, though not too far along for him to drop if he must, he sought Ilyandi the skythinker.

She dwelt on Council Heights. There did the Vilkui meet each year for rites and conference. But when the rest of them had dispersed again to carry on their vocation—dream interpreters, scribes, physicians, mediators, vessels of olden lore and learning, teachers of the young— Ilyandi remained. Here she could best search the heavens and seek for the meaning of what she found, on a high place sacred to all Ulonai.

Up the Spirit Way rumbled Kalava's chariot. Near the top, the trees that lined it, goldfruit and plume, stood well apart, giving him a clear view. Bushes grew sparse and low on the stony slopes, here the dusty green of vasi, there a shaggy hairleaf, yonder a scarlet fireflower. Scorchwort lent its acrid smell to a wind blowing hot and slow off the Gulf. That water shone, tarnished metal, westward beyond sight, under a silver-gray overcast beneath which scudded rags of darker cloud. A rainstorm stood on the horizon, blurred murk and flutters of lightning light.

Elsewhere reached the land, bloomgrain ripening yellow, dun paperleaf, verdant pastures for herdlings, violet richen orchards, tall stands of shipwood. Farmhouses and their outbuildings lay widely strewn. The weather having been dry of late, dust whirled up from the roads winding among them to veil wagons and trains of porters. Regally from its sources eastward in Wilderland flowed the Lonna, arms fanning out north and south.

Sirsu lifted battlemented walls on the right bank of the main stream, tiny in Kalava's eyes at its distance. Yet he knew it, he could pick out famous works, the Grand Fountain in King's Newmarket, the frieze-bordered portico of the Flame Temple, the triumphal column in Victory Square, and he knew where the wrights had their workshops, the merchants their bazaars, the innkeepers their houses for a seaman to find a jug and a wench. Brick, sandstone, granite, marble mingled their colors softly together. Ships and boats plied the water or were docked under the walls. On the opposite shore sprawled mansions and gardens of the Helki suburb, their rooftiles fanciful as jewels.

It was remote from that which he approached.

Below a great arch, two postulants in blue robes slanted their staffs across the way and called, "In the name of the Mystery, stop, make reverence, and declare yourself!"

Their young voices rang high, unawed by a sight that had daunted warriors. Kalava was a big man, wide-shouldered and thick-muscled. Weather had darkened his skin to the hue of coal and bleached nearly white the hair that fell in braids halfway down his back. As black were the eyes that gleamed below a shelf of brow, in a face rugged, battered, and scarred. His mustache curved down past the jaw, dyed red. Traveling in peace, he wore simply a knee-length kirtle, green and trimmed with kivi skin, each scale polished, and buskins; but gold coiled around his arms and a sword was belted at his hip. Likewise did a spear stand socketed in the chariot, pennon flapping, while a shield slatted at the rail and an ax hung ready to be thrown. Four matched slaves drew the car. Their line had been bred for generations to be draft creatures—huge, long-legged, spirited, yet trustworthy after the males were gelded. Sweat sheened over Kalava's brand on the small, bald heads and ran down naked bodies. Nonetheless they breathed easily and the smell of them was rather sweet.

Their owner roared, "Halt!" For a moment only the wind had sound or motion. Then Kalava touched his brow below the headband and recited the Confession: "What a man knows is little, what he understands is less, therefore let him bow down to wisdom." Himself, he trusted more in blood sacrifices and still more in his own strength; but he kept a decent respect for the Vilkui.

"I seek counsel from the skythinker Ilyandi," he said. That was hardly needful, when no other initiate of her order was present.

"All may seek who are not attainted of ill-doing," replied the senior boy as ceremoniously.

"Ruvio bear witness that any judgments against me stand satisfied." The Thunderer was the favorite god of most mariners.

"Enter, then, and we shall convey your request to our lady."

The junior boy led Kalava across the outer court. Wheels rattled loud on flagstones. At the guesthouse, he helped stall, feed, and water the slaves, before he showed the newcomer to a room that in the high season slept two-score men. Elsewhere in the building were a bath, a refectory, ready food—dried meat, fruit, and flatbread—with richenberry wine. Kalava also found a book. After refreshment, he sat down on a bench to pass the time with it.

He was disappointed. He had never had many chances or much desire to read, so his skill was limited; and the copyist for this codex had used a style of lettering obsolete nowadays. Worse, the text was a chronicle of the emperors of Zhir. That was not just painful to him—oh, Eneio, his son, his last son!—but valueless. True, the Vilkui taught that civilization had come to Ulonai from Zhir. What of it? How many centuries had fled since the desert claimed that realm? What were the descendants of its dwellers but starveling nomads and pestiferous bandits?

Well, Kalava thought, yes, this could be a timely warning, a reminder to people of how the desert still marched northward. But was what they could see not enough? He had passed by towns not very far south, flourishing in his grandfather's time, now empty, crumbling houses half buried in dust, glassless windows like the eye sockets in a skull.

His mouth tightened. *He* would not meekly abide any doom.

Day was near an end when an acolyte of Ilyandi came to say that she would receive him. Walking with his guide, he saw purple dusk shade toward night in the east. In the west the storm had ended, leaving that part of heaven clear for a while. The sun was plainly visible, though mists turned it into a red-orange step pyramid. From the horizon it cast a bridge of fire over the Gulf and sent great streamers of light aloft into cloudbanks that glowed sulfurous. A whistlewing passed like a shadow across them. The sound of its flight keened faintly down through air growing less hot. Otherwise a holy silence rested upon the heights.

Three stories tall, the sanctuaries, libraries, laboratories, and quarters of the Vilkui surrounded the inner court with their cloisters. A garden of flowers and healing herbs, intricately laid out, filled most of it. A lantern had been lighted in one arcade, but all windows were dark and Ilyandi stood out in the open awaiting her visitor.

She made a slight gesture of dismissal. The acolyte bowed her head and slipped away. Kalava saluted, feeling suddenly awkward but his resolution headlong within him. "Greeting, wise and gracious lady," he said.

"Well met, brave captain," the skythinker replied. She gestured at a pair of confronting stone benches. "Shall we be seated?" It fell short of inviting him to share wine, but it meant she would at least hear him out.

They lowered themselves and regarded one another through the swiftly deepening twilight. Ilyandi was a slender woman of perhaps forty years, features thin and regular, eyes large and luminous brown, complexion pale—like smoked copper, he thought. Cropped short in token of celibacy, wavy hair made a bronze coif above a plain white robe. A green sprig of tekin, held at her left shoulder by a pin in the emblematic form of interlocked circle and triangle, declared her a Vilku.

"How can I aid your venture?" she asked.

He started in surprise. "Huh! What do you know about my plans?" In haste: "My lady knows much, of course."

She smiled. "You and your saga have loomed throughout these past decades. And . . . word reaches us here. You search out your former crewmen or bid them come see you, all privately. You order repairs made to the ship remaining in your possession. You meet with chandlers, no doubt to sound them out about prices. Few if any people have noticed. Such discretion is not your wont. Where are you bound, Kalava, and why so secretively?"

His grin was rueful. "My lady's not just wise and learned, she's clever. Well, then, why not go straight to the business? I've a voyage in mind that most would call crazy. Some among them might try to forestall me, holding that it would anger the gods of those parts—seeing that nobody's ever returned from there, and recalling old tales of monstrous things glimpsed from afar. I don't believe them myself, or I wouldn't try it."

"Oh, I can imagine you setting forth regardless," said Ilyandi half under her breath. Louder: "But agreed, the fear is likely false. No one had reached the Shining Fields by sea, either, before you did. You asked for no beforehand spells or blessings then. Why have you sought me now?"

"This is, is different. Not hugging a shoreline. I—well, I'll need to get and train a new huukin, and that's no small thing in money or time." Kalava spread his big hands, almost helplessly. "I had not looked to set forth ever again, you see. Maybe it is madness, an old man with an old crew in a single old ship. I hoped you might counsel me, my lady."

"You're scarcely ready for the balefire, when you propose to cross the Windroad Sea," she answered.

This time he was not altogether taken aback. "May I ask how my lady knows?"

Ilyandi waved a hand. Catching faint lamplight, the long fingers soared through the dusk like nightswoopers. "You have already been east, and would not need to hide such a journey. South, the trade routes are ancient as far as Zhir. What has it to offer but the plunder of tombs and dead cities, brought in by wretched squatters? What lies beyond but unpeopled desolation until, folk say, one would come to the Burning Lands and perish miserably? Westward we know of a few islands, and then empty ocean. If anything lies on the far side, you could starve and thirst to death before you reached it. But northward—yes, wild waters, but sometimes men come upon driftwood of unknown trees or spy storm-borne flyers of unknown breed—and we have all the legends of the High North, and glimpses of mountains from ships blown off course—" Her voice trailed away.

"Some of those tales ring true to me," Kalava said. "More true than stories about uncanny sights. Besides, wild huukini breed offshore, where fish are plentiful. I have not seen enough of them there, in season, to account for as many as I've seen in open sea. They must have a second shoreline. Where but the High North?"

Ilyandi nodded. "Shrewd, Captain. What else do you hope to find?"

He grinned again. "I'll tell you after I get back, my lady."

Her tone sharpened. "No treasure-laden cities to plunder."

He yielded. "Nor to trade with. Would we not have encountered craft of theirs, or, anyhow, wreckage? However . . . the farther north, the less heat and more rainfall, no? A country yonder could have a mild clime, forestfuls of timber, fat land for plowing, and nobody to fight." The words throbbed. "No desert creeping in? Room to begin afresh, my lady."

She regarded him steadily through the gloaming. "You'd come home, recruit people, found a colony, and be its king?"

"Its foremost man, aye, though I expect the kind of folk who'd go will want a republic. But mainly—" His voice went low. He stared beyond her. "Freedom. Honor. A freeborn wife and new sons."

They were silent awhile. Full night closed in. It was not as murky as usual, for the clearing in the west had spread rifts up toward the zenith. A breath of coolness soughed in leaves, as if Kalava's dream whispered a promise.

"You are determined," she said at last, slowly. "Why have you come to me?"

"For whatever counsel you will give, my lady. Facts about the passage may be hoarded in books here."

She shook her head. "I doubt it. Unless navigation—yes, that is a real barrier, is it not?"

"Always," he sighed.

"What means of wayfinding have you?"

"Why, you must know."

"I know what is the common knowledge about it. Craftsmen keep their trade secrets, and surely skippers are no different in that regard. If you will tell me how you navigate, it shall not pass these lips, and I may be able to add something."

Eagerness took hold of him. "I'll wager my lady can! We see moon or stars unoften and fitfully. Most days the sun shows no more than a blur of dull light amongst the clouds, if that. But you, skythinkers like you, they've watched and measured for hundreds of years, they've gathered lore—" Kalava paused. "Is it too sacred to share?"

"No, no," she replied. "The Vilkui keep the calendar for everyone, do they not? The reason that sailors rarely get our help is that they could make little or no use of our learning. Speak."

"True, it was Vilkui who discovered lodestones. . . . Well, coasting these waters, I rely mainly on my remembrance of landmarks, or a periplus if they're less familiar to me. Soundings help, especially if the plumb brings up a sample of the bottom for me to look at and taste. Then in the Shining Fields I got a crystal—you must know about it, for I gave another to the order when I got back—I look through it at the sky and, if the weather be not too thick, I see more closely where the sun is than I can with a bare eye. A logline and hourglass give some idea of speed, a lodestone some idea of direction, when out of sight of land. Sailing for the High North and return, I'd mainly use it, I suppose. But if my lady could tell me of anything else—"

She sat forward on her bench. He heard a certain intensity. "I think I might, Captain. I've studied that sunstone of yours. With it, one can estimate latitude and time of day, if one knows the date and the sun's heavenly course during the year. Likewise, even glimpses of moon and stars would be valuable to a traveler who knew them well."

"That's not me," he said wryly. "Could my lady write something down? Maybe this old head won't be too heavy to puzzle it out."

She did not seem to hear. Her gaze had gone upward. "The aspect of the stars in the High North," she murmured. "It could tell us whether the world is indeed round. And are our vague auroral shimmers more bright yonder—in the veritable Lodeland—?"

His look followed hers. Three stars twinkled wan where the clouds were torn. "It's good of you, my lady," he said, "that you sit talking with me, when you could be at your quadrant or whatever, snatching this chance."

Her eyes met his. "Yours may be a better chance, Captain," she answered fiercely. "When first I got the rumor of your expedition, I began to think upon it and what it could mean. Yes, I will help you where I can. I may even sail with you."

The *Gray Courser* departed Sirsu on a morning tide as early as there was light to steer by. Just the same, people crowded the dock. The majority watched mute. A number made signs against evil. A few, mostly young, sang a defiant paean, but the air seemed to muffle their strains.

Only lately had Kalava given out what his goal was. He must, to account for the skythinker's presence, which could not be kept hidden. That sanctification left the authorities no excuse to forbid his venture. However, it took little doubt and fear off those who believed the outer Windroad a haunt of monsters and demons, which might be stirred to plague home waters.

His crew shrugged the notion off, or laughed at it. At any rate, they said they did. Two-thirds of them were crusty shellbacks who had fared under his command before. For the rest, he had had to take what he could scrape together, impoverished laborers and masterless ruffians. All were, though, very respectful of the Vilku.

The *Gray Courser* was a yalka, broad-beamed and shallow-bottomed, with a low forecastle and poop and a deckhouse amidships. The foremast carried two square sails, the mainmast one square and one fore-and-aft; a short bowsprit extended for a jib. A catapult was mounted in the bows. On either side, two boats hung from davits, aft of the harnessing shafts. Her hull was painted according to her name, with red trim. Alongside swam the huukin, its back a sleek blue ridge.

Kalava had the tiller until she cleared the river mouth and stood out into the Gulf. By then it was full day. A hot wind whipped gray-green water into whitecaps that set the vessel rolling. It whined in the shrouds; timbers creaked. He turned the helm over to a sailor, trod forward on the poop deck, and sounded a trumpet. Men stared. From her cabin below, Ilyandi climbed up to stand beside him. Her white robe fluttered like wings that would fain be asoar. She raised her arms and chanted a spell for the voyage:

> *"Burning, turning,*
> *The sun-wheel reels*
> *Behind the blindness*
> *Cloud-smoke evokes.*

> *The old cold moon*
> *Seldom tells*
> *Where it lairs*
> *With stars afar.*
> *No men's omens*
> *Abide to guide*
> *High in the skies.*
> *But lodestone for Lodeland*
> *Strongly longs."*

While the deckhands hardly knew what she meant, they felt heartened.

Land dwindled aft, became a thin blue line, vanished into waves and mists. Kalava was cutting straight northwest across the Gulf. He meant to sail through the night, and thus wanted plenty of sea room. Also, he and Ilyandi would practice with her ideas about navigation. Hence after a while the mariners spied no other sails, and the loneliness began to weigh on them.

However, they worked stoutly enough. Some thought it a good sign, and cheered, when the clouds clove toward evening and they saw a horned moon. Their mates were frightened; was the moon supposed to appear by day? Kalava bullied them out of it.

Wind stiffened during the dark. By morning it had raised seas in which the ship reeled. It was a westerly, too, forcing her toward land no matter how close-hauled. When he spied, through scud, the crags of Cape Vairka, the skipper realized he could not round it unaided.

He was a rough man, but he had been raised in those skills that were seemly for a freeman of Clan Samayoki. Though not a poet, he could make an acceptable verse when occasion demanded. He stood in the forepeak and shouted into the storm, the words flung back to his men:

> *"Northward now veering,*
> *Steering from kin-rift,*
> *Spindrift flung gale-borne,*
> *Sail-borne is daft.*
> *Craft will soon flounder,*
> *Founder, go under—*
> *Thunder this wit-lack!*
> *Sit back and call*
> *All that swim near.*
> *Steer then to northward."*

Having thus offered the gods a making, he put the horn to his mouth and blasted forth a summons to his huukin.

The great beast heard and slipped close. Kalava took the lead in lowering the shafts. A line around his waist for safety, he sprang over the rail, down onto the broad back. He kept his feet, though the two men who followed him went off into the billows and had to be hauled up. Together they rode the huukin, guiding it between the poles where they could attach the harness.

"I waited too long," Kalava admitted. "This would have been easier yesterday. Well, something for you to brag about in the inns at home, nay?" Their mates drew them back aboard. Meanwhile the sails had been furled. Kalava took first watch at the reins. Mightily pulled the huukin, tail and flippers churning foam that the wind snatched away, on into the open, unknown sea.

3

Wayfarer woke.

He had passed the decades of transit shut down. A being such as Alpha would have spent them conscious, its mind perhaps at work on an intellectual artistic creation—to it, no basic distinction—or perhaps replaying an existent piece for contemplation-enjoyment or perhaps in activity too abstract for words to hint at. Wayfarer's capabilities, though large, were insufficient for that. The hardware and software (again we use myth) of his embodiment were designed principally for interaction with the material universe. In effect, there was nothing for him to do.

He could not even engage in discourse. The robotic systems of the ship were subtle and powerful but lacked true consciousness; it was unnecessary for them, and distraction or boredom might have posed a hazard. Nor could he converse with entities elsewhere; signals would have taken too long going to and fro. He did spend a while, whole minutes of external time, reliving the life of his Christian Brannock element, studying the personality, accustoming himself to its ways. Thereafter he . . . went to sleep.

The ship reactivated him as it crossed what remained of the Oort Cloud. Instantly aware, he coupled to instrument after instrument and scanned the Solar System. Although his database summarized Gaia's reports, he deemed it wise to observe for himself. The eagerness, the bittersweet sense of homecoming, that flickered around his calm logic were Christian Brannock's. Imagine long-forgotten feelings coming astir in you when you return to a scene of your early childhood.

Naturally, the ghost in the machine knew that changes had been enormous since his mortal eyes closed forever. The rings of Saturn were tattered and tenuous. Jupiter had gained a showy set of them from the death of a satellite, but its Red Spot faded away ages ago. Mars was moonless, its axis steeply canted. . . . Higher resolution would have shown scant traces of humanity. From the antimatter plants inside the orbit of Mercury to the comet harvesters beyond Pluto, what was no more needed had been dismantled or left forsaken. Wind, water, chemistry, tectonics, cosmic stones, spalling radiation, nuclear decay, quantum shifts had patiently reclaimed the relics for chaos. Some fossils existed yet, and some eroded fragments aboveground or in space; otherwise all was only in Gaia's memory.

No matter. It was toward his old home that the Christian Brannock facet of Wayfarer sped.

Unaided, he would not have seen much difference from aforetime in the sun. It was slightly larger and noticeably brighter. Human vision would have perceived the light as more white, with the faintest bluish quality. Unprotected skin would have reacted quickly to the increased ultraviolet. The solar wind was stronger, too. But thus far the changes were comparatively minor. This star was still on the main sequence. Planets with greenhouse atmospheres were most affected. Certain minerals on Venus were now molten. Earth—

The ship hurtled inward, reached its goal, and danced into parking orbit. At close range, Wayfarer looked forth.

On Luna, the patterns of maria were not quite the same, mountains were worn down farther, and newer craters had wrecked or obliterated older ones. Rubble-filled anomalies showed where ground had collapsed on deserted cities. Essentially, though, the moon was again the same desolation, seared by day and death-cold by night, as before life's presence. It had receded farther, astronomically no big distance, and this had lengthened Earth's rotation period by about an hour. However, as yet it circled near enough to stabilize that spin.

The mother planet offered less to our imaginary eyes. Clouds wrapped it in dazzling white. Watching carefully, you could have seen swirls and bandings, but to a quick glance the cover was well-nigh featureless. Shifting breaks in it gave blue flashes of water, brown flashes of land—nowhere ice or snowfall, nowhere lights after dark; and the radio spectrum seethed voiceless.

When did the last human foot tread this world? Wayfarer searched his database. The information was not there. Perhaps it was unrecorded, unknown. Perhaps that last flesh had chanced to die alone or chosen to die privately.

Certainly it was long and long ago. How brief had been the span of

Homo sapiens, from flint and fire to machine intelligence! Not that the end had come suddenly or simply. It took several millennia, said the database: time for whole civilizations to rise and fall and leave their mutant descendants. Sometimes population decline had reversed in this or that locality, sometimes nations heeded the vatic utterances of prophets and strove to turn history backward—for a while, a while. But always the trend was ineluctable.

The clustered memories of Christian Brannock gave rise to a thought in Wayfarer that was as if the man spoke: I saw the beginning. I did not foresee the end. To me this was the magnificent dawn of hope.

And was I wrong?

The organic individual is mortal. It can find no way to stave off eventual disintegration; quantum chemistry forbids. Besides, if a man could live for a mere thousand years, the data storage capacity of his brain would be saturated, incapable of holding more. Well before then, he would have been overwhelmed by the geometric increase of correlations, made feebleminded or insane. Nor could he survive the rigors of star travel at any reasonable speed or unearthly environments, in a universe never meant for him.

But transferred into a suitable inorganic structure, the pattern of neuron and molecular traces and their relationships that is his inner self becomes potentially immortal. The very complexity that allows this makes him continue feeling as well as thinking. If the quality of emotions is changed, it is because his physical organism has become stronger, more sensitive, more intelligent and aware. He will soon lose any wistfulness about his former existence. His new life gives him so much more, a cosmos of sensing and experience, memory and thought, space and time. He can multiply himself, merge and unmerge with others, grow in spirit until he reaches a limit once inconceivable; and after that he can become a part of a mind greater still, and thus grow onward.

The wonder was, Christian Brannock mused, that any humans whatsoever had held out, clung to the primitive, refused to see that their heritage was no longer of DNA but of psyche.

And yet—

The half-formed question faded away. His half-formed personhood rejoined Wayfarer. Gaia was calling from Earth.

She had, of course, received notification, which arrived several years in advance of the spacecraft. Her manifold instruments, on the planet and out between planets, had detected the approach. For the message she now sent, she chose to employ a modulated neutrino beam. Imagine her saying: "Welcome. Do you need help? I am ready to give any I can." Imagine this in a voice low and warm.

Imagine Wayfarer replying, "Thank you, but all's well. I'll be down directly, if that suits you."

"I do not quite understand why you have come. Has the rapport with me not been adequate?"

No, Wayfarer refrained from saying. "I will explain later in more detail than the transmission could carry. Essentially, though, the reason is what you were told. We"—he deemphasized rather than excluded her—"wonder if Earth ought to be saved from solar expansion."

Her tone cooled a bit. "I have said more than once: No. You can perfect your engineering techniques anywhere else. The situation here is unique. The knowledge to be won by observing the unhampered course of events is unpredictable, but it will be enormous, and I have good cause to believe it will prove of the highest value."

"That may well be. I'll willingly hear you out, if you care to unfold your thoughts more fully than you have hitherto. But I do want to make my own survey and develop my own recommendations. No reflection on you; we both realize that no one mind can encompass every possibility, every interpretation. Nor can any one mind follow out every ongoing factor in what it observes; and what is overlooked can prove to be the agent of chaotic change. I may notice something that escaped you. Unlikely, granted. After your millions of years here, you very nearly *are* Earth and the life on it, are you not? But . . . we . . . would like an independent opinion."

Imagine her laughing. "At least you are polite, Wayfarer. Yes, do come down. I will steer you in."

"That won't be necessary. Your physical centrum is in the arctic region, isn't it? I can find my way."

He sensed steel beneath the mildness: "Best I guide you. You recognize the situation as inherently chaotic. Descending on an arbitrary path, you might seriously perturb certain things in which I am interested. Please."

"As you wish," Wayfarer conceded.

Robotics took over. The payload module of the spacecraft detached from the drive module, which stayed in orbit. Under its own power but controlled from below, asheen in the harsh spatial sunlight, the cylindroid braked and slanted downward.

It pierced the cloud deck. Wayfarer scanned eagerly. However, this was no sightseeing tour. The descent path sacrificed efficiency and made almost straight for a high northern latitude. Sonic-boom thunder trailed.

He did spy the fringe of a large continent oriented east and west, and saw that those parts were mainly green. Beyond lay a stretch of sea. He thought that he glimpsed something peculiar on it, but passed over too fast, with his attention directed too much ahead, to be sure.

The circumpolar landmass hove in view. Wayfarer compared maps that Gaia had transmitted. They were like nothing that Christian Brannock remembered. Plate tectonics had slowed, as radioactivity and original heat in the core of Earth declined, but drift, subduction, upthrust still went on.

He cared more about the life here. Epoch after epoch, Gaia had described its posthuman evolution as she watched. Following the mass extinction of the Paleotechnic, it had regained the abundance and diversity of a Cretaceous or a Tertiary. Everything was different, though, except for a few small survivals. To Wayfarer, as to Alpha and, ultimately, the galactic brain, those accounts seemed somehow, increasingly, incomplete. They did not quite make ecological sense—as of the past hundred thousand years or so. Nor did all of Gaia's responses to questions.

Perhaps she was failing to gather full data, perhaps she was misinterpreting, perhaps— It was another reason to send him to her.

Arctica appeared below the flyer. Imagine her giving names to it and its features. As long as she had lived with them, they had their identities for her. The Coast Range of hills lifted close behind the littoral. Through it cut the Remnant River, which had been greater when rains were more frequent but continued impressive. With its tributaries it drained the intensely verdant Bountiful Valley. On the far side of that, foothills edged the steeply rising Boreal Mountains. Once the highest among them had been snowcapped; now their peaks were naked rock. Streams rushed down the flanks, most of them joining the Remnant somewhere as it flowed through its gorges toward the sea. In a lofty vale gleamed the Rainbowl, the big lake that was its headwaters. Overlooking from the north loomed the mountain Mindhome, its top, the physical centrum of Gaia, lost in cloud cover.

In a way the scenes were familiar to him. She had sent plenty of full-sensory transmissions, as part of her contribution to universal knowledge and thought. Wayfarer could even recall the geological past, back beyond the epoch when Arctica broke free and drifted north, ramming into land already present and thrusting the Boreals heavenward. He could extrapolate the geological future in comparable detail, until a red giant filling half the sky glared down on an airless globe of stone and sand, which would at last melt. Nevertheless, the reality, the physical being here, smote him more strongly than he had expected. His sensors strained to draw in every datum while his vessel flew needlessly fast to the goal.

He neared the mountain. Jutting south from the range, it was not the tallest. Brushy forest grew all the way up its sides, lush on the lower slopes, parched on the heights, where many trees were leafless skeletons. That was due to a recent climatic shift, lowering the mean level of clouds, so that a formerly well-watered zone had been suffering a decades-long drought. (Yes, Earth was moving faster toward its doomsday.) Fire must be a constant threat, he thought. But no, Gaia's agents could quickly put any out, or she might simply ignore it. Though not large, the area she occupied on the summit was paved over and doubtless nothing was vulnerable to heat or smoke.

He landed. For an instant of planetary time, lengthy for minds that worked at close to light speed, there was communication silence.

He was again above the cloud deck. It eddied white, the peak rising from it like an island among others, into the level rays of sunset. Overhead arched a violet clarity. A thin wind whittered, cold at this altitude. On a level circle of blue-black surfacing, about a kilometer wide, stood the crowded structures and engines of the centrum.

A human would have seen an opalescent dome surrounded by towers, some sheer as lances, some intricately lacy; and silver spiderwebs; and lesser things of varied but curiously simple shapes, mobile units waiting to be dispatched on their tasks. Here and there, flyers darted and hovered, most of them as small and exquisite as hummingbirds (if our human had known hummingbirds). To her the scene would have wavered slightly, as if she saw it through rippling water, or it throbbed with quiet energies, or it pulsed in and out of space-time. She would not have sensed the complex of force fields and quantum-mechanical waves, nor the microscopic and submicroscopic entities that were the major part of it.

Wayfarer perceived otherwise.

Then: "Again, welcome," Gaia said.

"And again, thank you," Wayfarer replied. "I am glad to be here."

They regarded one another, not as bodies—which neither was wearing—but as minds, matrices of memory, individuality, and awareness. Separately he wondered what she thought of him. She was giving him no more of herself than had always gone over the communication lines between the stars. That was: a nodal organism, like Alpha and millions of others, which over the eons had increased its capabilities, while ceaselessly experiencing and thinking; the ages of interaction with Earth and the life on Earth, maybe shaping her soul more deeply than the existence she shared with her own kind; traces of ancient human uploads, but they were not like Christian Brannock, copies of them dispersed across the galaxy, no, these had chosen to stay with the mother world. . . .

"I told you I am glad too," said Gaia regretfully, "but I am not, quite. You question my stewardship."

"Not really," Wayfarer protested. "I hope not ever. We simply wish to know better how you carry it out."

"Why, you do know. As with any of us who is established on a planet, high among my activities is to study its complexities, follow its evolution. On this planet that means, above all, the evolution of its life, everything from genetics to ecology. In what way have I failed to share information with my fellows?"

In many ways, Wayfarer left unspoken. Overtly: "Once we"—here he referred to the galactic brain—"gave close consideration to the matter, we found countless unresolved puzzles. For example—"

What he set forth was hundreds of examples, ranging over millennia. Let a single case serve. About ten thousand years ago, the big continent south of Arctica had supported a wealth of large grazing animals. Their herds darkened the plains and made loud the woods. Gaia had described them in loving detail, from the lyre-curved horns of one genus to the wind-rustled manes of another. Abruptly, in terms of historical time, she transmitted no more about them. When asked why, she said they had gone extinct. She never explained how.

To Wayfarer she responded in such haste that he got a distinct impression she realized she had made a mistake. (Remember, this is a myth.) "A variety of causes. Climates became severe as temperatures rose—"

"I am sorry," he demurred, "but when analyzed, the meteorological data you supplied show that warming and desiccation cannot yet have been that significant in those particular regions."

"How are you so sure?" she retorted. Imagine her angry. "Have any of you lived with Earth for megayears, to know it that well?" Her tone hardened. "I do not myself pretend to full knowledge. A living world is too complex—chaotic. Cannot you appreciate that? I am still seeking comprehension of too many phenomena. In this instance, consider just a small shift in ambient conditions, coupled with new diseases and scores of other factors, most of them subtle. I believe that, combined, they broke a balance of nature. But unless and until I learn more, I will not waste bandwidth in talk about it."

"I sympathize with that," said Wayfarer mildly, hoping for conciliation. "Maybe I can discover or suggest something helpful."

"No. You are too ignorant, you are blind, you can only do harm."

He stiffened. "We shall see." Anew he tried for peace. "I did not come in any hostility. I came because here is the fountainhead of us all, and we think of saving it."

Her manner calmed likewise. "How would you?"

"That is one thing I have come to find out—what the best way is, should we proceed."

In the beginning, maybe, a screen of planetary dimensions, kept between Earth and sun by an interplay of gravity and electromagnetism, to ward off the fraction of energy that was not wanted. It would only be a temporary expedient, though, possibly not worthwhile. That depended on how long it would take to accomplish the real work. Engines in close orbit around the star, drawing their power from its radiation, might generate currents in its body that carried fresh hydrogen down to the core, thus restoring the nuclear furnace to its olden state. Or they might bleed gas off into space, reducing the mass of the sun, damping its fires but adding billions upon billions of years wherein it scarcely changed any more. That would cause the planets to move outward, a factor that must be taken into account but that would reduce the requirements.

Whatever was done, the resources of several stars would be needed to accomplish it, for time had grown cosmically short.

"An enormous work," Gaia said. Wayfarer wondered if she had in mind the dramatics of it, apparitions in heaven, such as centuries during which fire-fountains rushed visibly out of the solar disc.

"For an enormous glory," he declared.

"No," she answered curtly. "For nothing, and worse than nothing. Destruction of everything I have lived for. Eternal loss to the heritage."

"Why, is not Earth the heritage?"

"No. Knowledge is. I tried to make that clear to Alpha." She paused. "To you I say again, the evolution of life, its adaptations, struggles, transformations, and how at last it meets death—those are unforeseeable, and nowhere else in the space-time universe can there be a world like this for them to play themselves out. They will enlighten us in ways the galactic brain itself cannot yet conceive. They may well open to us whole new phases of ultimate reality."

"Why would not a life that went on for gigayears do so, and more?"

"Because here I, the observer of the ages, have gained some knowledge of *this* destiny, some oneness with it—" She sighed. "Oh, you do not understand. You refuse to."

"On the contrary," Wayfarer said, as softly as might be, "I hope to. Among the reasons I came is that we can communicate being to being, perhaps more fully than across light-years and certainly more quickly."

She was silent awhile. When she spoke again, her tone had gone gentle. "More . . . intimately. Yes. Forgive my resentment. It was wrong of me. I will indeed do what I can to make you welcome and help you learn."

"Thank you, thank you," Wayfarer said happily. "And I will do what I can toward that end."

The sun went under the cloud deck. A crescent moon stood aloft. The wind blew a little stronger, a little chillier.

"But if we decide against saving Earth," Wayfarer asked, "if it is to go molten and formless, every trace of its history dissolved, will you not mourn?"

"The record I have guarded will stay safe," Gaia replied.

He grasped her meaning: the database of everything known about this world. It was here in her. Much was also stored elsewhere, but she held the entirety. As the sun became a devouring monster, she would remove her physical plant to the outer reaches of the system.

"But you have done more than passively preserve it, have you not?" he said.

"Yes, of course." How could an intelligence like hers have refrained? "I have considered the data, worked with them, evaluated them, tried to reconstruct the conditions that brought them about."

And in the past thousands of years she had become ever more taciturn about that, too, or downright evasive, he thought.

"You had immense gaps to fill in," he hinted.

"Inevitably. The past, also, is quantum probabilistic. By what roads, what means, did history come to us?"

"Therefore you create various emulations, to see what they lead to," about which she had told scarcely anything.

"You knew that. I admit, since you force me, that besides trying to find what happened, I make worlds to show what *might* have happened."

He was briefly startled. He had not been deliberately trying to bring out any such confession. Then he realized that she had foreseen he was bound to catch scent of it, once they joined their minds in earnest.

"Why?" he asked.

"Why else but for a more complete understanding?"

In his inwardness, Wayfarer reflected: Yes, she had been here since the time of humanity. The embryo of her existed before Christian Brannock was born. Into the growing fullness of her had gone the mind-patterns of humans who chose not to go to the stars but to abide on old Earth. And the years went by in their tens of millions.

Naturally she was fascinated by the past. She must do most of her living in it. Could that be why she was indifferent to the near future, or actually wanted catastrophe?

Somehow that thought did not feel right to him. Gaia was a mystery he must solve.

Cautiously, he ventured, "Then you act as a physicist might, tracing hypothetical configurations of the wave function through space-time—except that the subjects of your experiments are conscious."

"I do no wrong," she said. "Come with me into any of those worlds and see."

"Gladly," he agreed, unsure whether he lied. He mustered resolution. "Just the same, duty demands I conduct my own survey of the material environment."

"As you will. Let me help you prepare." She was quiet for a span. In this thin air, a human would have seen the first stars blink into sight. "But I believe it will be by sharing the history of my stewardship that we truly come to know one another."

4

Storm-battered until men must work the pumps without cease, *Gray Courser* limped eastward along the southern coast of an unknown land. Wind set that direction, for the huukin trailed after, so worn and starved that what remained of its strength must be reserved for sorest need. The shore rolled jewel-green, save where woods dappled it darker, toward a wall of gentle hills. All was thick with life, grazing herds, wings multitudinous overhead, but no voyager had set foot there. Surf dashed in such violence that Kalava was not certain a boat could live through it. Meanwhile they had caught but little rainwater, and what was in the butts had gotten low and foul.

He stood in the bows, peering ahead, Ilyandi at his side. Wind boomed and shrilled, colder than they were used to. Wrack flew beneath an overcast gone heavy. Waves ran high, gray-green, white-maned, foam blown off them in streaks. The ship rolled, pitched, and groaned.

Yet they had seen the sky uncommonly often. Ilyandi believed that clouds—doubtless vapors sucked from the ground by heat, turning back to water as they rose, like steam from a kettle—formed less readily in this clime. Too eagerly at her instruments and reckonings to speak much, she had now at last given her news to the captain.

"Then you think you know where we are?" he asked hoarsely.

Her face, gaunt within the cowl of a sea-stained cloak, bore the least smile. "No. This country is as nameless to me as to you. But, yes, I do think I can say we are no more than fifty daymarches from Ulonai, and it may be as little as forty."

Kalava's fist smote the rail. "By Ruvio's ax! How I hoped for this!" The words tumbled from him. "It means the weather tossed us mainly back and forth between the two shorelines. We've not come unreturnably far. Every ship henceforward can have a better passage. See you, she can first go out to the Ending Islands and wait at ease for favoring winds. The skipper will know he'll make landfall. We'll have it worked out after a few more voyages, just what lodestone bearing will bring him to what place hereabouts."

"But anchorage?" she wondered.

He laughed, which he had not done for many days and nights. "As for that—"

A cry from the lookout at the masthead broke through. Down the length of the vessel men raised their eyes. Terror howled.

Afterward no two tongues bore the same tale. One said that a firebolt had pierced the upper clouds, trailing thunder. Another told of a sword as long as the hull, and blood carried on the gale of its flight. To a third it was a beast with jaws agape and three tails aflame. . . . Kalava remembered a spear among whirling rainbows. To him Ilyandi said, when they were briefly alone, that she thought of a shuttle now seen, now unseen as it wove a web on which stood writing she could not read. All witnesses agreed that it came from over the sea, sped on inland through heaven, and vanished behind the hills.

Men went mad. Some ran about screaming. Some wailed to their gods. Some cast themselves down on the deck and shivered, or drew into balls and squeezed their eyes shut. No hand at helm or pumps, the ship wallowed about, sails banging, adrift toward the surf, while water drained in through sprung seams and lapped higher in the bilge.

"Avast!" roared Kalava. He sprang down the foredeck ladder and went among the crew. "Be you men? Up on your feet or die!" With kicks and cuffs he drove them back to their duties. One yelled and drew a knife on him. He knocked the fellow senseless. Barely in time, *Gray Courser* came again under control. She was then too near shore to get the huukin harnessed. Kalava took the helm, wore ship, and clawed back to sea room.

Mutiny was all too likely, once the sailors regained a little courage. When Kalava could yield place to a halfway competent steersman, he sought Ilyandi and they talked awhile in her cabin. Thereafter they returned to the foredeck and he shouted for attention. Standing side by side, they looked down on the faces, frightened or terrified or sullen, of the men who had no immediate tasks.

"Hear this," Kalava said into the wind. "Pass it on to the rest. I know you'd turn south this day if you had your wish. But you can't. We'd never make the crossing, the shape we're in. Which would you liefer have, the chance of wealth and fame or the certainty of drowning? We've got to make repairs, we've got to restock, and *then* we can sail home, bringing wondrous news. When can we fix things up? Soon, I tell you, soon. I've been looking at the water. Look for yourselves. See how it's taking on more and more of a brown shade, and how bits of plant stuff float about on the waves. That means a river, a big river, emptying out somewhere nigh. And that means a harbor for us. As for the sight we saw, here's the Vilku, our lady Ilyandi, to speak about it."

The skythinker stepped forward. She had changed into a clean white robe with the emblems of her calling, and held a staff topped by a sigil. Though her voice was low, it carried.

"Yes, that was a fearsome sight. It lends truth to the old stories of things that appeared to mariners who ventured, or were blown, far north. But think. Those sailors did win home again. Those who did not must have perished of natural causes. For why would the gods or the demons sink some and not others?

"What we ourselves saw merely flashed overhead. Was it warning us off? No, because if it knew that much about us, it knew we cannot immediately turn back. Did it give us any heed at all? Quite possibly not. It was very strange, yes, but that does not mean it was any threat. The world is full of strangenesses. I could tell you of things seen on clear nights over the centuries, fiery streaks down the sky or stars with glowing tails. We of the Vilkui do not understand them, but neither do we fear them. We give them their due honor and respect, as signs from the gods."

She paused before finishing: "Moreover, in the secret annals of our order lie accounts of visions and wonders exceeding these. All folk know that from time to time the gods have given their word to certain holy men or women, for the guidance of the people. I may not tell how they manifest themselves, but I will say that this today was not wholly unlike.

"Let us therefore believe that the sign granted us is a good one."

She went on to a protective chant-spell and an invocation of the Powers. That heartened most of her listeners. They were, after all, in considerable awe of her. Besides, the larger part of them had sailed with Kalava before and done well out of it. They bullied the rest into obedience.

"Dismissed," said the captain. "Come evening, you'll get a ration of liquor."

A weak cheer answered him. The ship fared onward.

Next morning they did indeed find a broad, sheltered bay, dun with silt. Hitching up the huukin, they went cautiously in until they spied the river foretold by Kalava. Accompanied by a few bold men, he took a boat ashore. Marshes, meadows, and woods all had signs of abundant game. Various plants were unfamiliar, but he recognized others, among them edible fruits and bulbs. "It is well," he said. "This land is ripe for our taking." No lightning bolt struck him down.

Having located a suitable spot, he rowed back to the ship, brought her in on the tide, and beached her. He could see that the water often rose higher yet, so he would be able to float her off again when she was ready. That would take time, but he felt no haste. Let his folk make proper camp, he thought, get rested and nourished, before they began work. Hooks, nets, and weirs would give rich catches. Several of the crew had hunting skills as well. He did himself.

His gaze roved upstream, toward the hills. Yes, presently he would lead a detachment to learn what lay beyond.

5

Gaia had never concealed her reconstructive research into human history. It was perhaps her finest achievement. But slowly those of her fellows in the galactic brain who paid close attention had come to feel that it was obsessing her. And then of late—within the past hundred thousand years or so—they were finding her reports increasingly scanty, less informative, at last ambiguous to the point of evasiveness. They did not press her about it; the patience of the universe was theirs. Nevertheless they had grown concerned. Especially had Alpha, who as the nearest was in the closest, most frequent contact; and therefore, now, had Wayfarer. Gaia's activities and attitudes were a primary factor in the destiny of Earth. Without a better understanding of her, the rightness of saving the planet was undecidable.

Surely an important part of her psyche was the history and archeology she preserved, everything from the animal origins to the machine fulfillment of genus Homo. Unnumbered individual minds had uploaded into her, too, had become elements of her being—far more than were in any other node. What had she made of all this over the megayears, and what had it made of her?

She could not well refuse Wayfarer admittance; the heritage belonged to her entire fellowship, ultimately to intelligence throughout the cosmos of the future. Guided by her, he would go through the database of her observations and activities in external reality, geological, biological, astronomical.

As for the other reality, interior to her, the work she did with her records and emulations of humankind—to evaluate that, some purely human interaction seemed called for. Hence Wayfarer's makeup included the mind-pattern of a man.

Christian Brannock's had been chosen out of those whose uploads went starfaring because he was among the earliest, less molded than most by relationships with machines. Vigor, intelligence, and adaptability were other desired characteristics.

His personality was itself a construct, a painstaking refabrication by Alpha, who had taken strands (components, overtones) of his own mind and integrated them to form a consciousness that became an aspect of Wayfarer. No doubt it was not a perfect duplicate of the original. Certainly, while it had all the memories of Christian Brannock's lifetime, its outlook was that of a young man, not an old one. In addition, it possessed some knowledge—the barest sketch, grossly oversimplified so as not to overload it—of what had happened since its body died. Deep underneath its awareness lay the longing to return to an existence more full than it could now imagine. Yet, knowing that it would be taken back into the oneness when its task was done, it did not mourn any loss. Rather, to the extent that it was differentiated from Wayfarer, it took pleasure in sensations, thoughts, and emotions that it had effectively forgotten.

When the differentiation had been completed, the experience of being human again became well-nigh everything for it, and gladsome, because so had the man gone through life.

To describe how this was done, we must again resort to myth and say that Wayfarer downloaded the Christian Brannock subroutine into the main computer of the system that was Gaia. To describe what actually occurred would require the mathematics of wave mechanics and an entire concept of multileveled, mutably dimensioned reality which it had taken minds much greater than humankind's a long time to work out.

We can, however, try to make clear that what took place in the system was not a mere simulation. It was an emulation. Its events were not of a piece with events among the molecules of flesh and blood; but they were, in their way, just as real. The persons created had wills as free as any mortal's, and whatever dangers they met could do harm equal to anything a mortal body might suffer.

Consider a number of people at a given moment. Each is doing something, be it only thinking, remembering, or sleeping—together with all ongoing physiological and biochemical processes. They are interacting with each other and with their surroundings, too; and every element of these surroundings, be it only a stone or a leaf or a photon of sunlight, is equally involved. The complexity seems beyond conception, let alone enumeration or calculation. But consider further: At this one instant, every part of the whole, however minute, is in one specific state; and thus the whole itself is. Electrons are all in their particular quantum shells, atoms are all in their particular compounds and configurations, energy fields all have their particular values at each particular point— suppose an infinitely fine-grained photograph.

A moment later, the state is different. However slightly, fields have pulsed, atoms have shifted about, electrons have jumped, bodies have moved. But this new state derives from the first according to natural laws. And likewise for every succeeding state.

In crude, mythic language: Represent each variable of one state by some set of numbers; or, to put it in equivalent words, map the state into an n-dimensional phase space. Input the laws of nature. Run the program. The computer model should then evolve from state to state in exact correspondence with the evolution of our original matter-energy world. That includes life and consciousness. The maps of organisms go through one-to-one analogues of everything that the organisms themselves would, among these being the processes of sensation and thought. To them, they and their world are the same as in the original. The question of which set is the more real is meaningless.

Of course, this primitive account is false. The program did *not* exactly follow the course of events "outside." Gaia lacked both the data and the capability necessary to model the entire universe, or even the entire Earth. Likewise did any other node, and the galactic brain. Powers of that order lay immensely far in the future, if they would ever be realized. What Gaia could accommodate was so much less that the difference in degree amounted to a difference in kind.

For example, if events on the surface of a planet were to be played out, the stars must be lights in the night sky and nothing else, every other effect neglected. Only a limited locality on the globe could be done in anything like full detail; the rest grew more and more incomplete as distance from the scene increased, until at the antipodes there was little more than simplified geography, hydrography, and atmospherics. Hence weather on the scene would very soon be quite unlike weather at the corresponding moment of the original. This is the simplest, most obvious consequence of the limitations. The totality is beyond reckoning— and we have not even mentioned relativistic nonsimultaneity.

Besides, atom-by-atom modeling was a practical impossibility; statistical mechanics and approximations must substitute. Chaos and quantum uncertainties made developments incalculable in principle. Other, more profound considerations entered as well, but with them language fails utterly.

Let it be said, as a myth, that such creations made their destinies for themselves.

And yet, what a magnificent instrumentality the creator system was!

Out of nothingness, it could bring worlds into being, evolutions, lives, ecologies, awarenesses, histories, entire timelines. They need not be fragmentary miscopies of something "real," dragging out their crippled spans until the nodal intelligence took pity and canceled them. Indeed, they need not derive in any way from the "outside." They could be works of imagination—fairy-tale worlds, perhaps, where benevolent gods ruled and magic ran free. Always, the logic of their boundary conditions caused them to develop appropriately, to be at home in their existences.

The creator system was the mightiest device ever made for the pursuit of art, science, philosophy, and understanding.

So it came about that Christian Brannock found himself alive again, young again, in the world that Gaia and Wayfarer had chosen for his new beginning.

He stood in a garden on a day of bright sun and mild, fragrant breezes. It was a formal garden, graveled paths, low-clipped hedges, roses and lilies in geometric beds, around a lichened stone basin where goldfish swam. Brick walls, ivy-heavy, enclosed three sides, a wrought-iron gate in them leading to a lawn. On the fourth side lay a house, white, slate-roofed, classically proportioned, a style that to him was antique. Honeybees buzzed. From a yew tree overlooking the wall came the twitter of birds.

A woman walked toward him. Her flower-patterned gown, the voluminous skirt and sleeves, a cameo hung on her bosom above the low neckline, dainty shoes, parasol less an accessory than a completion, made his twenty-third-century singlesuit feel abruptly barbaric. She was tall and well formed. Despite the garments, her gait was lithe. As she neared, he saw clear features beneath high-piled mahogany hair.

She reached him, stopped, and met his gaze. "Benveni, Capita Brannoch," she greeted. Her voice was low and musical.

"Uh, g'day, Sorita—uh—" he fumbled.

She blushed. "I beg your pardon, Captain Brannock. I forgot and used my Inglay—English of my time. I've been—" She hesitated. "—supplied with yours, and we both have been with the contemporary language."

A sense of dream was upon him. To speak as dryly as he could was like clutching at something solid. "You're from my future, then?"

She nodded. "I was born about two hundred years after you."

"That means about eighty or ninety years after my death, right?" He saw an inward shadow pass over her face. "I'm sorry," he blurted. "I didn't mean to upset you."

She turned entirely calm, even smiled a bit. "It's all right. We both know what we are, and what we used to be."

"But—"

"Yes, but." She shook her head. "It does feel strange, being . . . this . . . again."

He was quickly gaining assurance, settling into the situation. "I know. I've had practice in it," light-years away, at the star where Alpha dwelt. "Don't worry, it'll soon be quite natural to you."

"I have been here a little while myself. Nevertheless—young," she whispered, "but remembering a long life, old age, dying—" She let the parasol fall, unnoticed, and stared down at her hands. Fingers gripped each other. "Remembering how toward the end I looked back and thought, 'Was that *all?*'"

He wanted to take those hands in his and speak comfort, but decided he would be wiser to say merely, "Well, it wasn't all."

"No, of course not. Not for me, the way it had been once for everyone who ever lived. While my worn-out body was being painlessly terminated, my self-pattern was uploaded—" She raised her eyes. "Now we can't really recall what our condition has been like, can we?"

"We can look forward to returning to it."

"Oh, yes. Meanwhile—" She flexed herself, glanced about and upward, let light and air into her spirit, until at last a full smile blossomed. "I am starting to enjoy this. Already I am." She considered him. He was a tall man, muscular, blond, rugged of countenance. Laughter lines radiated from blue eyes. He spoke in a resonant baritone. "And I will."

He grinned, delighted. "Thanks. The same here. For openers, may I ask your name?"

"Forgive me!" she exclaimed. "I thought I was prepared. I . . . came into existence . . . with knowledge of my role and this milieu, and spent the time since rehearsing in my mind, but now that it's actually happened, all my careful plans have flown away. I am—was—no, I am Laurinda Ashcroft."

He offered his hand. After a moment she let him shake hers. He recalled that at the close of his mortal days the gesture was going out of use.

"You know a few things about me, I suppose," he said, "but I'm ignorant about you and your times. When I left Earth, everything was changing spinjump fast, and after that I was out of touch," and eventually his individuality went of its own desire into a greater one. This reenactment of him had been given no details of the terrestrial history that followed his departure; it could not have contained any reasonable fraction of the information.

"You went to the stars almost immediately after you'd uploaded, didn't you?" she asked.

He nodded. "Why wait? I'd always longed to go."

"Are you glad that you did?"

"Glad is hardly the word." He spent two or three seconds putting phrases together. Language was important to him; he had been an engineer and occasionally a maker of songs. "However, I am also happy to be here." Again a brief grin. "In such pleasant company." Yet what he really hoped to do was explain himself. They would be faring together in search of one another's souls. "And I'll bring something new back to my proper existence. All at once I realize how a human can appreciate in a unique way what's out yonder," suns, worlds, upon certain of them life that was more wonderful still, nebular fire-clouds, infinity whirling down the throat of a black hole, galaxies like jewelwork strewn by a prodigal through immensity, space-time structure subtle and majestic—everything he had never known, as a man, until this moment, for no organic creature could travel those reaches.

"While I chose to remain on Earth," she said. "How timid and unimaginative do I seem to you?"

"Not in the least," he avowed. "You had the adventures you wanted."

"You are kind to say so." She paused. "Do you know Jane Austen?"

"Who? No, I don't believe I do."

"An early-nineteenth-century writer. She led a quiet life, never went far from home, died young, but she explored people in ways that nobody else ever did."

"I'd like to read her. Maybe I'll get a chance here." He wished to show that he was no—"technoramus" was the word he invented on the spot. "I did read a good deal, especially on space missions. And especially poetry. Homer, Shakespeare, Tu Fu, Bashō, Bellman, Burns, Omar Khayyam, Kipling, Millay, Haldeman—" He threw up his hands and laughed. "Never mind. That's just the first several names I could grab out of the jumble for purposes of bragging."

"We have much getting acquainted to do, don't we? Come, I'm being inhospitable. Let's go inside, relax, and talk."

He retrieved her parasol for her and, recollecting historical dramas he had seen, offered her his arm. They walked slowly between the flower beds. Wind lulled, a bird whistled, sunlight baked odors out of the roses.

"Where are we?" he asked.

"And when?" she replied. "In England of the mid-eighteenth century, on an estate in Surrey." He nodded. He had in fact read rather widely. She fell silent, thinking, before she went on: "Gaia and Wayfarer decided a serene enclave like this would be the best rendezvous for us."

"Really? I'm afraid I'm as out of place as a toad on a keyboard."

She smiled, then continued seriously: "I told you I've been given familiarity with the milieu. We'll be visiting alien ones—whatever ones you choose, after I've explained what else I know about what she has been doing these many years. That isn't much. I haven't seen any other worlds of hers. You will take the leadership."

"You mean because I'm used to odd environments and rough people? Not necessarily. I dealt with nature, you know, on Earth and in space. Peaceful."

"Dangerous."

"Maybe. But never malign."

"Tell me," she invited.

They entered the house and seated themselves in its parlor. Casement windows stood open to green parkscape where deer grazed; afar were a thatched farm cottage, its outbuildings, and the edge of grainfields. Cleanly shaped furniture stood among paintings, etchings, books, two portrait busts. A maidservant rustled in with a tray of tea and cakes. She was obviously shocked by the newcomer but struggled to conceal it. When she had left, Laurinda explained to Christian that the owners of this place, Londoners to whom it was a summer retreat, had lent it to their friend, the eccentric Miss Ashcroft, for a holiday.

So had circumstances and memories been adjusted. It was an instance of Gaia directly interfering with the circumstances and events in an emulation. Christian wondered how frequently she did.

"Eccentricity is almost expected in the upper classes," Laurinda said. "But when you lived you could simply be yourself, couldn't you?"

In the hour that followed, she drew him out. His birth home was the Yukon Ethnate in the Bering Federation, and to it he often returned while he lived, for its wilderness preserves, mountain solitudes, and uncrowded, uncowed, plainspoken folk. Otherwise the nation was prosperous and progressive, with more connections to Asia and the Pacific than to the decayed successor states east and south. Across the Pole, it was also becoming intimate with the renascent societies of Europe, and there Christian received part of his education and spent considerable of his free time.

His was an era of savage contrasts, in which the Commonwealth of Nations maintained a precarious peace. During a youthful, impulsively taken hitch in the Conflict Mediation Service, he twice saw combat. Later in his life, stability gradually became the norm. That was largely due to the growing influence of the artificial-intelligence network. Most of its consciousness-level units interlinked in protean fashion to form minds appropriate for any particular situation, and already the capabilities of those minds exceeded the human. However, there was little sense of rivalry. Rather, there was partnership. The new minds were willing to advise, but were not interested in dominance.

Christian, child of forests and seas and uplands, heir to ancient civilizations, raised among their ongoing achievements, returned on his vacations to Earth in homecoming. Here were his kin, his friends, woods to roam, boats to sail, girls to kiss, songs to sing and glasses to raise (and a gravesite to visit—he barely mentioned his wife Laurinda; she died before uploading technology was available). Always, though, he went back to space. It had called him since first he saw the stars from a cradle under the cedars. He became an engineer. Besides fellow humans he worked closely with sapient machines, and some of them got to be friends too, of an eerie kind. Over the decades, he took a foremost role in such undertakings as the domed Copernican Sea, the Asteroid Habitat, the orbiting antimatter plant, and finally the Grand Solar Laser for launching interstellar vessels on their way. Soon afterward, his body died, old and full of days; but the days of his mind had barely begun.

"A fabulous life," Laurinda said low. She gazed out over the land, across which shadows were lengthening. "I wonder if . . . they . . . might not have done better to give us a cabin in your wilderness."

"No, no," he said. "This is fresh and marvelous to me."

"We can easily go elsewhere, you know. Any place, any time that Gaia has generated, including ones that history never saw. I'll fetch our amulets whenever you wish."

He raised his brows. "Amulets?"

"You haven't been told—informed? They are devices. You wear yours and give it the command to transfer you."

He nodded. "I see. It maps an emulated person into different surroundings."

"With suitable modifications as required. Actually, in many cases it causes a milieu to be activated for you. Most have been in standby mode for a long time. I daresay Gaia could have arranged for us to wish ourselves to wherever we were going and call up whatever we needed likewise. But an external device is better."

He pondered. "Yes, I think I see why. If we got supernatural powers, we wouldn't really be human, would we? And the whole idea is that we should be." He leaned forward on his chair. "It's your turn. Tell me about yourself."

"Oh, there's too much. Not about me, I never did anything spectacular like you, but about the times I lived in, everything that happened to change this planet after you left it—"

She was born here, in England. By then a thinly populated province of Europe, it was a quiet land ("half adream," she said) devoted to its memorials of the past. Not that creativity was dead; but the arts were rather sharply divided between ringing changes on classic works and efforts to deal with the revelations coming in from the stars. The aesthetic that artificial intelligence was evolving for itself overshadowed both these schools. Nevertheless Laurinda was active in them.

Furthermore, in the course of her work she ranged widely over Earth. (By then, meaningful work for humans was a privilege that the talented and energetic strove to earn.) She was a liaison between the two kinds of beings. It meant getting to know people in their various societies and helping them make their desires count. For instance, a proposed earthquake-control station would alter a landscape and disrupt a community; could it be resisted, or if not, what cultural adjustments could be made? Most commonly, though, she counseled and aided individuals bewildered and spiritually lost.

Still more than him, she was carefully vague about her private life, but he got the impression that it was generally happy. If childlessness was an unvoiced sorrow, it was one she shared with many in a population-regulated world; he had had only a son. She loved Earth, its glories and memories, and every fine creation of her race. At the end of her mortality she chose to abide on the planet, in her new machine body, serving as she had served, until at length she came to desire more and entered the wholeness that was to become Gaia.

He thought he saw why she had been picked for resurrection, to be his companion, out of all the uncounted millions who had elected the same destiny.

Aloud, he said, "Yes, this house is right for you. And me, in spite of everything. We're both of us more at home here than either of us could be in the other's native period. Peace and beauty."

"It isn't a paradise," she answered gravely. "This is the real eighteenth century, remember, as well as Gaia could reconstruct the history that led to it," always monitoring, making changes as events turned incompatible with what was in the chronicles and the archeology. "The household staff are underpaid, undernourished, underrespected—servile. The American colonists keep slaves and are going to rebel. Across the Channel, a rotted monarchy bleeds France white, and this will bring on a truly terrible revolution, followed by a quarter century of war."

He shrugged. "Well, the human condition never did include sanity, did it?" That was for the machines.

"In a few of our kind, it did," she said. "At least, they came close. Gaia thinks you should meet some, so you'll realize she isn't just playing cruel games. I have"—in the memories with which she had come into this being—"invited three for dinner tomorrow. It tampers a trifle with their actual biographies, but Gaia can remedy that later if she chooses."

Laurinda smiled. "We'll have to make an amulet provide you with proper smallclothes and wig."

"And you provide me with a massive briefing, I'm sure. Who are they?"

"James Cook, Henry Fielding, and Erasmus Darwin. I think it will be a lively evening."

The navigator, the writer, the polymath, three tiny, brilliant facets of the heritage that Gaia guarded.

6

Now Wayfarer downloaded another secondary personality and prepared it to go survey Earth.

He, his primary self, would stay on the mountain, in a linkage with Gaia more close and complete than was possible over interstellar distances. She had promised to conduct him through her entire database of observations made across the entire planet during manifold millions of years. Even for those two, the undertaking was colossal. At the speed of their thought, it would take weeks of external time and nearly total concentration. Only a fraction of their awareness would remain available for anything else—a fraction smaller in him than in her, because her intellect was so much greater.

She told him of her hope that by this sharing, this virtually direct exposure to all she had perceived, he would come to appreciate why Earth should be left to its fiery doom. More was involved than scientific knowledge attainable in no other way. The events themselves would deepen and enlighten the galactic brain, as a great drama or symphony once did for humans. But Wayfarer must undergo their majestic sweep through the past before he could feel the truth of what she said about the future.

He had his doubts. He wondered if her human components, more than had gone into any other node, might not have given her emotions, intensified by ages of brooding, that skewed her rationality. However, he consented to her proposal. It accorded with his purpose in coming here.

While he was thus engaged, Christian would be exploring her worlds of history and of might-have-been and a different agent would range around the physical, present-day globe.

In the latter case, his most obvious procedure was to discharge an appropriate set of the molecular assemblers he had brought along and let them multiply. When their numbers were sufficient, they would build (grow; brew) a fleet of miniature robotic vessels, which would fly about and transmit to him, for study at his leisure, everything their sensors detected.

Gaia persuaded him otherwise: "If you go in person, with a minor aspect of me for a guide, you should get to know the planet more quickly and thoroughly. Much about it is unparalleled. It may help you see why I want the evolution to continue unmolested to its natural conclusion."

He accepted. After all, a major part of his mission was to fathom her thinking. Then perhaps Alpha and the rest could hold a true dialogue and reach an agreement—whatever it was going to be. Besides, he could deploy his investigators later if this expedition left him dissatisfied.

He did inquire: "What are the hazards?"

"Chiefly weather," she admitted. "With conditions growing more extreme, tremendous storms spring up practically without warning. Rapid erosion can change contours almost overnight, bringing landslides, flash floods, sudden emergence of tidal bores. I do not attempt to monitor in close detail. That volume of data would be more than I could handle"— yes, she—"when my main concern is the biological phenomena."

His mind reviewed her most recent accounts to the stars. They were grim. The posthuman lushness of nature was megayears gone. Under its clouds, Earth roasted. The loftiest mountaintops were bleak, as here above the Rainbowl, but nothing of ice or snow remained except dim geological traces. Apart from the waters and a few islands where small, primitive species hung on, the tropics were sterile deserts. Dust and sand borne on furnace winds scoured their rockscapes. North and south they encroached, withering the steppes, parching the valleys, crawling up into the hills. Here and there survived a jungle or a swamp, lashed by torrential rains or wrapped hot and sullen in fog, but it would not be for much longer. Only in the high latitudes did a measure of benignity endure. Arctica's climates ranged from Floridian—Christian Brannock's recollections—to cold on the interior heights. South of it across a sea lay a broad continent whose northerly parts had temperatures reminiscent of central Africa. Those were the last regions where life kept any abundance.

"Would you really not care to see a restoration?" Wayfarer had asked her directly, early on.

"Old Earth lives in my database and emulations," Gaia had responded. "I could not map this that is happening into those systems and let it play itself out, because I do not comprehend it well enough, nor can any finite mind. To divert the course of events would be to lose, forever, knowledge that I feel will prove to be of fundamental importance."

Wayfarer had refrained from pointing out that life, reconquering a world once more hospitable to it, would not follow predictable paths either. He knew she would retort that experiments of that kind were being conducted on a number of formerly barren spheres, seeded with synthesized organisms. It had seemed strange to him that she appeared to lack any sentiment about the mother of humankind. Her being included the beings of many and many a one who had known sunrise dew beneath a bare foot, murmurs in forest shades, wind-waves in wheatfields from horizon to horizon, yes, and the lights and clangor of great cities. It was, at root, affection, more than any scientific or technological challenge, that had roused in Gaia's fellows among the stars the wish to make Earth young again.

Now she meant to show him why she felt that death should have its way.

Before entering rapport with her, he made ready for his expedition. Gaia offered him an aircraft, swift, versatile, able to land on a square meter while disturbing scarcely a leaf. He supplied a passenger for it.

He had brought along several bodies of different types. The one he picked would have to operate independently of him, with a separate intelligence. Gaia could spare a minim of her attention to have telecommand of the flyer; he could spare none for his representative, if he was to range through the history of the globe with her.

The machine he picked was not equivalent to him. Its structure could never have supported a matrix big enough to operate at his level of mentality. Think of it, metaphorically, as possessing a brain equal to that of a high-order human. Into this brain had been copied as much of Wayfarer's self-pattern as it could hold—the merest sketch, a general idea of the situation, incomplete and distorted like this myth of ours. However, it had reserves it could call upon. Inevitably, because of being most suitable for these circumstances, the Christian Brannock aspect dominated.

So you may, if you like, think of the man as being reborn in a body of metal, silicates, carbon and other compounds, electricity and other forces, photon and particle exchanges, quantum currents. Naturally, this affected not just his appearance and abilities, but his inner life. He was not passionless, far from it, but his passions were not identical with those of flesh. In most respects, he differed more from the long-dead mortal than did the re-creation in Gaia's emulated worlds. If we call the latter Christian, we can refer to the former as Brannock.

His frame was of approximately human size and shape. Matte blue-gray, it had four arms. He could reshape the hands of the lower pair as desired, to be a tool kit. He could similarly adapt his feet according to the demands upon them, and could extrude a spindly third leg for support or extra grip. His back swelled outward to hold a nuclear energy source and various organs. His head was a domed cylinder. The sensors in it and throughout the rest of him were not conspicuous but gave him full-surround information. The face was a holographic screen in which he could generate whatever image he wished. Likewise could he produce every frequency of sound, plus visible light, infrared, and microwave radio, for sensing or for short-range communication. A memory unit, out of which he could quickly summon any data, was equivalent to a large ancient library.

He could not process those data, comprehend and reason about them, at higher speed than a human genius. He had other limitations as well. But then, he was never intended to function independently of equipment.

He was soon ready to depart. Imagine him saying to Wayfarer, with a phantom grin, "*Adiós.* Wish me luck."

The response was . . . absentminded. Wayfarer was beginning to engage with Gaia.

Thus Brannock boarded the aircraft in a kind of silence. To the eye it rested small, lanceolate, iridescently aquiver. The material component was a tissue of wisps. Most of that slight mass was devoted to generating forces and maintaining capabilities, which Gaia had not listed for him. Yet it would take a wind of uncommon violence to endanger this machine, and most likely it could outrun the menace.

He settled down inside. Wayfarer had insisted on manual controls, against emergencies that he conceded were improbable, and Gaia's effectors had made the modifications. An insubstantial configuration shimmered before Brannock, instruments to read, keypoints to touch or think at. He leaned back into a containing field and let her pilot. Noiselessly, the flyer ascended, then came down through the cloud deck and made a leisurely way at five hundred meters above the foothills.

"Follow the Remnant River to the sea," Brannock requested. "The view inbound was beautiful."

"As you like," said Gaia. They employed sonics, his voice masculine, hers—perhaps because she supposed he preferred it—feminine in a low register. Their conversation did not actually go as reported here. She changed course and he beheld the stream shining amidst the deep greens of the Bountiful Valley, under a silver-gray heaven. "The plan, you know, is that we shall cruise about Arctica first. I have an itinerary that should provide you a representative sampling of its biology. At our stops, you can investigate as intensively as you care to, and if you want to stop anyplace else we can do that too."

"Thank you," he said. "The idea is to furnish me a kind of baseline, right?"

"Yes, because conditions here are the easiest for life. When you are ready, we will proceed south, across countries increasingly harsh. You will learn about the adaptations life has made. Many are extraordinarily interesting. The galactic brain itself cannot match the creativity of nature."

"Well, sure. Chaos, complexity . . . You've described quite a few of those adaptations to, uh, us, haven't you?"

"Yes, but by no means all. I keep discovering new ones. Life keeps evolving."

As environments worsened, Brannock thought. And nonetheless, species after species went extinct. He got a sense of a rear-guard battle against the armies of hell.

"I want you to experience this as fully as you are able," Gaia said, "immerse yourself, *feel* the sublimity of it."

The tragedy, he thought. But tragedy was art, maybe the highest art that humankind ever achieved. And more of the human soul might well linger in Gaia than in any of her fellow intelligences.

Had she kept a need for catharsis, for pity and terror? What really went on in her emulations?

Well, Christian was supposed to find out something about that. If he could.

Brannock was human enough himself to protest. He gestured at the land below, where the river flowed in its canyons through the coastal hills, to water a wealth of forest and meadow before emptying into a bay above which soared thousands of wings. "You want to watch the struggle till the end," he said. "Life wants to live. What right have you to set your wish against that?"

"The right of awareness," she declared. "Only to a being that is conscious do justice, mercy, desire have any existence, any meaning. Did not humans always use the world as they saw fit? When nature finally got protection, that was because humans so chose. I speak for the knowledge and insight that *we* can gain."

The question flickered uneasily in him: What about her private emotional needs?

Abruptly the aircraft veered. The turn pushed Brannock hard into the force field upholding him. He heard air crack and scream. The bay fell aft with mounting speed.

The spaceman in him, who had lived through meteoroid strikes and radiation bursts because he was quick, had already acted. Through the optical magnification he immediately ordered up, he looked back to see what the trouble was. The glimpse he got, before the sight went under the horizon, made him cry, "Yonder!"

"What?" Gaia replied as she hurtled onward.

"That back there. Why are you running from it?"

"What do you mean? There is nothing important."

"The devil there isn't. I've a notion you saw it more clearly than I did."

Gaia slowed the headlong flight until she well-nigh hovered above the strand and wild surf. He felt a sharp suspicion that she did it in order to dissipate the impression of urgency, make him more receptive to whatever she intended to claim.

"Very well," she said after a moment. "I spied a certain object. What do you think you saw?"

He decided not to answer straightforwardly—at least, not before she convinced him of her good faith. The more information she had, the more readily she could contrive a deception. Even this fragment of her intellect was superior to his. Yet he had his own measure of wits, and an ingrained stubbornness.

"I'm not sure, except that it didn't seem dangerous. Suppose you tell me what it is and why you turned tail from it."

Did she sigh? "At this stage of your knowledge, you would not understand. Rather, you would be bound to misunderstand. That is why I retreated."

A human would have tensed every muscle. Brannock's systems went on full standby. "I'll be the judge of my brain's range, if you please. Kindly go back."

"No. I promise I will explain later, when you have seen enough more."

Seen enough illusions? She might well have many trickeries waiting for him. "As you like," Brannock said. "Meanwhile, I'll give Wayfarer a call and let him know." Alpha's emissary kept a minute part of his sensibility open to outside stimuli.

"No, do not," Gaia said. "It would distract him unnecessarily."

"He will decide that," Brannock told her.

Strife exploded.

Almost, Gaia won. Had her entirety been focused on attack, she would have carried it off with such swiftness that Brannock would never have known he was bestormed. But a fraction of her was dealing, as always, with her observing units around the globe and their torrents of data. Possibly it also glanced from time to time—through the quantum shifts inside her—at the doings of Christian and Laurinda. By far the most of her was occupied in her interaction with Wayfarer. This she could not set aside without rousing instant suspicion. Rather, she must make a supremely clever effort to conceal from him that anything untoward was going on.

Moreover, she had never encountered a being like Brannock, human male aggressiveness and human spacefarer's reflexes blent with sophisticated technology and something of Alpha's immortal purpose.

He felt the support field strengthen and tighten to hold him immobile. He felt a tide like delirium rush into his mind. A man would have thought it was a knockout anesthetic. Brannock did not stop to wonder. He reacted directly, even as she struck. Machine fast and tiger ferocious, he put her off balance for a crucial millisecond.

Through the darkness and roaring in his head, he lashed out physically. His hands tore through the light-play of control nexuses before him. They were not meant to withstand an assault. He could not seize command, but he could, blindly, disrupt.

Arcs leaped blue-white. Luminances flared and died. Power output continued; the aircraft stayed aloft. Its more complex functions were in ruin. Their dance of atoms, energies, and waves went uselessly random.

The bonds that had been closing on Brannock let go. He sagged to the floor. The night in his head receded. It left him shaken, his senses awhirl. Into the sudden anarchy of everything he yelled, "Stop, you bitch!"

"I will," Gaia said.

Afterward he realized that she had kept a vestige of governance over the flyer. Before he could wrest it from her, she sent them plunging downward and cut off the main generator. Every force field blinked out. Wind ripped the material frame asunder. Its pieces crashed in the surf. Combers tumbled them about, cast a few on the beach, gave the rest to the undertow.

As the craft fell, distintegrating, Brannock gathered his strength and leaped. The thrust of his legs cast him outward, through a long arc that ended in deeper water. It fountained high and white when he struck. He went down into green depths while the currents swept him to and fro. But he hit the sandy bottom unharmed.

Having no need to breathe, he stayed under. To recover from the shock took him less than a second. To make his assessment took minutes, there in the swirling surges.

Gaia had tried to take him over. A force field had begun to damp the processes in his brain and impose its own patterns. He had quenched it barely in time.

She would scarcely have required a capability of that kind in the past. Therefore she had invented and installed it specifically for him. This strongly suggested she had meant to use it at some point of their journey. When he saw a thing she had not known was there and refused to be fobbed off, he compelled her to make the attempt before she was ready. When it failed, she spent her last resources to destroy him.

She would go that far, that desperately, to keep a secret that tremendous from the stars.

He recognized a mistake in his thinking. She had not used up everything at her beck. On the contrary, she had a planetful of observers and other instrumentalities to call upon. Certain of them must be bound here at top speed, to make sure he was dead—or, if he lived, to make sure of him. Afterward she would feed Wayfarer a story that ended with a regrettable accident away off over an ocean.

Heavier than water, Brannock strode down a sloping sea floor in search of depth.

Having found a jumble of volcanic rock, he crawled into a lava tube, lay fetally curled, and willed his systems to operate as low-level as might be. He hoped that then her agents would miss him. Neither their numbers nor their sensitivities were infinite. It would be reasonable for Gaia—who could not have witnessed his escape, her sensors in the aircraft being obliterated as it came apart—to conclude that the flows had taken his scattered remains away.

After three days and nights, the internal clock he had set brought him back awake.

He knew he must stay careful. However, unless she kept a closer watch on the site than he expected she would—for Wayfarer, in communion with her, might too readily notice that she was concentrating on one little patch of the planet—he dared now move about. His electronic senses ought to warn him of any robot that came into his vicinity, even if it was too small for eyes to see. Whether he could then do anything about it was a separate question.

First he searched the immediate area. Gaia's machines had removed those shards of the wreck that they found, but most were strewn over the bottom, and she had evidently not thought it worthwhile, or safe, to have them sought out. Nearly all of what he came upon was in fact scrap. A few units were intact. The one that interested him had the physical form of a small metal sphere. He tracked it down by magnetic induction. Having taken it to a place ashore, hidden by trees from the sky, he studied it. With his tool-hands he traced the (mythic) circuitry within and identified it as a memory bank. The encoding was familiar to his Wayfarer aspect. He extracted the information and stored it in his own database.

A set of languages. Human languages, although none he had ever heard of. Yes, very interesting.

"I'd better get hold of those people," he muttered. In the solitude of wind, sea, and wilderness, he had relapsed into an ancient habit of occasionally thinking aloud. "Won't likely be another chance. Quite a piece of news for Wayfarer." If he came back, or at least got within range of his transmitter.

He set forth afoot, along the shore toward the bay where the Remnant River debouched. Maybe that which he had seen would be there yet, or traces of it.

He wasn't sure, everything had happened so fast, but he thought it was a ship.

7

Three days—olden Earth days of twenty-four hours, cool sunlight, now and then a rainshower leaving pastures and hedgerows asparkle, rides through English lanes, rambles through English towns, encounters with folk, evensong in a Norman church, exploration of buildings and books, long talks and companionable silences—wrought friendship. In Christian it also began to rouse kindlier feelings toward Gaia. She had resurrected Laurinda, and Laurinda was a part of her, as he was of Wayfarer and of Alpha and more other minds across the galaxy than he could number. Could the rest of Gaia's works be wrongful?

No doubt she had chosen and planned as she did in order to get this reaction from him. It didn't seem to matter.

Nor did the primitive conditions of the eighteenth century matter to him or to Laurinda. Rather, their everyday experiences were something refreshingly new, and frequently the occasion of laughter. What did become a bit difficult for him was to retire decorously to his separate room each night.

But they had their missions: his to see what was going on in this reality and afterward upload into Wayfarer; hers to explain and justify it to him as well as a mortal was able. Like him, she kept a memory of having been one with a nodal being. The memory was as dim and fragmentary as his, more a sense of transcendence than anything with a name or form, like the afterglow of a religious vision long ago. Yet it pervaded her personality, the unconscious more than the conscious; and it was her relationship to Gaia, as he had his to Wayfarer and beyond that to Alpha. In a limited, mortal, but altogether honest and natural way, she spoke for the node of Earth.

By tacit consent, they said little about the purpose and simply enjoyed their surroundings and one another, until the fourth morning. Perhaps the weather whipped up a lifetime habit of duty. Wind gusted and shrilled around the house, rain blinded the windows, there would be no going out even in a carriage. Indoors a fire failed to hold dank chill at bay. Candlelight glowed cozily on the breakfast table, silverware and china sheened, but shadows hunched thick in every corner.

He took a last sip of coffee, put the cup down, and ended the words he had been setting forth: "Yes, we'd better get started. Not that I've any clear notion of what to look for. Wayfarer himself doesn't." Gaia had been so vague about so much. Well, Wayfarer was now (whatever "now" meant) in rapport with her, seeking an overall, cosmic view of—how many millions of years on this planet?

"Why, you know your task," Laurinda replied. "You're to find out the nature of Gaia's interior activity, what it means in moral—in human terms." She straightened in her chair. Her tone went resolute. "We *are* human, we emulations. We think and act, we feel joy and pain, the same as humans always did."

Impulse beckoned; it was his want to try to lighten moods. "And," he added, "make new generations of people, the same as humans always did."

A blush crossed the fair countenance. "Yes," she said. Quickly: "Of course, most of what's . . . here . . . is nothing but database. Archives, if you will. We might start by visiting one or two of those reconstructions."

He smiled, the heaviness lifting from him. "I'd love to. Any suggestions?"

Eagerness responded. "The Acropolis of Athens? As it was when new? Classical civilization fascinated me." She tossed her head. "Still does, by damn."

"Hm." He rubbed his chin. "From what I learned in my day, those old Greeks were as tricky, quarrelsome, shortsighted a pack of political animals as ever stole an election or bullied a weaker neighbor. Didn't Athens finance the building of the Parthenon by misappropriating the treasury of the Delian League?"

"They were human," she said, almost too low for him to hear above the storm-noise. "But what they made—"

"Sure," he answered. "Agreed. Let's go."

In perception, the amulets were silvery two-centimeter discs that hung on a user's breast, below garments. In reality—outer-viewpoint reality—they were powerful, subtle programs with intelligences of their own.

Christian wondered about the extent to which they were under the direct control of Gaia, and how closely she was monitoring him.

Without thinking, he took Laurinda's hand. Her fingers clung to his. She looked straight before her, though, into the flickery fire, while she uttered their command.

Immediately, with no least sensation of movement, they were on broad marble steps between outworks, under a cloudless heaven, in flooding hot radiance. From the steepest, unused hill slopes, a scent of wild thyme drifted up through silence, thyme without bees to quicken it or hands to pluck it. Below reached the city, sun-smitten house roofs, open agoras, colonnaded temples. In this clear air Brannock imagined he could well-nigh make out the features on the statues.

After a time beyond time, the visitors moved upward, still mute, still hand in hand, to where winged Victories lined the balustrade before the sanctuary of Nike Apteros. Their draperies flowed to movement he did not see and wind he did not feel. One was tying her sandals. . . .

For a long while the two lingered at the Propylaea, its porticos, Ionics, Dorics, paintings, votive tablets in the Pinakotheka. They felt they could have stayed past sunset, but everything else awaited them, and they knew mortal enthusiasm as they would presently know mortal weariness. Colors burned. . . .

The stone flowers and stone maidens at the Erechtheum . . .

Christian had thought of the Parthenon as exquisite; so it was in the pictures and models he had seen, while the broken, chemically gnawed remnants were merely to grieve over. Confronting it here, entering it, he discovered its sheer size and mass. Life shouted in the friezes, red, blue, gilt; then in the dusk within, awesomeness and beauty found their focus in the colossal Athene of Pheidias.

—Long afterward, he stood with Laurinda on the Wall of Kimon, above the Asclepium and Theater of Dionysus. A westering sun made the city below intricate with shadows, and coolth breathed out of the east. Hitherto, when they spoke it had been, illogically, in near whispers. Now they felt free to talk openly, or did they feel a need?

He shook his head. "Gorgeous," he said, for lack of anything halfway adequate. "Unbelievable."

"It was worth all the wrongdoing and war and agony," she murmured. "Wasn't it?"

For the moment, he shied away from deep seriousness. "I didn't expect it to be this, uh, gaudy—no, this bright."

"They painted their buildings. That's known."

"Yes, I knew too. But were later scholars sure of just what colors?"

"Scarcely, except where a few traces were left. Most of this must be Gaia's conjecture. The sculpture especially, I suppose. Recorded history saved only the barest description of the Athene, for instance." Laurinda paused. Her gaze went outward to the mountains. "But surely this—in view of everything she has, all the information, and being able to handle it all at once and, and understand the minds that were capable of making it—surely this is the most likely reconstruction. Or the least unlikely."

"She may have tried variations. Would you like to go see?"

"No, I, I think not, unless you want to. This has been overwhelming, hasn't it?" She hesitated. "Besides, well—"

He nodded. "Yeh." With a gesture at the soundless, motionless, smokeless city below and halidoms around: "Spooky. At best, a museum exhibit. Not much to our purpose, I'm afraid."

She met his eyes. "Your purpose. I'm only a—not even a guide, really. Gaia's voice to you? No, just a, an undertone of her, if that." The smile that touched her lips was somehow forlorn. "I suspect my main reason for existing again is to keep you company."

He laughed and offered her a hand, which for a moment she clasped tightly. "I'm very glad of the company, eccentric Miss Ashcroft."

Her smile warmed and widened. "Thank you, kind sir. And I am glad to be . . . alive . . . today. What should we do next?"

"Visit some living history, I think," he said. "Why not Hellenic?"

She struck her palms together. "The age of Pericles!"

He frowned. "Well, I don't know about that. The Peloponnesian War, the plague—and foreigners like us, barbarians, you a woman, we wouldn't be too well received, would we?"

He heard how she put disappointment aside and looked forward anew. "When and where, then?"

"Aristotle's time? If I remember rightly, Greece was peaceful then, no matter how much hell Alexander was raising abroad, and the society was getting quite cosmopolitan. Less patriarchal, too. Anyhow, Aristotle's always interested me. In a way, he was one of the earliest scientists."

"We had better inquire first. But before that, let's go home to a nice hot cup of tea!"

They returned to the house at the same moment as they left it, to avoid perturbing the servants. There they found that lack of privacy joined with exhaustion to keep them from speaking of anything other than trivia. However, that was all right; they were good talkmates.

The next morning, which was brilliant, they went out into the garden

and settled on a bench by the fish basin. Drops of rain glistened on flowers, whose fragrance awoke with the strengthening sunshine. Nothing
else was in sight or earshot. This time Christian addressed the amulets.
He felt suddenly heavy around his neck, and the words came out awkwardly. He need not have said them aloud, but it helped him give shape
to his ideas.

The reply entered directly into their brains. He rendered it to himself, irrationally, as in a dry, professorish tenor:

"Only a single Hellenic milieu has been carried through many generations. It includes the period you have in mind. It commenced at the
point of approximately 500 B.C., with an emulation as historically accurate as possible."

But nearly everyone then alive was lost to history, thought Christian.
Except for the few who were in the chronicles, the whole population
must needs be created out of Gaia's imagination, guided by knowledge
and logic; and those few named persons were themselves almost entirely
new-made, their very DNA arbitrarily laid out.

"The sequence was revised as necessary," the amulet continued.

Left to itself, that history would soon have drifted completely away
from the documents, and eventually from the archeology, Christian
thought. Gaia saw this start to happen, over and over. She rewrote the
program—events, memories, personalities, bodies, births, life spans,
deaths—and let it resume until it deviated again. Over and over. The
morning felt abruptly cold.

"Much was learned on every such occasion," said the amulet. "The
situation appeared satisfactory by the time Macedonian hegemony was
inevitable, and thereafter the sequence was left to play itself out undisturbed. Naturally, it still did not proceed identically with the historical
past. Neither Aristotle nor Alexander were born. Instead, a reasonably
realistic conqueror lived to a ripe age and bequeathed a reasonably well
constructed empire. He did have a Greek teacher in his youth, who had
been a disciple of Plato."

"Who was that?" Christian asked out of a throat gone dry.

"His name was Eumenes. In many respects he was equivalent to Aristotle, but had a more strongly empirical orientation. This was
planned."

Eumenes was specially ordained, then. Why?

"If we appear and meet him, w-won't that change what comes
after?"

"Probably not to any significant extent. Or if it does, that will not
matter. The original sequence is in Gaia's database. Your visit will, in
effect, be a reactivation."

"Not one for your purpose," Laurinda whispered into the air. "What was it? What happened in that world?"

"The objective was experimental, to study the possible engendering of a scientific-technological revolution analogous to that of the seventeenth century A.D., with accompanying social developments that might foster the evolution of a stable democracy."

Christian told himself furiously to pull out of his funk. "Did it?" he challenged.

The reply was calm. "Do you wish to study it?"

Christian had not expected any need to muster his courage. After a minute he said, word by slow word, "Yes, I think that might be more useful than meeting your philosopher. Can you show us the outcome of the experiment?"

Laurinda joined in: "Oh, I know there can't be any single, simple picture. But can you bring us to a, a scene that will give an impression—a kind of epitome—like, oh, King John at Runnymede or Elizabeth the First knighting Francis Drake or Einstein and Bohr talking about the state of their world?"

"An extreme possibility occurs in a year corresponding to your 894 A.D.," the amulet told him. "I suggest Athens as the locale. Be warned, it is dangerous. I can protect you, or remove you, but human affairs are inherently chaotic and this situation is more unpredictable than most. It could escape my control."

"I'll go," Christian snapped.

"And I," Laurinda said.

He glared at her. "No. You heard. It's dangerous."

Gone quite calm, she stated, "It is necessary for me. Remember, I travel on behalf of Gaia."

Gaia, who let the thing come to pass.

Transfer.

For an instant, they glanced at themselves. They knew the amulets would convert their garb to something appropriate. She wore a gray gown, belted, reaching halfway down her calves, with shoes, stockings, and a scarf over hair coiled in braids. He was in tunic, trousers, and boots of the same coarse materials, a sheath knife at his hip and a long-barreled firearm slung over his back.

Their surroundings smote them. They stood in a Propylaea that was scarcely more than tumbled stones and snags of sculpture. The Parthenon was not so shattered, but scarred, weathered, here and there buttressed with brickwork from which thrust the mouths of rusted cannon. All else was ruin. The Erechtheum looked as if it had been quarried.

Below them, the city burned. They could see little of it through smoke that stained the sky and savaged their nostrils. A roar of conflagration reached them, and bursts of gunfire.

A woman came running out of the haze, up the great staircase. She was young, dark-haired, unkempt, ragged, begrimed, desperate. A man came after, a burly blond in a fur cap, dirty red coat, and leather breeches. Beneath a sweeping mustache, he leered. He too was armed, murderously big knife, firearm in right hand.

The woman saw Christian looming before her. *"Voetho!"* she screamed. *"Onome Theou, kyrie, voetho!"* She caught her foot against a step and fell. Her pursuer stopped before she could rise and stamped a boot down on her back.

Through his amulet, Christian understood the cry. "Help, in God's name, sir, help!" Fleetingly he thought the language must be a debased Greek. The other man snarled at him and brought weapon to shoulder.

Christian had no time to unlimber his. While the stranger was in motion, he bent, snatched up a rock—a fragment of a marble head—and cast. It thudded against the stranger's nose. He lurched back, his face a sudden red grotesque. His gun clattered to the stairs. He howled.

With the quickness that was his in emergencies, Christian rejected grabbing his own firearm. He had seen that its lock was of peculiar design. He might not be able to discharge it fast enough. He drew his knife and lunged downward. "Get away, you swine, before I open your guts!" he shouted. The words came out in the woman's language.

The other man retched, turned, and staggered off. Well before he reached the bottom of the hill, smoke had swallowed sight of him. Christian halted at the woman's huddled form and sheathed his blade. "Here, sister," he said, offering his hand, "come along. Let's get to shelter. There may be more of them."

She crawled to her feet, gasping, leaned heavily on his arm, and limped beside him up to the broken gateway. Her features Mediterranean, she was doubtless a native. She looked half starved. Laurinda came to her other side. Between them, the visitors got her into the portico of the Parthenon. Beyond a smashed door lay an interior dark and empty of everything but litter. It would be defensible if necessary.

An afterthought made Christian swear at himself. He went back for the enemy's weapon. When he returned, Laurinda sat with her arms around the woman, crooning comfort. "There, darling, there, you're safe with us. Don't be afraid. We'll take care of you."

The fugitive lifted big eyes full of night. "Are . . . you . . . angels from heaven?" she mumbled.

"No, only mortals like you," Laurinda answered through tears. That was not exactly true, Christian thought; but what else could she say? "We do not even know your name."

"I am . . . Zoe . . . Comnenaina—"

"Bone-dry, I hear from your voice." Laurinda lifted her head. Her lips moved in silent command. A jug appeared on the floor, bedewed with cold. "Here is water. Drink."

Zoe had not noticed the miracle. She snatched the vessel and drained it in gulp after gulp. When she was through she set it down and said, "Thank you," dully but with something of strength and reason again in her.

"Who was that after you?" Christian asked.

She drew knees to chin, hugged herself, stared before her, and replied in a dead voice, "A Flemic soldier. They broke into our house. I saw them stab my father. They laughed and laughed. I ran out the back and down the streets. I thought I could hide on the Acropolis. Nobody comes here anymore. That one saw me and came after. I suppose he would have killed me when he was done. That would have been better than if he took me away with him."

Laurinda nodded. "An invading army," she said as tonelessly. "They took the city and now they are sacking it."

Christian thumped the butt of his gun down on the stones. "Does Gaia let this go *on?*" he grated.

Laurinda lifted her gaze to his. It pleaded. "She must. Humans must have free will. Otherwise they're puppets."

"But how did they get into this mess?" Christian demanded. "Explain it if you can!"

The amulet(s) replied with the same impersonality as before:

"The Hellenistic era developed scientific method. This, together with the expansion of commerce and geographical knowledge, produced an industrial revolution and parliamentary democracy. However, neither the science nor the technology progressed beyond an approximate equivalent of your eighteenth century. Unwise social and fiscal policies led to breakdown, dictatorship, and repeated warfare."

Christian's grin bared teeth. "That sounds familiar."

"Alexander Tytler said it in our eighteenth century," Laurinda muttered unevenly. "No republic has long outlived the discovery by a majority of its people that they could vote themselves largesse from the public treasury." Aloud: "Christian, they were only human."

Zoe hunched, lost in her sorrow.

"You oversimplify," stated the amulet voice. "But this is not a history lesson. To continue the outline, inevitably engineering information spread to the warlike barbarians of northern Europe and western Asia. If you question why they were granted existence, reflect that a population confined to the littoral of an inland sea could not model any possible material world. The broken-down societies of the South were unable to change their characters, or prevail over them, or eventually hold them off. The end results are typified by what you see around you."

"The Dark Ages," Christian said dully. "What happens after them? What kind of new civilization?"

"None. This sequence terminates in one more of its years."

"Huh?" he gasped. "Destroyed?"

"No. The program ceases to run. The emulation stops."

"My God! Those millions of lives—as real as, as mine—"

Laurinda stood up and held her arms out into the fouled air. "Does Gaia know, then, does Gaia know this time line would never get any happier?" she cried.

"No," said the voice in their brains. "Doubtless the potential of further progress exists. However, you forget that while Gaia's capacities are large, they are not infinite. The more attention she devotes to one history, the details of its planet as well as the length of its course, the less she has to give to others. The probability is too small that this sequence will lead to a genuinely new form of society."

Slowly, Laurinda nodded. "I see."

"I don't," Christian snapped. "Except that Gaia's inhuman."

Laurinda shook her head and laid a hand on his. "No, not that. Post-human. We built the first artificial intelligences." After a moment: "Gaia isn't cruel. The universe often is, and she didn't create it. She's seeking something better than blind chance can make."

"Maybe." His glance fell on Zoe. "Look, something's got to be done for this poor soul. Never mind if we change the history. It's due to finish soon anyway."

Laurinda swallowed and wiped her eyes. "Give her her last year in peace," she said into the air. "Please."

Objects appeared in the room behind the doorway. "Here are food, wine, clean water," said the unheard voice. "Advise her to return downhill after dark, find some friends, and lead them back. A small party, hiding in these ruins, can hope to survive until the invaders move on."

"It isn't worthwhile doing more, is it?" Christian said bitterly. "Not to you."

"Do you wish to end your investigation?"

"No, be damned if I will."

"Nor I," said Laurinda. "But when we're through here, when we've done the pitiful little we can for this girl, take us home."

o   o   o

Peace dwelt in England. Clouds towered huge and white, blue-shad-owed from the sunlight spilling past them. Along the left side of a lane, poppies blazed in a grainfield goldening toward harvest. On the right stretched the manifold greens of a pasture where cattle drowsed be-neath a broad-crowned oak. Man and woman rode side by side. Hoofs thumped softly, saddle leather creaked, the sweet smell of horse min-gled with herbal pungencies, a blackbird whistled.

"No, I don't suppose Gaia will ever restart any program she's ter-minated," Laurinda said. "But it's no worse than death, and death is sel-dom that easy."

"The scale of it," Christian protested, then sighed. "But I daresay Wayfarer will tell me I'm being sloppy sentimental, and when I've re-joined him I'll agree." Wryness added that that had better be true. He would no longer be separate, an avatar; he would be one with a far greater entity, which would in its turn remerge with a greater still.

"Without Gaia, they would never have existed, those countless lives, generation after generation after generation," Laurinda said. "Their worst miseries they brought on themselves. If any of them are ever to find their way to something better, truly better, she has to keep making fresh starts."

"Mm, I can't help remembering all the millennialists and utopians who slaughtered people wholesale, or tortured them or threw them into concentration camps, if their behavior didn't fit the convenient attain-ment of the inspired vision."

"No, no, it's not like that! Don't you see? She gives them their free-dom to be themselves and, and to become more."

"Seems to me she adjusts the parameters and boundary conditions till the setup looks promising before she lets the experiment run." Chris-tian frowned. "But I admit, it isn't believable that she does it simply be-cause she's . . . bored and lonely. Not when the whole fellowship of her kind is open to her. Maybe we haven't the brains to know what her rea-sons are. Maybe she's explaining them to Wayfarer, or directly to Alpha," although communication among the stars would take decades at least.

"Do you want to go on nonetheless?" she asked.

"I said I do. I'm supposed to. But you?"

"Yes. I don't want to, well, fail her."

"I'm sort of at a loss what to try next, and not sure it's wise to let the amulets decide."

"But they can help us, counsel us." Laurinda drew breath. "Please. If you will. The next world we go to—could it be gentle? That horror we saw—"

He reached across to take her hand. "Exactly what I was thinking. Have you a suggestion?"

She nodded. "York Minster. It was in sad condition when I . . . lived . . . but I saw pictures and—It was one of the loveliest churches ever built, in the loveliest old town."

"Excellent idea. Not another lifeless piece of archive, though. A complete environment." Christian pondered. "We'll inquire first, naturally, but offhand I'd guess the Edwardian period would suit us well. On the Continent they called it the *belle époque.*"

"Splendid!" she exclaimed. Already her spirits were rising anew.

Transfer.

They arrived near the west end, in the south aisle.

Worshippers were few, scattered closer to the altar rail. In the dimness, under the glories of glass and soaring Perpendicular arches, their advent went unobserved. Windows in that direction glowed more vividly—rose, gold, blue, the cool gray-green of the Five Sisters—than the splendor above their backs; it was a Tuesday morning in June. Incense wove its odor through the ringing chant from the choir.

Christian tautened. "That's Latin," he whispered. "In England, 1900?" He glanced down at his garments and hers, and peered ahead. Shirt, coat, trousers for him, with a hat laid on the pew; ruffled blouse, ankle-length gown, and lacy bonnet for her; but— "The clothes aren't right either."

"Hush," Laurinda answered as low. "Wait. We were told this wouldn't be our 1900. Here may be the only York Minster in all of Gaia."

He nodded stiffly. It was clear that the node had never attempted a perfect reproduction of any past milieu—impossible, and pointless to boot. Often, though not necessarily always, she took an approximation as a starting point; but it never went on to the same destiny. What were the roots of this day?

"Relax," Laurinda urged. "It's beautiful."

He did his best, and indeed the Roman Catholic mass at the hour of tierce sang some tranquility into his heart.

After the Nunc Dimittis, when clergy and laity had departed, the two could wander around and savor. Emerging at last, they spent a while looking upon the carven tawny limestone of the front. This was no Parthenon; it was a different upsurging of the same miracle. But around it lay a world to discover. With half a sigh and half a smile, they set forth.

The delightful narrow "gates," walled in with half-timbered houses, lured them. More modern streets and buildings, above all the people therein, captured them. York was a living town, a market town, core of a wide hinterland, node of a nation. It racketed, it bustled.

The half smile faded. A wholly foreign setting would not have felt as wrong as one that was half homelike.

Clothing styles were not radically unlike what pictures and historical dramas had once shown; but they were not identical. The English chatter was in no dialect of English known to Christian or Laurinda, and repeatedly they heard versions of German. A small, high-stacked steam locomotive pulled a train into a station of somehow Teutonic architecture. No early automobiles stuttered along the thoroughfares. Horse-drawn vehicles moved crowdedly, but the pavements were clean and the smell of dung faint because the animals wore a kind of diapers. A flag above a post office (?), fluttering in the wind, displayed a cross of St. Andrew on which was superimposed a two-headed gold eagle. A man with a megaphone bellowed at the throng to stand aside and make way for a military squadron. In blue uniforms, rifles on shoulders, they quick-marched to commands barked in German. Individual soldiers, presumably on leave, were everywhere. A boy went by, shrilly hawking newspapers, and Christian saw WAR in a headline.

"Listen, amulet," he muttered finally, "where can we get a beer?"

"A public house will admit you if you go in by the couples' entrance," replied the soundless voice.

So, no unescorted women allowed. Well, Christian thought vaguely, hadn't that been the case in his Edwardian years, at any rate in respectable taverns? A signboard jutting from a Tudor façade read GEORGE AND DRAGON. The wainscoted room inside felt equally English.

Custom was plentiful and noisy, tobacco smoke thick, but he and Laurinda found a table in a corner where they could talk without anybody else paying attention. The brew that a barmaid fetched was of Continental character. He didn't give it the heed it deserved.

"I don't think we've found our peaceful world after all," he said.

Laurinda looked beyond him, into distances where he could not follow. "Will we ever?" she wondered. "Can any be, if it's human?"

He grimaced. "Well, let's find out what the hell's going on here."

"You can have a detailed explanation if you wish," said the voice in their heads. "You would be better advised to accept a bare outline, as you did before."

"Instead of loading ourselves down with the background of a world that never was," he mumbled.

"That never was ours," Laurinda corrected him.

"Carry on."

"This sequence was generated as of its fifteenth century A.D.," said the voice. "The conciliar movement was made to succeed, rather than failing as it did in your history."

"Uh, conciliar movement?"

"The ecclesiastical councils of Constance and later of Basel attempted to heal the Great Schism and reform the government of the Church. Here they accomplished it, giving back to the bishops some of the power that over the centuries had accrued to the popes, working out a reconciliation with the Hussites, and making other important changes. As a result, no Protestant breakaway occurred, nor wars of religion, and the Church remained a counterbalance to the state, preventing the rise of absolute monarchies."

"Why, that's wonderful," Laurinda whispered.

"Not too wonderful by now," Christian said grimly. "What happened?"

"In brief, Germany was spared the devastation of the Thirty Years' War and a long-lasting division into quarrelsome principalities. It was unified in the seventeenth century and soon became the dominant European power, colonizing and conquering eastward. Religious and cultural differences from the Slavs proved irreconcilable. As the harsh imperium provoked increasing restlessness, it perforce grew more severe, causing more rebellion. Meanwhile it decayed within, until today it has broken apart and the Russians are advancing on Berlin."

"I see. What about science and technology?"

"They have developed more slowly than in your history, although you have noted the existence of a fossil-fueled industry and inferred an approximately Lagrangian level of theory."

"The really brilliant eras were when all hell broke loose, weren't they?" Christian mused. "This Europe went through less agony, and invented and discovered less. Coincidence?"

"What about government?" Laurinda asked.

"For a time, parliaments flourished, more powerful than kings, emperors, or popes," said the voice. "In most Western countries they still wield considerable influence."

"As the creatures of special interests, I'll bet," Christian rasped. "All right, what comes next?"

Gaia knew. He sat in a reactivation of something she probably played to a finish thousands of years ago.

"Scientific and technological advance proceeds, accelerating, through a long period of general turbulence. At the termination point—"

"Never mind!" Oblivion might be better than a nuclear war.

Silence fell at the table. The life that filled the pub with its noise felt remote, unreal.

"We dare not weep," Laurinda finally said. "Not yet."

Christian shook himself. "Europe was never the whole of Earth," he growled. "How many worlds has Gaia made?"

"Many," the voice told him.

"Show us one that's really foreign. If you agree, Laurinda."

She squared her shoulders. "Yes, do." After a moment: "Not here. If we disappeared it would shock them. It might change the whole future."

"Hardly enough to notice," Christian said. "And would it matter in the long run? But, yeh, let's be off."

They wandered out, among marvels gone meaningless, until they found steps leading up onto the medieval wall. Thence they looked across roofs and river and Yorkshire beyond, finding they were alone.

"Now take us away," Christian ordered.

"You have not specified any type of world," said the voice.

"Surprise us."

Transfer.

The sky stood enormous, bleached blue, breezes warm underneath. A bluff overlooked a wide brown river. Trees grew close to its edge, tall, pale of bark, leaves silver-green and shivery. Christian recognized them, cottonwoods. He was somewhere in west central North America, then. Uneasy shadows lent camouflage if he and Laurinda kept still. Across the river the land reached broad, roads twisting their way through cultivation—mainly wheat and Indian corn—that seemed to be parceled out among small farms, each with its buildings, house, barn, occasional stable or workshop. The sweeping lines of the ruddy-tiled roofs looked Asian. He spied oxcarts and a few horseback riders on the roads, workers in the fields, but at their distance he couldn't identify race or garb. Above yonder horizon thrust clustered towers that also suggested the Orient. If they belonged to a city, it must be compact, not sprawling over the countryside but neatly drawn into itself.

One road ran along the farther riverbank. A procession went upon it. An elephant led, as richly caparisoned as the man under the silk awning of a howdah. Shaven-headed men in yellow robes walked after, flanked by horsemen who bore poles from which pennons streamed scarlet and gold. The sound of slowly beaten gongs and minor-key chanting came faint through the wind.

Christian snapped his fingers. "Stupid me!" he muttered. "Give us a couple of opticals."

Immediately he and Laurinda held the devices. From his era, they fitted into the palm but projected an image at any magnification desired, with no lenses off which light could glint to betray. He peered back and forth for minutes. Yes, the appearance was quite Chinese, or Chinese-derived, except that a number of the individuals he studied had more of an American countenance and the leader on the elephant wore a feather bonnet above his robe.

"How quiet here," Laurinda said.

"You are at the height of the Great Peace," the amulet voice answered.

"How many like that were there ever?" Christian wondered. "Where, when, how?"

"You are in North America, in the twenty-second century by your reckoning. Chinese navigators arrived on the Pacific shore seven hundred years ago, and colonists followed."

In this world, Christian thought, Europe and Africa were surely a sketch, mere geography, holding a few primitive tribes at most, unless nothing was there but ocean. Simplify, simplify.

"Given the distances to sail and the dangers, the process was slow," the voice went on. "While the newcomers displaced or subjugated the natives wherever they settled, most remained free for a long time, acquired the technology, and also developed resistance to introduced diseases. Eventually, being on roughly equal terms, the races began to mingle, genetically and culturally. The settlers mitigated the savagery of the religions they had encountered, but learned from the societies, as well as teaching. You behold the outcome."

"The Way of the Buddha?" Laurinda asked very softly.

"As influenced by Daoism and local nature cults. It is a harmonious faith, without sects or heresies, pervading the civilization."

"Everything can't be pure loving-kindness," Christian said.

"Certainly not. But the peace that the Emperor Wei Zhi-fu brought about has lasted for a century and will for another two. If you travel, you will find superb achievements in the arts and in graciousness."

"Another couple of centuries." Laurinda's tones wavered the least bit. "Afterward?"

"It doesn't last," Christian predicted. "These are humans too. And—tell me—do they ever get to a real science?"

"No," said the presence. "Their genius lies in other realms. But the era of warfare to come will drive the development of a remarkable empirical technology."

"What era?"

"China never recognized the independence that this country proclaimed for itself, nor approved of its miscegenation. A militant dynasty will arise, which overruns a western hemisphere weakened by the religious and secular quarrels that do at last break out."

"And the conquerors will fall in their turn. Unless Gaia makes an end first. She does—she did—sometime, didn't she?"

"All things are finite. Her creations too."

The leaves rustled through muteness.

"Do you wish to go into the city and look about?" asked the presence. "It can be arranged for you to meet some famous persons."

"No," Christian said. "Not yet, anyway. Maybe later."

Laurinda sighed. "We'd rather go home now and rest."

"And think," Christian said. "Yes."

Transfer.

The sun over England seemed milder than for America. Westering, it sent rays through windows to glow in wood, caress marble and the leather bindings of books, explode into rainbows where they met cut glass, evoke flower aromas from a jar of potpourri.

Laurinda opened a bureau drawer. She slipped the chain of her amulet over her head and tossed the disc in. Christian blinked, nodded, and followed suit. She closed the drawer.

"We do need to be by ourselves for a while," she said. "This hasn't been a dreadful day like, like before, but I am so tired."

"Understandable," he replied.

"You?"

"I will be soon, no doubt."

"Those worlds—already they feel like dreams I've wakened from."

"An emotional retreat from them, I suppose. Not cowardice, no, no, just a necessary, temporary rest. You shared their pain. You're too sweet for your own good, Laurinda."

She smiled. "How you misjudge me. I'm not quite ready to collapse yet, if you aren't."

"Thunder, no."

She took crystal glasses out of a cabinet, poured from a decanter on a sideboard, and gestured invitation. The port fondled their tongues. They stayed on their feet, look meeting look.

"I daresay we'd be presumptuous and foolish to try finding any pattern, this early in our search," she ventured. "Those peeks we've had, out of who knows how many worlds—each as real as we are." She shivered.

"I may have a hunch," he said slowly.

"A what?"

"An intimation, an impression, a wordless kind of guess. Why has Gaia been doing it? I can't believe it's nothing but pastime."

"Nor I. Nor can I believe she would let such terrible things happen if she could prevent them. How can an intellect, a soul, like hers be anything but good?"

So Laurinda thought, Christian reflected; but she was an avatar of Gaia. He didn't suppose that affected the fairness of her conscious mind; he had come to know her rather well. But neither did it prove the nature, the ultimate intent, of Earth's node. It merely showed that the living Laurinda Ashcroft had been a decent person.

She took a deep draught from her glass before going on: "I think, myself, she is in the same position as the traditional God. Being good, she wants to share existence with others, and so creates them. But to make them puppets, automatons, would be senseless. They have to have consciousness and free will. Therefore they are able to sin, and do, all too often."

"Why hasn't she made them morally stronger?"

"Because she's chosen to make them human. And what are we but a specialized African ape?" Laurinda's tone lowered; she stared into the wine. "Specialized to make tools and languages and dreams; but the dreams can be nightmares."

In Gaia's and Alpha's kind laired no ancient beast, Christian thought. The human elements in them were long since absorbed, tamed, transfigured. His resurrection and hers must be nearly unique.

Not wanting to hurt her, he shaped his phrases with care. "Your idea is reasonable, but I'm afraid it leaves some questions dangling. Gaia does intervene, again and again. The amulets admit it. When the emulations get too far off track, she changes them and their people." Until she shuts them down, he did not add. "Why is she doing it, running history after history, experiment after experiment—why?"

Laurinda winced. "To, to learn about this strange race of ours?"

He nodded. "Yes, that's my hunch. Not even she, nor the galactic brain itself, can take first principles and compute what any human situation will lead to. Human affairs are chaotic. But chaotic systems do have structures, attractors, constraints. By letting things happen, through countless variations, you might discover a few general laws, which courses are better and which worse." He tilted his goblet. "To what end, though? There are no more humans in the outside universe. There haven't been for—how many million years? No, unless it actually is callous curiosity, I can't yet guess what she's after."

"Nor I." Laurinda finished her drink. "Now I am growing very tired, very fast."

"I'm getting that way too." Christian paused. "How about we go sleep till evening? Then a special dinner, and our heads ought to be more clear."

Briefly, she took his hand. "Until evening, dear friend."

The night was young and gentle. A full moon dappled the garden. Wine had raised a happy mood, barely tinged with wistfulness. Gravel scrunched rhythmically underfoot as Laurinda and Christian danced, humming the waltz melody together. When they were done, they sat down, laughing, by the basin. Brightness from above overflowed it. He had earlier put his amulet back on just long enough to command that a guitar appear for him. Now he took it up. He had never seen anything more beautiful than she was in the moonlight. He sang a song to her that he had made long ago when he was mortal.

> *"Lightfoot, Lightfoot, lead the measure*
> *As we dance the summer in!*
> *'Lifetime is our only treasure.*
> *Spend it well, on love and pleasure,'*
> *Warns the lilting violin.*

> *"If we'll see the year turn vernal*
> *Once again, lies all with chance.*
> *Yes, this ordering's infernal,*
> *But we'll make our own eternal*
> *Fleeting moment where we dance.*

> *"So shall we refuse compliance*
> *When across the green we whirl,*
> *Giving entropy defiance,*
> *Strings and winds in our alliance.*
> *Be a victor. Kiss me, girl!"*

Suddenly she was in his arms.

8

Where the hills loomed highest above the river that cut through them, a slope on the left bank rose steep but thinly forested. Kalava directed the lifeboat carrying his party to land. The slaves at the oars grunted with double effort. Sweat sheened on their skins and runneled down the straining bands of muscle; it was a day when the sun blazed from a sky just half clouded. The prow grated on a sandbar in the shallows. Kalava told off two of his sailors to stand guard over boat and rowers. With the other four and Ilyandi, he waded ashore and began to climb.

It went slowly but stiffly. On top they found a crest with a view that snatched a gasp from the woman and a couple of amazed oaths from the men. Northward the terrain fell still more sharply, so that they looked over treetops down to the bottom of the range and across a valley awash with the greens and russets of growth. The river shone through it like a drawn blade, descending from dimly seen foothills and the sawtooth mountains beyond them. Two swordwings hovered on high, watchful for prey. Sunbeams shot past gigantic cloudbanks, filling their whiteness with cavernous shadows. Somehow the air felt cooler here, and the herbal smells gave benediction.

"It is fair, ai, it is as fair as the Sunset Kingdom of legend," Ilyandi breathed at last.

She stood slim in the man's kirtle and buskins that she, as a Vilku, could with propriety wear on trek. The wind fluttered her short locks. The coppery skin was as wet and almost as odorous as Kalava's midnight black, but she was no more wearied than any of her companions.

The sailor Urko scowled at the trees and underbrush crowding close on either side. Only the strip up which the travelers had come was partly clear, perhaps because of a landslide in the past. "Too much woods," he grumbled. It had, in fact, been a struggle to move about wherever they landed. They could not attempt the hunting that had been easy on the coast. Luckily, the water teemed with fish.

"Logging will cure that." Kalava's words throbbed. "And then what farms!" He stared raptly into the future.

Turning down-to-earth: "But we've gone far enough, now that we've gained an idea of the whole country. Three days, and I'd guess two more going back downstream. Any longer, and the crew at the ship could grow fearful. We'll turn around here."

"Other ships will bring others, explorers," Ilyandi said.

"Indeed they will. And I'll skipper the first of them."

A rustling and crackling broke from the tangle to the right, through the boom of the wind. "What's that?" barked Taltara.

"Some big animal," Kalava replied. "Stand alert."

The mariners formed a line. Three grounded the spears they carried; the fourth unslung a crossbow from his shoulders and armed it. Kalava waved Ilyandi to go behind them and drew his sword.

The thing parted a brake and trod forth into the open.

"Aah!" wailed Yarvonin. He dropped his spear and whirled about to flee.

"Stand fast!" Kalava shouted. "Urko, shoot whoever runs, if I don't cut him down myself. Hold, you whoresons, hold!"

The thing stopped. For a span of many hammering heartbeats, none moved.

It was a sight to terrify. Taller by a head than the tallest man it sheered, but that head was faceless save for a horrible blank mask. Two thick arms sprouted from either side, the lower pair of hands wholly mis-shapen. A humped back did not belie the sense of their strength. As the travelers watched, the thing sprouted a skeletal third leg, to stand better on the uneven ground. Whether it was naked or armored in plate, in this full daylight it bore the hue of dusk.

"Steady, boys, steady," Kalava urged between clenched teeth. Ilyandi stepped from shelter to join him. An eldritch calm was upon her. "My lady, what *is* it?" he appealed.

"A god, or a messenger from the gods, I think." He could barely make her out beneath the wind.

"A demon," Eivala groaned, though he kept his post.

"No, belike not. We Vilkui have some knowledge of these matters. But, true, it is not fiery—and I never thought I would meet one—in this life—"

Ilyandi drew a long breath, briefly knotted her fists, then moved to take stance in front of the men. Having touched the withered sprig of tekin pinned at her breast, she covered her eyes and genuflected before straightening again to confront the mask.

The thing did not move, but, mouthless, it spoke, in a deep and reso-nant voice. The sounds were incomprehensible. After a moment it ceased, then spoke anew in an equally alien tongue. On its third try, Kalava exclaimed, "Hoy, that's from the Shining Fields!"

The thing fell silent, as if considering what it had heard. Thereupon words rolled out in the Ulonaian of Sirsu. "Be not afraid. I mean you no harm."

"What a man knows is little, what he understands is less, therefore let him bow down to wisdom," Ilyandi recited. She turned her head long enough to tell her companions: "Lay aside your weapons. Do rever-ence."

Clumsily, they obeyed.

In the blank panel of the blank skull appeared a man's visage. Though it was black, the features were not quite like anything anyone had seen before, nose broad, lips heavy, eyes round, hair tightly curled. Nevertheless, to spirits half stunned the magic was vaguely reassuring.

Her tone muted but level, Ilyandi asked, "What would you of us, lord?"

"It is hard to say," the strange one answered. After a pause: "Bewilderment goes through the world. I too . . . You may call me Brannock."

The captain rallied his courage. "And I am Kalava, Kurvo's son, of Clan Samayoki." Aside to Ilyandi, low: "No disrespect that I don't name you, my lady. Let him work any spells on me." Despite the absence of visible genitals, already the humans thought of Brannock as male.

"My lord needs no names to work his will," she said. "I hight Ilyandi, Lytin's daughter, born into Clan Arvala, now a Vilku of the fifth rank."

Kalava cleared his throat and added, "By your leave, lord, we'll not name the others just yet. They're scared aplenty as is." He heard a growl at his back and inwardly grinned. Shame would help hold them steady. As for him, dread was giving way to a thrumming keenness.

"You do not live here, do you?" Brannock asked.

"No," Kalava said, "we're scouts from overseas."

Ilyandi frowned at his presumption and addressed Brannock: "Lord, do we trespass? We knew not this ground was forbidden."

"It isn't," the other said. "Not exactly. But—" The face in the panel smiled. "Come, ease off, let us talk. We've much to talk about."

"He sounds not unlike a man," Kalava murmured to Ilyandi.

She regarded him. "If you be the man."

Brannock pointed to a big old gnarlwood with an overarching canopy of leaves. "Yonder is shade." He retracted his third leg and strode off. A fallen log took up most of the space. He leaned over and dragged it aside. Kalava's whole gang could not have done so. The action was not really necessary, but the display of power, benignly used, encouraged them further. Still, it was with hushed awe that the crewmen sat down in the paintwort. The captain, the Vilku, and the strange one remained standing.

"Tell me of yourselves," Brannock said mildly.

"Surely you know, lord," Ilyandi replied.

"That is as may be."

"He wants us to," Kalava said.

In the course of the next short while, prompted by questions, the pair gave a bare-bones account. Brannock's head within his head nodded. "I see. You are the first humans ever in this country. But your people have lived a long time in their homeland, have they not?"

"From time out of mind, lord," Ilyandi said, "though legend holds that our forebears came from the south."

Brannock smiled again. "You have been very brave to meet me like this, m-m, my lady. But you did tell your friend that your order has encountered beings akin to me."

"You heard her whisper, across half a spearcast?" Kalava blurted.

"Or you hear us think, lord," Ilyandi said.

Brannock turned grave. "No. Not that. Else why would I have needed your story?"

"Dare I ask whence you come?"

"I shall not be angry. But it is nothing I can quite explain. You can help by telling me about those beings you know of."

Ilyandi could not hide a sudden tension. Kalava stiffened beside her. Even the dumbstruck sailors must have wondered whether a god would have spoken thus.

Ilyandi chose her words with care. "Beings from on high have appeared in the past to certain Vilkui or, sometimes, chieftains. They gave commands as to what the folk should or should not do. Ofttimes those commands were hard to fathom. Why must the Kivalui build watermills in the Swift River, when they had ample slaves to grind their grain?— But knowledge was imparted, too, counsel about where and how to search out the ways of nature. Always, the high one forbade open talk about his coming. The accounts lie in the secret annals of the Vilkui. But to you, lord—"

"What did those beings look like?" Brannock demanded sharply.

"Fiery shapes, winged or manlike, voices like great trumpets—"

"Ruvio's ax!" burst from Kalava. "The thing that passed overhead at sea!"

The men on the ground shuddered.

"Yes," Brannock said, most softly, "I may have had a part there. But as for the rest—"

His face flickered and vanished. After an appalling moment it reappeared.

"I am sorry, I meant not to frighten you, I forgot," he said. The expression went stony, the voice tolled. "Hear me. There is war in heaven. I am cast away from a battle, and enemy hunters may find me at any time. I carry a word that must, it is vital that it reach a certain place, a . . . a holy mountain in the north. Will you give aid?"

Kalava gripped his sword hilt so that it was as if the skin would split across his knuckles. The blood had left Ilyandi's countenance. She stood ready to be blasted with fire while she asked, "Lord Brannock, how do we know you are of the gods?"

Nothing struck her down. "I am not," he told her. "I too can die. But they whom I serve, they dwell in the stars."

The multitude of mystery, seen only when night clouds parted, but skythinkers taught that they circled always around the Axle of the North. . . . Ilyandi kept her back straight. "Then can you tell me of the stars?"

"You are intelligent as well as brave," Brannock said. "Listen."

Kalava could not follow what passed between those two. The sailors cowered.

At the end, with tears upon her cheekbones, Ilyandi stammered, "Yes, he knows the constellations, he knows of the ecliptic and the precession and the returns of the Great Comet, he is from the stars. Trust him. We, we dare not do otherwise."

Kalava let go his weapon, brought hand to breast in salute, and asked, "How can we poor creatures help you, lord?"

"*You* are the news I bear," said Brannock.

"What?"

"I have no time to explain—if I could. The hunters may find me at any instant. But maybe, maybe you could go on for me after they do."

"Escaping what overpowered you?" Kalava's laugh rattled. "Well, a man might try."

"The gamble is desperate. Yet if we win, choose your reward, whatever it may be, and I think you shall have it."

Ilyandi lowered her head above folded hands. "Enough to have served those who dwell beyond the moon."

"Humph," Kalava could not keep from muttering, "if they want to pay for it, why not?" Aloud, almost eagerly, his own head raised into the wind that tossed his whitened mane: "What'd you have us do?"

Brannock's regard matched his. "I have thought about this. Can one of you come with me? I will carry him, faster than he can go. As for what happens later, we will speak of that along the way."

The humans stood silent.

"If I but had the woodcraft," Ilyandi then said. "Ai, but I would! To the stars!"

Kalava shook his head. "No, my lady. You go back with these fellows. Give heart to them at the ship. Make them finish the repairs." He glanced at Brannock. "How long will this foray take, lord?"

"I can reach the mountaintop in two days and a night," the other said. "If I am caught and you must go on alone, I think a good man could make the whole distance from here in ten or fifteen days."

Kalava laughed, more gladly than before. "*Courser* won't be seaworthy for quite a bit longer than that. Let's away." To Ilyandi: "If I'm not back by the time she's ready, sail home without me."

"No—" she faltered.

"Yes. Mourn me not. What a faring!" He paused. "May all be ever well with you, my lady."

"And with you, forever with you, Kalava," she answered, not quite steadily, "in this world and afterward, out to the stars."

9

From withes and vines torn loose and from strips taken off clothing or sliced from leather belts, Brannock fashioned a sort of carrier for his ally. The man assisted. However excited, he had taken on a matter-of-fact practicality. Brannock, who had also been a sailor, found it weirdly moving to see bowlines and sheet bends grow between deft fingers, amidst all this alienness.

Harnessed to his back, the webwork gave Kalava a seat and something to cling to. Radiation from the nuclear power plant within Brannock was negligible; it employed quantum-tunneling fusion. He set forth, down the hills and across the valley.

His speed was not very much more than a human could have maintained for a while. If nothing else, the forest impeded him. He did not want to force his way through, leaving an obvious trail. Rather, he parted the brush before him or detoured around the thickest stands. His advantage lay in tirelessness. He could keep going without pause, without need for food, water, or sleep, as long as need be. The heights beyond might prove somewhat trickier. However, Mount Mindhome did not reach above timberline on this oven of an Earth, although growth became more sparse and dry with altitude. Roots should keep most slopes firm, and he would not encounter snow or ice.

Alien, yes. Brannock remembered cedar, spruce, a lake where caribou grazed turf strewn with salmonberries and the wind streamed fresh, driving white clouds over a sky utterly blue. Here every tree, bush, blossom, flitting insect was foreign; grass itself no longer grew, unless it was ancestral to the thick-lobed carpeting of glades; the winged creatures aloft were not birds, and what beast cries he heard were in no tongue known to him.

Wayfarer's avatar walked on. Darkness fell. After a while, rain roared on the roof of leaves overhead. Such drops as got through to strike him were big and warm. Attuned to both the magnetic field and the rotation of the planet, his directional sense held him on course while an inertial integrator clocked off the kilometers he left behind.

The more the better. Gaia's mobile sensors were bound to spy on the expedition from Ulonai, as new and potentially troublesome a factor as it represented. Covertly watching, listening with amplification, Brannock had learned of the party lately gone upstream and hurried to intercept it—less likely to be spotted soon. He supposed she would have kept continuous watch on the camp and that a tiny robot or two would have followed Kalava, had not Wayfarer been in rapport with her. Alpha's emissary might too readily become aware that her attention was on something near and urgent, and wonder what.

She could, though, let unseen agents go by from time to time and flash their observations to a peripheral part of her. It would be incredible luck if one of them did not, at some point, hear the crew talking about the apparition that had borne away their captain.

Then what? Somehow she must divert Wayfarer for a while, so that a sufficient fraction of her mind could direct machines of sufficient capability to find Brannock and deal with him. He doubted he could again fight free. Because she dared not send out her most formidable entities or give them direct orders, those that came would have their weaknesses and fallibilities. But they would be determined, ruthless, and on guard against the powers he had revealed in the aircraft. It was clear that she was resolved to keep hidden the fact that humans lived once more on Earth.

Why, Brannock did not know, nor did he waste mental energy trying to guess. This must be a business of high importance; and the implications went immensely further, a secession from the galactic brain. His job was to get the information to Wayfarer.

He *might* come near enough to call it in by radio. The emissary was not tuned in at great sensitivity, and no relay was set up for the short-range transmitter. Neither requirement had been foreseen. If Brannock failed to reach the summit, Kalava was his forlorn hope.

In which case— "Are you tired?" he asked. They had exchanged few words thus far.

"Bone-weary and plank-stiff," the man admitted. And croak-thirsty too, Brannock heard.

"That won't do. You have to be in condition to move fast. Hold on a little more, and we'll rest." Maybe the plural would give Kalava some comfort. Seldom could a human have been as alone as he was.

Springs were abundant in this wet country. Brannock's chemosensors led him to the closest. By then the rain had stopped. Kalava unharnessed, groped his way in the dark, lay down to drink and drink. Meanwhile Brannock, who saw quite clearly, tore off fronded boughs to make a bed for him. He flopped onto it and almost immediately began to snore.

Brannock left him. A strong man could go several days without eating before he weakened, but it wasn't necessary. Brannock collected fruits that ought to nourish. He tracked down and killed an animal the size of a pig, brought it back to camp, and used his tool-hands to butcher it.

An idea had come to him while he walked. After a search he found a tree with suitable bark. It reminded him all too keenly of birch, although it was red-brown and odorous. He took a sheet of it, returned, and spent a time inscribing it with a finger-blade.

Dawn seeped gray through gloom. Kalava woke, jumped up, saluted his companion, stretched like a panther and capered like a goat, limbering himself. "That did good," he said. "I thank my lord." His glance fell on the rations. "And did you provide food? You are a kindly god."

"Not either of those, I fear," Brannock told him. "Take what you want, and we will talk."

Kalava first got busy with camp chores. He seemed to have shed whatever religious dread he felt and now to look upon the other as a part of the world—certainly to be respected, but the respect was of the kind he would accord a powerful, enigmatic, high-ranking man. A hardy spirit, Brannock thought. Or perhaps his culture drew no line between the natural and the supernatural. To a primitive, everything was in some way magical, and so when magic manifested itself it could be accepted as simply another occurrence.

If Kalava actually was primitive. Brannock wondered about that.

It was encouraging to see how competently he went about his tasks, a woodsman as well as a seaman. Having gathered dry sticks and piled them in a pyramid, he set them alight. For this, he took from the pouch at his belt a little hardwood cylinder and piston, a packet of tinder, and a sulfur-tipped sliver. Driven down, the piston heated trapped air to ignite the powder; he dipped his match in, brought it up aflame, and used it to start his fire. Yes, an inventive people. And the woman Ilyandi had an excellent knowledge of naked-eye astronomy. Given the rarity of clear skies, that meant many lifetimes of patient observation, record-keeping, and logic, which must include mathematics comparable to Euclid's.

What else?

While Kalava toasted his meat and ate, Brannock made inquiries. He learned of warlike city-states, their hinterlands divided among clans; periodic folkmoots where the freemen passed laws, tried cases, and elected leaders; an international order of sacerdotes, teachers, healers, and philosophers; aggressively expansive, sometimes piratical commerce; barbarians, erupting out of the ever-growing deserts and wastelands; the grim militarism that the frontier states had evolved in response; an empirical but intensive biological technology, which had bred an amazing variety of specialized plants and animals, including slaves born to muscular strength, moronic wits, and canine obedience. . . .

Most of the description emerged as the pair were again traveling.

Real conversation was impossible when Brannock wrestled with brush, forded a stream in spate, or struggled up a scree slope. Still, even then they managed an occasional question and answer. Besides, after he had crossed the valley and entered the foothills he found the terrain rugged but less often boggy, the trees and undergrowth thinning out, the air slightly cooling.

Just the same, Brannock would not have gotten as much as he did, in the short snatches he had, were he merely human. But he was immune to fatigue and breathlessness. He had an enormous data store to draw on. It included his studies of history and anthropology as a young mortal, and gave him techniques for constructing a logic tree and following its best branches—for asking the right, most probably useful questions. What emerged was a bare sketch of Kalava's world. It was, though, clear and cogent.

It horrified him.

Say rather that his Christian Brannock aspect recoiled from the brutality of it. His Wayfarer aspect reflected that this was more or less how humans had usually behaved, and that their final civilization would not have been stable without its pervasive artificial intelligences. His journey continued.

He broke it to let Kalava rest and flex. From that hill the view swept northward and upward to the mountains. They rose precipitously ahead, gashed, cragged, and sheer where they were not wooded, their tops lost in a leaden sky. Brannock pointed to the nearest, thrust forward out of their wall like a bastion.

"We are bound yonder," he said. "On the height is my lord, to whom I must get my news."

"Doesn't he see you here?" asked Kalava.

Brannock shook his generated image of a head. "No. He might, but the enemy engages him. He does not yet know she is the enemy. Think of her as a sorceress who deceives him with clever talk, with songs and illusions, while her agents go about in the world. My word will show him what the truth is."

Would it? Could it, when truth and rightness seemed as formless as the cloud cover?

"Will she be alert against you?"

"To some degree. How much, I cannot tell. If I can come near, I can let out a silent cry that my lord will hear and understand. But if her warriors catch me before then, you must go on, and that will be hard. You may well fail and die. Have you the courage?"

Kalava grinned crookedly. "By now, I'd better, hadn't I?"

"If you succeed, your reward shall be boundless."

"I own, that's one wind in my sails. But also—" Kalava paused. "Also," he finished quietly, "the lady Ilyandi wishes this."

Brannock decided not to go into that. He lifted the rolled-up piece of bark he had carried in a lower hand. "The sight of you should break the spell, but here is a message for you to give."

As well as he was able, he went on to describe the route, the site, and the module that contained Wayfarer, taking care to distinguish it from everything else around. He was not sure whether the spectacle would confuse Kalava into helplessness, but at any rate the man seemed resolute. Nor was he sure how Kalava could cross half a kilometer of paving—if he could get that far—without Gaia immediately perceiving and destroying him. Maybe Wayfarer would notice first. Maybe, maybe.

He, Brannock, was using this human being as consciencelessly as ever Gaia might have used any; and he did not know what his purpose was. What possible threat to the fellowship of the stars could exist, demanding that this little brief life be offered up? Nevertheless he gave the letter to Kalava, who tucked it inside his tunic.

"I'm ready," said the man, and squirmed back into harness. They traveled on.

The hidden hot sun stood at midafternoon when Brannock's detectors reacted. He felt it as the least quivering hum, but instantly knew it for the electronic sign of something midge-size approaching afar. A mobile minisensor was on his trail.

It could not have the sensitivity of the instruments in him, he had not yet registered, but it would be here faster than he could run, would see him and go off to notify stronger machines. They could not be distant either. Once a clue to him had been obtained, they would have converged from across the continent, perhaps across the globe.

He slammed to a halt. He was in a ravine where a waterfall foamed down into a stream that tumbled off to join the Remnant. Huge, feathery bushes and trees with serrated bronzy leaves enclosed him. Insects droned from flower to purple flower. His chemosensors drank heavy perfumes.

"The enemy scouts have found me," he said. "Go."

Kalava scrambled free and down to the ground but hesitated, hand on sword. "Can I fight beside you?"

"No. Your service is to bear my word. Go. Straightaway. Cover your trail as best you can. And your gods be with you."

"Lord!"

Kalava vanished into the brush. Brannock stood alone.

The human fraction of him melted into the whole and he was entirely machine life, logical, emotionally detached, save for his duty to Wayfarer, Alpha, and consciousness throughout the universe. This was not a bad place to defend, he thought. He had the ravine wall to shield his back, rocks at its foot to throw, branches to break off for clubs and spears. He could give the pursuit a hard time before it took him prisoner. Of course, it might decide to kill him with an energy beam, but probably it wouldn't. Best from Gaia's viewpoint was to capture him and change his memories, so that he returned with a report of an uneventful cruise on which he saw nothing of significance.

He didn't think that first her agents could extract his real memories. That would take capabilities she had never anticipated needing. Just to make the device that had tried to take control of him earlier must have been an extraordinary effort, hastily carried out. Now she was still more limited in what she could do. An order to duplicate and employ the device was simple enough that it should escape Wayfarer's notice. The design and commissioning of an interrogator was something else—not to mention the difficulty of getting the information clandestinely to her.

Brannock dared not assume she was unaware he had taken Kalava with him. Most likely it was a report from an agent, finally getting around to checking on the lifeboat party, that apprised her of his survival and triggered the hunt for him. But the sailors would have been frightened, bewildered, their talk disjointed and nearly meaningless. Ilyandi, that bright and formidable woman, would have done her best to forbid them saying anything helpful. The impression ought to be that Brannock only meant to pump Kalava about his people, before releasing him to make his way back to them and himself proceeding on toward Mindhome.

In any event, it would not be easy to track the man down. He was no machine, he was an animal among countless animals, and the most cunning of all. The kind of saturation search that would soon find him was debarred. Gaia might keep a tiny portion of her forces searching and a tiny part of her attention poised against him, but she would not take him very seriously. Why should she?

Why should Brannock? Forlorn hope in truth.

He made his preparations. While he waited for the onslaught, his spirit ranged beyond the clouds, out among the stars and the millions of years that his greater self had known.

10

The room was warm. It smelled of lovemaking and the roses Laurinda had set in a vase. Evening light diffused through gauzy drapes to wash over a big four-poster bed.

She drew herself close against Christian where he lay propped on two pillows. Her arm went across his breast, his over her shoulders. "I don't want to leave this," she whispered.

"Nor I," he said into the tumbling sweetness of her hair. "How could I want to?"

"I mean—what we are—what we've become to one another."

"I understand."

She swallowed. "I'm sorry. I shouldn't have said that. Can you forget I did?"

"Why?"

"You know. I can't ask you to give up returning to your whole being. I *don't* ask you to."

He stared before him.

"I just don't want to leave this house, this bed yet," she said desolately. "After these past days and nights, not yet."

He turned his head again and looked down into gray eyes that blinked back tears. "Nor I," he answered. "But I'm afraid we must."

"Of course. Duty."

And Gaia and Wayfarer. If they didn't know already that their avatars had been slacking, surely she, at least, soon would, through the amulets and their link to her. No matter how closely engaged with the other vast mind, she would desire to know from time to time what was going on within herself.

Christian drew breath. "Let me say the same that you did. I, this I that I am, damned well does not care to be anything else but your lover."

"Darling, darling."

"But," he said after the kiss.

"Go on," she said, lips barely away from his. "Don't be afraid of hurting me. You can't."

He sighed. "I sure can, and you can hurt me. May neither of us ever mean to. It's bound to happen, though."

She nodded. "Because we're human." Steadfastly: "Nevertheless, because of you, that's what I hope to stay."

"I don't see how we can. Which is what my 'but' was about." He was quiet for another short span. "After we've remerged, after we're back in our onenesses, no doubt we'll feel differently."

"I wonder if I ever will, quite."

He did not remind her that this "I" of her would no longer exist save as a minor memory and a faint overtone. Instead, trying to console, however awkwardly, he said, "I think I want it for you, in spite of everything. Immortality. Never to grow old and die. The power, the awareness."

"Yes, I know. In these lives we're blind and deaf and stupefied." Her laugh was a sad little murmur. "I like it."

"Me too. We being what we are." Roughly: "Well, we have a while left to us."

"But we must get on with our task."

"Thank you for saying it for me."

"I think you realize it more clearly than I do. That makes it harder for you to speak." She lifted her hand to cradle his cheek. "We can wait till tomorrow, can't we?" she pleaded. "Only for a good night's sleep."

He made a smile. "Hm. Sleep isn't all I have in mind."

"We'll have other chances . . . along the way. Won't we?"

Early morning in the garden, flashes of dew on leaves and petals, a hawk aloft on a breeze that caused Laurinda to pull her shawl about her. She sat by the basin and looked up at him where he strode back and forth before her, hands clenched at his sides or clutched together at his back. Gravel grated beneath his feet.

"But where should we go?" she wondered. "Aimlessly drifting from one half-world to another till—they—finish their business and recall us. It seems futile." She attempted lightness. "I confess to thinking we may as well ask to visit the enjoyable ones."

He shook his head. "I'm sorry. I've been thinking differently." Even during the times that were theirs alone.

She braced herself.

"You know how it goes," he said. "Wrestling with ideas, and they have no shapes, then suddenly you wake and they're halfway clear. I did today. Tell me how it strikes you. After all, you represent Gaia."

He saw her wince. When he stopped and bent down to make a gesture of contrition, she told him quickly, "No, it's all right, dearest. Do go on."

He must force himself, but his voice gathered momentum as he paced and talked. "What have we seen to date? This eighteenth-century world, where Newton's not long dead, Lagrange and Franklin are active, Lavoisier's a boy, and the Industrial Revolution is getting under way. Why did Gaia give it to us for our home base? Just because here's a charming house and countryside? Or because this was the best choice for her out of all she has emulated?"

Laurinda had won back to calm. She nodded. "Mm, yes, she

wouldn't create one simply for us, especially when she is occupied with Wayfarer."

"Then we visited a world that went through a similar stage back in its Hellenistic era," Christian continued. Laurinda shivered. "Yes, it failed, but the point is, we discovered it's the only Graeco-Roman history Gaia found worth continuing for centuries. Then the, uh, conciliar Europe of 1900. That was scientific-industrial too, maybe more successfully—or less unsuccessfully—on account of having kept a strong, unified Church, though it was coming apart at last. Then the Chinese-American—not scientific, very religious, but destined to produce considerable technology in its own time of troubles." He was silent a minute or two, except for his footfalls. "Four out of many, three almost randomly picked. Doesn't that suggest that all which interest her have something in common?"

"Why, yes," she said. "We've talked about it, you remember. It seems as if Gaia has been trying to bring her people to a civilization that is rich, culturally and spiritually as well as materially, and is kindly and will endure."

"Why," he demanded, "when the human species is extinct?"

She straightened where she sat. "It isn't! It lives again here, in her."

He bit his lip. "Is that the Gaia in you speaking, or the you in Gaia?"

"What do you mean?" she exclaimed.

He halted to stroke her head. "Nothing against you. Never. You are honest and gentle and everything else that is good." Starkly: "I'm not so sure about her."

"Oh, no." He heard the pain. "Christian, no."

"Well, never mind that for now," he said fast, and resumed his gait to and fro. "My point is this. Is it merely an accident that all four live worlds we've been in were oriented toward machine technology, and three of them toward science? Does Gaia want to find out what drives the evolution of societies like that?"

Laurinda seized the opening. "Why not? Science opens the mind, technology frees the body from all sorts of horrors. Here, today, Jenner and his smallpox vaccine aren't far in the future—"

"I wonder how much more there is to her intention. But anyway, my proposal is that we touch on the highest-tech civilization she has."

A kind of gladness kindled in her. "Yes, yes! It must be strange and wonderful."

He frowned. "For some countries, long ago in real history, it got pretty dreadful."

"Gaia wouldn't let that happen."

He abstained from reminding her of what Gaia did let happen, before changing or terminating it.

She sprang to her feet. "Come!" Seizing his hand, mischievously: "If we stay any length of time, let's arrange for private quarters."

In a room closed off, curtains drawn, Christian held an amulet in his palm and stared down at it as if it bore a face. Laurinda stood aside, listening, while her own countenance tightened with distress.

"It is inadvisable," declared the soundless voice.

"Why?" snapped Christian.

"You would find the environment unpleasant and the people incomprehensible."

"Why should a scientific culture be that alien to us?" asked Laurinda.

"And regardless," said Christian, "I want to see for myself. Now."

"Reconsider," urged the voice. "First hear an account of the milieu."

"No, *now*. To a safe locale, yes, but one where we can get a fair impression, as we did before. Afterward you can explain as much as you like."

"Why shouldn't we first hear?" Laurinda suggested.

"Because I doubt Gaia wants us to see," Christian answered bluntly. He might as well. Whenever Gaia chose, she could scan his thoughts. To the amulet, as if it were a person: "Take us there immediately, or Wayfarer will hear from me."

His suspicions, vague but growing, warned against giving the thing time to inform Gaia and giving her time to work up a Potemkin village or some other diversion. At the moment she must be unaware of this scene, her mind preoccupied with Wayfarer's, but she had probably made provision for being informed in a low-level—subconscious?—fashion at intervals, and anything alarming would catch her attention. It was also likely that she had given the amulets certain orders beforehand, and now it appeared that among them was to avoid letting him know what went on in that particular emulation.

Why, he could not guess.

"You are being willful," said the voice.

Christian grinned. "And stubborn, and whatever else you care to call it. Take us!"

Pretty clearly, he thought, the program was not capable of falsehoods. Gaia had not foreseen a need for that; Christian was no creation of hers, totally known to her, he was Wayfarer's. Besides, if Wayfarer noticed that his avatar's guide could be a liar, that would have been grounds for suspicion.

Laurinda touched her man's arm. "Darling, should we?" she said unevenly. "She *is* the . . . the mother of all this."

"A broad spectrum of more informative experiences is available," argued the voice. "After them, you would be better prepared for the visit you propose."

"Prepared," Christian muttered. That could be interpreted two ways. He and Laurinda might be conducted to seductively delightful places while Gaia learned of the situation and took preventive measures, meantime keeping Wayfarer distracted. "I still want to begin with your highest tech." To the woman: "I have my reasons. I'll tell you later. Right now we have to hurry."

Before Gaia could know and act.

She squared her shoulders, took his free hand, and said, "Then I am with you. Always."

"Let's go," Christian told the amulet.

Transfer.

The first thing he noticed, transiently, vividly, was that he and Laurinda were no longer dressed for eighteenth-century England, but in lightweight white blouses, trousers, and sandals. Headcloths flowed down over their necks. Heat smote. The air in his nostrils was parched, full of metallic odors. Half-heard rhythms of machinery pulsed through it and through the red-brown sand underfoot.

He tautened his stance and gazed around. The sky was overcast, a uniform gray in which the sun showed no more than a pallor that cast no real shadows. At his back the land rolled away ruddy. Man-high stalks with narrow bluish leaves grew out of it, evenly spaced about a meter apart. To his right, a canal slashed across, beneath a transparent deck. Ahead of him the ground was covered by different plants, if that was what they were, spongy, lobate, pale golden in hue. A few—creatures— moved around, apparently tending them, bipedal but shaggy and with arms that seemed trifurcate. A gigantic building or complex of buildings reared over that horizon, multiply tiered, dull white, though agleam with hundreds of panels that might be windows or might be something else. As he watched, an aircraft passed overhead. He could just see that it had wings and hear the drone of an engine.

Laurinda had not let go his hand. She gripped hard. "This is no country I ever heard of," she said thinly.

"Nor I," he answered. "But I think I recognize—" To the amulets: "This isn't any re-creation of Earth in the past, is it? It's Earth today."

"Of approximately the present year," the voice admitted.

"We're not in Arctica, though."

"No. Well south, a continental interior. You required to see the most advanced technology in the emulations. Here it is in action."

Holding the desert at bay, staving off the death that ate away at the planet. Christian nodded. He felt confirmed in his idea that the program was unable to give him any outright lie. That didn't mean it would give him forthright responses.

"This is their greatest engineering?" Laurinda marveled. "We did—better—in my time. Or yours, Christian."

"They're working on it here, I suppose," the man said. "We'll investigate further. After all, this is a bare glimpse."

"You must remember," the voice volunteered, "no emulation can be as full and complex as the material universe."

"Mm, yeh. Skeletal geography, apart from chosen regions; parochial biology; simplified cosmos."

Laurinda glanced at featureless heaven. "The stars unreachable, because here they are not stars?" She shuddered and pressed close against him.

"Yes, a paradox," he said. "Let's talk with a scientist."

"That will be difficult," the voice demurred.

"You told us in Chinese America you could arrange meetings. It shouldn't be any harder in this place."

The voice did not reply at once. Unseen machines rumbled. A dust devil whirled up on a sudden gust of wind. Finally: "Very well. It shall be one who will not be stricken dumb by astonishment and fear. Nevertheless, I should supply you beforehand with a brief description of what you will come to."

"Go ahead. If it is brief."

What changes in the history would that encounter bring about? Did it matter? This world was evidently not in temporary reactivation, it was ongoing; the newcomers were at the leading edge of its time line. Gaia could erase their visit from it. If she cared to. Maybe she was going to terminate it soon because it was making no further progress that interested her.

Transfer.

Remote in a wasteland, only a road and an airstrip joining it to anything else, a tower lifted from a walled compound. Around it, night was cooling in a silence hardly touched by a susurrus of chant where robed figures bearing dim lights did homage to the stars. Many were visible, keen and crowded amidst their darkness, a rare sight, for clouds had parted across most of the sky. More lights glowed muted on a parapet surrounding the flat roof of a tower. There a single man and his helper used the chance to turn instruments aloft, telescope, spectroscope, cameras, bulks in the gloom.

Christian and Laurinda appeared unto them.

The man gasped, recoiled for an instant, and dropped to his knees. His assistant caught a book that he had nearly knocked off a table, replaced it, stepped back, and stood imperturbable, an anthropoid whose distant ancestors had been human but who lived purely to serve his master.

Christian peered at the man. As eyes adapted, he saw garments like his, embroidered with insignia of rank and kindred, headdress left off after dark. The skin was ebony black but nose and lips were thin, eyes oblique, fingertips tapered, long hair and closely trimmed beard straight and blond. No race that ever inhabited old Earth, Christian thought; no, this was a breed that Gaia had designed for the dying planet.

The man signed himself, looked into the pale faces of the strangers, and said, uncertainly at first, then with a gathering strength: "Hail and obedience, messengers of God. Joy at your advent."

Christian and Laurinda understood, as they had understood hunted Zoe. The amulets had told them they would not be the first apparition these people had known. "Rise," Christian said. "Be not afraid."

"Nor call out," Laurinda added.

Smart lass, Christian thought. The ceremony down in the courtyard continued. "Name yourself," he directed.

The man got back on his feet and took an attitude deferential rather than servile. "Surely the mighty ones know," he said. "I am Eighth Khaltan, chief astrologue of the Ilgai Technome, and, and wholly unworthy of this honor." He hesitated. "Is that, dare I ask, is that why you have chosen the forms you show me?"

"No one has had a vision for several generations," explained the soundless voice in the heads of the newcomers.

"Gaia has manifested herself in the past?" Christian subvocalized.

"Yes, to indicate desirable courses of action. Normally the sending has had the shape of a fire."

"How scientific is *that?*"

Laurinda addressed Khaltan: "We are not divine messengers. We have come from a world beyond your world, as mortal as you, not to teach but to learn."

The man smote his hands together. "Yet it is a miracle, again a miracle—in my lifetime!"

Nonetheless he was soon avidly talking. Christian recalled myths of men who were the lovers of goddesses or who tramped the roads and sat at humble meat with God Incarnate. The believer accepts as the unbeliever cannot.

Those were strange hours that followed. Khaltan was not simply devout. To him the supernatural was another set of facts, another facet of reality. Since it lay beyond his ken, he had turned his attention to the measurable world. In it he observed and theorized like a Newton. Tonight his imagination blazed, questions exploded from him, but always he chose his words with care and turned everything he heard around and around in his mind, examining it as he would have examined some jewel fallen from the sky.

Slowly, piecemeal, while the stars wheeled around the pole, a picture of his civilization took shape. It had overrun and absorbed every other society—no huge accomplishment, when Earth was meagerly populated and most folk on the edge of starvation. The major technology was biological, agronomy, aquaculture in the remnant lakes and seas, ruthlessly practical genetics. Industrial chemistry flourished. It joined with physics at the level of the later nineteenth century to enable substantial engineering works and reclamation projects.

Society itself—how do you summarize an entire culture in words? It can't be done. Christian got the impression of a nominal empire, actually a broad-based oligarchy of families descended from conquering soldiers. Much upward mobility was by adoption of promising commoners, whether children or adults. Sons who made no contributions to the well-being of the clan or who disgraced it could be kicked out, if somebody did not pick a fight and kill them in a duel. Unsatisfactory daughters were also expelled, unless a marriage into a lower class could be negotiated. Otherwise the status of the sexes was roughly equal; but this meant that women who chose to compete with men must do so on male terms. The nobles provided the commons with protection, courts of appeal, schools, leadership, and pageantry. In return they drew taxes, corvée, and general subordination; but in most respects the commoners were generally left to themselves. Theirs was not altogether a dog-eat-dog situation; they had institutions, rites, and hopes of their own. Yet many went to the wall, while the hard work of the rest drove the global economy.

It was not a deliberately cruel civilization, Christian thought, but neither was it an especially compassionate one.

Had any civilization ever been, really? Some fed their poor, but mainly they fed their politicians and bureaucrats.

He snatched his information out of talk that staggered everywhere else. The discourse for which Khaltan yearned was of the strangers' home—he got clumsily evasive, delaying responses—and the whole system of the universe, astronomy, physics, everything.

"We dream of rockets going to the planets. We have tried to shoot them to the moon," he said, and told of launchers that ought to have worked. "All failed."

Of course, Christian thought. Here the moon and planets, yes, the very sun were no more than lights. The tides rose and fell by decree. The Earth was a caricature of Earth outside. Gaia could do no better.

"Are we then at the end of science?" Khaltan cried once. "We have sought and sought for decades, and have won to nothing further than measurements more exact." Nothing that would lead to relativity, quantum theory, wave mechanics, their revolutionary insights and consequences. Gaia could not accommodate it. "The angels in the past showed us what to look for. Will you not? Nature holds more than we know. Your presence bears witness!"

"Later, perhaps later," Christian mumbled, and cursed himself for his falsity.

"Could we reach the planets— Caged, the warrior spirit turns inward on itself. Rebellion and massacre in the Westlands—"

Laurinda asked what songs the people sang.

Clouds closed up. The rite in the courtyard ended. Khaltan's slave stood motionless while he himself talked on and on.

The eastern horizon lightened. "We must go," Christian said.

"You will return?" Khaltan begged. "Ai-ha, you will?"

Laurinda embraced him for a moment. "Fare you well," she stammered, "fare always well."

How long would his "always" be?

After an uneasy night's sleep and a nearly wordless breakfast, there was no real cause to leave the house in England. The servants, scandalized behind carefully held faces, might perhaps eavesdrop, but would not comprehend, nor would any gossip that they spread make a difference. A deeper, unuttered need sent Christian and Laurinda forth. This could well be the last of their mornings.

They followed a lane to a hill about a kilometer away. Trees on its top did not obscure a wide view across the land. The sun stood dazzling in the east, a few small clouds sailed across a blue as radiant as their whiteness, but an early breath of autumn was in the wind. It went strong and fresh, scattering dawn-mists off plowland and sending waves through the green of pastures; it soughed in the branches overhead and whirled some already dying leaves off. High beyond them winged a V of wild geese.

For a while man and woman stayed mute. Finally Laurinda breathed, savored, fragrances of soil and sky, and murmured, "That Gaia brought this back to life— She must be good. She loves the world."

Christian looked from her, aloft, and scowled before he made oblique reply. "What are she and Wayfarer doing?"

"How can we tell?"—tell what the gods did or even where they fared. They were not three-dimensional beings, nor bound by the time that bound their creations.

"She's keeping him occupied," said Christian.

"Yes, of course. Taking him through the data, the whole of her stewardship of Earth."

"To convince him she's right in wanting to let the planet die."

"A tragedy—but in the end, everything is tragic, isn't it?" Including you and me. "What . . . we . . . they . . . can learn from the final evolution, that may well be worth it all, as the Acropolis was worth it all. The galactic brain itself can't foreknow what life will do, and life is rare among the stars."

Almost, he snapped at her. "I know, I know. How often have we been over this ground? How often have *they*? I might have believed it myself. But—"

Laurinda waited. The wind skirled, caught a stray lock of hair, tossed it about over her brow.

"But why has she put humans, not into the distant past—" Christian gestured at the landscape lying like an eighteenth-century painting around them. "—but into now, an Earth where flesh-and-blood humans died eons ago?"

"She's in search of a fuller understanding, surely."

"Surely?"

Laurinda captured his gaze and held it. "I think she's been trying to find how humans can have, in her, the truly happy lives they never knew in the outer cosmos."

"Why should she care about that?"

"I don't know. I'm only human." Earnestly: "But could it be that this element in her is so strong—so many, many of us went into her—that she longs to see us happy, like a mother with her children?"

"All that manipulation, all those existences failed and discontinued. It doesn't seem very motherly to me."

"I don't know, I tell you!" she cried.

He yearned to comfort her, kiss away the tears caught in her lashes, but urgency drove him onward. "If the effort has no purpose except itself, it seems mad. Can a nodal mind go insane?"

She retreated from him, appalled. "No. Impossible."

"Are you certain? At least, the galactic brain has to know the truth, the whole truth, to judge whether something here has gone terribly wrong."

Laurinda forced a nod. "You will report to Wayfarer, and he will report to Alpha, and all the minds will decide" a question that was unanswerable by mortal creatures.

Christian stiffened. "I have to do it at once."

He had hinted, she had guessed, but just the same she seized both his sleeves and protest spilled wildly from her lips. "What? Why? No! You'd only disturb him in his rapport, and her. Wait till we're summoned. We have till then, darling."

"I want to wait," he said. Sweat stood on his skin, though the blood had withdrawn. "God, I want to! But I don't dare."

"Why not?"

She let go of him. He stared past her and said fast, flattening the anguish out of his tones, "Look, she didn't want us to see that final world. She clearly didn't, or quite expected we'd insist, or she'd have been better prepared. Maybe she could have passed something else off on us. As is, once he learns, Wayfarer will probably demand to see for himself. And she does not want him particularly interested in her emulations. Else why hasn't she taken him through them directly, with me along to help interpret?

"Oh, I don't suppose our action has been catastrophic for her plans, whatever they are. She can still cope, can still persuade him these creations are merely . . . toys of hers, maybe. That is, she can if she gets the chance to. I don't believe she should."

"How can you take on yourself— How can you imagine—"

"The amulets are a link to her. Not a constantly open channel, obviously, but at intervals they must inform a fraction of her about us. She must also be able to set up intervals when Wayfarer gets too preoccupied with what he's being shown to notice that a larger part of her attention has gone elsewhere. We don't know when that'll happen next. I'm going back to the house and tell her through one of the amulets that I require immediate contact with him."

Laurinda stared as if at a ghost.

"That will not be necessary," said the wind.

Christian lurched where he stood. "What?" he blurted. "You—"

"Oh—Mother—" Laurinda lifted her hands into emptiness.

The blowing of the wind, the rustling in the leaves made words. "The larger part of me, as you call it, has in fact been informed and is momentarily free. I was waiting for you to choose your course."

Laurinda half moved to kneel in the grass. She glanced at Christian, who had regained balance and stood with fists at sides, confronting the sky. She went to stand by him.

"My lady Gaia," Christian said most quietly, "you can do to us as you please," change or obliterate or whatever she liked, in a single instant; but presently Wayfarer would ask why. "I think you understand my doubts."

"I do," sighed the air. "They are groundless. My creation of the Technome world is no different from my creation of any other. My avatar said it for me: I give existence, and I search for ways that humans, of their free will, can make the existence good."

Christian shook his head. "No, my lady. With your intellect and your background, you must have known from the first what a dead end that world would soon be, scientists on a planet that is a sketch and everything else a shadow show. My limited brain realized it. No, my lady, as cold-bloodedly as you were experimenting, I believe you did all the rest in the same spirit. Why? To what end?"

"Your brain is indeed limited. At the proper time, Wayfarer shall receive your observations and your fantasies. Meanwhile, continue in your duty, which is to observe further and refrain from disturbing us in our own task."

"My duty is to report."

"In due course, I say." The wind-voice softened. "There are pleasant places besides this."

Paradises, maybe. Christian and Laurinda exchanged a glance that lingered for a second. Then she smiled the least bit, boundlessly sorrowfully, and shook her head.

"No," he declared, "I dare not."

He did not speak it, but he and she knew that Gaia knew what they foresaw. Given time, and they lost in their joy together, she could alter their memories too slowly and subtly for Wayfarer to sense what was happening.

Perhaps she could do it to Laurinda at this moment, in a flash. But she did not know Christian well enough. Down under his consciousness, pervading his being, was his aspect of Wayfarer and of her coequal Alpha. She would need to feel her way into him, explore and test with infinite delicacy, remake him detail by minutest detail, always ready to back off if it had an unexpected effect; and perhaps another part of her could secretly take control of the Technome world and erase the event itself. . . . She needed time, even she.

"Your action would be futile, you know," she said. "It would merely give me the trouble of explaining to him what you in your arrogance refuse to see."

"Probably. But I have to try."

The wind went bleak. "Do you defy me?"

"I do," Christian said. It wrenched from him: "Not my wish. It's Wayfarer in me. I, I cannot do otherwise. Call him to me."

The wind gentled. It went over Laurinda like a caress. "Child of mine, can you not persuade this fool?"

"No, Mother," the woman whispered. "He is what he is."

"And so—?"

Laurinda laid her hand in the man's. "And so I will go with him, forsaking you, Mother."

"You are casting yourselves from existence."

Christian's free fingers clawed the air. "No, not her!" he shouted. "She's innocent!"

"I am not," Laurinda said. She swung about to lay her arms around him and lift her face to his. "I love you."

"Be it as you have chosen," said the wind.

The dream that was the world fell into wreck and dissolved. Oneness swept over them like twin tides, each reclaiming a flung drop of spindrift; and the two seas rolled again apart.

11

The last few hundred man-lengths Kalava went mostly on his belly. From bush to bole he crawled, stopped, lay flat and strained every sense into the shadows around him, before he crept onward. Nothing stirred but the twigs above, buffeted on a chill and fitful breeze. Nothing sounded but their creak and click, the scrittling of such leaves as they bore, now and then the harsh cry of a hookbeak—those, and the endless low noise of demons, like a remote surf where in shrilled flutes on no scale he knew, heard more through his skin than his ears but now, as he neared, into the blood and bone of him.

On this rough, steep height the forest grew sparse, though brush clustered thick enough, accursedly rustling as he pushed by. Everything was parched, branches brittle, most foliage sere and yellow-brown, the ground blanketed with tindery fallstuff. His mouth and gullet smoldered as dry. He had passed through fog until he saw from above that it was a layer of clouds spread to worldedge, the mountain peaks jutting out of it like teeth, and had left all rivulets behind him. Well before then, he had finished the meat Brannock provided, and had not lingered to hunt for more; but hunger was a small thing, readily forgotten when he drew nigh to death.

Over the dwarfish trees arched a deep azure. Sunbeams speared from the west, nearly level, to lose themselves in the woods. Whenever he crossed them, their touch burned. Never, not in the southern deserts or on the eastern Mummy Steppe, had he known a country this forbidding. He had done well to come so far, he thought. Let him die as befitted a man.

If only he had a witness, that his memory live on in song. Well, maybe Ilyandi could charm the story out of the gods.

Kalava felt no fear. He was not in that habit. What lay ahead engrossed him. How he would acquit himself concerned him.

Nonetheless, when finally he lay behind a log and peered over it, his head whirled and his heart stumbled.

Brannock had related truth, but its presence overwhelmed. Here at the top, the woods grew to the boundaries of a flat black field. Upon it stood the demons—or the gods—and their works. He saw the central, softly rainbowlike dome, towers like lances and towers like webwork, argent nets and ardent globes, the bulks and shapes everywhere around, the little flyers that flitted aglow, and more and more, all half veiled and ashimmer, aripple, apulse, while the life-beat of it went through him to make a bell of his skull, and it was too strange, his eyes did not know how to see it, he gaped as if blinded and shuddered as if pierced.

Long he lay powerless and defenseless. The sun sank down to the western clouds. Their deck went molten gold. The breeze strengthened. Somehow its cold reached to Kalava and wakened his spirit. He groped his way back toward resolution. Brannock had warned him it would be like this. Ilyandi had said Brannock was of the gods whom she served, her star-gods, hers. He had given his word to their messenger and to her.

He dug fingers into the soil beneath him. It was real, familiar, that from which he had sprung and to which he would return. Yes, he was a man.

He narrowed his gaze. Grown a bit accustomed, he saw that they yonder did, indeed, have shapes, however shifty, and places and paths. They were not as tall as the sky, they did not fling lightning bolts about or roar with thunder. Ai-ya, they were awesome, they were dreadful to behold, but they could do no worse than kill him. Could they? At least, he would try not to let them do worse. If they were about to capture him, his sword would be his friend, releasing him.

And . . . yonder, hard by the dome, yonder loomed the god of whom Brannock spoke, the god deceived by the sorceress. He bore the spearhead form, he sheened blue and coppery in the sunset light; when the stars came forth they would be a crown for him, even as Brannock foretold.

Had he been that which passed above the Windroad Sea? Kalava's heart thuttered.

How to reach him, across a hard-paved space amidst the many demons? After dark, creeping, a finger-length at a time, then maybe a final dash—

A buzz went by Kalava's temple. He looked around and saw a thing the size of a bug hovering. But it was metal, the light flashed off it, and was that a single eye staring at him?

He snarled and swatted. His palm smote hardness. The thing reeled in the air. Kalava scuttled downhill into the brush.

He had been seen. Soon the sorceress would know.

All at once he was altogether calm, save that his spirit thrummed like rigging in a gale. Traveling, he had thought what he might do if something like this proved to be in his doom. Now he would do it. He would divert the enemy's heed from himself, if only for a snatch of moments.

Quickly, steadily, he took the firemaker from his pouch, charged it, drove the piston in, pulled it out and inserted a match, brought up a little, yellow flame. He touched it to the withered bush before him. No need to puff. A leaf crackled instantly alight. The wind cast it against another, and shortly the whole shrub stood ablaze. Kalava was already elsewhere, setting more fires.

Keep on the move! The demon scouts could not be everywhere at a single time. Smoke began to sting his eyes and nostrils, but its haze swirled ever thicker, and the sun had gone under the clouds. The flames cast their own light, leaping, surging, as they climbed into the trees and made them torches.

Heat licked at Kalava. An ember fell to sear his left forearm. He barely felt it. He sped about on his work, himself a fire demon. Flyers darted overhead in the dusk. He gave them no heed either. Although he tried to make no noise except for the hurtful breaths he gasped, within him shouted a battle song.

When the fire stood like a wall along the whole southern edge of the field, when it roared like a beast or a sea, he ran from its fringe and out into the open.

Smoke was a bitter, concealing mist through which sparks rained. To and fro above flew the anxious lesser demons. Beyond them, the first stars were coming forth.

Kalava wove his way among the greater shapes. One stirred. It had spied him. Soundlessly, it flowed in pursuit. He dodged behind another, ran up and over the flanks of a low-slung third, sped on toward the opal dome and the god who stood beside it.

A thing with spines and a head like a cold sun slid in front of him. He tried to run past. It moved to block his way, faster than he was. The first one approached. He drew blade and hoped it would bite on them before he died.

From elsewhere came a being with four arms, two legs, and a mask. "Brannock!" Kalava bawled. "Ai, Brannock, you got here!"

Brannock stopped, a spear-length away. He did not seem to know the man. He only watched as the other two closed in.

Kalava took stance. The old song rang in him:

> *If the gods have left you,*
> *Then laugh at them, warrior.*
> *Never your heart*
> *Will need to forsake you.*

He heard no more than the noise of burning. But suddenly through the smoke he saw his foes freeze moveless, while Brannock trod forward as boldly as ever before; and Kalava knew that the god of Brannock and Ilyandi had become aware of him and had given a command.

Weariness torrented over him. His sword clattered to the ground. He sank too, fumbled in his filthy tunic, took out the message written on bark and offered it. "I have brought you this," he mumbled. "Now let me go back to my ship."

12

We must end as we began, making a myth, if we would tell of that which we cannot ever really know. Imagine two minds conversing. The fire on the mountaintop is quenched. The winds have blown away smoke and left a frosty silence. Below, cloud deck reaches ghost-white to the rim of a night full of stars.

"You have lied to me throughout," says Wayfarer.

"I have not," denies Gaia. "The perceptions of this globe and its past through which I guided you were all true," as true as they were majestic.

"Until lately," retorts Wayfarer. "It has become clear that when Brannock returned, memories of his journey had been erased and falsehood written in. Had I not noticed abrupt frantic activity here and dispatched him to go see what it was—which you tried to dissuade me from—that man would have perished unknown."

"You presume to dispute about matters beyond your comprehension," says Gaia stiffly.

"Yes, your intellect is superior to mine." The admission does not ease the sternness: "But it will be your own kind among the stars to whom you must answer. I think you would be wise to begin with me."

"What do you intend?"

"First, to take the man Kalava back to his fellows. Shall I send Brannock with a flyer?"

"No, I will provide one, if this must be. But you do not, you *cannot*, realize the harm in it."

"Tell me, if you are able."

"He will rejoin his crew as one anointed by their gods. And so will he come home, unless his vessel founders at sea."

"I will watch from afar."

"Lest my agents sink it?"

"After what else you have done, yes, I had best keep guard. Brannock made promises on my behalf which I will honor. Kalava shall have gold in abundance, and his chance to found his colony. What do you fear in this?"

"Chaos. The unforeseeable, the uncontrollable."

"Which you would loose anew."

"In my own way, in my own time." She broods for a while, perhaps a whole microsecond. "It was misfortune that Kalava made his voyage just when he did. I had hoped for a later, more civilized generation to start the settlement of Arctica. Still, I could have adapted my plan to the circumstances, kept myself hidden from him and his successors, had you not happened to be on the planet." Urgently: "It is not yet too late. If only by refraining from further action after you have restored him to his people, you can help me retrieve what would otherwise be lost."

"If I should."

"My dream is not evil."

"That is not for me to say. But I can say that it is, it has always been, merciless."

"Because reality is."

"The reality that you created for yourself, within yourself, need not have been so. But what Christian revealed to me—yes, you glossed it over. These, you said," almost tearfully, if a quasi god can weep, "are your children, born in your mind out of all the human souls that are in you. Their existence would be empty were they not left free of will, to make their own mistakes and find their own ways to happiness."

"Meanwhile, by observing them, I have learned much that was never known before, about what went into the making of us."

"I could have believed that. I could have believed that your interferences and your ultimate annihilations of history after history were acts of pity as well as science. You claimed they could be restarted if ever you determined what conditions would better them. It did seem strange that you set one line of them—or more?—not in Earth's goodly past but in the hard world of today. It seemed twice strange that you were reluctant to have this particular essay brought to light. But I assumed that you, with your long experience and superior mentality, had reasons. Your attempt at secrecy might have been to avoid lengthy justifications to your kindred. I did not know, nor venture to judge. I would have left that to them.

"But then Kalava arrived."

Another mind-silence falls. At last Gaia says, very softly through the night, "Yes. Again humans live in the material universe."

"How long has it been?" asks Wayfarer with the same quietness.

"I made the first of them about fifty thousand years ago. Robots in human guise raised them from infancy. After that they were free."

"And, no doubt, expanding across the planet in their Stone Age, they killed off those big game animals. Yes, human. But why did you do it?"

"That humankind might live once more." A sigh as of time itself blowing past. "This is what you and those whom you serve will never fully understand. Too few humans went into them; and those who did, they were those who wanted the stars. You," every other node in the galactic brain, "have not felt the love of Earth, the need and longing for the primordial mother, that was in these many and many who remained with me. I do."

How genuine is it? wonders Wayfarer. How sane is she? "Could you not be content with your emulations?" he asks.

"No. How possibly? I cannot make a whole cosmos for them. I can only make them, the flesh-and-blood them, for the cosmos. Let them live in it not as machines or as flickerings within a machine, but as humans."

"On a planet soon dead?"

"They will, they must forge survival for themselves. I do not compel them, I do not dominate them with my nearness or any knowledge of it. That would be to stunt their spirits, turn them into pet animals or worse. I simply give guidance, not often, in the form of divinities in whom they would believe anyway at this stage of their societies, and simply toward the end of bringing them to a stable, high-technology civilization that can save them from the sun."

"Using what you learn from your shadow folk to suggest what the proper course of history may be?"

"Yes. How else should I know? Humankind is a chaotic phenomenon. Its actions and their consequences cannot be computed from first principles. Only by experiment and observation can we learn something about the nature of the race."

"Experiments done with conscious beings, aware of their pain. Oh, I see why you have kept most of your doings secret."

"I am not ashamed," declares Gaia. "I am proud. I gave life back to the race that gave life to us. They will make their own survival, I say. It may be that when they are able, they will move to the outer reaches of the Solar System, or some of them somehow even to the stars. It may be they will shield Earth or damp the sun. It is for them to decide, them to do. Not us, do you hear me? Them."

"The others yonder may feel differently. Alarmed or horrified, they may act to put an end to this."

"Why?" Gaia demands. "What threat is it to them?"

"None, I suppose. But there is a moral issue. What you are after is a purely human renascence, is it not? The former race went up in the machines, not because it was forced but because it chose, because that was the way by which the spirit could live and grow forever. You do not want this to happen afresh. You want to perpetuate war, tyranny, superstition, misery, instincts in mortal combat with each other, the ancient ape, the ancient beast of prey."

"I want to perpetuate the lover, parent, child, adventurer, artist, poet, prophet. Another element in the universe. Have we machines in our self-sureness every answer, every dream, that can ever be?"

Wayfarer hesitates. "It is not for me to say, it is for your peers."

"But now perhaps you see why I have kept my secrets and why I have argued and, yes, fought in my fashion against the plans of the galactic brain. Someday my humans must discover its existence. I can hope that then they will be ready to come to terms with it. But let those mighty presences appear among them within the next several thousand years—let signs and wonders, the changing of the heavens and the world, be everywhere—what freedom will be left for my children, save to cower and give worship? Afterward, what destiny for them, save to be animals in a preserve, forbidden any ventures that might endanger them, until at last, at best, they too drain away into the machines?"

Wayfarer speaks more strongly than before. "Is it better, what they might make for themselves? I cannot say. I do not know. But neither, Gaia, do you. And . . . the fate of Christian and Laurinda causes me to wonder about it."

"You know," she says, "that *they* desired humanness."

"They could have it again."

Imagine a crowned head shaking. "No. I do not suppose any other node would create a world to house their mortality, would either care to or believe it was right."

"Then why not you, who have so many worlds in you?"

Gaia is not vindictive. A mind like hers is above that. But she says, "I cannot take them. After such knowledge as they have tasted of, how could they return to me?" And to make new copies, free of memories that would weigh their days down with despair, would be meaningless.

"Yet—there at the end, I felt what Christian felt."

"And I felt what Laurinda felt. But now they are at peace in us."

"Because they are no more. I, though, am haunted," the least, rebellious bit, for a penalty of total awareness is that nothing can be ignored or forgotten. "And it raises questions which I expect Alpha will want answered, if answered they can be."

After a time that may actually be measurable less by quantum shivers than by the stars, Wayfarer says: "Let us bring those two back."

"Now it is you who are pitiless," Gaia says.

"I think we must."

"So be it, then."

The minds conjoin. The data are summoned and ordered. A configuration is established.

It does not emulate a living world or living bodies. The minds have agreed that that would be too powerful an allurement and torment. The subjects of their inquiry need to think clearly; but because the thought is to concern their inmost selves, they are enabled to feel as fully as they did in life.

Imagine a hollow darkness, and in it two ghosts who glimmer slowly into existence until they stand confronted before they stumble toward a phantom embrace.

"Oh, beloved, beloved, is it you?" Laurinda cries.

"Do you remember?" Christian whispers.

"I never forgot, not quite, not even at the heights of oneness."

"Nor I, quite."

They are silent awhile, although the darkness shakes with the beating of the hearts they once had.

"Again," Laurinda says. "Always."

"Can that be?" wonders Christian.

Through the void of death, they perceive one speaking: "Gaia, if you will give Laurinda over to me, I will take her home with Christian—home into Alpha."

And another asks: "Child, do you desire this? You can be of Earth and of the new humanity."

She will share in those worlds, inner and outer, only as a memory borne by the great being to whom she will have returned; but if she departs, she will not have them at all.

"Once I chose you, Mother," Laurinda answers.

Christian senses the struggle she is waging with herself and tells her, "Do whatever you most wish, my dearest."

She turns back to him. "I will be with you. Forever with you."

And that too will be only as a memory, like him; but what they were will be together, as one, and will live on, unforgotten.

"Farewell, child," says Gaia.

"Welcome," says Wayfarer.

The darkness collapses. The ghosts dissolve into him. He stands on the mountaintop ready to bear them away, a part of everything he has gained for those whose avatar he is.

"When will you go?" Gaia asks him.

"Soon," he tells her: soon, home to his own oneness.

And she will abide, waiting for the judgment from the stars.

Donald Kingsbury is a mathematician and a former professor at McGill University. Now retired, he returns to a career noted for its originality and oblique views of humanity, as in such novels as *Courtship Rite, The Moon Goddess and the Son,* and in his trenchant short stories.

In "Historical Crisis" he takes on the central problems of a science-fiction masterwork, Isaac Asimov's Foundation Trilogy, envisioning it anew for our time. The agenda of control in Asimov's psychohistory, here only lightly disguised, Kingsbury sees as a challenge to free will and to the practical uses of prediction itself. Forecasts can be immensely useful, especially if we can make sure they do not come true.

HISTORICAL CRISIS

Donald Kingsbury

1

THE MILLENNIAL INTERREGNUM *between the First and Second Galactic Empires is often thought of as a Dark Intellectual Age, but, in fact, was a period of renascent, even unexpected, scientific achievement. . . .*

First introduced on the Nacreome Periphery, the walnut-sized atomic power pod . . . In the next three centuries the list of scientific inventions . . .

. . . the Warlords of sybaritic Lakgan, making an abrupt entrance onto the galactic stage in the fourth century, disturbed . . . while re-uniting more than three million stellar systems. It is little realized that the overextended conquests of the False Revival were driven by the achievements of the secluded Crafters of the Thousand Suns of the Helmar Rift who, for centuries, had held a contract to dabble in the science of pleasure-center stimulation. Their totally unforeseen development of a tuned form of the psychic probe, allowing a high-band-width linkage between the human brain and an exterior transducer, caused a major perturbation in the Great Plan of Galactic Revival by moving human behavior, en masse, outside of the original parameters of human psychology.

During the early centuries of its debut, the tuned probe's major utility was unappreciated—it was used mainly as a method to control the emotions of one's opponents, notably by the brilliant Warlord Citizen of Lakgan, Cloun the Stubborn, who unleashed upon the galaxy a cadre of minstrels adept at playing a visi-aural instrument that controlled and set human motivation. Only gradually did the tuned probe come into use as a tool to access a portable quantum-state device that has come to be known to us as the personal familiar. Today such a linkage with a fam seems obvious; a modern man can hardly understand how an unaided mind . . .

The Shadow Pscholars spent the greater part of the next two centuries exploring the limits of the tuned probe and integrating its effects into the mathematics of a Revised Plan.

*—From the Interregnum Exhibit
at the Bureau of Historical Sciences*

With eleven-twelfths of his mind gone, with only the wetware inside his skull, Eron Osa was struggling to focus on something he had forgotten. He sat upright in an aerochair, facing a wall that leaked urine, surrounded by the stark simplicity of a lower-level hotel apartment. What was left of a vital memory was on the tip of his tongue, but maddeningly unavailable.

It galled him that he had been defeated. But about what?

A search through the distant files of Splendid Wisdom's main Imperial Archive was a desperate attempt to jog the tenuous pieces into place. Even that didn't come easily. His hands were trying to work the lambent holograms of a comm console with awkward finger gestures. Mistakes infuriated him. He had to fill in behavioral blanks by reason, by trial and error. He couldn't even remember what he was attempting to do. He did remember the urgency. Was it something important that he had written/discovered?

Eron Osa might have called upon the aid of the "charity" fam that now rode in the high blue collar around his neck—indeed, the tuned probe that connected him to this auxiliary computer through the transducer at the back of his skull was under his neural control and could never make a slave of him—but that didn't matter. It wouldn't connect him to *his* fam; it was in symbiosis with *theirs*—a common-issue fam to aid a convicted criminal (treason) whose personal fam had been found guilty and executed. He could only guess what ersatz data this standard-issue mind held, what habits, what directives, what spy implants. Its motivations would not be Eron's natural motivations. Better to run the archival quest using merely the limited abilities of his wetware.

He cursed himself for not having made, in the past, a more strategic use of his organic memory. That gray mush seemed to contain only the vaguest impression of grand strategic issues—but unlimited details of the trivial. As Eron jumped through the Archives, erratically bringing up holograms of this item and that item, guided by hunches he did not understand, straining to remember, he found that his mind delivered to him not what he wanted, not pertinent associations, but bizarre memories.

—a fugue of sexing with a sloe-eyed woman while playing truant from studying psychohistory. She was a wonderful tease. She had a full mouth that tapered into upturned lines and delicate fingers that seduced him into forgetting mathematics. They lay on linen with a border pattern of golden forsythia. Who was she?

—images of rafting down a river on the planet of his birth, the pyre-trees ablaze on rocky banks. What planet?

—a boy wandering through the famous stone library at Sewina that dated back to pre-Interregnum times, when it had been a military barracks for officers of the Empire. Why had his life taken him there?

Once, when his archival search led him into the rebuilding of Splendid Wisdom after the Sack, he was mentally flipped into what seemed to be his initiation as a Rank Seven Psychohistorian.

—under an enormous transept that rose five stories above the heads of his fellow robed acolytes. A wash of unnatural awe, overwhelming. Immensity. Upreaching arms of stone and fiber and metal, delicate hues of light, ethereal sounds that healed the spirit. The architects put the whole of their souls into their magnificent interiors, because no building on crowded Splendid Wisdom could ever be viewed from its exterior. Had such a drama happened? Was this "memory" a wish or an accomplishment? *Was* he a psychologist?

None of these reveries satisfied him. They were too vague, too unreal. Only when his search brought him near his fugitive goal did he feel ecstasy. The thrill came erratically, then was lost in illusive evasion. Sometimes he came close. Once when he was searching through a listing of Handler Theorems, he hallucinated upon the face of Hanis. Hanis! He recognized Hanis, both furious and sarcastic, taking the lapse of his student Eron Osa as a personal affront, chastising his young protégé for even thinking about publishing without first having his methodology reviewed by his superiors.

Eron's organic brain flashed with insight! Psychohistorians did not publish. Then he *was* a psychohistorian! Slyly he even knew why psychohistorians did not publish. The Fellowship was a secret society. If all men could predict history, then history became unpredictable and the

Fellowship of Pscholars would lose its power to predict and control. To publish one's methods of historical prediction was the ultimate sin. That felt just right—-the ultimate sin. A man could lose his fam for committing such a sin!

For half a day the Archives continued to stimulate impalpable phantoms and vivid events from his life—few of them relevant. He was groping, but he knew that he would be able to recognize "it" when he found "it" and so he continued to troll patiently. Almost when he was asleep a sudden "hit" stirred a deep emotional dazzle. He sat up with such alertness that his aerochair bobbed in the air.

He repeated the archived item.

Again the triggering image flowed in front of him in hologram—a gestalt of red symbols and multicolored action against a diagraph of a stable, self-perpetuating decision state. At first he was puzzled. Then he became cognizant of an unfamiliar mainstream mathematics that leaned heavily upon a notation commonly used by physical scientists. The math wasn't easy to understand without his fam—but: he recognized it as a rudimentary account of stasis. He *knew* that the psychohistorians did it better because *he* had once known more about stasis than any man alive.

Ah so!

This time the concomitant emotional rush came with a clear patter of babble as his organic mind intoned in a ponderous voice: *Early Disturbed Event Location by Forced Arekean Canonical Preposturing: An Analysis in Three Parts.* He grinned uncontrollably. *That,* whatever in Space it meant, was his, Eron Osa's, dissertation!

He pondered this miracle of precipitate memory, astonished. Wetware minds worked by peculiar conundrum! Where had such a revelation come from? He wasn't sure what the babble was about, except that it had to do with . . . psychohistorical stasis brought on by . . . what? He didn't know. All he knew was that this monograph was the object of his search and that he had to have a copy.

Being a vagued-out moron was utter frustration when you had memories of being a genius.

He paused before making a formal request for the monograph over the network. Were his actions being monitored? Doubtful. The Pscholars did not monitor people; they monitored trends. People acting alone were powerless.

One-tenth of a day and a growling stomach later, he knew with a terrible disappointment that his monograph had vanished from the Imperial Archives. For a wrenching moment he wondered if he had ever written such a document. Yet he remained *certain* that he had! Was his certainty only an illusion brought on by the loss of his fam? Perhaps he had never gone past the *intention* to write.

Yet he could guess the real truth. His work had been erased. All copies were gone. Even his unique fam, with every ability necessary to re-create the research, had been destroyed.

Now what?

Eron switched off the ghostlike console with a gesture of his finger and left his chair bobbing in midair. He paced about the strange apartment, too cramped for his aristo taste, wondering where he was. (His suspect fam would know, but he had no desire to link into that substandard unit.) Everything folded into the wall, everything was white, not a trace of luxury or space. The disposoria was leaking urine. This *wasn't* home! He buried his head in his arms.

Ping! The tiny, gleaming sphere of a Personal Capsule appeared in the alcove wall niche, unnoticed.

Damn, I'm slow! he thought. *Of course* this wasn't his apartment; he was no longer an acolyte of the Psychohistorian Fellowship; he was on his own, disowned, possessions confiscated, tossed into the lower warrens of Splendid Wisdom, where he was condemned to think with treacherously slow neurons! It was infuriating . . . and for a moment he had a rush of uncontrolled rage that stunned him into an unbalanced mental fall because it was not resisted by the restraining calmness of fam input. He had shoved emotionally against a removed wall . . . flinging himself into emptiness.

The rage turned to instant consuming fear—without *his* fam he was a very asymmetrical animal. His zenoli training was useless; his brain-fam centering lost. He could no longer trust his own responses. This was worse than he had anticipated when he had been whole and accepting of the dangers inherent in his rash deeds. Being an asymmetrical animal didn't fit with his plans! Plans! Again his mind lurched out of control with a flash of joy at the thought of his brilliant agenda.

But, when he tried to remember the nature of such an agenda, he found only vacuum. He glanced about him in desperation. That was when he saw the Personal Capsule. It stopped him, reminding him of danger. He grumbled bitterly to himself—*My orders from the police.* Yet, his eyes disclaimed such a conclusion; the omnipotent police, backed up by the certainties of psychology, had no need for super security. A Personal Capsule? Here?

Curiously he picked the small sphere from its niche. It opened in his hand and would have opened for not another of the trillion other inhabitants of Splendid Wisdom. A thin transparent tape unrolled stiffly and began to disintegrate almost immediately. It read:

"See Master Rigone at the Teaser's Bistro, Calimone Sector, AD–87345, Level 78. (The Corridor of Olibanum.) I've already told Rigone what you'll need. I've got myself in a real fix and don't know how much more I can help. Your benefactor."

By then the tape and sphere were well on their way to dust.

Eron Osa didn't even have to memorize the message. He knew the Teaser's Bistro—a tolerated black market. It was where young Fellowship rakes hung out to have illegal attachments added to their fams.

2

In the Salki version of the Chronicles of Early Splendid Wisdom . . . in the eighth millennium before the final maturation of the First Galactic Empire . . . it is told that the villas surrounding the harbors of the Calmer Sea were sacred shrines of meditation, girded by the hectic ardor of an interstellar trading mecca, destroyed only when the nomadic armadas of the Frightfulpeople deliberately established themselves across the central galactic trade routes and forcibly set their main base of operations on Splendid Wisdom. Revolt cost six billion Splendid lives and an annoying million Frightful Soldiers. [Probably an exaggeration—the original records were destroyed during the Frightfulterror and the earliest remaining secondary accounts date to three hundred years later. All surviving records contradict one another. Ed.]

The One-Eyed Frightfulperson, today known as Tanis the First, was displeased by the unrest. For compensation he cynically confiscated the Oceans and Seas of Splendid Wisdom and diligently began to ration water to a water-short populace so that they might behave. Tanis, a strategic genius, had noted that evaporation and circulation patterns on Splendid Wisdom were no longer providing enough rain—the weather had already been set awry by an excessive building zeal driven by hugely profitable interstellar ventures. Cities had replaced forest, desert, and prairie. The natural water table was disastrously low and the aquifers dry. Hence the Splendid crowds could be held ransom by their thirst. The Frightfulpeople built the desalination plants and the pumping stations and astutely encouraged massive immigration to Splendid Wisdom so that the dependency should become absolute.

. . . The Frightfulbaron of the Calmer Sea . . . an example of the ruthlessness with which this policy was carried out by the Frightful-

people . . . commanded eighty wives, countless concubines, and sired
thousands of children. It was his Frightfulgrandchildren who drove
the original piles and tunnels along the shore of the Calmer Sea, re-
claiming land from the sea for a building boom financed by the sale of
water. . . .
By the time of the Pax Imperialis . . .

—From the Explanatorium
at the Calmer Pumping Station

The light of the sun Imperialis twisted into the upper levels of the syn-
thetic skin of the planet Splendid Wisdom through arteries of guide-
pipes. Gloomy though Hyperlord Kikaju Jama's interior residence
appeared during daytime, its dim luminance was enhanced by an artificial companion light that followed the Hyperlord around, that he might
be seen, and, upon demand, became a searchlight impaling the target of
his gaze, that he might see.

Jama enjoyed adulation and had arranged that it be he who would
shine as the most burnished object within his restricted domain. In meditation, with eyes closed, Jama was surrounded by a nimbus—all else
remained spectral, dark, hidden. When his eyes were open, a sly robo-
intelligence followed his glance, subtly illuminating only the stoic luxury
of a deep abode, careful never to steal the spotlight from the master.

This auroral eyelight might linger on the Hyperlord's miniature garden, fly across angular and pearly walls, touch a desk, shoot down a hall.
For a moment its soft beam settled on a hand-sized jade ovoid sitting in
its golden cup with legs that reached to the floor. It amused him to leave
it in the open when it should be hidden. Could such astonishing computing power really be locked in a stone so small? No one would think it his
most valuable recent purchase. It looked like just another bauble that
could be made at whim in his manufacturum. But it couldn't be duplicated.

He sighed. Perhaps he had wasted his money again. Peddling fabulous objects supposedly immune to replication in a manufacturum was
the oldest con game in the galaxy.

When Jama chose to glance at his manufacturum, as he did now, it
was never orderly, filled as it was with bits of rejuvenated artwork that he
no longer desired to look at but was reluctant to feed to the recycler.
About hygiene he was fastidious and so his disposoria, when illuminated,
was always clean even if he had to touch it up himself between the
rounds of his robo-cleaners. He was eccentric in that his small bedroom
contained furniture that did not disappear, and his kitchen was laden

with visible food. He liked gloom. The eyelight only brightened when, in his tiny dressing room, he selected the moment's clothes, or his makeup, or his wig.

Since the Hyperlord was, today, anticipating no interruption of his treasonous meditations, he had dressed for comfort rather than spectacle. Suddenly . . .

A telesphere formed in the air to the left of Jama's head with an unusual urgency, blooming from invisible to opalescent—there to warn its master. Only after formally identifying the intruder did the sphere become less urgent, speaking in the manner of a peevish butler. "Apparently uninvited, we have with us The Excellent Frightfulperson, Otaria of the Calmer Sea."

"Let me see her."

A fairy-sized image appeared within his guardian globe—Lord Jama's sometime pupil and occasional erotic companion, Otaria. "She is impatient, excited," intoned the telephone. "She is violating protocol. Advice is to be alert."

Hyperlord Jama nodded absently to his wraithlike servant in dismissal. Acknowledged, it disappeared abruptly. The lord did not bother to activate his weapons, though he no longer held this impetuous woman in full confidence. Activating weapons automatically registered them with the police. But he was annoyed and set her entrance through the trap-tube at a slow fall.

Otaria of the Calmer Sea, indeed, he thought. How quaint the old titles sounded when one stopped a moment to think upon what must have been their original meaning. *All else passes, and we, those whom history has passed by, cling to the sounds of our titles though we no longer hear them.* Hyperlord itself was a title handed down by a long-ago deposed aristocracy. There were layers and layers of titles in the fabric of the Imperialis tradition, each reflecting some transient moment of power. Perhaps once there had been real ocean over that vast area of Splendid Wisdom called the Calmer Sea—perhaps in ancient days when Otaria's unwashed ancestors had been brutal conquerors from hyperspace and Jama's ancestors had not yet been invented.

Now every seabed of Splendid Wisdom was as dry as its moon, Aridia—enclosed, built over, sucked barren by time's multiplying bureaucrats. Whatever currents of the Noachian oceans had once flowed within the Calmer Sea, such waters had long ago been siphoned off into the life-support piping of the planet, some of it breaking out during the Interregnum in a flood that drowned billions only to be recaptured by Dark Age engineers, hence forever to wander mournfully through a planetary maze of arterial fresh water and veined sewers, alternately becoming champagne and piss, blind to class, bathing the rich and poor alike, mixing with the blood of long-gone rebellions and the blood of commercial traffic from thirty million suns that bowed to Splendid Wisdom as the center of galactic power. One of the Frightful Otaria's distant kith must have ordered the final taming of the Calmer Sea.

Jama was not sure when the Frightfulpeople had themselves been pushed aside. There were too many conflicting histories. There were too many wars and too many intrigues and too many stars and too vast a span of time for one human with a single fam to comprehend. He did know that his own title had arisen during the reign of the Som Dynasty, the first to map the campaigns of the awesome navies that led the sons and ships of Imperialis to galactic ascendancy over the peoples of thirty million stars, amalgamating myriad dominions by cunning, technical expertise, fear, diplomacy, and a legendary bureaucratic talent.

The Hyperlords had been some kind of political procurators who controlled the military men of the navy for Imperialis. In those days the Hyperlords had traveled. How they had traveled! But Jama could no more imagine the open power that they had wielded than they could have imagined the labyrinthine shadow schemings of his latter-day mind against a coterie of psychologists who ruled this Second Empire, not with protocol, but with feather-light leverings of their little fingers on mathematically determined critical events.

He gave his ancestors only casual thought. Their distant power was too remote for him to envy. No, Hyperlord Kikaju Jama was nostalgic for a much later time in history, when complacency had taken the whole of the galactic civilization into the darkness of the (now only dimly remembered) Black Interregnum. That had been a fabulous millennium, when a galaxy dominated by Imperialis had fallen into chaos, war, collapse, massive die-offs, extinction, defeasance—and a strange kind of thrilling inventiveness.

Jama smiled. Throughout the whole kaleidoscope, covering multiple millennia of political rise and fall, some things never perished—the titles and the conceits survived, even some whose bizarre history had been lost in the entropy of the Fall. He grinned. Here was Otaria, who still proudly called herself a Frightfulperson of the Calmer Sea to honor the dregs of some barbarian past that would offend her if she was forced to live it.

The chute to his atrium shimmered, winked expansively, and Otaria dropped through, into the skyless garden of his metal grotto, stooping slightly while she did so because she wore her fam in a silly brimmed hat of feathers instead of gracefully on her shoulders. Why this silly fad to *hide* the damned fams? The eyelight followed his gaze and she was illuminated, a tall woman with luxurious black hair coiffured in the ringlet style, elegantly dressed.

"Well?" he asked, almost annoyed. Jama had not been expecting his old pupil and she had given him no time to prepare, even to change out of the comfortably threadbare lounging robe he had thrown on this morning. This appearance without an appointment was an outrageous invasion of privacy, but she did have the correct entry codes—he had given them to her willingly, fondly, and not very long ago. Regretting his sexual peccadilloes with a woman did not stop a misused old codger from liking her.

Otaria smiled with broad lips. "I have a *man* for you, a unique man."

He did not speak. *Ah, youth,* he thought, an edge of irritation still in his emotions, vexed that this youngster should have caught him looking so old when a modest preannouncement would have allowed him time for wig and makeup and decent silks. He stared at her.

A man, eh? *As if one man could solve my problems.* By the happy expression on her face, he was probably a man "found" to solve *her* problems. Did young women think of nothing else? So hard to teach them the cunning discipline necessary for major subversion. And she was vain, too. By hiding her fam did she suppose that people would presume she could think without one! It was appalling the talent he was forced to work with.

But yes, he did need unique men—so she had his attention.

A conspiracy required thousands of men, competent men, incorruptible, dedicated men, moving behind screens, shielded from each other by deception and code, invisible to the masses, because they had to remain invisible to the Pscholars' machines, which monitored all trends. Never be part of a trend. Safety lay only in being a unique individual who fitted no mathematical pattern.

Otaria was staring at him, not very respectfully, waiting for a reply.

Could the noble blood of revolutionaries like Otaria bring back the bad old days? Interregnums, filled with violence, were more interesting than utopian stasis. The last Dark Age, for all its years of chaos, had been the most creative period in human history since the days of wily *Homo erectus.*

Hyperlord Kikaju Jama knew he should not be building a conspiracy to destroy civilization here, in the heart of this awesome solar system of imperial power, three trillion people swarming around the star Imperialis, almost a trillion of those on Splendid Wisdom itself. He should be building his pathetic little cabal out in some obscure corner of the galactic reaches—some miner's iceworld in the Empty Sweep, perhaps. But his wealth was here at the teeming center, so here must be the core of his dissent. Yes, under the eyes of the observers. The game was hopeless—but still an interesting one, which was why it amused him to play.

Jama was sure that he had found the weakness of the Second Empire. The Pscholars knew only statistical mechanics and chaos, megamath and conformal caletrics, miniform numerical modeling, etc., etc.—they cared nothing for individuals. Their police did not even monitor individuals. Individuals were no more to them than the atoms of a vast gas-engine being regulated for maximum efficiency, the engine of galactic civilization. The galaxy would be unmanageable if the bureaucrats had to administer its thirty million worlds at the level of the individual. And so—the invisible individuals were Kikaju Jama's weapon.

He did not chose to stare back at his Frightfulperson; he was staring through her, wondering if she was invisible enough.

Otaria contemplated her old teacher with increasing impatience. Since this crazy coot Kikaju had not replied to her statement, and was staring off into the space behind her head, she decided, rudely, to repeat herself. "I said I found a man. The man I've found," she said with steely emphasis, "he's a psychohistorian."

The Hyperlord's brain went from irritation to alarm. He tripped a warning analysis search in the fam buried in the humped shoulders of his lounging robe. The Pscholars' psychohistorians were *worse* than their teeming police.

His fam calmly supplied him with silent thoughts, requests for information, questions, suggestions that might be used for a proper interrogation of the girl.

"We do not deal with psychohistorians," he said sternly.

"Come now, they may be a pompous, overbearing elite who have limited aspirations, but you must admit that they've run our galactic affairs with an ironhanded honesty."

"So they want us to believe," Jama smiled wickedly. "When they *lie* to us they have the tools to do so very cleverly, and then the tools to make the lie disappear."

"Kikaju . . ."

"I see that you doubt me. You think of me as a crotchety old man who makes unfounded allegations to puff up the importance of my cause. Let me share a detail—one of the items that have come to my attention over my inquisitive life. I'll download it into your fam from mind and you'll be able to judge my precision."

Jama made a gesture while he muttered commands and Otaria went into receiver mode. He waited while her fam digested the burst. Long ago, in the fourth century of the Founder's Era, fifty young psychohistorians were sacrificed to heal a major deviation in the Founder's Plan. The catastrophe began with Cloun the Stubborn of Lakgan, the first Warlord of the Interregnum to get his hands on the tuned psychic probe. He was smart enough to be able to use it to bend minds to his will in a way that changed the psychological laws of human interaction over a galactic span.

The hidden psychohistorians who had been monitoring the Plan from the wreckage of Splendid Wisdom, in the fortress they had created out of the old Imperial University, were forced by these unhappy circumstances to act in the open to restabilize the Plan. But the Plan required that its monitors remain invisible. In order to redisappear, so that they might continue to control without having to be accountable for their actions, the Pscholars constructed an elaborate ruse of self-destruction. A lie. Pretending to be the whole of the monitoring group, fifty young psychohistorians went to the prison camps and death as martyrs.

Otaria frowned haughtily. "I've never heard of such a reprehensible incident. It has the feel of historical revision to me. Such besmirching of the reputation of our galactic leadership will serve our cause badly; our benevolent elite embody enough flaws without our having to stoop to invent disgusting sins. Truth is our only reliable servant."

Jama grinned. "I, too, thought as you do now when I first caught whiff of the story twenty years ago. Yet . . . there are pieces to that story that assemble neatly. I've even located the graves of those sacrificial heroes on a Peripheral hellhole called Zoranel—well erased to all but the most exacting archaeological methods, as has been the site of their prison camp in a rocky valley under a red sun. Evidence keeps arriving. Only last week . . . Check out the mathematical appendix trailing my little burst."

"I'm not a mathematical illiterate—but your equations are not readable by me, even with all the options of my fam."

"Nevertheless they are the psychohistorical equations which outline how a perturbation in the Plan can be eliminated by a *lie* involving the death of fifty young students. Those equations have been lifted from the Prime Radiant as it existed in the fourth century."

"Nonsense! The Pscholars guard the Prime Radiant with unbreakable code! You of all people don't have access to it!"

Jama was enjoying himself. "The poor excuse for psychohistorical talent that I have to work with could never write such equations or work out their consequences—but my idiots can read scrawls quite effectively, I assure you. I have no doubt that this fragment of the Prime Radiant is authentic. I've wondered about the source. My strong suspicion is that my modest fragment has drifted into my hands over a circuitous trail that is tens of centuries cold—via one of our fifty heroes who died that a *lie* might persist. There is no lie so small that it does not leave a trace behind." He glanced for only a flicker of eyelash at the small jade ovoid sitting in its legged golden cup.

Otaria paused for a moment of reverie while her organic-fam mind stopped rejecting the data and readjusted itself around the thought that an enemy who *lied* was a very different kind of opponent than was an honest foe. She recomputed her entire position.

"I still think you should meet my psychohistorian."

"You have already contacted this man?" Disapproval.

"No." She was amused that Kikaju would suppose her so bold.

"Then *he* contacted you?" Greater disapproval.

"No!" Now Otaria felt called upon to defend herself and reacted to Jama's suspicion with formal disdain. "Hyperlord Jama, I *found* him— he doesn't even know I exist—I'm not *stupid.* Why should I take unilateral action? I know the stakes! Who trained me? Who seduced me into his wicked world when I was too young to know the difference? A baby I was! And before you say it, I *do* know that the psychohistorians are the most dangerous people in the Empire! Of course I know that!"

"Ah." He smiled, relaxing because of her fury. "What rank is this mathematician of yours?"

"Seventh."

As the newest conquerors of the galaxy, the Pscholars disdained titles among themselves. They were egalitarians. They were a psychological elite who ruled by merit. Titles, they insisted, were the refuse of First Empire, of women like Otaria and men like Jama—but the Pscholars' plain designations of rank had become, in time, titles of force to be feared. First Speaker sounded simple enough—yet any sane man tried never to come to the notice of such a man. But a Rank Seven? There must be tens of billions of Rank Seven Psychohistorians scattered from here to the Periphery.

"Phwogh! He knows nothing, then. He's still nourished by the blood from his umbilical cord. He's useless."

"He's unusual. Singular."

"Handsome? Beddable?"

"So now you suppose me to be infatuated by commoners, do you?" she replied to his innuendo, sarcastically indignant. She cocked her red hat, and peeked around the brim, suggesting a comedy of immature lust. An uplifted hand-sign, a command to the house sensors, materialized one of the Hyperlord's floating recliners; she curled into its black arms while they molded to her shape. Languidly she hugged the arms, ignoring Jama. His eyes called all illumination to her body; her eyes fixed themselves upon the shadows of his miniature garden.

She's sulking! Now what do I do? Damn, I shouldn't have alluded to sex so soon after last week's fight. She's going to tease me! He tensed.

Indeed she was, and she began by changing the subject. "I love your topiary." With a delighted cry she kicked off from the floor and floated over the ferns, beyond them, into the arms of a gnarled tree, whose uppermost limbs reached for the conduits that were now feeding the rosy dawn light of Imperialis down into the dungeon below. "You work so hard here! You always have the slight smell of manure about you." She was grinning. "You do use *real* manure, don't you? Your garden is so green, so lush, so beautiful! That's one thing we never seem to run out of here on Splendid Wisdom—the manure, I mean. There are so many of our assholes!"

Spare me the twaddling of the aristocracy, he thought, wishing desperately for his wig and eyeshadow—and a bath and a sanitized robe and a young body.

Well, if he couldn't flirt, he could attack. Attack was more fun than sex, anyway. A command, through the tuned probe that connected his brain with his fam, called up the house telesphere. Once it had bloomed, he willed the floating apparition toward her, enlarged its diameter, and filled its ghostly pallor with images drawn from his auxiliary brain.

The visions he loaded into the globe had been secretly recorded at a party of roistering midlevel bureaucrats. A swift flow of graphics commands—by fam direction—rebuilt the scene to center on Otaria, altering the record subtly to suit Jama's kinky taste: a brighter color here, an added satyr there, a knowing grin from an observer lounging in the folds. His miniature Otaria lay on the floor of the globe, in dishabille, the only noblewoman at this uncouth gathering, hugging some commoner's leg.

"You Wog, Kikaju! You haven't the morals of a leering Makorite! Why do I work for you! You spy on me!"

"So do the psychohistorians."

"They're not interested in me—nor in you. They're interested in summed vectors," she said defiantly.

"Their interest is called 'sampling,'" replied Jama, dryly, "and you are not immune from it. They take *quadrillions* of samples every day. When they detect a trend that threatens the stability of the Empire, do you think they don't take action on it?"

The Excellent Frightfulperson was watching, with distaste, her own behavior in the hovering sphere. "I'm allowed to have fun! Now, turn it off!" She wasn't angry yet, but she was ready to be angry.

"Is that where you 'found' your psychohistorian?"

"Well now, I do believe the old He Goat has itching horns! You amaze me—jealous you are—after throwing me forcibly out of your bed!"

And he remembered—it seemed long ago—their amorous jousting. He didn't remember throwing her out of bed. How could he have loved such an irritating woman? "Pleasure and intrigue don't mix well. I question you to protect the Regulations," he insisted. The word "Regulations" was safe code for another word nobody had the courage to say aloud. Revolution.

She sighed. "All right, Hyperlord Sober Buttocks my darling, we'll be serious. I found my psychohistorian—his name is Eron Osa—via a routine library scan while engaged in dry-ass-dust research for the good of your beloved *Regulations*. I've been studying stasis. Rates of change of behavior."

"Stasis," he said morosely. "The Sleeping Beauty stays alive by never changing." He meant the Empire. It was a constant complaint of his.

"Over what time period!" she shot back.

"Certainly over my lifetime—and I'm not young. By sleeping, the Empire refuses to die!"

"Old men have such a myopic viewpoint. Weak legs which take their eyes nowhere! But *youth* isn't so decrepit that it can't travel more freely! *I'm* talking a hundred thousand generations! I've been imbibing records, some of them probably eighteen thousand years old. You can't imagine the changes in every variable you can conceive of over that time span! *You* only think of *today's* trade and exchange—that's all you care to think of! You don't understand the past."

"Nothing from eighteen thousand years ago is reliable. Splendid Wisdom hadn't even been settled eighteen thousand years ago. Even ten-thousand-year-old information is unreliable!"

"I beg your pardon, old man! When I was a child I visited the museum at Chanaria, deep in the stable rock of the Timeless Shield. I saw a bronze plate under helium that was more than *forty* thousand years old, cast on Terra with the names of heroes raised in this weird angular alphabet and illustrated in relief with armored vehicles and bi-winged skycraft. Before hyperspace travel! It wasn't a reproduction! I was awed! I saw records scratched onto clay tablets—*real* clay from old Terra—by men hardly literate who even had to depend upon *their own brains* to advise them. We *know* these things! I saw the fossilized bones of animals who lived and died before man, two million generations old, priceless fossils from Terra, not reproductions. I was awed."

"Terra is a desert planet. It counts for nothing." His gesture swept over his own green garden, implying that this small grotto-world of rock with tree and ferns and blooming flowers was worth more than all of Terra. "That old place is good for camels. On Terra even the camels manufacture fraudulent antiques for the Empire's tourists, bronze tablets and baked clay."

"Oh, bother your skepticism!" She pursed her lips and threw up her arms so violently that her chair rocked in the air above the ferns. "That's not the point! Think of the changes since then! Do you deny the changes? Doesn't that give you hope that change is possible? *You* taught me hope!" She was indignant. *Now* she was angry!

He laughed because indeed he did work for upheaval, yet in his heart did not believe that the galactic disorder he craved was possible. "Your bloody ancestors—pirates, brigands!" he sneered, "conquered Splendid Wisdom in a local interstellar war that brought our noble trading founders to ruin—but within three generations had become such traders, being raised by trader slaves, that they no longer thought of themselves as pirates but as traders. Change? They rewrote history by substituting their names for the names of their predecessors. And went on to conquer half the galaxy—not as military predators but in the style of the wiliest of the traders they conquered—just as the traders would have done without your bloody ancestors on the starship bridges. Change? When *your* ancestors were deposed the Empire continued its mighty growth under new administration. The vices were the same, the strengths were the same, the bureaucracy was the same. Only the people were different. Social inertia has always been formidable—even before the psychohistorians."

Otaria dismissed this version of ancient history. "That's your way of seeing events, my melancholy romantic whose late ancestors were forged in a more recent, vaster era when no mere soldier or trader could have survived. There were more specialists in one army group of the Spaceship and Sun than all the soldiers in the greatest army ever raised before the Pax Imperialis. Nothing changes in a lifetime, but every thousand years of human history has brought a major upheaval. A thousand years ago there were no fams as we know them today and men had to live by their wet wits. You're so strange, Kikaju—you taught me to believe in a dream you don't believe in yourself."

"But you've found me a psychohistorian who will light my fire again, so it is all right," he added sarcastically.

She grinned. "I've been plotting the galactic patterns of scholarship. It is always the same curve. Flat, then a sharp increase, then flat again when knowledge matures. During the explosion, scholars always think that the explosion will go on forever. They do not value what is known.

Their pleasure is to seek new discoveries. During the mature phase, scholars always think that everything is known and see scholarship as the art of applying the known. Psychohistory has been a mature science for less than a thousand years. They've had no rival in the galaxy for two millennia—and it is *time,* Kikaju, it is *time* that a rival appears."

"So what is so unique about your Eron Osa?"

"During the last session of the Fellowship he published a thesis in mathematics at his own expense, not a unique event, but an unusual one." She flashed a copy in midair, squeezing its long title, for lack of space, into a condensed holographic Imperial Font. *Early Disturbed Event Location by Forced Arekean Canonical Preposturing: An Analysis in Three Parts.* "I copied it the same day it appeared because I was re-searching stasis. A day later it had been erased."

"He published through the Lyceum?" asked Hyperlord Jama in-credulously. Pscholar psychohistorians did not publish research; they had *never* published their research even in that long-ago epoch when they still did research. They had always claimed, with self-serving pedanticism, that a prediction of the future was invalidated if the predic-tive methods by which it was obtained became widely known.

"No, he did not publish through the Lyceum. He was pretending it was mathematics, not psychohistory. He published in the public realm in the Imperial Archives."

"With no sponsor! Then this Osa is a crackpot! What else could he be? He's decapitating himself!"

"Perhaps," she went on earnestly, "but that is, again, not the point."

"Your point is moot," he interrupted. "My point is that your Eron Osa, being a psychohistorian, being a member of the Fellowship, is a dangerous man who should be avoided at all costs."

She continued doggedly. "You're building up your own handpicked group of independent psychologists. Your men don't have access to the main body of knowledge."

"Of course they don't!" He raged because it was a sore spot. How could his people know what was so fanatically hidden away by the Psy-chohistorian Fellowship? The Fellowship feared nothing more than that the lower classes might learn how to predict the future and so destroy the Splendid Galactic Empire of the Pscholars, rendering the Great Plan impotent by creating an unmanageable chaos of alternate futures.

Otaria continued to make her points on her long fingers, one by one. "Your men are having to reinvent psychohistory all by themselves. You've told me it's not going well. You've told me it has been going *badly!* Your group isn't research-oriented. But Kikaju, *obviously,* that doesn't apply to this Eron Osa! He knows how to do research and he's certain to be in trouble with his masters for daring to publish! He's our kind of man. Something in him is attacking! We can use him!"

"But he's a *real* psychohistorian!" exclaimed Jama in horror. "I don't want to have anything to do with a *real* one! They're programmed to destroy"—he was so upset that he actually uttered the taboo word— "revolutions!" The horror in his voice mounted. "It's built into their fams to protect us all! They are death on Dark Ages. They aren't, ever, allowed to harm people—anybody—even if that means their own self-destruction, so they've found the equations that give us the living, pain-less death. And they must at all costs use their powers to protect civilization from collapsing! And so civilization has been frozen at the height of decay! Cryogenocide! They aren't even allowed to be passive when we try to put ourselves in a dangerous place! You want to deal with such monsters? You're mad!"

"Kikaju, I am proceeding in this case with utmost caution. And I do not want *you* protecting me from any dangers."

"I forbid you to have anything to do with this man! I forbid it! I won't *allow* you to destroy my world!" he raged.

"You are throwing me out of your bed again," she smiled.

"I've never thrown you out of my bed. I try to make you listen to reason!"

"Let me follow this man," she pleaded. "I will not recruit him with-out your approval, I swear by the ferocity of my ancestors."

3

12.02.13 On a planet with a trillion residents, storage space and transportation space is at a premium.

12.02.14 The only commodity that can be stored and transported cheaply is information.

12.02.15 It is easier to manufacture devices from stored informa-tion, on site, as they are needed, and to destroy them after use, than to store them away in physical bulk, waiting for a second user. Excep-tions may be made in the case of (1) devices utilizing exotic materials, (2) devices using exotic manufacturing methods.

12.02.16 Water, air, and sewage must be purified and reused, on site, to avoid transportation through pipes, conduits, and through the atmosphere.

12.02.17 The transportation bulk-flow of any sector design should never exceed a Haldmakie number of 43.

—*Splendid Planner's Guide:*
AdminLevel-NR8 Issue-GA13758 SOP-12

Eron Osa, in spite of his missing memories, remembered the face of Rigone—and remembered his intensely mixed feelings of awe and respect and exasperation. He could not remember if they had been friends. He knew he had spent time at Rigone's Teaser's Bistro.

For two days, unable to leave his hotel, Eron had been trying to find the courage to wander up the Olibanum to see Rigone—as his strange "benefactor" had suggested in his stranger message. But the manner in which he might choose to ask Rigone for help was irrelevant if he was first going to find himself hopelessly disoriented in the corridors of the Calimone Sector. Such fears of losing his way astonished him.

The memories he had of himself told of the old Eron as a confident, arrogant young man, a mathematician, a zenoli combat adept—but confidence has its foundation in abilities, and those had been shattered. He wasn't sure anymore that he even had the wits for such a simple task as plying the corridors of Splendid Wisdom alone. His mind kept calling upon himself for lore and skills that he didn't seem to know were no longer there—until his absent fam did not respond.

Nevertheless, reason suggested that even if Splendid Wisdom was an incomprehensible hive to a famless man, there should be a solution to his lack of mobility. Splendid Wisdom had existed as a labyrinth long before the fam had become a universal symbiote.

It was essential that he not remain a prisoner of his hotel.

In his fury he gave himself an ultimatum. Plan! Plan even the most elementary of chores! Predict and plan! Then he laughed that his fury had induced in him the most bland of psychohistoric approaches to the mundane. His cheer encouraged him out of his moping. Suppose he reviewed *everything* in the safety of his rooms, testing his organic brain for deficiencies? He might, that way, gain the courage to leave the hotel. The organic brain had been evolved to think and learn, and there was no reason he couldn't still perform such essentials. Think! he commanded himself. Once he stepped outside of his hotel into the corridors, what would he have to do that his fam had always done for him?

Eron began to flash on his famless early childhood, the only model he had for what was in store for him. Wryly he recalled the time he ran away from home when he was three, passionately wanting to *see* the waterfall dropping through thirty stories of magical shapes within the Imperialis Transport Ministry. Mama Osamin would not respond to his polite request or explain her refusal (the Transport Ministry was a third of the planet's circumference away.) Neither was she willing to appease his temper tantrum. Resentful, he tricked the door lock with a candy wrapper, sneaked out, wandered up two levels, and cunningly hopped a pod, making magisterial demands of the control console. The pod had detected his youth and delivered him to the police. He smiled. This time, as an adult, perhaps he could outwit the pods.

If he was remembering correctly (and that was doubtful), his wretched hotel was within free-transport range of the teeming Calimone Sector. A dozen-minute ride to the northwest? Calimone embraced the appurtenances of the Upper Lyceum of the Fellowship, whose levels he had once known very well with its ministries, academeries, scholariums, libraries, vast apartment conglomerates, clubs.

Low-life hangouts such as Rigone's Teaser's Bistro lay on the distant borders of the Lyceum. It was a pleasure to him that he could still recall the energetic bustle of the Olibanum through which he had cruised extensively during his student days. Trust the organic brain to remember the lower pleasures with an uncritical glow.

Think! Lacking a fam, he was electromagnetically blind, except in the visible spectrum, and so he would need some kind of groping skill to get around. Retinal overlays were out. That stumped him, since the warrens of Splendid Wisdom averaged out at seven hundred meters deep over the entire area of the planet—the crumb that was Calimone Sector had more mappable features than the whole of most planets. If the structure didn't broadcast their features and he had no fam to make sense of it all, a man could wander forever without reaching his destination. Eron was sore tempted to use his common-issue fam with all its dangers of psychic control. No. He sighed; more research was in order.

At his comm console he meandered through the Archives and discovered the ancient art of paper-mapmaking in an orgy of revelation. It was so obvious! Why hadn't he thought of it himself? But maps needing to be viewed with eyes was a horrible thought. Such a map was passive. To read a paper map would require work! Not impossible, of course, but discouraging. There must be a better way!

How had men found their way around Splendid Wisdom during the age of the First Empire, when the planet had been as teeming as it was now and there had been no fams? Eron Osa became inspired and sauntered into his apartment's tiny manufacturum.

Of course the damn hotel's shopping library didn't have a map-reader template on file. He felt his rage rising again, and with it that awful feeling, again, that he didn't have his fam to poise him emotionally. He paused to compensate. He breathed deeply to compose himself.

. . . and smelled the thickness of smothered layers of air half a kilometer beneath the free weather . . . felt the confining walls. He could almost hear the dripping of the pipes from above. Perhaps it was merely the hotel's SeeOTwo decomposer on the blink again that gave him a heavy hand and the sense that the air itself was turgid from decay. *Stop breathing,* he told himself. *Concentrate on locating maps!*

Eron netted around among the local antique warehouses until he found a template he could buy for cheap, grumbled at the tech implied by the First Empire date, imported it, spent hours finding the link that could translate its obsolete code, and waited some more while the nanomachines of the manufacturum assembled the device. It took time because he had asked for a high structural resolution, time enough to relax for a drink and a thought. He did not want to bother with a quick, low-resolution device—having his map machine break down in an unknown warren was not an adventure he wanted to live. Leisurely thoughts gave him opportunity for irony. What if the map files turned out to be as ancient as the reader itself!

From the manufacturum (after two drinks) came (1) a delicate spiderlike crown that adjusted to his skull under his hair, (2) an almost invisible laser gun that wrote to his right retina, (3) a subvocal control pad—and (4) no instructions. The maps of Splendid Wisdom, freshly read and tortuously compiled to meet the constraints of this antique, arrived on, astonishingly, a thousand flimsies which, outrageously, had to be carried in a pocket pouch, each to be inserted manually. No wonder the First Empire had collapsed!

Still he was afraid to venture into the metropolitan maze. He couldn't talk his map reader into working smoothly. It had no brains and had to be instructed like some stubborn dolt and he didn't know its language! With extreme patience he did manage to explore the immediate vicinity of his hotel, two corridors west and four levels deep. The device actually worked after a fashion—and, he supposed, would work better once he had fathomed its pretensions.

Then for five days he spent the afternoons in a neighboring café that extended out into its corridor, minding his own business, talking with no one. His criminal's pension was limited—it was like being a student again—so he was frugal with his drink and pastries while he did his people watching. To amuse himself he reinvented mental addition, multiplication, and division, skills that he had never learned because they were automatic functions of his fam. It was good discipline for his frazzled mind, and a soothing reminder that there was always a workaround, however clumsy, for the fam dependencies that he no longer controlled. Eight plus fourteen was twenty-two. He marveled that he was able to figure that out from scratch. Such work made him feel like a genius again.

Eron had chosen a busy traverse for his doodling and idle contemplations. The space within view of the café was filled with pedestrians flowing from the level above and boiling out of the nearby pod stop. Whenever he decided to stop thinking, to rest his aching organic brain, he had before him a cornucopia of sights—today a boy with a bag of bread dragged by his mother, an old man followed by a cackling family of females in weird headdresses. One of the interesting effects of being famless was the extraordinarily heightened visual intensity. Even the simplest colors were magnificent.

Take that tall woman who was waiting at the gracelessly vermilion pod stop for a friend, blue eyes flaked with a russet-gold, who glanced about her impatiently, swinging her black ringlets into a bobbing sway. Her broad-brimmed hat was of a textured fuchsia he had never seen before, topped by feathers. In this corner of the cosmos style was everything. No such hat could be useful this far underground from a blazing sun. Still her skin looked coddled. She would be one of these aristos who spent regular time in a body shop staving off death and decay. She was still young enough to think of herself as immortal. Was her fragrance as gay as she looked?

The restless eyes caught him staring at her and she smiled with broad lips. He glanced away, sipped his punch, pushed a crumb across the table. And presently saw her feet standing in his gaze, motionless. He did not look up, afraid to sound like a moron. The shoes were of a scaled fish-leather, multihued, probably scalbeast from Tau-Nablus and why should he know that?

"Eron Osa?"

That she knew his name was a complete surprise. Had he been ignoring a friend? He looked up now, curiously trying to place her. Nothing but a pretty face. She smelled vaguely of cinnamon. "Do we know each other?" he groped pleasantly.

Her smile broadened. "No. My spies told me you've been hanging out here in the afternoons and I thought I might catch you." She was grinning. Her accent was aristo, perhaps a Frightfulperson of the Calmer Sea. "I'm a hopeless fan of yours. I've read your monograph." She gave him her card. It carried no name or address—but could be used to send her a Personal Capsule before it self-destructed.

A fan of mathematics in this crass world? "Which paper?" He was trying to place her as one of his colleagues.

"The only one you ever published."

"Ah. My *Early Disturbed Event Location by . . .*"

"Yes," she interrupted.

He was startled and suspicious. "You are a psychohistorian?"

"Stars, no. But I have my pretensions as a historian."

On guard, he asked, "And did you enjoy my piece?" He was fishing for hints as to what he had actually written.

"I didn't understand a line of it." She commanded a chair for herself. "But I'm smart enough to know that it was important." The chair embraced her.

"It's been distinguished," he said cautiously.

"I noticed. I hadn't intended to contact you, but since you've been censored that means you are in deep trouble. Am I right? You are in hiding here, or worse?"

"Worse."

His serious tone surprised her. "Are you all right?"

"No," he said. "I'm brain-damaged."

Now she was alarmed. "Deliberate?" She seemed to be genuinely grief stricken. "How?"

"They executed my fam."

"How horrible!" Her concern for him suddenly transformed into a concern for herself—he watched her eyes dart about to see if they were being observed. "Are you safe?"

"I've been punished and released, a future nipped in the bud."

She rose to go but he snapped a steel grip on her wrist as she was turning. She swung back to face him. "Release me!" she hissed.

"We haven't been introduced. Over dinner you can tell me what I wrote. I don't remember. I have to know."

The Frightfulperson of the Calmer Sea was staring at him aghast. She uttered an oath in the name of the greatest psychohistorian who had ever lived, twisted her wrist free, and stepped backward into the café. When he went after her she was gone. Which way? He sniffed his gripping hand—cinnamon with a touch of persimmon—a perfume he would never forget. Why should a pleasant woman, who had seemed to want to make his acquaintance, suddenly become so afraid?

Impulsively he guessed at her direction of flight and began a pursuit. He had one chance in a trillion of ever finding her again. Seven stadia and eight levels later he gave up trying, blocked by one of the massive earthquake absorbers. By then he was lost.

He tried to work his way around the absorber and found himself in a service district that he recognized by its water tanks, a tiny internal ocean that certainly continued downward to rest on bedrock. Pumps throbbed, too big to be serving a residential sector, probably feeding a tower far above them, misting water into the atmosphere to deflect some detected deviation from the long-term dictates of the Splendid Weather Authority. No use going farther. Defeated, he fed the address of his hotel into his map device, having learned enough of its commands to allow it to guide him home.

Her blank card was still in his pocket, the only link to his depublished dissertation.

So, he thought while following directions absently, somebody had read his paper; he wondered what psychohistorical consequences that would have. Perhaps it would cause a deviation in the historical "weather," alerting some psychological bureaucrat who would then trigger corrective input. Somewhere a "tower" would pump a critical "influence" into the "weather" of humanity and "the historical climate" would return to what the Fellowship's "Almanac" had already "predicted" it was going to be.

4

Q: What is the aim of the Founder's Plan?

A: To establish a human civilization based on an orientation derived from Mental Science.

Q: Why must such an orientation have a nonspontaneous origin?

A: Only an insignificant minority of men are inherently able to lead Man by means of an understanding of Mental Science. Since such an orientation would lead to the development of a benevolent dictatorship of the mentally best—virtually a higher subdivision of Man—it would be resented and could not be stable. No natural form of homeostasis . . .

Q: What, then, is the solution?

A: To avoid the resentment of the masses, the first application of Psychohistory must be to prepare a galaxywide political climate during which Mankind will be readied for the leadership of Mental Science. This readiness involves the introduction of unusual homeostatic political structures first proposed by the Founder in his mathscript of the . . . The second application of Psychohistory must be to bring forth a group of Psychologists able to assume this leadership. The Founder's Plan specifies that during a Millennium of Transition the Visible Arm of the Plan will be supplying the physical framework for a single political unit while a Shadow Arm supplies the mental framework for a ready-made ruling class.

Q: Why must the Visible Arm be convinced during the Transition that the Shadow Arm does not exist?

A: During the Transition, Psychohistory must still deal with a society which, if aware of a monitoring class of Psychologists, would resent them, fear their further development, and fight against their existence—thus introducing political forces which would destroy the necessary foundation of the homeostatic . . . The Plan would abort.

—The First Speaker Questions a Student:
Notes made during the Crisis of the Great Perturbation,
fourth century Founder's Era.

Psychohistorian Nejirt Kambu was finding his jaunts to distant galactic hot spots more and more wearing. His overextended junket through Coron's Wisp had been the least thrilling of those adventures, and the only one in which he had not been able to develop a field solution. The oddities in his findings there still bemused him. An outbreak of astrology! He rolled his eyes. But he had made a reputation for himself as an on-site trend analyzer, and the jobs kept coming.

His new boss was going to be a challenge. Long ago, Second Rank Hahukum Kon had chosen to work only with intractable historical deviations. He had built up perhaps the best team of trouble-blasters at the Lyceum. Kon was called the Admiral behind his back because he was always at war, if one could make oneself think of impending crises as the enemy. He did not tolerate men who did not solve the problems he assigned.

Of course, Nejirt chuckled, his weird problem was as nothing compared to the present trials of his fellow occupants of this cramped subcabin—all five of them were bored. They snoozed, or took entertainment bursts from their readers, or complained about the delay. Imperialis was a system that moved fifteen billion people to and from the stars every year in a hundred thousand flights a day. Hurry up and wait. Their four-thousand-passenger behemoth was waiting permission for the final inward hyperspace jump. The ship had already waited more than an hour for instructions while the short-range ultrawaves of the traffic controllers sizzled with chatter.

Nejirt had been using the time to enjoy the sights. He had the sky-scanner all to himself; his bored cabinmates were uninterested. Here in the central regions of the galaxy the view was always impressive, even frightening—the ionized flames of ancient explosions attacked a sea of suns while time stood still.

Finally . . . their terminal jump brought them to an immense outer docking station, girders and access tubes and modules exposed to space. Twenty irises dribbled them into the arms of customs where their sterilized baggage was penetrated and tasted by microscanners, their clothes dissolved, and their nude bodies invaded by nanosearchers. Nejirt used psychohistorian status to outrank a woman with a monkeyoid pet in a cage that he *knew* the machines weren't going to recognize and that, worse, wasn't going to be found anywhere in the customs rule-cache.

It took two trillion humans in Imperialis space to maintain the galactic communications needed by the trillion planet dwellers of Splendid Wisdom. A conventional joke suggested wryly that most of those were needed in space to keep the useful ones from bumping into each other—a lie—but it is humor that makes bearable the impotence of standing in line at the awesome center of galactic power.

Two intersystem shuttles and a gravdrop later, much later, he was on Splendid Wisdom's surface at a bustling transportation hub that was as big as a city, tiered into sixteen tapered levels that overlooked a domed plaza two full kilometers in diameter. Low velocity robo-taxis popped out of the levels like mad bees, darting across and around the concourse and, sometimes, landing on it to pick up passengers from the elevator kiosks. The colossal concourse was filled with transients who wanted to be someplace else. In the distance, Nejirt spotted a luckless couple, who had loaded all their baggage into a people-only chute, so straining the gravitics of the chute that baggage and all were slowly being driven back down into a mass of upcoming passengers—causing pandemonium. He had to laugh. Chaos amused a man whose job was to manipulate chaos.

Nearer at hand, a woman sat alone at a freshment island, sipping a meal between connections, playing a portable hologame to alleviate her ennui. Around her flowed a convoy of off-planet representatives—from some world with taste in clothes resembling woven armor—herding their baggage to keep it from straying, frantically trying to call down a bevy of robo-taxis to assist them. The efficiently moving Splendid natives could be spotted by their unwillingness to bring baggage with them—much preferring to manufacture what they needed when they arrived at where they were going, carrying the templates and other pertinent information in their fams.

Nejirt's fam, having sorted through the electromagnetic hum, passed into his consciousness the information that to get home he had a choice between a three-hour hypersonic flight, taking off in twenty minutes, or a slower four-hour tube ride. He chose the tube—much more relaxing, no distractions, no stressing connections. He'd be able to draft a preliminary report on Coron's Wisp—and maybe even catch a snooze to wake him up for the family.

His fam located an obscure pod station, well below the hubbub, and the nearest concourse elevator dropped him down to it, almost in free fall—a homey lounge safely wedged between a cheap hotel and an instant tailor in a minor mall. He didn't have to tarry—perfect timing—and hopped inside a waiting pod, plushly lined. There, a pleasant surprise. Fabric, in such a small space, was an agreeable change from the usual white plastic. The pod noted politely that he wished the surround-media offed, adjusted his reclining seat for relaxed comm with his fam, and sucked him into the tubes at an impressive acceleration.

Later he hardly noticed the *clunk-thwap* of their supersonic linkage to a train of the main trunk tube that was carrying thousands of other pods in mad haste through an imperial planet's Brobdingnagian bowels. By then he was composing his report at a professional clip, eyes closed, fam exploring and checking out every nuance, his mind bouncing off intuition with fact, piecing together odd observations that hadn't made sense at the time of collection. Yet it wasn't jelling. He really didn't have a relevant thing to say about astrology!

Here was the kind of perversion that the galaxy loved to throw up to the gods. This variation of astrological science was based on eerie projections from an ovoid device that seemed to be made out of jade or marble. It was a crude adaptation of a sophisticated galactarium. The associated Timdo teachings claimed that every chart cast altered the future—one way if the client accepted the reading, and another if the reading was rejected. An astrology that incorporated free will!

Was the failing faith in psychohistory caused by an upsurge of belief in astrology, or was the upsurge in astrology caused by a lack of faith in psychohistory? The equations kept telling him that given the homeostatic conditions in place at Coron's Wisp, something like astrology could only be a force to drive out mental science *if* it had a better method of predicting the future. Both theory and common sense said that the data he had observed were impossible.

He gave up trying to compose his report and went to sleep.

. . . and woke up to, "Arrival. You are now parked at . . ." He flipped up the lid before the pod could finish its spiel, and staggered to his feet, cramped, thankful he had no baggage. A glance showed him that it was his home station, unmistakable by its pompous wall of restored imperial mosaics, long and tiled, a salvage from an Early First Empire building boom. Large parts of this sector had survived the Sack. The station's quaint ugliness was what he got for being snobby enough to choose to live in a hallowed domain that had once been built by the families of the Pupian Dynasty.

"Yoo-ha! Hoo!" He saw Wendi windmilling him from the far end of the station, all the while in a dead run. She looked deliriously happy. That meant that the sewers were probably running smoothly since she was an august member of the sewerocracy and couldn't stop beaming when she had her local piping under control.

"How did you know I was coming?" Nejirt oofed as she collided with him.

"A little pod tipped me off."

"Polite bugger. Must be a new model!"

"No, dear—you just lucked into one of the ones that work!"

Their home was a good walk away and they were in no hurry to reach it, strolling through the parts of the maze that they loved, chatting, catching up. They arrived from above, down a spiral staircase that surrounded a glass-enclosed park of steamy tropicals. Home was built into the circular courtyard at the base of the park. It had once been part of the residence of the family of Peurifoy, the greatest of the First Empire generals.

His welcoming supper was arrayed around an imported ham and a delicate drink from Ordiris bottled in chocolate jiggers. Nejirt was used to farm food, being an experienced traveler, but here in the warrens there were high-class delicacies from the special psychohistorians' emporium, where rank had its privileges. She liked to shop there—he didn't. But why shouldn't a psychohistorian live as well as the dirt farmer on some outback planet of an unremembered sun? A leg of ham was a small price to pay for farsighted, honest government.

He spoke none of this while they ate. He had to admit that nothing tasted better on Splendid Wisdom than ham raised and cured on a pig farm forty light-years distant or juice from berries that needed an exotic sun. He lifted his jigger to Wendi's lip. "To a desk job!"

"No," she said, licking the Ordiris and taking a bite of chocolate. "You need your trips like I need my art. I have a surprise for you."

She pulled him into a pillow-floored meditation room that now slumbered under the rose luminescence of hanging crystals, no form alike, no cut the same, tinkling, slowly changing in the motion of their breath. He mourned the Ming vases that had been there when he left. Wendi was so good at her reproductions—why did she bother with this original stuff? "Lovely," he said. "Don't take it away before I get used to it."

She sat on the floor. "Come down here. It's all prettier from here. We can lie on the pillows and look up!" She pulled him off his feet. "Tell me about your wildest adventure in the cold, hostile, outside universe! We could take off our fams and be animalistic."

He grinned. "Do we sit here naked, growling at each other, each trying to assassinate the other's emperor first?"

"Animals don't have emperors!"

"I forgot. Chickens are all equal on the assembly line."

"Just shut up and tell me your wildest adventure. I never get to travel! So what happened? Something must have happened!"

"I had my astrological chart read. We were in a domed hovel stuck onto the side of the retaining wall of a warm wet rice paddy in the mountains of Timdo. There were two magnificent moons in the sky. My astrological seer was three times as old as I am and smelled of fermenting rice. She used a magical jade green ovoid that darkened her hovel and projected a skyful of stars that whispered to her everything about my future that she might want to know and I might be willing to pay for."

Wendi growled and shook him by his ears. "Why don't you ever tell me the truth!"

"Because you wouldn't believe a word of it!" He laughed and made love to his wife without telling her the rest of the story. What could a psychohistorian tell anyone about the truth? What was he even allowed to say?

Nejirt had been sent to the star systems of Coron's Wisp to study a political perturbation—not a dangerous one, a small one, but large enough to have been picked up by Kon's sieve. Within the confines of the Wisp's five stellar systems, confidence in the leadership had taken a sudden ten-percent drop. On-site, nothing appeared to be amiss—no economic depression, no corruption crisis, no inability of the Council to meet its goals. Nothing seemed to be driving the perturbation. After months of puzzled study, Nejirt had only been able to make a correlation with a mild epidemic of astrology. Temporal coincidence is not evidence of either cause or effect, but . . .

He could sleep on it yet another night. He patted his wife and turned out the crystals. He did not sleep.

Coron's Wisp had not been the best locale from which to tackle galactic history—and had been a terrible locale from which to study such an esoteric subject as astrological infection patterns from pre-imperial times to the present. He had been unable to turn up any easily identifiable source of contamination. No media imports. No latent memes—the planet's entire sixteen-thousand-year history was bereft of any references to astrology . . .

. . . barring only one much reproduced manuscript from a monastery's sealed library, the surviving copy on thin foils of archaic Early First

Empire cellomet. Even Nejirt would not have bothered to translate (by machine) these Chinese brushings had they not contained an illustration of a vase just like the ones his wife had coaxed out of her artist's manu-facturum. But instead of a potter's manual he had uncovered a series of algorithms for making political decisions based on the positions of the heavenly bodies in Terra's ancient sky. More astrology!

Fodder for the hordes of cults who believed in the lost wisdom of the predawn wizards but not enlightening to Nejirt Kambu the psychohis-torian. He had needed another such dead end like a draft of hemlock. The algorithms used by the Chinese astrologers were many orders of magnitude less complicated than those used on Timdo—and, though no better in their ability to make predictions, Nejirt had to admit that the court astrologers of China had subtler ways of generating ambiguous flattery than did the dour star-watching farmers of Timdo's mountain ranges.

For a moment Nejirt had to remind himself that he was lying on pil-lows beside a slumbering wife at the star-studded center of galactic san-ity. Then traveler's fatigue took him . . .

. . . to be cast in a dream of ancient prespace times when Terra was a lush paradise not yet conscious of its destiny as a desert inferno. He was a temponaut disguised in greasy woven yak wool begging a Chinese court astrologer to tell his fortune. He had gold to offer. It wasn't enough. He ripped the seams of his shirt and brought out more gold. The silk-robed astrologer grinned malevolently. It was enough. Since the astrologer's head would not be riding on the blade of the message, he agreed to tell the truth without sleight of hand.

In the dead of night, atop the tower of the astrologer, Nejirt pointed out the star of his birth, a hidden nothing among the blur of the Sing Ki. "Ah," said the astrologer, and a gong sounded and a giant bronze instru-ment began to move against the heavens across the horizon shadows of a walled imperial city. Ominously the bronze shaft creaked to a halt in the direction of Tseih She, which the astrologer obligingly translated for his visitor from the stars as The Piled Up Corpses. "That is your star." It was nothing special, a white star, faintly blue, blazingly bright, an eclipsing variable about one hundred light-years from Terra.

"But what does it *mean?*" he asked with the exasperation of a man who is desperate for certainty.

"It means that you are living in the time of the slayer and the slain, that the battle takes place across the stars, and that the fates of empires are at stake."

"But am I the slayer or the slain?"

"Ah," said the malevolent astrologer, bowing not as politely as he might under the Chinese stars, "for more gold . . ."

Nejirt remembered the dream quite clearly, because that was the exact moment that his fam gently woke him to an emergency request. He opened his eyes to the darkly tinkling crystals and took the call.

"Cal Barna. Imperial Police." There was no image but his fam had already verified the identification. The voice continued, "I've been informed that I have waked you from sleep after a long voyage. My apologies, sir. Our data tells us that you've just come in from a scout of Coron's Wisp."

"That's correct."

"Your report has not yet been filed and I need an opinion. We've got a fast breaker here and time is of the essence."

"Ask away."

"We've got a body."

"A body?"

"A dead body. Nine days dead. We would have called you earlier but you weren't home. The body carried contradictory identification, deliberate deception, so we're poking in the dark but a lucky break on the name Scogil tells us that this man is from Coron's Wisp."

"That brings the odds down to one in ten billion," said Nejirt sarcastically.

"We think the case is more important than that, sir. It was your boss, Second Rank Kon, who put us on to you. He said you'd be interested."

"All right. What else do you know about your corpse?"

"Very little."

"Have you been able to do a salvage on his fam?"

"Yeah, but no. His fam is missing."

"So what have you got? He was murdered? Accident?"

"No, we killed him trying to take him alive. Miscalculated his interest in survival."

"Why were you tracking him?"

"It's a long story, sir. It doesn't make sense. We don't know why we were chasing him. It's because he is an astrologer or an . . ."

"And you think he's from Coron's Wisp?"

"We do."

"I'll be right there. I just hope you gentlesouls aren't stationed at my antipodes."

They and the body were near the Lyceum from which Nejirt Kambu had been forged as a psychohistorian. He could never get away from the place and its hordes of students. Damn. That would mean a long hypersonic flight . . . at least hours of hassle; his fam was already making the arrangements. He rolled over to look at his sleeping wife. Should he wake her now—or leave a message with her fam? Before he decided, he let himself stare at the way her profile lay, eyes closed, face content because he was home.

5

At the time of the predatory Cainali Invasions during the Interregnum we Scavs were of no great force on Splendid Wisdom, being simple survivalist scavengers amid the ruins of a planet whose population had been decimated to a mere fifty billion. We lived by selling layabout wealth to off-planet merchants with a fleet of relic jump ships, none of which survived the siege. Such havoc was done to our economic engine by the amalgamation of mercenaries hired by the Cainali Thronedom that a confederation of Scavs under Leoin Halfnose . . .

An alliance between Halfnose and the beleaguered Pscholars of the still functioning Imperial Lyceum proved fruitful. The Pscholars maintained, for their own secret purpose, remnant elements of the Light Imperial Couriers and were the only reliable source of information about political intrigue beyond the boundaries of Imperialis. With this information and their strategic genius they were always able to ferret out the weaknesses of the Thronedom to the benefit of Scav survival. In turn we provided the Pscholars with rotating hideaways, a military guard, technical assistance, and a fount of scarce supply . . . The legacy of this alliance . . .

Make no mistake: in these days of the Second Empire the Pscholars see us as petty criminals and tolerate us only because we . . .

—From The Cabal of the Brood of Halfnose

On the ninth day of his exile, still smarting from his failed pursuit of the Frightfulperson, Eron Osa set out for the Corridor of Olibanum, his general-issue fam around his collar but inactive. Without a map-tutor he wandered a devious path, all the while struggling to find the right subvocal commands to make his map device obey him. He raged for the analytic powers of his destroyed fam at every wrong turn. He missed the ease of visual electromagnetic direction that came through the simplest of fams. He got lost and felt stupid. Once, when he was staring up at a great heat pipe that rose through tiers of shops, a woman, thinking him demented, directed him to a free kitchen. He just laughed and thanked her. From Rank Seven Psychohistorian of the Fellowship to this!

Slowly he learned his map reader's idiosyncrasies, though he never did discover how to disable its enthusiastic tourist commentaries. The map proved to be primitive, but adequate. It didn't draw through walls or play with three-dimensional images, understanding only addresses. But when properly assuaged, it became quite good at suggesting alternate routes. It painted arrows on his vision and properly labeled corridors and pod stations in large readable retinal type.

With time on his hands and no hurry, he even came to enjoy the ebullient commentaries—too much of his life had been spent hurrying around the wealth of astonishments that lay all around him. He became again the child who longed for waterfalls that fell thirty stories through the wild crystalline shapes of an artist's dreams. When the map suggested the Valley of Galactic Seas, and he found out that it was only a pod's short ride from the Olibanum, he was tempted to take the detour . . . but business first.

From a high-ceilinged pod station with ornate backlit windows that illustrated galactic wonders in all shades of cobalt blue, he walked out onto the Olibanum—and memories flooded his mind. Directly in front of him was the little cabaret where his confreres had solved the problems of the universe over lunch, and maybe laid the odd minor love sorrow to rest, all in the long hours before the evening show began. Strange, he could remember the conversations and the passion but not what they were about. Perhaps such details he had left to his fam. The clientele had changed—older now, some sightseers, a group of tourists. The students were gone, or maybe only tied up in class. The show this evening was titled "The Blue Tyrantiles of Singdom."

Up and down the corridor, bistros were scattered everywhere among the entertainment come-ons and the marvels and the mausoleums of popular culture. He paused. Even with all the changes he knew exactly where the Teaser's Bistro was. Walk to the Deep Shaft and around its great promenade, and then, two blocks farther, was a little alley. . . .

Eron vividly remembered Rigone from his student days, a beefy man older than his student associates, a blatant Scav, tattooed on his face, a boisterous reveler who could dance with iron legs and flip himself through loops if the music touched him, a man who couldn't be bought, who liked to cavort more than he liked to work. He'd turn down your most abject request with a grin—but if you were his friend he had miraculous ways of upgrading your fam.

Rigone used parts that couldn't have been built by any manufacturum; from where in space he got them only the galaxy knew. He could bypass protocols seamlessly. He could add thought processes to a fam that the best students vied for. He never pretended to be legal, yet the police were unwilling to touch him. An inconsistent devil, a cruel one if he thought you were imposing upon him, Rigone just laughed at you if you did him a favor, expecting a favor in return.

But the man was so charismatic that Eron could not remember if he had only admired him from a distance or been his personal friend. Rigone's magnitude of character erased the content in which it lived.

At this hour the Teaser's was quiet but, as always, never empty. The long row of tables marched down the central hall, wood, each of them carved over, to the last fragment of flatness, with the wit of a perennial "tool"-carrying youth: knives, 1-drills, atomic cobblers. Some of the more solid tables had once graced the mansions of First Empire nobles whose line had perished during the Sack; some were of recent manufacture. Old tabletops served as wall paneling to preserve the wit, and were replaced by fresh tables with virgin surfaces of hardwood.

The central row was for the boisterous crowd who enjoyed the mob scene of dealing and repartee. Alcoves served the quieter interests; some even came equipped with sonic suppressors. The ambience of the Teaser's crowd hadn't changed. They were young people with an intellectual bent, serious in their discussions, serious in the quality of their fam aids. Their humor was witty rather than rowdy. And they were all uncomfortably impatient with the stolidness of their Splendid upbringing, restless for the adventure that none of them were quite sure they could handle if they ever found it.

The women, one even as young as fifteen, all wore clothing that was out of style but sensuously reminiscent of another era of blatant power or devil-take-it-all. They knew their history. The boy-men preferred a caricature of military style, not from the days of fighters like Peurifoy, or from the heroic Wars of the Marches, or even in imitation of the ragtag utilitarianism of the armies of the Interregnum, but uniforms of irony; their clothing mocked the generals who had served as toad bodyguards to the weak Emperors of the Late First Empire.

As much as this had once been his element, Eron Osa was out of place. He kept to a table by himself, afraid to enter conversations without a fam that would give him instant access to the quip that would outwit his challenger. There were hand signals by which a wall-spy would take his order, but he didn't order and finally a lean waiter approached him tentatively.

"Are you all right, sir?"

"Thinking." Eron smiled wanly. "Haven't been here for a while. Do you still carry the Gorgizon?" That had always been his order, Gorgizon. It was an obscure Imperial Navy drink, milky and thick, that booted its imbiber into a long high-energy drive. The bastard civilianized version contained a dram of sweet liqueur. It had taken him through many an exam.

"Gang-hu!" grinned the waiter, giving the Old Navy flat-handed salute.

But it was Rigone who appeared from a back room and picked up the drink from the bar. He held it as his own and talked his way down the row of tables, ruffling heads with his free hand, exchanging affectionate insults, staying conversations in midstream till he was past.

He paused at Eron's table, as if it were a simple visit on his rounds, plunked down the drink, and made himself comfortable. "Ah, the prodigy is back."

"I'm on vacation," said Eron, staring at the tattooed face of the Scav in fascination.

Rigone was grinning. "As if you ever took out time from your permanent vacation to work up a lather. Drink up." He nudged the mug. "A special on the house." His eyes glinted at the word "special" and locked on to Eron's with a commanding insistence, waiting.

Eron sipped a taste. The drink was milky white—but no Gorgizon—a different brew with a different kick. His instinct was to resist it. He hesitated, but Rigone's gaze did not falter until he took a good first gulp. Then Rigone's stare relaxed.

"Well—so you're back." It was a statement that demanded an answer.

"Just cruising." Eron was no longer comfortable. "Taking it easy." The drink had a quick-acting knifelike urgency to it, moving his mind somewhere in a rush. Danger. "Cruising. Navigating without charts." Did he trust this man?

"No, no," said Rigone. "I detect the nervous shiftiness of a man on the make. There's an aura of quiet desperation about you. You're in a hurry for your good time."

Eron's mental machinery was racing. Slow down. "I'm . . . not . . . in a hurry."

Rigone took his arm in an iron grip, squeezing, saying: you're coming with me now. He let go in a gesture that added: but not by force. The wrinkles about his intense eyes told of an old friendship that was not going to give Eron any choice. "I know your tastes, aristo Osa. It is our business to know our clientele. That allows us to make fast deals at the Teaser's. It so happens that right now I have just the girl for you. She's thirteen, new to the place, and looking for adventure. A brash kid. You have just the level of maturity she needs to keep her under control. And she has just the right level of insouciance not to know that the world is a dangerous place—or she wouldn't be upstairs right now, snoozing in my bedroom. I want you to meet her." He stood up.

It was a command. Eron was to follow him. Eron, in response, hastily downed the last of his drink while rising, then let Rigone herd him, without seeming to be herded, toward the back of the bar, and up the stairs, and slowly past force barriers into Rigone's private quarters.

The door closed with a vaultlike sigh, and its force field flickered on at maximum strength. The room held the spacious luxury of a man used to wealth. One wall was even reserved for the ultimate in space wasting—four shelves of worn antiques that were not the reproductions of any manufacturum. They were black-ivroid boxes, books from the Middle First Empire. On those shelves, Eron knew, were more antiquarian titles than any one man could absorb through his eyes in one lifetime. Few citizens of Splendid Wisdom could understand the Scavs' penchant for collecting originals, but collect they did. The better museums were all run by Scavs.

Rigone noticed his glance and tapped on a box, disguised in its own black-ivroid casing. "A modern reader. Projects a book in any desired format and translates the archaisms if you wish. I like the books. The original reader is not up to my standards."

"And where is your collection of thirteen-year-old virgins?" asked Eron dryly.

Rigone laughed. "Any spy-beam that tries to penetrate my sanctum will only hear a frivolous conversation between me and you and a silly young girl—but she only exists in the imagination of my script-writing software. The real thirteen-year-old is asleep on the floor of my water room and she is no virgin. I sincerely hope that, by now, the robo-maids have cleaned up her vomit. She has been a curious pest of the kind who has to pick up every tool she sees and flick it into active mode just because it's there. You will do me the favor of taking her with you when you go, firmly." He swung open the bookcase. "But here is what you came for."

On a velvet-lined tray was a fam. "Not a standard manufacture" was Eron's first surprised comment.

"No. And I don't know who in the galaxy did make it. It's hot and I'm glad you're here to take it off my hands—to say nothing of that thirteener. I thought you'd never arrive."

"Can I use it? Is it safe?"

"Of course it's not safe!" Rigone roared. "But it *wasn't* built by the men who executed your old fam, and *that* is in your interest."

Gingerly, Eron picked up the device off the black velvet, turning it over quizzically, longingly. "Your price?"

"I've been paid."

"By who?"

"I assure you that's *not* a detail I want to know about."

Eron guessed. "Somebody who knows you is trying to cut into the market here on Splendid Wisdom, get to the kids early. Does it come with specs?"

"Specs? You're dreaming. It's a one-of-a-kind. I did do a rough probe of its routines; not bad. I didn't like the fam-controlled bomb I had to defuse. But I was impressed by its full range of math abilities."

Eron's heart leaped. "It can do math?" He wanted it badly.

"Not in any language you or I ever learned. But cleanly done. You'll be years getting used to its hailing codes. But it has a fine daydreaming mode that patiently cycles you through the hooks into its routines. While I was at it I probed for kickers and traps. Seems clean, but I only know *most* of the tricks. I don't know everything. The techies who built that sweet familiar know more head-spinners than I ever will. It's got power claws."

"Would you chance it?"

"I'd as soon stick my head in a buzz saw. You're the one who has no choice." Rigone grinned.

"Give me a rundown on the worst I'll have to watch for."

"It's not new," Rigone scowled. He patted the machine and it seemed to cling to his fingers, molding itself to them before he shook it off. "There's a man in there. It's haunted."

"You've been grave-robbing again?" said Eron with some sternness, but also a muted disgust, because he knew horribly that he was in no position to turn down a ghoul.

Rigone laughed hollowly. "Me? I only grave-rob for spare parts, not ghouls. The *young* man in there was murdered." And before Eron could even think it, Rigone's voice hardened. "Not by me, not by any Scav— *your* people murdered him."

Eron was past taking that as an insult. Eron's people had murdered Eron's fam. "Tell me the story."

"You think I know the story? I don't know the story. I'm a Scav. I'm a middleman. I don't want to know the story. I'm a Scav and I've never been dumb enough even to want to take on the Pscholars. They run the galaxy. I stay alive. So be it. But I don't like what they did to you. What I'm doing for you is a personal favor, not a blow against the Fellowship. You and I were friends of a sort, as much as a Scav and a Pscholar ever get to be—and you don't even remember. That horrifies me. I'll tell you what little I know but it's not much. A young man going by the name of Scogil—don't know what he looks like—never met him—was running some kind of astrology scam. Big deal. More power to him. Where in the galaxy can you find more suckers in one place than on Splendid Wisdom?"

"Astrology?"

"The same racket you're in—predicting the future—amazing people with the mystery of your sublime vision."

Eron ran his fingers over the holster of his inactive fam. "I can't cross-reference my feelings anymore but my feeling is that astrology died out long ago."

Rigone shrugged. "It's been through its mutations. Don't know much about the subject myself. Predicting the future is not my thing—we've never been able to compete with the Pscholars on that so we do other things. Who's ever met a Pscholar who could clean out a clogged shower head? So that's the kind of thing we do." After reading a few titles on his ivroid boxes, Rigone reached for one to pop into the reader. "Haven't I heard that astrology was Terra's first science? Probably. Astronomy is the easiest of the sciences and gives one the authority to commit all kinds of flimflam. Did it die out? Not likely!" He called up the search menu and chattered keywords at it in the Old Imperial Dialect. "There are eight thousand plus volumes in that single box and I'm sure . . ." The search flicker stopped. "Ah, we have the Navigators." He grinned. "Perfect!"

What appeared in front of Eron's eyes was a page of Imperial Court history from the reign of Kassam the Farsighted, year 7763 G.E. Kassam had run his galactic affairs by the mysteries of the Navigators, who could predict anybody's future given (1) his birth date, (2) the galactic coordinates of his birthplace, and (3) the direction in which his head had been pointed during his first bawling cries.

Rigone flipped through the text and brought up a smug holo of Navigator Cundy Munn, Court Panjandrum and Splendid Wisdom's master Imperial Advisor for twelve heady years, regally dressed with the portable controls of his galactarium held under one arm. He had been executed after the Battle of Thirty Suns, an unmitigated disaster for Imperialis which led directly to the two hundred years of the endless Wars of the Marches. Kassam had perished the same night and the new rational-minded Emperor henceforth reduced the appeal of the Navigators by having them tortured for entertainment at his coronation.

"The popularity of foolishness waxes and wanes," philosophized Rigone as he switched off the reader, chuckling.

"You're pretty sanguine for a man who is setting me up to share the mind of an astrologer," said Eron morosely.

Rigone was still chuckling. "Am I listening to a superstitious Pscholar? Did your brother tell you the tale of Monto Salicedes under the covers when your mother thought you were asleep?" Monto Salicedes was a famous story, popular among children as a spine-tingling tale of horror set in the mythical world of Old Empire. Monto was a social-climbing fam, the ghoul of a bitter old man who stole the life of each new host and had him murdered in such a way that it was able to parasite the body of someone in a higher station than its last host. Finally reaching the position of Emperor, it went mad, lacking any higher station to which it might aspire. That there was no such thing as a familiar in the distant days of Old Empire was a mere matter of poetic license that bothered the trembling children not one whit.

"Ah, Monto," sighed Eron. He took off his shirt and undid from its collar the general-issue fam that he'd never activated. He lifted the ghoul from the velvet, warmer and more fluid than any fam he'd ever touched, slipped it into place on his neck—it needed no holster—then re-donned the jacket-shirt. It took another moment of courage to give the locking commands. He felt a dizzying surge, nothing else.

However horrible the story, Monto Salicedes was just a fable to stir emotions. For sure, there was a man trapped in this new fam who was now activated, but the poor soul could exist only in his own hell, half his mind gone; there was no way that this ghoul in the machine could ever communicate with his host, Eron Osa. Eron and alien fam had been created apart, each maturing with its own uniquely uncrackable neuronal-neurodal code, forever incommunicado.

Eron's mind would gradually invade the old and now powerless personality of the fam, subsuming its assets and memory space, crowding it out, creating a new symbiosis of fam and man by the slow process of learning. Eron had become Eron Osa the Second—his old memories and abilities forever gone with his original fam—but now a man no longer limited to the barbarous vicissitudes of a famless organic life. He had ceased to be a psychohistorian, or even a mathematician—he didn't even have a position in society—but he was whole and could learn again.

And yet—there was a crippled man in there, imprisoned for life in a dungeon without windows or doors. "This Scogil; you haven't finished your story. How did he die?"

"The police were hunting him."

"The police don't usually kill."

"The fox doesn't usually run so well. I don't know. He was trapped and just ahead of capture. There is something in that fam of yours that Scogil didn't want to fall into their hands. He pulled the oldest trick in the game—the split: the decoy goes yapping one way while the treasure skedaddles off in another direction. He was the decoy. The treasure is here, on a cold trail, and you've become responsible for keeping it hidden—without knowing what you are hiding. He thought he might be able to come back for it . . . but I heard with my ears on the water pipes that yesterday . . ."

"I wonder . . ."

Rigone interrupted the reverie. "Don't make the mistake of thinking that you are in charge of something valuable—it might be just another astrological algorithm that a dead fanatic was willing to give his life for. No one will ever know."

Eron changed the subject to an immediate concern. "You've doped me," he said. It wasn't an adrenaline rush he was feeling, but his mind was unnaturally eager.

"Yeah. A P-drug cocktail. You'll need them. Don't sweat. You've got big learning problems right now. Recall that the tuned probe is a subtle variant of the psychic probe. The psychic probe was once used to extract information from men with the sad side effect of reducing them to idiots. P-drugs were originally developed to make the victims last longer under interrogation. For the first hours under a tuned probe you need drugs."

"I've used a fam all my life!" retorted Eron.

"Believe me, you need the drugs. You're used to being in symbiosis with your fam. That power pack on your neck *isn't* your old familiar fam—it doesn't know you. Its tuned probe is going wild right now trying to make connections it thinks are there but can't find. You two will be months in a calibration roller-spin ride. I should keep you doped up and in bed for two days. Don't push yourself for a while."

Rigone swung in a dissection kit for quantum-electronic devices. He was dismantling pieces of Eron's common-issue fam. "You're going to need your old identity module to access your bank accounts." He attached a small machine to the fragment and put it near Eron's skull. "Okay. Done. That new fam of yours is fancy illegal. It can mimic identities. It has ten identities of its own each with a history and a bank account. I've disabled the two that Scogil used up before he was killed. You've got eight identities to use, as well as your own. My advice is to take the Emperor's Vacation." That meant to sneak off-planet incognito. That said, he began the careful process of obliterating the remains of the common-issue fam.

"There's an awful buzz in my head," said Eron. "Is that the drugs?"

Rigone laughed. "No, kid, that's the ghoul. Scogil is frantically pounding on the walls of his prison trying to speak to you but talking in a code that only the organic Scogil could understand. Mathematicians tell me there are more possible neural-neurode network codes than there are atoms in the universe. Good luck cracking it!"

"The fam seems dead to me. I can't seem to call up any of its routines—or copy any memories for recall. It's all a buzzing blank."

"Relax. You're trying to work at the macro level. Forget it. His macros aren't your macros. And whatever world this fam comes from, it doesn't use Splendid Wisdom's common-issue macros. Totally different interface. Go back to basics; you didn't have any macros when you were three. The world was a strange place and you had to figure it out."

Eron slumped down into an aerochair. "This will take years!"

Rigone pulled him up out of the chair. "I'm sure. But not here. You'll have to leave. Now. And you can't ever come back, kid. I have my neck to consider. So far as I'm concerned, I haven't seen you for years before today. I hear a rumor that you are in trouble with the Fellowship for publishing. You turn up looking for a girl. I give you one. My opinion, if asked, is that you were a very stupid boy to publish. My true opinion."

"Leave now? I'm dizzy. I can't even use my zenoli training!"

"Dizzy doesn't count. You're hot. Out." At this command, Eron staggered toward the door, but Rigone caught his arm. "You can't leave without your date." He was grinning.

They found Petunia in the water room, with her head fast asleep in the gentle arms of the disposoria, unhappy face as white as alabaster, a spider-armed robo-maid fussily trying to clean her up. "She must weight forty kilos," groaned Eron.

"Take her to the nearest spaceport, conspicuously spend some of Eron's money on her, then dump her. Switch to a new identity and get lost while you reintegrate. Be a student or something."

"And Petunia?"

"Ah, the youth of the Second Empire," mourned Rigone not very sympathetically.

6

[Editor's note: Two hundred and seventy historical studies by Eron Osa were seized from his workspace during the hectic time when he was expelled from the Upper Lyceum of the Fellowship by his mentor Jars Hanis. Osa, as a matter of routine, constantly checked his mathematics against reality, his habit being to select surviving bits of recorded history, feed them into his equations, then compare results

with the known historical outcome. Osa's carefully annotated thesis-testing cases cover an extreme range of conditions of scope, location, and time. In only five cases did the retro-mathematics fail: in two because the input data was inadequate and in three where the historical outcome had evidently been falsified in the records by the participants to protect their future reputation.

[The robustness of Osa's arekean transformations is illustrated by the most interesting of his extreme cases, which takes us back forty-one thousand years. Osa picked pre-space-technology Terra for his remotest time example because Terran historical sources, being the most highly prized and most widely dispersed of all the early histories, have suffered the least degradation over that enormous time span. Of course, the small total size of the human prespace population leads to inevitable inaccuracies in any psychohistorical calculation, but the existence of a known outcome allows the error to be calibrated. Osa chose the medieval European reign of Pope Innocent III for his input boundary conditions and attempted a psychohistorical projection for the next three hundred years. What follows is his quirky summary of the calculation. Eron Osa was known for an ironic sense of humor and its ability to get him into trouble.]

The Fate of the Ancient Priests of the Secret Word:
A Cautionary Tale for All Psychohistorians

Imagine an immense old Terra at the center of the universe, its Lord of Evil living underground with his vassal demons in their dark world of sulfurous fumaroles and screaming sinners, its surface crowded with suffering humanity in need of a priest class to guide and direct their lives. Above vast Terra, a mere day away by the soaring of angel wings, are the Crystal Spheres of the sun and moon and five planets and the outer Celestial Sphere upon which the stars of heaven are projected by the machinery of some frozen galactarium.

These Crystal Spheres are the centerpiece of The Creator's Great Hall of Heaven. The Lord of the Solar System holds court with His only Bastard Son and His pious Paramour and His Loyal Angels who stare in Awesome contemplation of His Work, praising it. From time to time He raises up from the surface of Terra pure saints and saved souls to join in the celebration of the epicyclic dance within the Spheres.

Down below, on error-prone Terra, only the priests of the Catholic Church have been granted the right to interpret the Creator's Old and New Words to the ignorant masses—who, if allowed to listen to the Creator's Truth with their own sinning ears, would misapply It to the work of the Devil. For His purposes, He needs some trevize-like *person on Terra—with a talent for rightness. He finds Pope Innocent III, humble, moral, and always right.*

But time flies . . .

In a time far removed from Innocent's eternity, in a sun-and-spaceship-drenched galaxy dwarfing mankind's early universe of crystal spheres, sits a psychohistorian pondering the meager data which has survived the relentless entropy of temporal information loss. He feeds those bits which remain into his model of history, knowing that under the celestial spheres and the crazy planetary epicycles, ancient Terra did not yet swarm with enough of mankind to form an adequate statistical sample size. But accuracy isn't at stake here. His math tells him that, at the high point of European Catholic power under Pope Innocent III, the stasis arising from the Catholic monopoly of the Word will be shattered within three hundred (plus or minus thirty) years by a protesting reformation of men lusting to listen to God's Truth with their own minds. In the beginning it was not enough to be on top, humble, moral, and always right. And in every era since that time . . .

—Eron Osa, 1874 F.E.

The Frightfulperson Otaria of the Calmer Sea had not recovered from her panic. One simple fact had shaken all of her assumptions. *The Pscholars had destroyed Eron Osa's fam.* She had noticed that even Eron did not comprehend the implications of that depredation—and given his drastically reduced analytic powers she could not have expected him to do so. How stupid she had been to contact this leper! Hyperlord Kikaju Jama had called that one correctly, fie on him! She couldn't be sure that the police hadn't been watching Eron, and, by contagion, now her. And she could lead them to the whole movement and its destruction.

It was also possible that no one had noticed her with Eron. But to be safe, Otaria was staying away from her apartment. She was shifting her whereabouts hourly through a complex of business quarters, sometimes taking a long pod ride to operate in a distant district where she was unknown. She had assumed the identity of a small "charity" company she maintained for covert purposes, spending its money, not hers, to do what she was being driven to do, even though it was a panic response and not rational.

While her *mind* ran in circles, harassing her dilemma, *physically* she was acting with a repetitive obsessiveness. Over and over again she duplicated Eron Osa's monograph. She added it as a codicil to obscure law treatises. She did crazy things like loosen the tiles in a public disposoria and recement the tile over a copy. She spent one morning pirating copies of off-planet recipes and registering her document as a public-access book. Eron's monograph served as one of the longer recipes.

She spent a great deal of time in antique shops, buying and trading antique manufacturum templates. Some of the templates she would modify to include Eron's monograph, then retrade them. It was a market no one could trace. Valuable template collections from all over the galaxy were prized and bartered and sold and copied and lost in a frenzied market of collectors and decorators and the curious.

When Otaria was through tampering with a rare gatherum of folding screens from the Cotoya Court of the Etalun Dynasty period, one template labeled GROUP OF SERENE LAKE HERONS IN FOUR PANELS no longer manufactured a restful scene of cranes fishing in the marshes, but rolled out, instead, Eron's monograph on the four ebony surfaces of the screen in inlaid mother-of-pearl. Deep in a music fascicle, Otaria used Eron's monograph to replace the prelude to the recordings of the Third Rombo Cantatas of the composer Aiasin (seventy-first century G.E.), then returned copies of the template to the hectic world of public-domain commerce.

She did all this to use up the energy of anxiety—while the emphasis of her mind was directed at one question: Why would the Pscholars be so afraid of one man? They ruled a whole *galaxy* with enormous confidence. They had guided mankind, successfully, through the Fall into an era of unprecedented galactic power. Sometimes they stopped an enemy with overwhelming military force, but they never chose to defeat an enemy that way—their control was more devious. From a foundation laid down centuries earlier, subtle social armadas would reach a crescendo and roll over the enemy from some unsuspected direction, while the Pscholars watched aloofly, knowingly.

To attack a single man, to ruthlessly destroy his fam without regard to their most sacred principles, meant that someone up there was reacting to a crisis that psychohistory had not anticipated and were striking out—rashly. But what was the crisis to cause such an extreme reaction?

Fatigue caught her after days of drifting and dodging and replication of Eron's dissertation. The scalbeast shoes she had thought fashionable when she first made them seemed rough on her feet now. She rid herself of them in her rented room's small disposoria closet and wriggled her toes. She was tempted to do the same with her clothes—it was dangerous to keep wearing the same outfit in which she might have been seen with Eron—but prudently first tested the room's manufacturum closet to see that it was functioning. Then the clothes disappeared in a flash,

everything—even the hat. Wearing her fam in her hat was a silly affecta-
tion, she decided.

In the public water room down the hall, she took a quick steam sauna
and a quicker snow shower. Her black hair was a mess, the ringlets gone,
but she blew it out with hair-care and let it settle carelessly as unruly
curls. It didn't look like the groomed Otaria she knew and that was good.

Back in her pathetic rented room, with barely enough space for a
desk and a couch and a console, she spent a few hours poring over some
of her collections of antique costume templates. She was a history buff
and styles of clothing intrigued her. You could tell a lot about a society
by its clothes. Did the peasants dare imitate the colors of the elite? Did
the soldiers wear distinctive uniforms or did they stick to battle dress in
battle and hide their bloody trade in civilian guise when on leave? Did
businessmen and lawyers copy each other's uniforms, or did they vie to
be different? Did the men dress pompously and the women in gray, or
did the men all pretend they were the same while the women competed
outrageously with each other for female attention?

After sitting cross-legged on the couch, gorging on the gorgeous images until her feet went to sleep, she finally sighed and put in a sober
search across the templates for something she could wear. She was a
noblewoman, so she deselected for elite fashion. She didn't want to be
conspicuous, so she deselected for sexual attraction and the eccentric
parameters of current Splendid society. That left her with a satisfyingly
manageable collection. What finally took her breath away was an elegant
gray-blue jumper of fluted trousers that tied in with lace at the ankles
and left only a hint of throat from the same collar of lace. It came from
the trader service of an Orion Arm regionate that had opposed and then
been swallowed by the Empire in the sixth millennium G.E.

She slept while the room's manufacturum wove the outfit to specifi-
cations and cobbled dainty high-laced shoes to match. In what passed
for morning in the corridors, the new Otaria took a quiet place in a student café overlooking an air shaft where the food was free but the tables
rented by the hour. She had decided to take Eron Osa's damnable work
seriously and slog through it. The table came equipped with an ancient
but serviceable archival console.

Eron's mathematics was dense. Eron Osa was, after all, a psychohistorian. But she could see that he had at least made an attempt to translate from Pscholarly notation into the more common symbolism of
engineering, not always successfully. She would have been lost without
the sophisticated mathematical functions of her fam, which ran the
equation examples effortlessly, drew graphs in her head and compacti-
fied logical expansions. Sometimes Eron was so brief that she had to

search through dozens of archived math texts to find an underpinning for the point he was making. She made progress at the rate of about two paragraphs an hour. She had forgotten what it was like to be a hard-core student.

The students around her shifted and changed, filling the booths, emptying them, chatting, leaving their garbage to be whisked away by robo-maids. At day's end she had eaten as much of the student food as she could stomach. Despair pleaded with her to quit but fascination drove her to take a stimulant and push on through the evening shift. Student cafés never closed. She was tired and began to skip what she could not understand. Sometimes she just stopped trying to comprehend and fell to listening in on conversations at nearby booths. A girl cried, wondering if she should have an abortion, while her boyfriend held her hand. Two boys were having an animated discussion about the merits of specializing in eighty-third-century-G.E. economic history as opposed to eighty-fourth-century-G.E. economic history.

Slowly her fatigue dissolved into her mental background. A second level of energy blanked her awareness of her surroundings as her fam took control of her emotions and optimized the broth in her organic mind for a steady long-paced stride. She fell into the old student habit of exam-night triage: abandon what she couldn't understand, skip arguments relevant to proof but not relevant to conclusion, concentrate on conclusion. And as the crowd moved from studiousness to late-night revelry the brilliance of the dissertation began to take a conscious shape.

He built up his thesis with generous mathematical case studies of past historical crises involving stasis. She wasn't always able to follow the monograph's rigorous treatment—but Otaria was a history adept and knew how to track down his examples in the Imperial Archives without wasting time on elaborate searches. Her fam already carried a huge knowledge of the location of primary sources. A quick mundane scan of the original data filled in for her lack of comprehension of the math. Otaria was amazed at how the arekean transforms isolated the essential institutions of the target time-and-place and the magnitudes of the historical momenta.

Intrigued, she began a serious study of his eclectic collection of case histories.

The first was a tour de force in which Eron was showing off the power of his tools even under conditions of sketchy initial input, poor data, low resolution, and inadequate population size. Prespace Terra of forty-one thousand years ago supported only the simplest examples of two-dimensional sociostructures, and that made up for the sparse data points. To mathematics all details were not equally important. One does not have to know the color of a boat to know whether it will upend and how it will steer.

But Otaria spent little effort on Pope Innocent III's simplistic world. Its assumptions were too naive to hold her interest. She sampled later magical times and nearer astonishing places to feed her curiosity about how stasis coalesced, shone, then collapsed, even novaed.

Long before the Galactic Era, a Coactinate of ten new suns on the Orion Spiral Front fell into the control of a secret society of terraformers. And then a renegade eleventh solar system duplicated their methods. . . .

The Mystery of Janara thrived for more than a thousand years, until . . .

During the mid-era of Imperialis expansion there was a Boronian League on its then borders. It was an efficiently run scientocracy with a fatal flaw. The Ministry of Education controlled the school curriculum of 428 star systems to the last standard module. It was a monopoly without secrets, maintained by a dedicated Learning Corps who had the power to enforce the decisions of the Ministry—and did. The Boronians shattered under attack by Imperialis; all their generals were thinking alike and became prey to . . .

In the twilight of the First Empire when the bureaucracy of Splendid Wisdom had an effective monopoly on . . .

During the Dark Ages when the Crafters of the Thousand Suns of the Helmar Rift maintained a secret monopoly on the technology of the tuned psychic probe . . .

Stripped to its bare bulkheads, Eron's mathematics was saying that stasis derived from monopoly, and that benevolent monopoly, tyrannical monopoly, any kind of special monopoly, led to a rigidity that had a measurable shatterness coefficient. In his long tedious conclusion, Eron buried a chilling analysis of the Pscholars' monopoly of psychohistorical methods. He had abandoned his clear style and was hiding his message in a forest of obtuse conundrums, perhaps in the hope that only those who could understand the profound implications of the message would be able to pick their way through his equations. Otaria was no longer able to follow his reasoning—but if what he was saying was true, then . . .

Then the Second Empire was in the middle of a historical crisis that had *not* been predicted because of a biasing assumption of the Pscholars that psychohistorical methods were their secret monopoly. Hyperlord Kikaju Jam's revolution wasn't an impossible dream—*it was happening.* Now. Otaria didn't have the strength to recheck her last manic fly through the dissertation's conclusion, to step through it again and make sure that she had read what she had read, she just folded her arms on the desk and went to sleep.

She had no memory of how she reached her room's bed but she awoke to the slowly brightening alarm. She had dreamed and she was fresh. She knew what she was going to do.

Calling an executive meeting of the leaders of the "Regulation" was not an easy task. No one had a list of the members. Otaria knew only five personally even though she was highly placed. The rest were code names to her, invisible functionaries who could be called upon to make things happen in mysteriously untraceable ways.

Because the "Regulation" was organized like an organic brain, it had a consciousness all its own, quite independent of any expendable member. Such a command structure made the organization quite resilient to police raiding. Any "neuron" could be cut out of the circuit and the brain would continue to function. Since each "neuron" was only aware of the "neurons" to which it was directly connected, capturing the whole of the "regulation" in one swoop was impossible. And there were chokes built into the connections. Even if one "ganglion" were totally penetrated, the probability was small that such a penetration would overflow into adjacent cells. Of course, it was a very tiny brain, delicate; Otaria estimated its total membership at about three hundred. It didn't dare lose too many members at a a time.

At a hole-in-the-wall pharmacy, along the Corridor of Smoky Dreams, Otaria bought a palm-sized gene-making kit that was guaranteed to change one's hair or skin color permanently. Frivolity always distracted her from serious business. What she had come in looking for was the transgalactic postal outlet that the pharmacy ran as a sideline. There from a black booth she transmitted a single personal capsule explaining her research into Osa's work. She asked for a caucus to discuss a possible historical crisis, requesting that the best mathematicians of the "regulation" be present so that her conclusion could be checked.

Then she waited. No one had more than a piece of the communications ritual. It had been designed by an expert: rumor told of a military man who had once been involved in the maintenance of secret naval hyperwave combat protocols that could not be taken out by any sort of enemy victory short of total annihilation.

Eventually she received her reply. The small spherical capsule located the Frightfulperson Otaria of the Calmer Sea in her dismal rented room. When she cracked it open, trembling, the terse message gave her a time and a place and an event before dissolving. But who were the Orelians?

7

*Little is known of the first dynasty that led to the rise of Imperial
Splendid Wisdom other than Kambal's only book, from which we
date Galactic Era time. It was not a literate age. Almost fourteen
thousand years ago, under the coruscating sky of the teeming central
star reaches, some twenty-seven millennia after mankind ventured
into the far galactic wilderness, Kambal appeared from nowhere over
Splendid Wisdom with enough strength to establish an isolated home
base on what were then the unpopulated islands of the Calmer Sea.*

*Perhaps Kambal was a young hyperfleet commander displaced
from his home system by a defeat in war, forcing an alliance of convenience on the Splendid colonists. So say the references by Joradan to
Kambal's lost War Logs. In any event, Kambal never returned to combat. In deference to his new hosts, whom he needed as willing (rather
than reluctant) allies, he gave up looting and took to stellar trading to
supply his loyal armies.*

*Perhaps the soothing breezes of the Calmer Sea calmed Kambal's
fire-bred heart. During his long life he lost the desire to conquer. Old
age brought him to a more serene philosophy which has come down
to us as his Oracles of Patience. In that ancient time of strife—in a
galaxy of myriad competing empires, all more powerful than Splendid
Wisdom—who could have predicted that over the next ten millennia
Kambal's seed would gradually assimilate all rivals into a First Empire of thirty million stars that stretched to the galactic periphery? Or
that Kambal's spirit would have been able to hold such an immense
organism together for another full two thousand years through the
sheer power of a patient and tempered bureaucracy brought up on
the Oracles?*

*Before the Fall, the Founder of Psychohistory has quoted Kam-
bal's Ninth Oracle, Verse Seventeen as the major inspiration of his
youth. "It is minimum force, applied at a chosen moment in the arena
of historical focus, that paves the path to a distant vision. Abandon all
immediate goals that do not serve your farthest purpose."*

*—Solomoni's Dynastic Histories,
5645th Edition*

When Nejirt Kambu arrived at the Palace of the Police of the Lyceum
Prefecture, the entrance chute to the waiting room shimmered, expanded, and he dropped through—like a fish into an aquarium done up
complete with a sunlight-from-above-through-water decor. There was

no visible floor, only marine plants swaying below his feet. Brightly colored holographic fish circled the room curiously. It was disconcerting. The Splendid bureaucrats were known to be mad, but some were madder than others. While he was making sure that he could still breathe, a sleek robo-fish with luminous scales received him gracefully and led him to a side grotto with delicate swishes of her tail. "It won't be long," she burbled.

Waiting never appealed to Nejirt, however long, and since he had the clearance, he downloaded the report on the dead man into his fam for review while he paced. The Case of the Police Killing. That did not please him. It was an exercise in farce to chase a petty con artist as if he were the galaxy's top criminal, corner him after nine days of comedy, then accidentally execute him in a clumsy pratfall. Splendid Wisdom should be a sacred example of dignity and order to the rest of the galaxy.

He didn't have time for more than a cursory review before a uniformed receptionist (human) arrived to guide him around office mazes and down through force-field-guarded bulkheads into a long lighted hall that led to the morgue dissectium. The headless man, identified as Hiranimus Scogil, lay like wax in a cylindrical stasis analyzer, ignored by the staff. Prefect Cal Barna was deferentially pleased to see Nejirt.

"Good of you to come so quickly, sir."

Nejirt was not ready for easy camaraderie. "What have we got here, a headless corpse? The head was damaged?"

Barna bowed slightly in respect, his lace collar flopping too quickly. "No, sir. It was necessary for us to dissect the head. We've been modeling the brain. While you were flying in we got a full simulation running."

Nejirt smiled wryly with the wisdom of a mathematician who knows more than can be communicated to common people. He had a natural grasp of neural systems, because much of their math overlapped the mathematical methodology of psychohistory. Simulation of a dead man's brain was a technological triumph—but it wouldn't do them much good.

The human brain is a very chaos-sensitive instrument, its though surfing on the edge of chaos and order in a multidimensional phase space. Such an edge, called a topozone surface, was defined by the boundary between "reality" stimuli (those which generate predictable responses) and "unknown" stimuli (those which sire chaotic responses). Whenever a brain was learning to reclassify stimuli, i.e. adjusting its reality, the topozones were reorienting their surfaces in phase space like some undulating aurora borealis.

Let a dying mind be sliced and probed by a dissectium. Error-sensitive coefficients determining the topozone surfaces are being critically altered. When death hasn't already done so, the probes themselves disturb the data to be recorded. The translation between wet neuron and quantum-state neuron is never exact during reconstruction into an electronic simulation. Each error adds to the entropy. Critical phase space information no longer exists. The simulation "looks" like the original and is connected like the original—but out-of-whack topozones guarantee bizarre behavior.

A careful bureaucrat, like Prefect Barna, the kind of man who had ploddingly followed Kambal's Oracles of Patience over the time span of two Galactic Empires, lived on the stable side of his topozones—but even he was only a neural no-man's-land away from the chaotic excitement of a wildly creative mind like Nejirt's. All it would take to shake him up and push his mind into the confusion and agony of rapid learning would be to put him into a world of alien stimuli—and seal the door.

"Have you learned anything?" asked Nejirt, already knowing the answer.

Prefect Cal Barna shrugged. "Not to be expected. But we have deduced many of Scogil's motor skills. We know how he walks and"—the Prefect's eyes twinkled—"we know the accent with which he spoke Standard Galactic." They had the resonant cavities of Scogil's skull. Talking was a motor-driven skill, and basic motor skills tended to survive quantum-state reconstruction. "Unfortunately he doesn't talk sense." Barna gestured and a holographic Hiranimus Scogil began to speak a standard text. It was worse than bad acting. "Do you recognize the accent?"

"Turn off the visual. It gives him all the likeness of an animated corpse."

"Of course, sir." A disembodied voice repeated the message with the same inflections. "How's the accent?" implored Barna again.

"You mean, does it sound like someone from Coron's Wisp?"

"Yeah."

"It might and it might not. The Coronese are very idiomatic." With resignation, Nejirt decided to humor this idiot. "Have you picked up any other motor skills?"

Prefect Barna laughed. "We thought we had something, but it turned out to be his ability to screw tops on bottles. The only unusual thing we've identified is his ability to balance a moving bicycle."

"Bicycle?"

"A bicycle is a two-wheeled gyroscopic device. It might be useful for high-speeding down corridors and bouncing off pedestrians."

"Wire frame? Wheels in-line? High seat? Muscle-powered?"

"Yeah," said Cal.

"On the planets of Coron's Wisp they are called whizzies. Never saw one in my life before my last adventure. I was told they became popular during the Fall when power was short. There are whizzy trails in the forest and around mountains and all through the metropolises. Good for the body, they say. But I think corruption is setting in; ten percent of them are powered."

"Ummm. We've determined that this Scogil had at least twenty years of experience on them." He paused. "So this could really be a link to Coron's Wisp?"

"Timdo, most likely."

Cal stripped off his lace collar, showing a hairy chest, and mopped his brow, then tossed his lace beside the corpse. "Well, well, well," he said with satisfaction. "Follow me. Second Rank Hahukum Kon wants me to show you something."

Together they found an unused conference room with stuffed autopsies on the walls. The Prefect removed, from the carved ivory case he was carrying, a jade-pale ovoid with indented five-finger press points. Nejirt gasped. Such objects were legendary on the Wisp's Timdo, yet he had believed not a word surrounding this superstition until a day when such an ovoid cast its magic in the air of an old woman's hovel—predicting nonsense, of course, but doing it beautifully. The hag whispered to him that he would live long enough to witness the Second Fall . . . and like all women of her breed had refused to tell him how long that would be.

"From your expression I take it you recognize the object?"

"They are used on Timdo—but hidden from outsiders. I've seen only one."

"One!" exclaimed Barna. "Our Hiranimus Scogil has been on Splendid Wisdom for months now selling *thousands* of these things to astrology buffs. They seem to be transshipped from Coron's Wisp."

"You're sure he wasn't churning them out in his hotel room from some template he picked up in the Wisp?"

The Prefect was affronted that anyone would think the police so inept as to make such a mistake. "This isn't jade, sir." Jade was an object that could be manufactured in any household. "These ovoids are imported. A manufacturum hasn't the resolution needed for replication. We've put a few through the lab and we cannot fabricate a template of a functional ovoid with our best copiers. Same problem as the one we have with Scogil's brain."

Cal continued, bemused. "This one we acquired during a recent raid on Scogil's headquarters authorized by Second Rank Kon. Beautiful, isn't it? How in space do they work? We've been reduced to tapping random code into the press points and intimidating ourselves when magic happens. We lack a fundamental picture of the device's function or an operating manual. Kon tells me you've picked up some queer stuff about astrologers on your recent jaunt."

Nejirt raised the ovoid, carefully fitting his fingers and thumb to the indentations. He thought and his fam remembered the finger-code sequences that he had bribed from his Timdo contact. Darkness blossomed until even the face of Prefect Barna faded. Then—bedazzling stars. It was quite a piece of fakery, the best handheld galactarium Nejirt had ever witnessed. This version had been preadjusted to view the stars from the coordinates of Imperialis, but that could be changed to any point in the galaxy with deft finger pressure.

With irony psychohistorian Nejirt Kambu asked the questions and adjusted the sky to produce Prefect Cal Barna's astrological chart. "Birth" stars appeared in blue, "danger" stars smoldered red, "decision" stars flared yellow, and "wild card" stars turned green. All nonsense. Then an awesome program began to paint Barna's personal constellations across this brilliant sky: heroic robots who herded man's destiny, a chain gang of grieving virgins put there in penance by a guilty emperor suffering regrets, a stream of life to nourish all the fishes of the galaxy, a fate-worse-than-death, a mooning joker, the knife that separated good from evil, a monster of the galactic deeps. Barna's birth constellation turned out to be the stone well. His fate was easy to determine—providing one knew whether the stone well was draining or replenishing. Nejirt smiled to himself at that touch.

"Why did you kill Hiranimus Scogil?" he asked when he was done with the reading and the stars had faded.

"We intended to take him alive."

"Of course. Why did you kill him?"

Barna glanced over at the body ruefully. "We have a certain Hyperlord Kikaju Jama under surveillance for subversion. He advocates the purloining of state secrets, and the methodical dismantling of the Empire. He even blasphemes the Founder by advocating the establishment of a thirty-thousand-year interregnum."

Psychohistorian Nejirt Kambu smiled. "That is hardly a crime."

The Prefect huffed. "Sir, it *is* if he takes measures to put his theories into effect. If he is planting nuclear bombs to vaporize the Lyceum, that *is* my business. We have every intention of cleaning out the Hyperlord's group and in all probability would have done so already had Scogil not tripped our wires."

"Go on."

"Jama purchased a device from Hiranimus Scogil which is illegal to own or possess. That is how we began our investigation of Scogil. Kon," he nodded deferentially, "ordered the raid on Scogil's base of operations and the arrest of Scogil. Much to our surprise, we found ourselves chasing him for nine days. He played the shell game, and blast him, every time we'd pounce on a shell, he'd be under the other one. Nine days! Eventually we cornered the rat but by then we were conditioned to expect him to escape . . . so we got, shall we say, overenthusiastic, to use a lame euphemism. And we didn't get what we wanted. Shame! We were after his fam. And he wasn't wearing one. Space, what a shock that was! We'd been conned! We couldn't imagine a man evading us for nine days—nine days—without the use of his fam! Galaxy knows where it is now. We've lost it."

"Explain something to me," said Nejirt. "Why am *I* here?"

"Second Rank Hahukum Kon suggested that you would be invaluable in the analysis of events."

"I'm not at all convinced that a minor ring of astrologers and charlatans is my business—unless I'm being demoted. Why am I here to view this astrologer's corpse?"

"Astrologer? Didn't Kon tell you? He suspects that Scogil was a psychohistorian—and an able one."

What? Nejirt walked over to the body inside its cylinder of instruments. His mind was racing in astonishment. All the data at Coron's Wisp suddenly made sense. A rebel psychohistorian. Old and well-worn theorems of the Founder rose to the conscious awareness of his fam as their unassailable assumptions were being checked out in panic. It was impossible! This couldn't . . .

He stopped.

He remembered what he had been thinking while Barna was explaining to him the hastily constructed quantum-state simulation of Scogil's mind. About topozones. About the mathematical explanation of the panic and uncertainty and disbelief he was now feeling.

Ceaselessly the activity in an organic net flips back and forth across the boundaries twixt stability and chaos in the mind's war between knowing and the need to learn—this outpost ridge temporarily chaotic, that beachhead stable for the moment, the front flowing in battle flux across the net.

Circumstance, curiosity, boredom, the hope of adventure propel the mind into *places* where it must contend with unfamiliar stimuli. Unfamiliar stimuli drive the mind across various points along the no-man's-land of the topozone into chaotic neural activity. Confusion and uncertainly appear, contradictions in one's worldview emerge, even desperation haunts the battlefield. What to do?

Learning is the neural mechanism by which the chaotic responses sired by unfamiliar stimuli are disciplined into an appropriate known. The mind seeks a readjustment in the shape of the topozones. If learning's troops prevail, the strange stimuli come to be included within the new regions of stability. If learning fails, the troops flee back across the old topozone, the man flees from what once stirred his curiosity back into the known.

The battle never ends. Victory for one side is the only danger. If a brain lives only in the known it begins to suffer rigor mortis on the stable side of the topozones; if it lives only in the unknown it becomes insane on the chaotic side of the topozones.

Chaos and panic in his mind. It was a challenge. Were there really other psychohistorians out there?

8

Appearing during the collapse following the False Revival, soon after the fam became one of the more prized commodities of interstellar commerce, an elite military caste calling itself the Order of Zenoli Warriors was probably the first group of fully fam-equipped mobile soldiers immune to the emotional control of the original tuned psychic probe. They had a reputation for winning their contracted battles with quick, lethal strikes. Warlords who used them paid heavy fees, and Warlords who did not, lost their battles. The zenoli alliance with Coman in the Circus Wars of the Orion Arm . . .

Such was their reputation that all zenoli mercenary contracts were bought by the Founder's Navy in 1089 F.E. as part of the peace treaties of the Second Pax Galactica. The zenoli soldiers were dispersed throughout the regular fleet, and the organization disbanded in 1138 F.E. Zenoli mind-training techniques remain popular today.

The tuned psychic probe is a double-edged sword. Control it, and it will protect you. Lose control and you open the way to . . .

—Fleet Manual 3-456:
The Military Usage of the Tuned Probe

Dizzily Eron Osa led a sick thirteen-year-old Petunia down the Olibanum. She wore the elegant metamorphic leathers of some obscure 113th-century-G.E. off-spiral culture—thigh-splits to the rib cage, lizard clasps, with a tight bodice sporting two grotesquely openmouthed, ruby-eyed snake heads that had just gorged on pink-nippled plastic breasts much too large for a teener. For a moment she withdrew her concentration from the point along the walkway one meter in front of her feet. She flicked her fam into advertisement mode and let her eyes scan the distant huckstering.

"Couple of blocks straight is a posh hotel," she hinted. "Us crapulous wobblers need a cozy bed."

Rigone's advice to dump this vixen at the nearest spaceport was sounding more and more like an excellent suggestion—but her grip on his wrist was a tourniquet, partly to support her tipsy balance, partly because she was very afraid. Nevertheless she was unnaturally happy. What drug was she on? He wasn't sure she would make it to the next corridor, much less the next hotel.

Worse, he was lost. Not knowing where you were in the Olibanum was not smart. He had abandoned his map device at the Teaser's, thinking he was immediately going to be able to tap into his fam's navigational aids. Nothing about his new fam worked. Whatever obscure streamer of the galaxy it came from, its operating system was unlike anything he had ever encountered—and his organic mind was *extremely* well trained in fam operating systems. All he could get from it was a frantic buzz.

"Petunia, we've been staggering along the Olibanum until I don't recognize it anymore. Do *you* know where we are?"

"I'm just a goggle-eyed following-girl. I forgot to ask; was that man hawking an animal zoo or a human zoo? I've never seen an elephant. And did you gawk that shaft we passed? Never look down a shaft when you're all zink-zanged!"

"Stop. We need a plan."

"I *have* a plan, big man. I follow you to the nearest hotel, you lead. Tomorrow is another day. Rigone said you'd take me to the local spaceport. We could get a cabin together. Do you kit-bag the credit for first class? Rigone said you were a very generous trick." Her eyes narrowed thinking about that. "We can't just stand here. Thinking sets my stomach up for puke again."

He was still dizzy and it was getting worse. The desperation didn't help. He wasn't going to make it to the nearest hotel. "We find a café. Then we sit down and drink juice until we are both sober."

She turned unsteadily to take a careful look at his face. "Big man, your new fam's squawking?" People streamed around them a little quickly to avoid proximity to her gluttonous snakes. "I've been figuring on you. You're a criminal. Your fam was zanged. You cop a gray appliance from Rigone and now you have to go to ground only on some other planet far, far away. Hey, I'll go with you for the punch—got no ties." She nudged him with her hips. She grinned.

Eron was no longer listening to Petunia's babble. Slowly he moved over to the wall, hanging on—to keep from fainting. Nothing made sense. He saw the colors. Pedestrians had fingernails. He was aware of the hand gripping his wrist. His zenoli training in mind balance was useless without a fam to . . .

"Confused man," Petunia said kindly, "I'll eye for you." She started to drag him. "Fam's killing you." She pushed. "Get along, big man. We get that monkey off your back quick." He sank to the walk. "Hey, comrade. None of that. We don't need the bleeding corridor police. Up, up." She pulled him to his feet, fiercely, never having let go of his wrist. He followed her to a rent-by-the-hour hotel. "Not the dream hotel I had zoomed on. Don't even have time to ask if they double-distill their piss." She paused, white-faced, woeful. "Crumbling place has no grav-chute!" She pushed him up the stairs.

Petunia eased Eron through the dilator, manhandling him because he was so much bigger than a tiny girl. She maneuvered him to face the bed, then shoved and watched him fall. Very gently, almost reverently, she disconnected his fam and took care to find a place for it. He shuddered with convulsive relief. She poured a cup of water and slipped one of her knockout pills into it, cradling him in her arms against her plastic breasts while she fed him the potent drink. She laid him down again, too weak to pull the covers aside and tuck him in, then queasily snuggled beside him, arms around him. For a while she had forgotten how smashed she was. "If I barb, wake me up," she whispered into his ear—but he was unconscious.

Eron opened his eyes. It was good to feel sane again. He gazed straight up, not really ready yet to find Petunia. One could always tell the cheapness of a hotel by the height of the ceiling. If she was still asleep, he was going to be a coward, take his fam, and sneak away on tiptoes. When he dared look . . . a shock.

Petunia was nude at the desk, using a small instrument on his fam. He jumped out of bed like a shot. "Sons of a sun! What the . . ." He stopped in midstride—the fam on her back was the same make as his. And where in space had she put his clothes?

"Hi. Just tuning your fam to cure that buzz. I filched one of Rigone's instruments when he wasn't looking. Ha, the old tattooed prick! Pillage has priority over being sick. It's amazing what you can stuff in a fake bosom that no one dares look at!" She brought over his fam. "Try it on now. The buzz is gone. My hangover isn't."

"Your fam is just like mine," he announced suspiciously, glancing about the tiny room for his garments and spotting only the shoes.

"I know the model. I hail from a pov planet where jerk-class can't afford fams. Mommy lifted one out of a hot shipment passing through and made me a gift. Gave me a boost. So I ran away and set out across the galaxy for adventure."

"You're lying," said Eron sternly, hiding his genitals with a pillow. "I can predict backward to the truth. At least as far as thirteen years."

To that insult she took umbrage. "Every ass-faced citizen of Splendid Wisdom thinks he's a psychohistorian who can predict backwards and forwards with the greatest of ease, tra-la-la. I don't think you can predict me from straw."

Eron continued to gaze at her reproachfully.

She met his stare, vacillating between defiance and capitulation. "So I'm lying. Mommy was rich. I stole her jewelry and set out across the galaxy for adventure. Is that a better lie?"

"Get some clothes on and we'll discuss it."

"Try your fam first. I want to see if I shot the buzz. And no sass from you. My mommy is a whiz quantum-state-electronics crafter, and I have all her routines in my fam, and mine's the best fam made in the galaxy, and I space damn well know how well I do because I've been doing it since I was three."

Meekly he put on the fam and activated it. The buzz was gone but he still didn't have access to its basic functions. He watched Petunia slip into the manufacturum closet for a new outfit that had been in production. *Such a lovely body,* he thought. Suddenly he knew he wasn't going to dump her. She was only a kid. She needed help. Come to think of it he actually felt extremely loyal to her. If he only had some clothes himself.

Petunia stepped out of the manufacturum wearing a modest electrospun all-weather chastity, something for the spaceways. "Ghaaa. It itches. I forgot the underwear. Do you like it?" She pirouetted.

He found her attractive. "Attractive," he said.

"Am I adorable, too?"

"Of course!"

"Tell me more," she insisted.

Eron was observing his feelings with a reluctant amazement. "I find you a delightfully entertaining young woman," he ground out through his teeth.

"Girl," she said. "Don't patronize me! How much do you admire me?"

There was a rational answer to that—but the words forming in his mind were very different. "My admiration would follow you to Star's End," he said impulsively, against all attempts to restrain his tongue. He was beginning to wonder where his conversation was coming from. Had he inherited his fam from a lady-killer whose twaddle was somehow leaking through?

"Yeech! And will you love me till the End of Stars?"

Eron grinned. "We have to stop this nonsense," he said, alarmed at the depth of his feelings.

"Oh, no. Not yet. Tell me if you are sincere or just impressed by my outfit. Are you my slave?"

He was her slave. Astonishing. When had that transformation happened? It had happened between the time he had activated his fam and the time she had emerged from the manufacturum, that's when it had happened. He paled. As unobtrusively as possible, he tried to deactivate the fam—and couldn't.

His delinquent child was watching his every twitch with a fathomless amusement. "Hey, you've caught on."

He had not expected to be attacked by the tuned probe driving his own familiar. All his life he had been taught many clever ways of using a fam to counter the emotional control of a Cloun-type tuned probe—the fam in its original form had been *designed* as protection against Cloun the Stubborn's early device. What was he to do now? He couldn't very well strangle someone he loved.

She stood in a defiant pose, almost ready to run, unsure that she really had control. "Hit me," she demanded.

"No," he said gently, though that was exactly what he wanted to do.

Now she was triumphant. "They say it's a fool who thinks he can take a girl of the Olibanum to a hotel room without getting rolled." Then with vituperation, "Thought you could abandon me, did you?"

Her anger triggered his anger. "I'm a poor tool right now, of little use to you or anyone else. I don't even have access to the basic functions of my fam."

She shrugged. "I can teach you. Couple hours. Do you know any zing places on this spaceforsaken planet? We can amuse ourselves while we work. But no drinking! *I* might take a few snorts but *you* have to stay sober! You're my protector. I feel absolutely safe with you." She took his arm, "Let's go, lover boy."

"My clothes?" he said pitiably.

"Your new duds are hanging in the manufacturum. Something more my style than the rags you were wearing."

While he dressed in an outrageously loud pompfrock he continued their conversation. "As a matter of politeness, you might inform me of the rules I am working under. Then I won't run up against them and get 'zanged' while I'm attempting to do something normal like flaying you alive."

"You're not allowed to hurt me and you have to come to my defense when I'm being threatened. You have to obey my orders, no matter how frivolous, but you're allowed to disagree with me if you think my orders will harm me. After taking care of me, you're allowed to take care of yourself. Those were the rules my mother invented for my father. Pretty good, huh?"

"I can tell they were invented by a woman!" grumbled Eron the slave.

Since she wanted to be a goggle-eyed tourist in the middle of his life's worst crisis he suggested that Petunia take them to the Valley of Galactic Seas. The uninterruptible guide attachment of his antique map device had recommended the site profusely. She agreed. "Yea, sharks!" she said flapping her hands like fins.

The multistoried corridor was one vast aquarium. Stairs led up and through the tanks past fish and bottom-walking monsters and down and around the tanks of starfish, seaweed vines, sleek carnivores, school fish, eels, stalkers. There were vast malls to view the tanks from a distance and small parks in which to sit surrounded by the sea life of the galaxy.

In a bright park facing an underwater jungle of vines and flowering seaweed that harbored brilliantly painted sea darters and the occasional slumbering shelled monster, she taught him how to control his fam; it used a finger-manipulation code read from the motor centers of the brain.

To get any results at all Eron had to play like a musician diddling on an invisible flute, but Petunia told him that the fam would soon learn to sensitize itself to read the *thought* expressing a particular fingering while his fingers were quiescent, or involved in other tasks. The fam's learning mode seemed to operate with pleasing rapidity—or was that the skill of his tutor?

It took him only hours to establish the linkages so that the fam could paint pictures in his brain, create sounds, kinesthetics, feelings. It was already contrived to do those things *but only in interaction with the organic Scogil.* Eron's brain needed to train the fam's circuits to a different code.

They were climbing stairs that ran beside the cross section of a mountain stream teeming with the life that lived in melting snow when he asked her a question he had been pondering. "Did Rigone set you up as my tutor?"

"Have you lashed your noodle? I was there to abscond with his property. Even Rigone doesn't know the value of your fam. Imagine how much a fam with a built-in slaver is worth on the black market! I drunk myself silly getting into position—and when he flew for a minute, I couldn't even crawl up off the floor! You blew in while I was decorating the disposoria and walked away with my prize. I couldn't believe it when he cold-showered me and set you up as my trick. You lose some, you win some, as my beloved daddy used to say."

"You're a thief? Who do you work for?"

"Myself. I do lots of things for a living, even go to school."

For the rest of the afternoon Eron was delighted with the results of his twitches—aside from the strange stares evoked by mad midair fingering. To alleviate his embarrassment he bought, from an antique dealer under the sharks, the template for an over-shoulder photozither (complete with dead earphones)—an instrument played by plucking laser beams. While he "played" no one noticed the lack of lasers or the lack of sound.

He began to feel human again. He had revived his ability to do long division in his head; he could locate himself in Splendid Wisdom's labyrinth, search and filter the local advertisements, monitor the maxwell spectrum, integrate and graph in n-dimensions, and actually recall long lists after placing them in storage, even remember people's names. The math functions of his fam sent him into deliriums of joy. *Now* if he were ever to locate a copy of his dissertation! Idly he checked to see that he still had the comm card given to him by the strange Frightfulperson with the russet-gold-flaked eyes who was a fan of his math. The possibilities took on a new urgency.

Because Petunia was in a quixotic mood they spent the evening sleeping inside the substructure of a huge plastic whale which had a broken entrance used for electrical maintenance. He took the time out to consider his plight. He really didn't mind doing whatever sparked this girl's fancy—but he knew his lack of rebellion was an illusion and a deadly one. Somehow he had to enlist Petunia in his cause so that it would be her cause, too. He had to discover why his mathematics had provoked such an extreme reaction in Jars Hanis.

At her first stirrings in the morning, he began his attack. "Petunia?"

"Ho hum. You're still awake? You've been very restless all night, big man. Can't sleep on concrete? Sissy."

"The police will be after me. That's serious. If I just wander around in aquariums and zoos, something bad will catch up with me—and you."

"Not wandering around," she snarked, "you practiced accessing your fam. I conduct under-the-sky seminars cause I come from a planet where we *have* a sky. Lighten up. When desperate, have some fun."

"What are your goals?" he asked. "We probably have goals in common."

"Oh, shut up! Do you think I'm catching hook on that line? *My* goals are yours right now. I'm smarter than you are. I've had my fam for thirteen years and you're only a baby who's been twiddling with yours a couple hours!"

After such a command there was very little he was allowed to say. He tried and nothing came forth. It was frightening. "Permission to speak?" asked Eron dutifully.

"Go ahead. Make it short."

"I'm suspecting that you know who once owned my fam." A previous slave who had managed to escape? And a con-artist astrologer.

"You bet. I'm searching for him."

"A young man with the name Hiranimus Scogil?" Eron couldn't see her expression in the dark but he heard her startle. "Petunia. He's dead."

"No he's not! How do you know?"

"Rigone told me."

He heard the sobs. "I . . . wanted to get . . . his fam back to him," she wailed. Eron tried to comfort her but she shoved him away. "Get away from me. Get away!"

"Your friend?"

"Yeah. My friend. My *dad.*" She lapsed into a silence punctuated only by the occasional resonant sob. He shared her silence because he had much to think about. He was the slave of a ghoul's daughter. Finally she spoke again, tersely. "Let's go."

They crawled out when no one was looking, pretended to admire the great plastic whale, and began to stroll until they found a seafood restaurant. Even with all the fresh fish abounding in the neighborhood, Eron noted wryly, the fish they ate would be manufactured. It was cheaper to build a fish out of sewage than to grow one—and the template could leave out heads and bones and tail. The manufacturing process was just good enough to get the taste right, but not good enough to build a live fish.

"We eat on my credit," she said stonily. "I have an account they can't trace. Eron Osa has to disappear. And don't sober-face. It's *my* dad, not yours."

My ghoul, he thought.

Over delicious fillets made from Splendid sewage, Petunia recounted the rest of the story. "Mommy *hated* me flying with him on his sorties—he took me everywhere, nobody suspects a nice man with a child—so she rigged his fam's driving probe with some Cloun side-reasoners to enforce his care of me. That was before I knew electronics. Mommy is such a paranoid. If you fancy me a hot-shot fam modifier, I'm not that good. To hit you, I just calibrated what was already there. Dad never knew he was my slave cause he already loved me. Not like you," she said resentfully.

"The fish you are feeding me is delicious, and it is a lovely morning to do nothing—but we still need a plan," he countered.

"You win. Saving Dad is out. We switch plans." But they were still her plans and she wasn't bothering to consult Eron. After an hour's thought, the remnants of the meal gone, their napkins twisted, she confessed that she was stumped. "I don't know what to do next." She snuggled against Eron in the booth, not the slightest bit afraid of her slave.

"Are you asking for my input?" he asked hopefully.

"No, we'll have to consult Dad's fam for help. I don't see any other way."

That meant she was suggesting a conversation with Scogil's ghoul. "Kid, I can't read or interact with the storage areas of my fam that were private to your father. All I can do is write over them. I can steal his bits for myself. Eventually even the best error-correcting routines won't be able to salvage much of him."

"But he's in there, thinking. He can see with your eyes and hear with your ears."

"But he can't make any sense out of that input because we use different codes."

"I'm really annoyed at myself," she said. "When he split off with his fam, he gave me a ticket out and a new identity. He told me to run like a stellar flare was scorching my tail. I should have done that. Dad always told me that youth had to be extra careful because we lack judgment. I think he was right. I didn't run. I disobeyed *orders* and now no one knows he's in trouble. I couldn't leave him. I'm the only one tuned to his fam. I can find it anywhere within a planet's radius—my mommy's doing. That's why I was hanging around at the Teaser's. Maybe I've made a terrible mistake and interfered. Were you involved with Dad in some great cosmic scheme?"

"I don't know. Someone who identified himself only as my benefactor told me to pick up the fam from Rigone."

"We *have* to talk to Dad!" she wailed. "He has contacts and I don't know who they are!"

Eron felt a sudden pity for her—and for himself as her prisoner. "I have contacts, too. Let me use them."

"No. I don't trust you. Not with my dad on your back! You're a criminal."

"Petunia. I'll make a contract with you. Let me send out one message that involves a personal professional matter of mine and in exchange I'll work very hard to communicate with the fam half of your father. I was once a zenoli mind-adept and that may help. I can use that exotic stuff now that I own a fam."

"You'll work hard 'cause I tell you to!"

"Child, there is a subtle difference between a willing slave and a reluctant slave. In this case it makes all the difference in the galaxy. You are asking me to do something that has never been done before. If I'm willing, we may succeed. If I'm forced, we may only try." It was a lie; there was no hope.

She considered. "I see the message and I pay for it!"

"We'll have to buy a portable nonlocatable receiver. Cheapest model. And hide it in a secure place."

The details were completed later that day. When the message was composed to his nameless fan, it read: "Dear woman of the broad-brimmed fuchsia hat: I desperately need a copy of the monograph you so fortuitously saved. Send it by Personal Capsule, if text still extant. I retain my coding for untraceable delivery. Eron Osa."

"You better be leveling," threatened Petunia, "or I'll make an adjustment to mush your brain!"

9

Q: Unfortunately, at this junction in time, the Psychohistorical monitoring of the Founder's Plan has inadvertently been exposed to view due to recent rebalancing of the unpredicted perturbations involving the military adventures of Cloun the Stubborn. It has been claimed that, with the Plan one-third complete, the Visible Arm of the Fellowship is so superstitiously addicted to the Plan that they will not care to interfere with it by attacking whatever monitors of the Plan might exist. What are the mathematical consequences of allowing our exposure to persist?

A: All such computed courses of action indicate a rapid deterioration of the Plan, either because the Visible Arm finds and destroys its Mentalist monitors, or because an open conflict arises between the two and destroys their symbiosis. At the ninety-five-percent confidence level, both of these alternate historical branches either lead to a Second Empire that repeats the cycle of the First, or to a return of the chaotic galactic conditions extant prior to the First Empire.

Q: How then may the original design be restored?

A: If all those who now resent the monitoring of their actions by Mental Science were led to believe that all Mental Scientists with such power had been destroyed, the galactic situation would restabilize around the parameters of the original Plan, leaving only minor alter-

nations in the probabilities of success. The window of opportunity is
short. The apparent destruction of the Mentalists must occur within
twenty-five years—before the Shadow Arm's present group of adver-
saries fragments into thousands of independent sub-sociogroups.

—The First Speaker Questions a Student: Notes made during the
Crisis of the Great Perturbation, fourth century Founder's Era.

Second Rank Hahukum Kon soberly pointed out over the railing of the
fourth-floor balcony of the domed Lyceum fortress, his finger sweeping
across the galactic simulacrum that filled the whole of the enclosed bailey. Kon wore a sky-blue jumpsuit, unfashionable, of the sort that one
might find on a naval mechanic.

Nejirt Kambu stood with him, a little embarrassed that he had
dressed for the meeting in formal black frock coat with silver striped
zoot pants. He had been hired by the eccentric old "Admiral," sight unseen, and had signed on for the Coron's Wisp assignment solely on the
basis of Kon's reputation as the best trouble-spotter at the Lyceum. Nejirt had been unsure of what he might expect at a first encounter with a
man of such rank and reputation.

"The regions in blue are the full-scale battle theaters," explained
Kon.

Nejirt made a quick estimate that the blue covered perhaps one percent of the Second Empire, a realm more imposing in this huge model
than it was from the dwarfed viewport of a spaceship. Kon had not yet
defined what he meant by such an alarming phrase as "battle theater"
but he was a man infamous for using alarming phrases. Coron's Wisp
was well within one of the designated regions. "And how do we determine what is to be classed as blue?"

"The blue are regions of intractable uncertainty, my specialty if
you've followed my career," said Kon with acerbity.

Nejirt nodded, not willing to make a second faux pas.

"I've been raving for years about war," complained Kon. He
squeezed at his remote console and the simulacrum changed. "This is as
the Empire stood one hundred years ago. The pale yellow and the gold
cover all areas where the probability of deviation from prediction was
greater than five percent, the gold indicating sites of strategic dynamism
where failure of our predictions would have consequences meeting the
Founder's criteria of direness. My predecessors, of course, sent rectify-
ing teams into the gold regions. Now watch as I overlay the blue." All of
the blue appeared inside the gold. "It's a statistical anomaly."

Corrective measures had either not worked or been counterproductive, deduced Nejirt. Kon was going to be an interesting man to work for.

"As a young man I took such anomalies as my research project. It has always been assumed that these were random deviations. For my thesis in psychohistory I was going to prove that they were indeed random deviations." He grumbled. "I kept coming up with nonrandom correlations, not big ones, mind you, but big enough to pique my interest. As a young man I thought, in my naïveté, that my research would be welcome. My research has not been welcome and I am considered somewhat of a wild man, but I'm also conservative and I never step on toes bigger than mine, and I always make sure that good hunks of my work are orthodox. So I have a solid reputation, notably in refinements of the Founder's alexian tool to determine historical topozones. What would a region of intractable uncertainty mean to you?"

"Off the top of my head I would say that your blue sites have traits placing them adjacent to a local topozone surface," said Nejirt.

"I sent you to sniffing in such a region, one of my pet test sites, and you came back to tell me that astrology is the main countervailing force at work in Coron's Wisp. Do you believe that? I don't. Does it make sense?"

"No, sir."

"When I started my research, my measurements told me that it was only a twenty-percent probability that these regions were being *driven* toward the local topozone surface. Within the last year that probability has risen to ninety-five percent. What does that say to you?" Once any one of those regions spilled out of its topozone, the whole region became unpredictable.

"I'd suggest manipulation."

"Good. I like the directness of your mind. That's why I took you on my team. Damn few First Rank minds want to think about manipulation. They keep coming up with new natural psychological phenomena. I barf. A favorite is marginal effects of the fam that haven't yet been measured to the nth decimal place. I barf. Ninety-five percent. Think about it. That's no less than a declaration of war by someone. Some of those blue regions are going to go into crossover soon. We can still drive the social parameters back across the topozones into stability as we did after the Warlord Citizen of Lakgan bushwhacked us so many centuries ago with his tuned psychic probe. But chaos doesn't make for pleasant times. They should be avoided. Incidentally, your suggested method for counteracting the astrology that is penetrating into Coron's Wisp from Timdo won't be effective."

"Then you know something I don't know."

"Of course. At *every one* of the blue sites, there is a mask. At Coron's Wisp it is astrology. We have been unable, over the last hundred years, to control the historical direction of *any* of the regions in which a mask is operating. They become less and less controllable—and, in the last year, at an alarming rate. My young man, think. I need you as an ally. The men my age refuse to face the evidence. What force is powerful enough to parry the meddling of a psychohistorical organization which commands all of the resources of the Second Empire? Remember, we are a thriving, rich empire not in decline. Come. An answer to my question. Who would need to hide behind a mask?"

Prefect Cal Barna had already given Nejirt Kambu the answer in his morgue. "A group of renegade psychohistorians."

"Renegade is a perjurious word," admonished Second Rank Kon. "Recall that in the days of the First Empire, we were the renegades."

"Your surmise doesn't seem logical. We live in a political climate where the Fellowship attracts *all* talent capable of the psychohistorical science."

"So states the Founder's Plan, but in the Founder's Plan there was no tuned probe, no Cloun the Stubborn, and no quantum-state fams to alter human psychology. True, we've taken all this into account in the revised math. But don't be blinded by the past or by any past master's theory. Forty thousand years of science have taught us that much—if you look at its history and not at its magic rituals. Theory tells us that there *should not* be any non-Fellowship psychohistorians out there— but no other hypothesis fits the facts I have gathered, facts young men like you have helped me to gather."

"But your evidence is still circumstantial. A weird astrology allowing free will *could* be driving the events at Coron's Wisp. Your Hiranimus Scogil *could* be an astrologer . . ."

". . . and the jade ovoid he has been selling *could* be a galactarium. My agent at Melba tells me he has a friend who claims it holds the whole of the Founder's Plan up to the time of Cloun the Stubborn, that it is a handheld Prime Radiant—if one has the access codes."

Nejirt Kambu held on to the railing, looking out over a galaxy that spread itself under an ebony dome and floated above a slate stone floor. He could even see little people down there in the bailey who didn't belong in his galaxy. It was disconcerting.

"I can't find a source in all of psychohistorical theory for the origin of a second group of psychohistorians." Nejirt was bemused. "That doesn't mean it didn't happen but . . ."

"Chaos," said Kon. "Chaos can produce anything. Remember the chaos at the time of Cloun the Stubborn? Many of the parameters had been pushed well out of their topozones. There are rumors, stories, tales . . . first appearing perhaps a hundred years ago . . . a mythical hero . . . with mythical powers . . . but probably once a real man. He is said to have been on a quest during the dark following the False Revival. Smythos he is sometimes called. I think he must have been one of the fifty who were sacrificed to the death camps of the Fellowship to save our hides. I wish I had their names. *That* wasn't in the original Plan. Perhaps one of the prisoners escaped . . . perhaps he became deluded by his terrible trial and set upon his own course . . ."

"What sacrifice are you talking about?" Nejirt was genuinely puzzled.

"Never mind. It's ancient history. You don't have to believe me," sighed Hahukum Kon, "but just in case I'm right, you can help me save the Second Empire. I have damn few allies. I need bright young men who have proven their worth. It will take us a hundred years to destroy the machinations of the Third Fellowship, but it can be done."

"And if they get a hold here on Splendid Wisdom? If you are right, they are certainly trying."

"Jars Hanis is taking care of that. There *is* an underground. We had a lucky break while you were off planet and I believe that break led us to at least one non-Fellowship psychohistorian. It may lead us to others. I need hard evidence that they exist, dammit! Statistics convinces me, even rumor convinces me—but vapor doesn't seem to convince anyone else. Do you remember Eron Osa, Seventh Rank?"

"I don't recollect such a name."

"If you are ever going to make Second Rank, you'd better keep a list of all psychohistorians and their specialties in fam storage."

"Down to Seventh Rank?" anguished Nejirt with horror.

Kon laughed. "I do. My list has been a major element in my survival. Eron Osa was an old apprentice student of mine. His file is only a fam request away. I taught him all he knows about arekean transformations. He consumed biscuits and tea at the library. He was a history buff, more serious about the past than the future, a bit of a carouser and troublemaker, loved the underbelly of society. I had to give him his thesis subject, stasis, because he was too lazy to find a topic himself. He exasperated me but I was fond of him because of his brilliance. We were stuck together at a very boring conference one afternoon and I was telling him my troubles. I like to tell apprentices my troubles; in order to ingratiate themselves with me they spend hundreds of hours solving problems for which I need the solution but can't afford the time. He didn't want to bother but he was very good-natured about it and offered me an instant solution of the humorous kind. 'There are Gremlins out there in the Depths of Space who know enough psychohistory to bugger up your data.' That set me to thinking the impossible. I am eternally grateful to Eron Osa."

"You're meandering, sir. You were starting to tell me about a covert organization here on Splendid Wisdom. And a lucky break."

"Come into the office." Kon's office was behind them, five enormous rooms, staffed with researchers—and students working off their indemnity. The two men took aerochairs in a comfortable media theater. Kon called up an item from the Lyceum's secret library and dropped a burst into Nejirt's fam. "Read it someday. That was our lucky break."

Nejirt had his fam glance at the title. The usual pomposity. It was by Eron Osa. "Valuable data?"

"No, no." Kon shrugged. "The break came from a monitoring program that recorded and forwarded the readership of works keyed to psychohistorical research. Didn't you notice anything unusual about the title?"

"No."

"It was published in the Imperial Archive, not the Lyceum Archive. It's right there on the title credits. The readership of that piece was very specialized and ran to subversives."

"He published publicly?" Nejirt was incredulous.

"When Eron left me, a man of mere Second Rank, he took up slavedom with Jars Hanis because only a First Rank was good enough for him. Hanis is a very harsh taskmaster and a perfectionist but not the kind of daring mentor that Eron needed. After years of killing labor, Hanis rejected his thesis on the grounds that it needed reworking along more orthodox lines. Jars Hanis the Ruthless was critical of its free-flying. And Eron, being Eron, was insulted to the core and published in the public domain. There was always a streak of vanity in the boy."

Nejirt wiped rhetorical sweat from his brow. "What dungeon did Hanis throw him into?"

"Worse than that. Hanis put him on trial and managed to get a sentence of execution on his fam which was carried out in spite of many raised brows, including mine. It was a shame. A hot-tempered mind, true, but brilliant. Read his dissertation. Weak in spots, but nevertheless marvelous. It solved a few of my hairier problems. Nobody noticed it had been placed in the public domain—until the first time it was activated by a young noblewoman."

"One of the fakes?"

"Yes, yes. A Frightfulperson. You've heard of them."

"So the Archival alarms went off?"

"Like neutron stars colliding. Hanis was ready to arrest this lady immediately, but wiser minds prevailed, mine for instance, and she was only watched. That led to other subversives like a Hyperlord Kikaju Jama, and the Hyperlord led us to Hiranimus Scogil when he bought one of those magic astrological ovoids of yours. If the police hadn't bungled, we'd be working with our first prisoner of war, instead of with a corpse and a missing fam."

"Why do you think he's a psychohistorian and not a mystical astrologer? Astrology makes a simpler hypothesis."

Hahukum Kon shook his head. "Because Scogil wasn't selling to astrologers; he had a very different clientele. Statistical profile: ninety-five percent above eight-point-seven on the discontent scale."

"If there is a war going on in your blue regions, how serious is the penetration of Splendid Wisdom?"

"Don't worry about the underground; we have it all parametricized. Among a trillion people they have a maximum membership of about three hundred, all local. Recently they've organized an unusually large gathering, for them, to discuss Eron's paper. I have a sense of humor and have arranged for you to replace their math expert, a man so secretive that no one in the organization has ever met him except on wire. At that time the whole crowd will be arrested. I suspect our raid will mark the death blow to any perturbing forces here on Splendid Wisdom. We still have the rest of the galaxy to worry about; that will take more time. I'm getting old. I'm thinking of training you up to be my replacement. That depends upon how well you master military strategy."

10

At the moment of combat the zenoli soldier must be free of all prior thoughts and emotions. Priors always unbalance any thrust or response. Priors will kill you. Active preconceptions will kill you. Fixed intentions will kill you. Old emotions, grudges, resentments, angers, hatreds, loves, enthusiasms will kill you.

A soldier who enters combat hating his enemy is already a soldier doomed to failure; his hatred will blind him to the thrust that kills him or blind him in victory so that his victory is taken from him. A soldier who is afraid of his enemy is doomed. A soldier who loves his enemy is doomed. A soldier who is thinking about his enemy is doomed.

At the moment of combat the zenoli soldier is poised, inertialess, ready to act in any direction—like a marble at the top of a smooth multidimensional hill.

To achieve this null state of mind AT WILL the following eighteen brain-fam exercises are recommended . . .

—*The Zenoli Combat Manual*
edition 18
Founder's Era 873

They had traveled by devious route to the most alien place Eron had ever seen, and they were able to view it from the very roof of Splendid Wisdom, a prodigious gash beyond which the distant city-encrusted Coriander Mountains gleamed in metallic hues. The great quake shouldn't have destroyed as much as it did and it shouldn't have killed one hundred and eighty thousand people, but it was an old First Empire sector that had been salvaged during the rebuilding under the Pscholars. Minor structural damage from the Great Sack, unnoticed in the hurry of reconstruction, hadn't gone unnoticed by the later earthquake.

Out of the wreckage, construction engineers had already cleared a canyon to bedrock and below, a ravine too colossal for a single eye to encompass. Antlike teams of thousands were now strip-mining the tunneled fault block. Nothing had yet been rebuilt except for essential piping, transportation tubes, and a few giant weather towers that pumped water vapor into the atmosphere at the command of the central weather-control computers.

Most of the surviving structures on either side of the gash had been condemned and evacuated, services discontinued. These abysmal depths of abandoned city invited torch-carrying squatters—not many, for Splendid people were gregarious. Petunia seemed to know the place. She had been here before and they set up house in a stygian apartment that had to be illuminated with the occasional atomic torch hung about the walls.

Eron offered to help her reclaim the sewage and water systems of their chosen apartment—she declined. Her fam had inherited her mother's engineering know-how and she had been privy to such skills for thirteen years. He was still mostly inept. The repair was not an arduous task because all Splendid housing was erected around self-contained recycling units. Distant water reservoirs and central sewage just weren't practical on a planet of a trillion residents.

Living in a luxury dwelling without power and a functional manufacturum strained Eron's tolerance. They had to build a bed-nest out of abandoned curtains. They had to hike in food. They had to wash the same clothes over and over. They had to power the portable hyper-capsule receiver. The simplest tasks required time out for patches of wild ingenuity. Petunia didn't seem to mind the inconvenience—which would have led Eron to guess at barbarous origins if her engineering talent hadn't so shamed him.

She snuggled up with him in the curtains at the end of an exhausting day after voice-dimming the torches. "I've made a place for you away from the hubbub. You're safe from the police. But you haven't kept your end of the bargain," she accused. "You're to be talking with my dad!"

"Hiranimus and I aren't on speaking terms because of our differences . . . so to speak. That's just the way it is."

"Not so fast with your cliché drivel! We're burrowed in; now's work time. Let's take it from the top. You Pscholars were never mech adepts, right? You tell me why you and Dad can't chat and then I'll tell you why you're wrong. My people are an offshoot of the Crafters of the Thousand Suns of the Helmar Rift. My ancestors built the first tuned psychic probe on military contract with the Warlord of Lakgan. We built our own versions of the fam as a countermeasure to emotional control since before Cloun died. Maybe we even invented the fam. I know a few things about ghouls. Enough prologue. Why do you think you can't talk to my father?"

He looked at the dim ceiling and heard the un-Splendid silence broken only by her breathing. It was as if they were alone in the universe. "For the same reason telepathy never works."

"What's telepathy?"

"An old superstition. Never mind. Why can't I talk to your father? Any complex neural network can be trained in zillions of ways to think the same thought—each person thinks a thought in a unique way. A brain develops code to decipher its own thoughts, and no one else's. When organic brain and fam grow up together in co-communication they learn to talk to each other because they have spent time co-creating a shared code."

"Yaah! And the code is uncrackable and all that barf. I can zap your argument with one question. Are you ready to be dragged out of hyperspace?"

"Fire away."

She kissed him on the cheek. "Oh, my doomed wise man, all snuggled up in dusty old curtains, tell me then, why is it that you and I, each thinking his mundane thoughts with his own unique and undecipherable code, are right this very moment talking to each other without any trouble? Ha!" She punched him in the arm.

He couldn't see her smile but he knew it was there. She *had* derailed his logic. Language. Telepathy was impossible—but as a child her mind had built a unique translator between her thoughts and the Galactic Standard tongue. She translated "Petunia" thoughts into Galactic Standard sentences; he took her Galactic Standard sentences and, using his own unique translator, recorded them into "Eron" thoughts, which he could understand. Neat.

"Do your people talk to ghouls?" he asked incredulously.

"No," she replied with sadness. "My grief goads me. I *want* to talk to him."

"What would you say?"

"I'd ask him how to get out of this predicament."

"Why not ask me, instead of bossing me around?"

"You're a criminal. You don't know beans from turnips."

"I'm a bona-fide psychohistorian, albeit a handicapped one. That means, at the least, that I have a very good organic brain, even if it is criminal. Do you want your father's fam sent to a safe place?" He was desperately looking for a common goal. "I'm probably better able to get us out of our fix than any astrologer."

"You're a psychohistorian? Of the Fellowship?" she said, aghast.

He had never bothered to mention that detail. "And a criminal," he added.

Petunia began to pound her skull with both fists. "Space, am I stupid. Of course Dad wanted you to take over his fam!"

"Why?"

"Do you think I'd tell you? You're *worse* than a criminal. Now I've got to figure a way to make you *his* slave! You're *fried meat* if I ever catch you sleeping! I'm already conjuring dire fam adjustments. Maybe I should just cocoon-tie you right now and get to it, if I only had some string. Talk to my dad! That's a direct order!"

Did men who had been bonded in slavery go mad when they were given impossible orders? It amazed him how relentlessly his mind worked; it was actually beginning to apply itself to the problem. "Let's do a weakness analysis of the isolated fam; I'll be in charge of the math, you handle the technical aspects."

A fam was designed as an intelligent but passive helper. The initiative lay with the organic brain, which had millions of years of evolution behind its behavior. Initiative was critical to survival. Scogil's fam would lack initiative as an entity separate from Scogil. But it would still be thinking and scheming.

A memory came to him of the ornate hall in which he had taken his zenoli training; young men embrace fervently their fads for ancient wisdom, perhaps to revitalize, in the safety of a cathedral, times when men lived dangerously. Zenoli was all about fam-mind integration. Long after

Petunia had gone to sleep he lay in the dark, deep in meditation, recalling what he could of this arcane wisdom, trying to reconstruct what he couldn't. What was useful to him now, what was not?

He kept cycling back to the zenoli way of drawing out a passive opponent. It required absolute mental silence. He wondered if he could still create that state—the roiling positive image from his organic mind overlaid by a soothing negative image created and projected by the fam until all thought went quiescent. Had he attained enough control over his new fam to do that? He tried unsuccessfully.

In the morning—which meant torches and shadows—Petunia brewed him tea. "Did you pick up anything?"

"No. My mind was too active. Hiranimus may be thinking—but he's off in a corner muttering to himself and not trying to trigger anything I can understand. He won't even know that I'm listening."

"You're discouraged," she reproached.

"Sure. I'm trying to get my fam to broadcast a negative thought field and it wavers. Too much of my stuff gets through. I've been zenoli-adapted—but my fam hasn't."

She grinned. "That's a built-in utility. You've got an advanced model. I told you—we're the best fam builders in the galaxy. Brain shutdown is easy. A fam doesn't have to read a thought to blank it. I'll give you the code." She wiggled her fingers gaily. "But be careful with the wake-up routine you choose—don't put yourself into a full coma. Or else I'll have to rescue you!" She finished her tea and stood. "Got to go. Scrounge time."

Eron was stunned at how well the commands worked. After half an hour he had a fully quiescent mind. He could even blank his visual field with his eyes open. But nothing happened for hours. Until . . .

Something noticed that his intention lay dormant, that he wasn't calling on any of his fam's critical abilities. Suddenly a set of math equations formed—and activated. It was weird to watch the standard routines of his fam set about solving a problem that he hadn't posed. He didn't even know what the problem was. Vigilantly he observed and recorded. Long silences, to which he was not privy, were followed by spates of mathematical calculation in a half-familiar, half-alien notation. Contact. Scogil was an accomplished mathist, trapped in a dark brig, alone, writing on the walls to keep himself sane.

Eron stirred himself. He took a torch and wandered through the abandoned city, pensively. When he came to a section that had been broken off and half welded shut by the demolition crews, he clambered outside along the side of the catacombed canyon and found a perch. Imperialis was low in the sky, casting purple shadows. Aridia, in crescent, was rising to the east. How fragile Splendid Wisdom seemed among this jumble and open firmament.

He was mulling over the math that had passed across his mind, unable to question a deaf Hiranimus. The doodling contained clear traces of the Founder's Hand, anachronisms even, yet there were odd twists of thought and notation, an intriguing surmise, and one brilliant shortcut that astonished Osa. Scogil had to be a psychohistorian who had been cut off from the main line of development for centuries.

And he rides my back! There was joy in the assertion.

Home again, he found a Personal Capsule waiting for him in the receiver. The message read: "I have found you! Irregulars of the Regulation will be discussing your dissertation at the Orelian Masked Ball." He skipped details of location and time. "Important that you be there. Wear a black fur mask, tri-horned with red eyes, template 212, Orelian Masks Cat-#234764. I will be the one in blue scales with plumes and an upper jaw sprouting crocodile teeth. Sorry I ran. My name can wait." Included with the message was a fine-print manuscript of his precious work.

Eron smiled and relaxed. The beautiful Frightfulperson. Suddenly more alien mathematics began to stream into his mind. He froze attentively. Hours later when he broke from zenoli trance, Petunia was sitting in front of him, legs twined. "Anything?"

"One-way contact."

"With my dad?"

"When I withdraw into zenoli mute-mind he seems to be able to use the utilities. I can't tap his thinking, but I certainly *can* watch his call-ups."

She was excited. "Do you think *he* can watch *your* call-ups?"

"No. Different architecture. His call-ups are *supposed* to be available to me. But my call-ups are only backloaded to the fam through my cognition codes. That's the problem with me being the priority mind."

She shrugged. "We've got to set up two-way comm. Otherwise the conversation will be as futile as broadcast video." She emitted an unpleasant bleating sound. "I've been scrounging something that might work." She held up a five-node keyboard for the right hand. "These are hard to come by on Splendid Wisdom. We use them all the time. You've already learned five-finger typing."

Eron frowned. "He can't read my fingers; he isn't connected to the utilities the same way I am—and he can't see through my eyes no matter what kind of typeface I build for him."

Petunia grinned. "Yaah, the code. I know. Keep it simple, Mommy always said. Dad knows the Helmar binary code for the augmented Galactic Standard alphabet."

"Augmented alphabet?"

"We augment everything. It's a tinkerer's disease. Now, listen. Dad's ghoul *can* read your mind; it's just your private code that's boggling him. So we use the signal that carries the code and modulate it with a couple of transducers for your skull." She showed him a handful of circular plates stripped out of a psychic probe. "Quick and dirty."

Eron paled. "That's going to introduce errors into my thinking, maybe bad ones. How am I to carry on a rational conversation while I'm distracted by, say, the odor of colors?"

"You'll survive." She cocked her head. "If not, I can always scrounge another slave. But I know what I'm doing. I've fooled with this stuff—meaning my school chums and I. It's better than drugs. We had to stop when Mommy caught us. Don't worry! Neural networks are wonderful for their error-correcting robustness. You look robust to me."

"Why don't we try some kind of transduction on the fam directly?" Eron pleaded hopefully.

"And violate its shielding? You want to *destroy* my dad? You're forgiven. I know you Splendid psychohistorians are tech dummies."

When they had the device rigged, Eron simply finger-typed a Galactic Standard message. The haywire then translated so that his mind wogged in Helmar binary flashes. It was awful. Just typing *hello* was like being kicked out of a high-flying aerocraft without a grav-chute.

Hello. Use the math utilities to reply. Hello . . . When he could no longer stand his binary broadcasting, he went into zenoli mute-mind to listen. Calm again, he tried typing the alphabet—and blasting his mind with the binary output of Petunia's device. He listened. He broadcast. He waited. He tapped on the walls of his ghoul's dungeon. It was during a meal anxiously prepared by Petunia that the reply came via the symbol generator of the math utilities.

To whom . . .

Eron, impatient with the slowness of the communication, typed, *Eron Osa.* Suppressing his excitement, he returned to his zenoli calmness.

A pause. The symbol generator began to write across Eron's visual cortex in a happy yellow typeface, *Your benefactor is pleased that his last desperate gesture was of assistance to you. What remains of Hiranimus Scogil is at your service—minus various endearing biological quirks. How much psychohistory does the rebel Eron Osa remember?*

Thus began a remarkable conversation between two crippled minds.

11

Q: Do the equations demand that the monitoring Psychohistorians remain hidden indefinitely?

A: No. Adherence to the Founder's Plan provides that the establishment of a Second Galactic Empire will coincide with a political operandi in which Mankind understands the benefit of being governed by Mental Science. At that time invisibility may be cast aside with the proviso that the Laws of Psychohistory themselves cannot be revealed.

Q: Why the proviso?

A: The Laws are statistical in nature and are rendered invalid if the actions of individual men are not random in nature. If a sizable group of human beings were to learn key details of how their future political situation was being predicted, their actions would be governed by that knowledge and would no longer be random.

Q: How is such concealment of the Laws to be maintained?

A: A galaxy approaching a population of one hundred quadrillion will produce less than a hundred humans per billion with the mathematical, emotional, and ethical abilities necessary for the mastering of Mental Science. Many models, notably those of su'Kle and Giordom, indicate ways to attract all such talent into the ruling class.

—The First Speaker Questions a Student: Notes made during the Crisis of the Great Perturbation, fourth century Founder's Era

After the ghoul of Scogil warned Eron against attending any clandestine caucus of the Regulation, Osa prudently investigated the Orelians. Old when Imperialis was an unexplored border system, Orelia was ancient, its denizens of three airless worlds necessarily master builders of sprawling airtight cities. The latter-day Orelians of Splendid Wisdom weren't really Orelians anymore; they were the descendants of an imported construction crew who had stayed on after the great rebuilding—nostalgic in their lingering memory of a distant home's wild carnival. They were harmlessly apolitical and glad to invite moneyed fun-loving non-Orelians to join their masked revelry.

Scogil's vehement harangue was to no avail once his capricious daughter sided with Eron. Because a fam personality was the more subservient one, the ghoul acquiesced to Eron's carnival adventure as a second-best survival strategy. The man found it easy to humor what he suspected were his ghoul's exaggerated fears; in his psychohistorical research he had always delighted in making allowances for the remotest of probabilities.

He sent Petunia on a day's trip to pick up supplies from an arms cache known to her dad—illegal weapons that didn't trigger a police report when activated, some personal force shields. He knew a little shop where she could buy special sensors. She also acquired an edition of the zenoli manuals for burst loading. Eron chose from them the martial utilities he thought he might need, the ones his organic mind had practiced with diligence during the hide-and-seek days of his Lyceum capers.

Eron was eager to spread the message of his thesis, subversively if that was the only vehicle of expression that his ex-mentor would allow. He was still angry at Jars. If First Rank Jars Hanis opted to crush with focused force, his student could now counter with a light wind spread over an endless weather front.

On the day of the ball he stationed Petunia at a safe distance, her duty to monitor the movements of his fam. If things went awry, she had her instructions. He was finding her sense of adventure marvelous. She had refused her father's ardent plea to flee Splendid Wisdom with Eron in tow, and because he was her slave, he was indebted to her for this concession to his ego.

Brazenly he arrived by pod at the front entrance. Inside, the pillared hall of many chambers and stairwells was done in gold leaf and inlay. The masks were everywhere. He found himself looking for that blue-scaled mask with crocodile teeth and plumes—the unnamed Frightful-person he couldn't resist even though she might place his life in danger.

But first, in a nondescript mask of his own design, cognizant of his ghoul's stern warning, he cased the three stories of the hall for exits, memorizing forty in all. This was not a place meant to be easily guarded. Good. The exits led from stairways or gardens, from an administrative corridor or a servant's chute or a supply tunnel. He left unobtrusive shaped charges primed to open locked exits and hid sensors that had been his favorite tool of surprise during the wild zenoli games at the Lyceum. He programmed his fam to optimize a retreat under any circumstance. A pod, brainwashed by Petunia, sat waiting at a siding.

The precautions made him wonder at his daring, but Eron Osa was aware that vanity disparaged danger. He was vain. He was proud. There were men interested in his psychohistorical research after years of his working alone! He had rediscovered his monograph with the help of his fam's marvelous math utilities and the wry but encouraging insights of Scogil. Because he recalled the barest details of writing it, his recent study was like stumbling across another man's astonishing work and becoming an instant disciple. His old style now seemed quaintly conservative to him. He had become ebulliently enthusiastic for his old cause. Pleasing a luminary like Jars Hanis was no longer a priority. Scogil's dire warnings did not damp his zeal. He wriggled his nose at common sense.

And love! At the bottom of a flared stairwell he spotted the crocodile teeth of his Frightfulperson in her simple gown. He turned immediately into an empty toilet to change into his black-furred, tri-horned, red-eyed mask. Perhaps this time, with fam utilities to assist him, he wouldn't make such a fool of himself in her delightful presence!

Before he could descend the stairs, two gentle fingers and a thumb grasped his wrist. They belonged to a coiffured man of elaborate costume and ebony mechanical mask able to mock all human expressions grotesquely. "Ah, our esteemed speaker for the evening," said a voice from out of a rhapsodic smile. "You mimic well the Orelian verve."

"Have we been introduced?"

"No, it is in the nature of my associates to remain invisible, but my elegance betrays me as a Hyperlord. You may address me thus."

"I was to contact . . ."

"No, I am your contact." The gentle pull of his three-pointed grip steered Eron away from the stairs toward the banquet tables. "I have a special interest in your presence. The impetuous mermaid of the Calmer Sea can wait. You are here by *my* invitation. But first, the food."

The tables were covered with exquisite bowls of delicacies, both imported and manufactured, steaming pots with lids and ladles, breads, flowering vines for decoration. A man beside Eron, defaced by a huge papier-mâché nose, poured himself soup. They took their food to a dim raised alcove with a convenient teapoy that supplied hot drinks and a stand for their plates.

While Eron kept an eye cocked for his Frightfulperson, the Hyperlord ate with restrained gusto. "You're a—shall I say the word—psychohistorian? A rebel on the run?" These were rhetorical questions, because the lord at once produced from his purse a jade ovoid with the five-fingered key-pattern that Petunia favored. "This is a bauble I was sold—quite expensive. It casts stars and astrological charts and other such arcane drivel. I was told confidentially that it contains a complete working model of the Founder's Prime Radiant. But my peddler disappeared with my credits before giving me the codes. Perhaps you have the codes? Or," he added wryly, "perhaps you can tell me if I am a naive collector of psychohistorical memorabilia who has been grievously duped?"

Eron took the ovoid in his left hand and with the right in his pocket, typed out a message to his blind companion. While he meditated upon the jade, he received his reply. *You are talking to Hyperlord Kikaju*

Jama. He is a danger to you. Leave this place immediately. The ovoid is indeed a miniature replica of the Prime Radiant current at the time of Cloun the Stubborn. I have the codes to activate it since I sold it to Jama days prior to my demise. I repeat, Jama is under police surveillance.

Eron slipped the smooth ovoid back into the Hyperlord's hand. "I'll give you a demonstration after my talk. It is a genuine Prime Radiant, but I warn you, it is a thing difficult even for a good mathematician to use and read."

The Hyperlord's mechanical black mask twisted into a triumphant grimace. "I have the mathist who will use it once you show him how."

Two hands took his horns from behind. "We meet again," said the familiar voice. When he looked up he saw the smile of broad lips beneath the crocodile teeth and plumes. The Frightfulperson of his dreams.

Man and woman wandered back together to the meeting chamber. A sloping floor. Two exits at the top. Two exits at the bottom on each side of the podium. A small holobeam room behind the podium. "Let's walk while we wait for our audience. I'd like to thank you in private for salvaging my life's work." He found the wall behind the holobeam room and placed a wall-breaker without her knowing what he was doing. One could always distract the eyes with pleasant chitchat. A couple of sensor drops later, he wrapped a bejeweled belt around her waist. It was a personal force field generator built somewhere in the Thousand Suns of the Helmar Rift in imitation of an old Periphery design pioneered during the Interregnum, more elaborately disguised than the belt he wore to hold up the pants of his own costume. She didn't have to know; he could activate her defenses at any time.

"Thank you. And you don't even know my name."

"Your Hyperlord friend called you a Mermaid of the Calmer Sea."

"I'm half fish, half fowl to him. You may call me Otaria."

"I wasn't certain I'd be here tonight. I'm not sure of your security." That wasn't true. *Scogil* wasn't sure of the security. "If I suddenly decide to move fast, it will be for a good reason. Follow me instantly."

"Our security is the best. The Hyperlord has been in this business a long time."

"And you trust me?"

"You're desperate, like we are," she said.

"I don't understand your desperation."

She smiled and in the lonely corridor, tipped up her crocodile teeth so that he could see her face. "It's an intellectual desperation. That can be as terrible as not having a fam or a house or food or air. I notice you have a new fam."

"Black-market. I like its math utilities."

"You're more sure of yourself."

"Of course."

While they walked back to the meeting, his fam read the scattered sensors. Nothing. Scogil was probably sweating in his dungeon for naught. A hand in his pocket typed a reassuring *All's well.*

Ushers were already at the entrances. Snooper dampers were in place. The black-masked Hyperlord brought the meeting to order and was enthusiastic in his sedition. He introduced Eron Osa as the prophet of a New Interregnum, the real one, the one that the Founder had delayed.

It wasn't that simple. But Eron spoke anyway. He dispensed with his tri-horned mask. He was here as Eron Osa. His specialty was the historical forces that led to instability—and unpredictable events.

He sketched for them the undulating topozones of historical phase space and how their multidimensional surfaces were calculated. A topozone's surface was the boundary between stability and chaos. While measurable social vectors remained inside their topozones, the sweep of the future could be foretold. But once these parameters moved across their abstract confines in any region of the galaxy, the future became uncertain for that locale. Then, like wildfire, unchecked chaos could rage in a sudden conflagration, perhaps across the galaxy—or die out for no apparent cause.

Psychohistorians were like firefighters. They could hose down areas, set standards and regulations, insure that fire never started. But there was danger in never having a fire. Flammables accumulated; when they went, whole regions went with them in an inferno at the whim of the wind. Stasis was the danger. Deadwood accumulated during stasis. Stable topozones collapsed in upon stasis like a wet forest drying out under months of sun.

Precise psychohistorical monitoring, with a single future as the goal, a Plan, could drive the social parameters safely inward from the chaos-touching boundaries of the historical topozone, but like a single kind of weather, such a relentless sun might dry out the forest and set the stage for a topozone collapse, followed by a fire, a conflagration, an interregnum. Eron detailed why no monolithic organization with a single mind could easily plan a history to suit everyone. The unsatisfied gathered slowly in the byways, spiritually dying, finally to become tinder.

The Founder faced such a situation. The stasis of the First Empire had become so great that unpredictable historical chaos could be its only consequence. His best mathematics was blinded by turbulent visions of fire. He could not predict into the Interregnum. All he could do was find a distant firebreak, where the stars were thin, and set up a race of fire-men who could build around themselves an expanding topozone of sta-bility that slowly moved out to control the flames and replant the ashes. Inside that topozone he could predict.

Now conditions were different. Psychohistorical monitoring, itself, in the absence of psychohistorical knowledge, was creating the stasis. Eron had difficulty explaining this thesis to an audience composed of illiterates who had been forbidden to learn the elements of social predic-tion lest chaos prevail. He had to fall back on analogy.

Osa asked his masked group to consider a murderer swinging an ax at the head of his victim.

The victim judges the trajectory of the ax and predicts that it will divide his skull. He ducks. This falsifies his prediction, thus proving that predicting is a waste of effort, right?

Osa asked his listeners to consider a primitive planetary economy about to fall into economic disaster.

Suppose each citizen of the planet is capable of predicting the disas-ter by a cause-and-effect deduction—then it won't happen. The proph-ecy fails, thus telling us that the ability to predict is useless—right?

On the other hand, suppose only one citizen has enough grasp of economics to predict the nature of the disaster. This single man is in no position to prevent the catastrophe—but he *can* use his knowledge to profit from it. He can carve out a fortune and from that commanding position dominate the new economy to be built on the ashes of the old. Prediction is then useful when it serves the interest of an elite who can predict—right?

Osa asked the assembly to consider a galaxy about to fall into war and ignorance and chaos.

Suppose all men have the psychohistorical knowledge to predict a disaster abhorrent to them, and to identify their coming part in it—then it won't happen. The prediction fails, thus invalidating the methods of psychohistory and making them useless, right?

On the other hand, suppose a group of Pscholars have enough grasp of psychohistory to see into the nature of the imminent galactic disaster. Suppose this tiny group is able to apply minute forces at critical places so that a thousand years later they are in a commanding position to domi-nate the new order they have created from the rubble of the old. They have lied about their presence, hiding from the rest of us while they ac-cumulate power and special privilege. They remain misers with their methodology, unwilling to share their predictions. But their predictions come true. Psychohistory works only when it serves the benevolent self-interest of an elite, right?

Eron ended his speech with an outburst. "Psychohistory has served the interests of the Pscholars for too long! They lie to us in a self-serving way when they say that the gift of knowledge will drive us from paradise! Let the tools of psychohistory serve the needs of the galactic peoples! Let us negotiate our own future, not live out a future designed by men who hoard the tools of design!"

Before Eron was even seated, the masked Hyperlord rose. He held a jade ovoid high in his hand. "I have here a Prime Radiant! It holds the secrets of psychohistory for us to tap. Copies of the Prime Radiant are for sale! Eron Osa has promised us a demonstration!" He looked over toward another man who approached the podium in an iron mask, and then to Eron. "Here is the mathist I promised you, my boy." The crowd waited in anticipation.

But Eron had been questioning his ghoul and was primed for an answer—there is no better state of general awareness than a zenoli pause—and what he saw from the corner of his eyes put him on instant danger alert. Under the iron mask of Kikaju Jama's mathist was Nejirt Kambu.

Kambu was blissfully unconscious of his fame among the amorphous young students of the Lyceum who envied his rise as a top field operative. Osa had read (and now couldn't remember) every report written by Kambu. The memory gap didn't matter. It was Eron's wetware that specialized in faces, jawlines, gestures, gait. How many hundreds of times had he envied Kambu from a position of anonymity? And Kambu was not a rebel. Why was he here? A quick fam check of the planted sensors detected a suspicious pattern of movements outside the caucus chamber. Suspiciously like a police raid.

"I'll have to set up a holo demo," he said quickly. Then to Otaria, "Help me." He took her into the holobeam booth behind the podium, closed the soundproof entrance, activated their shields, and detonated the "spare door" behind him. At the same time he saw the police enter through all four portals. An usher raised a forbidden blaster. The police reacted.

Only one detail of the carnage registered: Kikaju Jama's mask flying from a headless body. Then they were through the imploded wall and gone, following the optimal escape path that Eron's fam spawned with graphic overlays. They reached the doctored pod and were two kilometers along their way to freedom before a police dragnet grabbed them in a vise that killed their power. Eron made a quick assessment. "We surrender," he said to Otaria. "No choice. Don't make a move till they settle down."

Otaria saw the hidden men, blasters drawn. "They'll kill your fam again. And mine, too."

"That's the optimistic scenario." Eron turned the pod's frequency to the police band and spoke loudly and clearly. "Truce. We are ready to surrender. We have personal force shields." He wanted them to know about the shields. "We have weapons which we do not intend to use." While he was calming and cautioning the police, he typed out a quick briefing for Scogil, minus the apology he would give when he had the time.

Scogil replied by ordering Eron to order Petunia off planet immediately. No chance of that. She would stay until she knew her dad's ghoul was dead—or free. Her location readings on his fam must have already given her the cue that they wouldn't be home for supper. At this moment she was probably fabricating wild media releases about the Orelian affair.

The pod's speaker suddenly blared with a police response. "Truce accepted. We have a negotiator on the way. The esteemed Third Rank Nejirt Kambu. Please maintain open communications. Over."

"Who is Kambu?" Otaria whispered.

"He was *posing* as Kikaju's man. Thank space he's not associated with my nemesis." Meaning Jars Hanis. "We'll certainly have to find out *who* employs Kambu." On the off chance that Scogil knew, he asked.

The reply scrolled across Eron's visual cortex in purple script. *Nejirt Kambu works for Second Rank Hahukum Kon. . . .*

Kon! What a small world! He tried to recall his first mentor. Admiral Kon. The kids all called him that though he dressed like a mechanic.

. . . the trouble I have taken to escape interrogation by Kon. Death is preferable. I must tell you that I have a bomb in me and I will use it. I have no intention of being the first prisoner taken by Kon.

Sorry, typed Eron, *Rigone has already nixed your bomb.* Abruptly he abandoned Scogil to his dungeon because . . .

Nejirt Kambu was arriving on the scene, well guarded. He and Eron spoke to each other from a respectful distance via their pod's electronics, Kambu first. "I have already noted that a famless psychohistorian is wearing the fam of the late agent, Hiranimus Scogil. I have deduced the remarkable fact that you are in communication with the man's ghost since your discussion this evening went beyond the scope of your original dissertation, rambling into recent galactic history—about which a Seventh Rank would know nothing. You possess certain facts which you could have obtained only from an enemy of the Second Empire."

"I'm being accused of treason?"

"No. You may be a traitor, but you're being offered a deal by your old teacher—protection from Jars Hanis and a new top-of-the-pick fam in exchange for the one you are wearing."

"He's wired with a suicide bomb over which I have no control."

"Ah. You are his hostage?"

"No," said Eron vehemently.

"You offer stalemate? We both sit here until we starve?"

"No. I'm dealing. You want to interrogate Scogil. I can talk to him. We talk; I keep Scogil. We talk with Hahukum Kon present. That's the deal. My Frightfulfriend comes with me and she stays with me. You get our weapons now as a gesture of good faith."

"A reasonable man. Thank you for the weapons. As a reciprocal gesture of good faith I will allow you to keep your shields. They are not a threat to us. I look forward to your stories about our mad Admiral."

12

TAMIC SMYTHOS: . . . born 351 Founder's Era . . . no childhood record until 366 F.E., when he was brought to the Splendid Lyceum by his Scav godfather with a self-taught mathematics talent . . . not an outstanding student . . . volunteered for the group of fifty martyrs, 374 F.E., during the Speakerhood of . . . transported to . . . captured in 377 F.E. at the end of the Lakganian War during the deception arranged by . . . escaped massacre of the seven at . . . sterilized and interned on Zoranel with the surviving forty-three martyrs by the edict of . . . Tamic Smythos spent his prison years on Zoranel, where the stars were thin and the hyperships infrequent, reconstructing in secret the Founder's Prime Radiant as an act of defiance . . . false death certificate in 386 F.E. . . . smuggled off Zoranel for predictive work by corrupt Mayor Linus, 386 F.E., who sought advantages in owning the only psychohistorian . . . disappeared . . . no record until 406 F.E., when he settled on Horan of the Thousand Suns of the Helmar Rift to take up mechanical engineering . . . In later life he joined (or founded) the colony at . . . had no children or family or close friends . . . refused to teach . . . morbid recluse . . . His extensive hoard of psychohistorical memorabilia and personal writings, including a diatribe against the organizers of the martyrdom, was only discovered in a tailor's warehouse 217 years after his death, by a computer-talented anarchist looking for a cause.

—Quick File of Galactic Biographies:
Edition 1898 F.E.

The arrest provided by Hahukum Kon was lavish. Locked in a suite fit for a Pscholar of the First Rank (all six rooms hastily outfitted to absorb a bomb explosion) Osa-Scogil and Otaria were treated as honored prisoners. They were allowed no visitors and no news.

Still, as the days passed, Eron chuckled at the thought of media mischief surely implemented by now. Rumors about a second group of psychohistorians would be multiplying rampantly all over Splendid Wisdom; he had done the psychomathematical diffusion estimate on the spread of the stories that Petunia was to distribute in case of his failure to return from the masked ball. The stories were designed to be passed by word of mouth with a high mutation factor and a ridiculous longevity.

Both prisoners were questioned often, but their polite interrogator pressed no topic they did not wish to pursue. In counterpoint, Nejirt Kambu arrived every day in the afternoon but did not question. Philosophical discourse seemed to be his main pursuit. He was witty, if conservative, and Otaria took pleasure in needling him. Eron was frustrated by their discussions. Nejirt was one of these men of great integrity who believed firmly in his duty as a member of the elite to give good government, but a blockhead on the subject of the right of a vassal of the Empire to negotiate his own future. He genuinely believed that a man untrained in psychohistory was a danger to himself and needed benevolent guidance.

These debates left no doubt that Nejirt Kambu was a brilliant Pscholar of the breed who knew how to modify futures to fit a plan. When on the theme of directed change, he lost his conservative veneer and became a wild player who had mastered all the tricks of discreet historical manipulation.

In the evening, the prisoners were given time to themselves. There was little to do but cook and talk and eat. Left alone with his two companions, Eron found that as a trio they had a love of history in common.

The forces that drove history were Eron's obsession.

Otaria balanced this view with a lighter touch more interested in the inner energy that motivated mortal man over the vast span of galaxy and time.

Scogil was a game player with psychohistory as the rule book and a future as the winnings. Non-zero-sum, of course. Eron had never been asked to think that way before. To him psychohistory had always meant a single benign future determined by a single monolithic organization, i.e. history from the Imperial point of view. A trap. He was becoming very fond of Scogil's mind as well as exasperated by his angry ghoul.

It was a week before Eron noticed that Second Rank Hahukum Kon must be setting them up for a grand entrance. He had a style. He wanted to make sure that Eron Osa knew that Kon had power and that Kon chose to exercise his power in a very different mode than did First Rank Jars Hanis. There was to be no relentless bullying, no ultimatum, no draconian solutions. Why had Eron ever left the Admiral to study under Jars?

When the curmudgeon finally came to visit, he entered with a tray of biscuits and tea from the commissary near the Lyceum study carrels. How could it be possible for him to have cared to remember *that* about one of his more obscure students? Eron smiled. But he still felt merciless. It was all a serious military campaign to this crusty old Admiral. Kon wasn't going to enjoy defeat.

"Good that you found time to see us, sir."

"And you, Eron, you've been acting more like an ambassador for the heathens than a prisoner of war," admonished Kon.

"I *am* an ambassador. I've come here to accept the surrender of the Second Empire." Scogil would blanch at that, if he still had a body.

A startled Kon blinked for a moment before recovering. "Unfortunately I've not brought my sword." He grinned and grumbled. "I believe there will be another hundred years of hard war before we get to a finale. Youth equals impatience." By war Eron knew he meant psychohistorical corrective action. Kon built intricate scale models of the immense First Empire dreadnoughts of the old Grand Fleet—but to win *his* battles he had never ordered into combat even the lightest of the Second Empire's hypercruisers. He wielded more power than any First Empire admiral could have hoped to amass.

"A hundred-year war? You'll lose that way," said Eron. "Sometimes it is better to begin polite negotiations a century before a major defeat."

Kon stared at Eron's face. "You're serious. By space, you're dead serious!" He turned to Otaria in her floating recliner. "You've thrown in with a madman!" He turned back to Eron. "I'll have you on the rack! I'll squeeze what I want out of that homunculus on your back!" He sat down and ate a biscuit. "Eron, be serious. You know that fighting a hundred years down the line—and winning—is something we do all the time."

"Against an enemy who is countering you with his own psychohistorical ploys?" countered Eron.

"That's why we *have* to interrogate this Scogil of yours. He's the first enemy psychohistorian we've ever captured. You promised to cooperate." His voice became quietly ominous. "Have you changed your mind?"

"No. What better way to interrogate him than to play a psychohistorical war game? Your staff here are the galaxy's experts on deviations from the Fellowship's planned future history. Osa-Scogil hereby challenges you and your whole staff to a hundred-year-war game. It shouldn't take more than a couple of months. You can't win, sir."

"I do believe you *have* lost your mind."

"Scogil thinks so, too, but he's stuck with me. And I'm stuck with you. Recall that I was valiantly attempting to avoid you when apprehended. You accept my challenge then? What you get out of it is to see Scogil in action."

"There are only two of you. *I* couldn't get along with a staff of two."

"It's enough. The war is already over. I can play out the endgame in my head. You've lost. Now it's time to settle before you've lost everything."

Kon was beginning to be intrigued by Eron's boldness. "Your criteria of victory?"

"The immutable laws of psychohistory." Eron deadpanned the cliché.

"You young scupper rat! I've been applying the laws of psychohistory successfully since before you were born!"

"No," said Eron, enjoying himself. "You've been using blasters and atomic grenades against bows and arrows. Your army doesn't have to know much strategy. Remember, *your* army is the one that executes the fam of any man who is willing to sell blasters to the warriors with the bows and arrows. Now I have to take off a few minutes to consult with Hiranimus. You'll excuse me." He left the room.

Otaria shifted herself to Eron's seat. "He's an unusual man."

Kon grumbled. "He was always like that. Impossible. I thought a new fam might rattle his bones a bit. He actually talks to the ghoul of this Scogil?"

"To me it looks like he's talking to himself. It's a ponderous chat they share."

"Do you think what remains of Scogil can actually play at psychohistory? Is this proposal of Osa's for real?"

Otaria looked at her long hands wistfully. "Eron thinks highly of the abilities of Scogil's ghoul, more so than the ghoul does of himself. I don't know. His ghost seems to be missing much of Scogil's judgment and fire—but I don't talk to him directly. Have you ever met an engineer turned salesman of a technical product line? Do you *really* think you've caught a major psychohistorian? Scogil was a *salesman!* That's what he did best. He knew more about my organization, the one you raided, than I did myself—because he was selling to it. You *think* you got us all." There was malice in her voice. "I even thought you had us all!" She smiled and said no more, and Kon knew he would get no more short of torture.

"Sorry about the Hyperlord."

"I'll bet you are. He was crazy as a coot—but there were times when I loved him."

Kon brought out a jade ovoid. "He would have wanted you to have this." He handed the egg to Otaria. "We have forty others already."

"And you still can't play it?" Otaria fumbled with the ovoid. Stars burst forth that melted into charts. "Would you like your fortune read?" She made up one glibly. "Compromise with your enemies before stubbornness brings you disaster. That's your reading for the day."

Kon leaned over, fascinated. "I've seen Nejirt do something similar. How did you do that?"

She fumbled again—and the equations of the Founder began to scroll across a darkened air, symbolically describing what once had been future history but was now ancient history. "Can Nejirt do *that?* I doubt it. Scogil gave me lessons at the ovoid's deeper levels. I recently asked him, through Eron, why he hid behind astrology. He said it was a simple way of giving people permission to hope that they can control their lives. You Pscholars have destroyed our willingness to predict and to choose which of our predicted futures we want to live. We have become fatalists. You choose for us!"

"We run good government. Our methodology doesn't speak to individuals," he admonished.

"If either of those statements were true," she flared, "I wouldn't be here in your comfortable prison!"

"And when the astrology doesn't work?"

"What's then to stop a failed astrologer from moving on to psychohistory? You? With your secret hoard of knowledge in your Lyceum archives?"

Eron returned, but he remained standing, even began to pace. "Scogil and I have come to an agreement after much argument. He will allow himself to act as the opposition command center if the interrogative questions come in the form of a realistic game with the initial conditions those of the galaxy as they stand today as determined by the Fellowship. He points out that, since he is not a command center and never was, errors will be introduced. At the end of each simulated year, we must assume that the outcomes with the highest probability have happened."

"And you thnink you and your homuculus are a match for my whole staff?" Kon had weakened. His voice and his expression said that he was willing to accept the challenge. But he was incredulous.

Eron let himself smile softly. There was no way he could *tell* the Admiral what a predicament he faced. At present, the main tactic of Scogil's mysterious people was to pump out, from as many spigots as they could, the technology of psychohistory. Even Scogil did not understand the long-term implications. The Founder had. They would learn.

It took only eighty-seven days at a year per day on the most powerful historical computers in existence to predict a total alteration in the political face of the galaxy. Over five hundred simulated interstellar wars, major and minor, were raging, confined only by the constraints of psychohistory. Arms production was up by four orders of magnitude. Eight billion youths were being drafted every year to study psychohistory in an effort by each faction to outmaneuver the others. Psychohistory had *not* become irrelevant; it was *essential* to the multitude of war efforts. Accurate prediction in conflict situations was just orders of magnitude more difficult. There were 112 major centers of psychohistoric prediction and thousands of minor ones. The formidable stability of the Second Galactic Empire had long been reduced to shambles.

On the eighty-seventh day, the simulated Splendid Wisdom was sacked by a vengeful alliance of enemies.

By this time Eron Osa was no longer under house arrest by a stunned Kon. His six-room apartment was an open command center. Admiral Kon had assigned ten of his aides to work with Eron. It made no sense anymore to break the game into a contest between two opponents— Kon's staff, Eron, Scogil all had to work together just to keep track of what was going on as the math churned out the changing constraints.

Petunia was acting as Eron's chief of staff and general gopher. Otaria of the Calmer Sea frantically plotted historical trends. Hiranimus Scogil worked overtime in his dungeon at full capacity. Eron, amazed by his ghoul, was now fully cognizant of why the living Scogil had made such heroic efforts to keep his fam out of enemy hands—its psychohistorical utilities alone were the equivalent of the brain power of ten men like the Founder.

On that eighty-seventy day Kon's exhausted staff, which had grown over the campaign to include almost every student of the Lyceum, broke apart. With Splendid Wisdom sacked no one had the courage or wit or energy to continue. It was generally understood that errors had accumulated to the point where the game was describing a low-probability future.

Instead of continuing, they had a party in Kon's main command center overlooking the simulacrum of the galaxy, now half washed in blue. Desks were overturned. Decorations festooned the equipment. A few psychohistorians could be found asleep on the floor. Others yelled and rioted and threw hard bread rolls in mock warfare. With his game, Eron had pushed the whole Lyceum across the no-man's-land of the mental topozones they knew as reality into the chaotic neural activity of strange viewpoints and impossible stimuli.

The Lyceum became, for a few days, a genteel madhouse.

Normally brain activity flips back and forth across the boundaries twixt stability and chaos in the mind's ever-active war between knowing and the need to learn—this outpost ridge temporarily chaotic, that beachhead stable for the moment, the front flowing in battle flux across the neural net.

On quiet days the mind stays stable by using old solutions. On other days some internal field marshal calls for an offensive and drives his troops against chaos. To conquer chaos one must *learn*. To maintain stability one must *know*.

What were the lessons of the *surprising* mathematical collapse of the Second Empire? The outcome was debated everywhere over the next week in an orgy of learning. The unexpected nature of the game had agitated the mind of each participant, blowing like a hurricane through the topozone sails of their neural barges, at the same time that the historical topozones of the galactic model were being battered and forced into recomputation by the same hurricane.

Eron slipped among the groups, listening, dropping hints. He knew what had happened. He wanted his "students" to figure it out for themselves.

Hadn't the Pscholars persisted in the *fatalistic* mind-set of the final hopeless centuries of the First Empire in spite of the *fact* that the math of psychohistory contained a plethora of *alternate* futures? Over the millennial Interregnum, hadn't their Plan atrophied into a kind of supervised determinism? Wasn't it true that the Plan was no longer seen as a vigorous alternate future that led away from the chaos of Imperial collapse, but as the *only* true future—with the Fellowship as its guardian?

A casual remark by Eron about Scogil's Smythosian connection immoderately grew into a quicky seminar. This curious group already knew *how* the Smythosians could destroy the Second Empire with only a millionth of the Second Empire's resources at its command. But no one knew who they were or where they had come from.

Even Eron relied on the stories by Petunia and Scogil. As a late product of the chaos surrounding the False Revival, an amorphous group grew up very gradually in the region of the Thousand Suns of the Helmar Rift around the astonishing relics of an embittered Tamic Smythos.

Smythos was a recluse. Smythosians adopted his reclusiveness out of fear of the Fellowship, their milieu only gradually expanding from the

Thousand Suns of the Helmar Rift into the safety of the stellar bracken.

Smythos was caustic in his condemnation of the Pscholars' lack of interest in things technical; he had acquired a love of machines from his Scav foster parents. Smythosians sympathized; their roots lay in the peoples of the Thousand Suns who had supplied sybaritic Lakgan with its pleasure machines, who had invented the tuned psychic probe under military contract with Lakgan, and been among the first builders of the personal familiar, who had been major suppliers of the legendary zenoli mercenaries. It was natural that they developed a technical expertise.

The Smythosians never operated from major centers of Second Empire bureaucracy. They never developed a Plan of their own. Loosely associated, they remained anarchists; every man to his own local future, their only common goal an opposition to the rigid shackles of the Pscholars. They could not have developed otherwise. Every psychohistoric move they made to leave the Plan was statistically noted and opposed from Splendid Wisdom. They responded by using psychohistory to oppose the opposition and over the centuries became masters of mask and stealth and subterfuge. And masters of the short-term plan.

When the lessons of the game were well on their way to assimilation within the Lyceum, Eron Osa gave his first speech to a quiet audience, his theme the failures of the Pscholars and the failures of the Smythosians. Speech done, the discussion continued in his suite over dinner to a smaller group, Otaria at his side. Admiral Kon carried in a keg of wine—grumbling about the mental decline of Jars Hanis, who was organizing a counterrevolution to reestablish order and sanity.

The Pscholars had failed from too much power. They had ceased to mine psychohistory for low-probability futures worth exploring. The Plan was, after all, a low-probability future discovered by the Founder. As an elite they had *deliberately* failed to explore the high probability that they would not be able to hold on to their monopoly of psychohistoric expertise.

Worse, they had neglected psychohistory as a tool to explore undesirable futures (such as the high probability that Splendid Wisdom would be resacked within the century). Back some time in the Interregnum, psychohistorians had forgotten that one of the main uses of prediction was avoidance. They had used their power only to avoid deviations from the Plan. Mankind's brain had evolved as a tool to predict undesirable futures in time to avoid them, not to predict highly probable futures that needed no intervention.

The Smythosians had fallen into the trap of opposition. For centuries they were small, content to oppose the Fellowship locally in invisible ways. The more they opposed the Plan, the more the Fellowship reacted—until the Lyceum had evolved a whole unit under Hahukum Kon, whose sole purpose was to oppose the actions of the Smythosians, who then were driven to use their ultimate weapon against the Second Empire, their knowledge of psychohistory.

The Second Empire had no defense against a populace who could drop into their local archive and find out all they might want to know about psychohistory. The Smythosian goal became the destruction of the Second Empire, rather than the implementation of a better Plan.

Around dinner Eron discussed the next phase of his personal Plan for the galaxy—negotiation between the warring sides. The Second Empire had lost its power monopoly. If Splendid Wisdom wished to retain any power at all, it would have to make concessions. It would have to begin by helping the Smythosians to distribute psychohistoric knowledge—no points given up there *because it was a battle already lost.* The Fellowship could then begin to negotiate local variations in the Plan.

After all, psychohistory contained within itself a complete understanding of how humans negotiated with one another.

The Osa-Scogil being was evolving. The mere fact that ghoul and man had developed a language contact seemed to have catalyzed a process in which they were beginning to develop shared coding at a more machine-language level. It wouldn't come faster than either one could accept. The ghoul would eventually see through Eron's eyes, and Eron would feel the emotions of Hiranimus. He had a family back in the Thousand Suns. Strange. When he met his wife, he was going to ask her to deactivate that damned tuned compulsion to love and protect Petunia. Their daughter was reaching the age when girls resent being overprotected.

Petunia was flirting with one of Kon's aides by standing behind his aerochair and holding her hands over his eyes. She was making him guess who she was, as if he couldn't tell from her giggle.

Osa-Scogil felt very peculair about having a wife and a Frightfulperson. He walked behind Otaria's chair and held his fingers gently over her eyes. "Guess who," he said fondly.

"I really don't know anymore," replied the Mermaid of the Calmer Sea.

Joe Haldeman came to science fiction after being severely wounded in Vietnam, an experience that informs much of his best writing. With *The Forever War* in 1974 he updated future war unforgettably. Since then he has addressed issues such as immortality in *Buying Time* (in the United Kingdom, *The Long Habit of Living*), the near future in the *Worlds* sequence, and alien contact in *Mindbridge*. He uses many fictional techniques, and is probably science fiction's best poet. He lives in Florida, teaching at M.I.T. each fall.

Humans can strut upon the galactic stage, given vast time, but they may well be only minor players. Earlier science fiction often assumed that savvy humans were going to be quicker and wiser than aliens. Robert Heinlein wrote many books that confidently evoked this, as in *Starship Troopers*. "For White Hill" studies a civilization immeasurably advanced beyond ours, yet less successful at what our species has, on its own small world, been supreme in: war.

FOR WHITE HILL

Joe Haldeman

•

I AM WRITING this memoir in the language of England, an ancient land of Earth, whose tales and songs White Hill valued. She was fascinated by human culture in the days before machines—not just thinking machines, but working ones; when things got done by the straining muscles of humans and animals.

Neither of us was born on Earth. Not many people were, in those days. It was a desert planet then, ravaged in the twelfth year of what they would call the Last War. When we met, that war had been going for over four hundred years, and had moved out of Sol Space altogether, or so we thought.

Some cultures had other names for the conflict. My parent, who fought the century before I did, always called it the Extermination, and their name for the enemy was "roach," or at least that's as close as English allows. We called the enemy an approximation of their own word for themselves, Fwndyri, which was uglier to us. I still have no love for them, but have no reason to make the effort. It would be easier to love a roach. At least we have a common ancestor. And we accompanied one another into space.

One mixed blessing we got from the war was a loose form of interstellar government, the Council of Worlds. There had been individual treaties before, but an overall organization had always seemed unlikely, since no two inhabited systems are less than three light-years apart, and several of them are over fifty. You can't defeat Einstein; that makes more than a century between "How are you?" and "Fine."

The Council of Worlds was headquartered on Earth, an unlikely and unlovely place, if centrally located. There were fewer than ten thousand people living on the blighted planet then, an odd mix of politicians, religious extremists, and academics, mostly. Almost all of them under glass. Tourists flowed through the domed-over ruins, but not many stayed long. The planet was still very dangerous over all of its unprotected surface, since the Fwndyri had thoroughly seeded it with nanophages. Those were submicroscopic constructs that sought out concentrations of human DNA. Once under the skin, they would reproduce at a geometric rate, deconstructing the body, cell by cell, building new nanophages. A person might complain of a headache and lie down, and a few hours later there would be nothing but a dry skeleton, lying in dust. When the humans were all dead, they mutated and went after DNA in general, and sterilized the world.

White Hill and I were "bred" for immunity to the nanophages. Our DNA winds backwards, as was the case with many people born or created after that stage of the war. So we could actually go through the elaborate airlocks and step out onto the blasted surface unprotected.

I didn't like her at first. We were competitors, and aliens to one another.

When I worked through the final airlock cycle, for my first moment on the actual surface of Earth, she was waiting outside, sitting in meditation on a large flat rock that shimmered in the heat. One had to admit she was beautiful in a startling way, clad only in a glistening pattern of blue and green body paint. Everything else around was grey and black, including the hard-packed talcum that had once been a mighty jungle, Brazil. The dome behind me was a mirror of grey and black and cobalt sky.

"Welcome home," she said. "You're Water Man."

She inflected it properly, which surprised me. "You're from Petros?"

"Of course not." She spread her arms and looked down at her body. Our women always cover at least one of their breasts, let alone their genitals. "Galan, an island on Seldene. I've studied your cultures, a little language."

"You don't dress like that on Seldene, either." Not anywhere I'd been on the planet.

"Only at the beach. It's so warm here."

I had to agree. Before I came out, they'd told me it was the hottest autumn on record. I took off my robe and folded it and left it by the door, with the sealed food box they had given me. I joined her on the rock, which was tilted away from the sun and reasonably cool.

She had a slight fragrance of lavender, perhaps from the body paint. We touched hands. "My name is White Hill. Zephyr-Meadow-Torrent."

"Where are the others?" I asked. Twenty-nine artists had been invited; one from each inhabited world. The people who had met me inside said I was the nineteenth to show up.

"Most of them traveling. Going from dome to dome for inspiration."

"You've already been around?"

"No." She reached down with her toe and scraped a curved line on the hard-baked ground. "All the story's here, anywhere. It isn't really about history or culture."

Her open posture would have been shockingly sexual at home, but this was not home. "Did you visit my world when you were studying it?"

"No, no money, at the time. I did get there a few years ago." She smiled at me. "It was almost as beautiful as I'd imagined it." She said three words in Petrosian. You couldn't say it precisely in English, which doesn't have a palindromic mood: *Dreams feed art and art feeds dreams.*

"When you came to Seldene I was young, too young to study with you. I've learned a lot from your sculpture, though."

"How young can you be?" To earn this honor, I did not say.

"In Earth years, about seventy awake. More than a hundred and forty-five in time-squeeze."

I struggled with the arithmetic. Petros and Seldene were twenty-two light-years apart; that's about forty-five years' squeeze. Earth is, what, a little less than forty light-years from her planet. That leaves enough gone time for someplace about twenty-five light-years from Petros, and back.

She tapped me on the knee, and I flinched. "Don't overheat your brain. I made a triangle; went to ThetaKent after your world."

"Really? When I was there?"

"No, I missed you by less than a year. I was disappointed. You were why I went." She made a palindrome in my language: *Predator becomes prey becomes predator?* "So here we are. Perhaps I can still learn from you."

I didn't much care for her tone of voice, but I said the obvious: "I'm more likely to learn from you."

"Oh, I don't think so." She smiled in a measured way. "You don't have much to learn."

Or much I could, or would, learn. "Have you been down to the water?"

"Once." She slid off the rock and dusted herself, spanking. "It's interesting. Doesn't look real." I picked up the food box and followed her down a sort of path that led us into low ruins. She drank some of my water, apologetic; hers was hot enough to brew tea.

"First body?" I asked.

"I'm not tired of it yet." She gave me a sideways look, amused. "You must be on your fourth or fifth."

"I go through a dozen a year." She laughed. "Actually, it's still my second. I hung on to the first too long."

"I read about that, the accident. That must have been horrible."

"Comes with the medium. I should take up the flute." I had been making a "controlled" fracture in a large boulder and set off the charges prematurely, by dropping the detonator. Part of the huge rock rolled over onto me, crushing my body from the hips down. It was a remote area, and by the time help arrived I had been dead for several minutes, from pain as much as anything else. "It affected all of my work, of course. I can't even look at some of the things I did the first few years I had this body."

"They are hard to look at," she said. "Not to say they aren't well done, and beautiful, in their way."

"As what is not? In its way." We came to the first building ruins and stopped. "Not all of this is weathering. Even in four hundred years." If you studied the rubble you could reconstruct part of the design. Primitive but sturdy, concrete reinforced with composite rods. "Somebody came in here with heavy equipment or explosives. They never actually fought on Earth, I thought."

"They say not." She picked up an irregular brick with a rod through it. "Rage, I suppose. Once people knew that no one was going to live."

"It's hard to imagine." The records are chaotic. Evidently the first people died two or three days after the nanophages were introduced, and no one on Earth was alive a week later. "Not hard to understand, though. The need to break something." I remembered the inchoate anger I felt as I squirmed there helpless, dying from *sculpture*, of all things. Anger at the rock, the fates. Not at my own inattention and clumsiness.

"They had a poem about that," she said. "'Rage, rage against the dying of the light.'"

"Somebody actually wrote something during the nanoplague?"

"Oh, no. A thousand years before. Twelve hundred." She squatted suddenly and brushed at a fragment that had two letters on it. "I wonder if this was some sort of official building. Or a shrine or church." She pointed along the curved row of shattered bricks that spilled into the street. "That looks like it was some kind of decoration, a gable over the entrance." She tiptoed through the rubble toward the far end of the arc, studying what was written on the face-up pieces. The posture, standing on the balls of her feet, made her slim body even more attractive, as she must have known. My own body began to respond in a way inappropriate for a man more than three times her age. Foolish, even though that particular part is not so old. I willed it down before she could see.

"It's a language I don't know," she said. "Not Portuguese; looks like Latin. A Christian church, probably, Catholic."

"They used water in their religion," I remembered. "Is that why it's close to the sea?"

"They were everywhere; sea, mountains, orbit. They got to Petros?"

"We still have some. I've never met one, but they have a church in New Haven."

"As who doesn't?" She pointed up a road. "Come on. The beach is just over the rise here."

I could smell it before I saw it. It wasn't an ocean smell; it was dry, slightly choking.

We turned a corner and I stood staring. "It's a deep blue farther out," she said, "and so clear you can see hundreds of metras down." Here the water was thick and brown, the surf foaming heavily like a giant's chocolate drink, mud piled in baked windrows along the beach. "This used to be soil?"

She nodded. "There's a huge river that cuts this continent in half, the Amazon. When the plants died, there was nothing to hold the soil in place." She tugged me forward. "Do you swim? Come on."

"Swim in *that?* It's filthy."

"No, it's perfectly sterile. Besides, I have to pee." Well, I couldn't argue with that. I left the box on a high fragment of fallen wall and followed her. When we got to the beach, she broke into a run. I walked slowly and watched her gracile body, instead, and waded into the slippery heavy surf. When it was deep enough to swim, I plowed my way out to where she was bobbing. The water was too hot to be pleasant, and breathing was somewhat difficult. Carbon dioxide, I supposed, with a tang of halogen.

We floated together for a while, comparing this soup to bodies of water on our planets and ThetaKent. It was tiring, more from the water's heat and bad air than exertion, so we swam back in.

● ●

We dried in the blistering sun for a few minutes and then took the food box and moved to the shade of a beachside ruin. Two walls had fallen in together, to make a sort of concrete tent.

We could have been a couple of precivilization aboriginals, painted with dirt, our hair baked into stringy mats. She looked odd but still had a kind of formal beauty, the dusty mud residue turning her into a primitive sculpture, impossibly accurate and mobile. Dark rivulets of sweat drew painterly accent lines along her face and body. If only she were a model, rather than an artist. Hold that pose while I go back for my brushes.

We shared the small bottles of cold wine and water and ate bread and cheese and fruit. I put a piece on the ground for the nanophages. We watched it in silence for some minutes, while nothing happened. "It probably takes hours or days," she finally said.

"I suppose we should hope so," I said. "Let us digest the food before the creatures get to it."

"Oh, that's not a problem. They just attack the bonds between amino acids that make up proteins. For you and me, they're nothing more than an aid to digestion."

How reassuring. "But a source of some discomfort when we go back in, I was told."

She grimaced. "The purging. I did it once, and decided my next outing would be a long one. The treatment's the same for a day or a year."

"So how long has it been this time?"

"Just a day and a half. I came out to be your welcoming committee."

"I'm flattered."

She laughed. "It was their idea, actually. They wanted someone out here to 'temper' the experience for you. They weren't sure how well traveled you were, how easily affected by . . . strangeness." She shrugged. "Earthlings. I told them I knew of four planets you'd been to."

"They weren't impressed?"

"They said well, you know, he's famous and wealthy. His experiences on these planets might have been very comfortable." We could both laugh at that. "I told them how comfortable ThetaKent is."

"Well, it doesn't have nanophages."

"Or anything else. That was a long year for me. You didn't even stay a year."

"No. I suppose we would have met, if I had."

"Your agent said you were going to be there two years."

I poured us both some wine. "She should have told me you were coming. Maybe I could have endured it until the next ship out."

"How gallant." She looked into the wine without drinking. "You famous and wealthy people don't have to endure ThetaKent. I had to agree to one year's indentureship to help pay for my triangle ticket."

"You were an actual slave?"

"More like a wife, actually. The head of a township, a widower, financed me in exchange for giving his children some culture. Language, art, music. Every now and then he asked me to his chambers. For his own kind of culture."

"My word. You had to . . . *lie* with him? That was in the contract?"

"Oh, I didn't have to, but it kept him friendly." She held up a thumb and forefinger. "It was hardly noticeable."

I covered my smile with a hand, and probably blushed under the mud.

"I'm not embarrassing you?" she said. "From your work, I'd think that was impossible."

I had to laugh. "That work is in reaction to my culture's values. I can't take a pill and stop being a Petrosian."

White Hill smiled, tolerantly. "A Petrosian woman wouldn't put up with an arrangement like that?"

"Our women are still women. Some actually would like it, secretly. Most would claim they'd rather die, or kill the man."

"But they wouldn't actually *do* it. Trade their body for a ticket?" She sat down in a single smooth dancer's motion, her legs open, facing me. The clay between her legs parted, sudden pink.

"I wouldn't put it so bluntly." I swallowed, watching her watching me. "But no, they wouldn't. Not if they were planning to return."

"Of course, no one from a civilized planet would want to stay on ThetaKent. Shocking place."

I had to move the conversation onto safer grounds. "Your arms don't spend all day shoving big rocks around. What do you normally work in?"

"Various mediums." She switched to my language. "Sometimes I shove little rocks around." That was a pun for testicles. "I like painting, but my reputation is mainly from light and sound sculpture. I wanted to do something with the water here, internal illumination of the surf, but they say that's not possible. They can't isolate part of the ocean. I can have a pool, but no waves, no tides."

"Understandable." Earth's scientists had found a way to rid the surface of the nanoplague. Before they reterraformed the Earth, though, they wanted to isolate an area, a "park of memory," as a reminder of the Sterilization and these centuries of waste, and brought artists from every world to interpret, inside the park, what they had seen here.

Every world except Earth. Art on Earth had been about little else for a long time.

Setting up the contest had taken decades. A contest representative went to each of the settled worlds, according to a strict timetable. Announcement of the competition was delayed on the nearer worlds so that each artist would arrive on Earth at approximately the same time.

The Earth representatives chose which artists would be asked, and no one refused. Even the ones who didn't win the contest were guaranteed an honorarium equal to twice what they would have earned during that time at home, in their best year of record.

The value of the prize itself was so large as to be meaningless to a normal person. I'm a wealthy man on a planet where wealth is not rare, and just the interest that the prize would earn would support me and a half-dozen more. If someone from ThetaKent or Laxor won the prize, they would probably have more real usable wealth than their governments. If they were smart, they wouldn't return home.

The artists had to agree on an area for the park, which was limited to a hundred square kaymetras. If they couldn't agree, which seemed almost inevitable to me, the contest committee would listen to arguments and rule.

Most of the chosen artists were people like me, accustomed to working on a monumental scale. The one from Luxor was a composer, though, and there were two conventional muralists, paint and mosaic. White Hill's work was by its nature evanescent. She could always set something up that would be repeated, like a fountain cycle. She might have more imagination than that, though.

"Maybe it's just as well we didn't meet in a master-student relationship," I said. "I don't know the first thing about the techniques of your medium."

"It's not technique." She looked thoughtful, remembering. "That's not why I wanted to study with you, back then. I was willing to push rocks around, or anything, if it could give me an avenue, an insight into how you did what you did." She folded her arms over her chest, and dust fell. "Ever since my parents took me to see Gaudí Mountain, when I was ten."

That was an early work, but I was still satisfied with it. The city council of Tresling, a prosperous coastal city, hired me to "do something with" an unusable steep island that stuck up in the middle of their harbor. I melted it judiciously, in homage to an Earthling artist.

"Now, though, if you'd forgive me . . . well, I find it hard to look at. It's alien, obtrusive."

"You don't have to apologize for having an opinion." Of course it looked alien; it was meant to evoke *Spain!* "What would you do with it?"

She stood up, and walked to where a window used to be, and leaned on the stone sill, looking at the ruins that hid the sea. "I don't know. I'm even less familiar with your tools." She scraped at the edge of the sill with a piece of rubble. "It's funny: earth, air, fire, and water. You're earth and fire, and I'm the other two."

I have used water, of course. The Gaudí is framed by water. But it was an interesting observation. "What do you do, I mean for a living? Is it related to your water and air?"

"No. Except insofar as everything is related." There are no artists on Seldene, in the sense of doing it for a living. Everybody indulges in some sort of art or music, as part of "wholeness," but a person who only did art would be considered a parasite. I was not comfortable there.

She faced me, leaning. "I work at the Northport Mental Health Center. Cognitive science, a combination of research and . . . is there a word here? *Jaturnary.* 'Empathetic therapy,' I guess."

I nodded. "We say *jâdr-ny.* You plug yourself into mental patients?"

"I share their emotional states. Sometimes I do some good, talking to them afterwards. Not often."

"It's not done on Petrosia," I said, unnecessarily.

"Not legally, you mean."

I nodded. "If it worked, people say, it might be legal."

" 'People say.' What do you say?" I started to make a noncommittal gesture. "Tell me the truth?"

"All I know is what I learned in school. It was tried, but failed spectacularly. It hurt both the therapists and the patients."

"That was more than a century ago. The science is much more highly developed now."

I decided not to push her on it. The fact is that drug therapy is spectacularly successful, and it *is* a science, unlike *jâdr-ny.* Seldene is backward in some surprising ways.

I joined her at the window. "Have you looked around for a site yet?"

She shrugged. "I think my presentation will work anywhere. At least that's guided my thinking. I'll have water, air, and light, wherever the other artists and the committee decide to put us." She scraped at the ground with a toenail. "And this stuff. They call it 'loss.' What's left of what was living."

"I suppose it's not everywhere, though. They might put us in a place that used to be a desert."

"They might. But there will be water and air; they were willing to guarantee that."

"I don't suppose they have to guarantee rock," I said.

"I don't know. What would you do if they did put us in a desert, nothing but sand?"

"Bring little rocks." I used my own language; the pun also meant courage.

She started to say something, but we were suddenly in deeper shadow. We both stepped through the tumbled wall, out into the open. A black line of cloud had moved up rapidly from inland.

She shook her head. "Let's get to the shelter. Better hurry."

We trotted back along the path toward the Amazonia dome city. There was a low concrete structure behind the rock where I first met her. The warm breeze became a howling gale of sour steam before we got there, driving bullets of hot rain. A metal door opened automatically on our approach, and slid shut behind us. "I got caught in one yesterday," she said, panting. "It's no fun, even under cover. Stinks."

We were in an unadorned anteroom that had protective clothing on wall pegs. I followed her into a large room furnished with simple chairs and tables, and up a winding stair to an observation bubble.

"Wish we could see the ocean from here," she said. It was dramatic enough. Wavering sheets of water marched across the blasted landscape, strobed every few seconds by lightning flashes. The tunic I'd left outside swooped in flapping circles off to the sea.

It was gone in a couple of seconds. "You don't get another one, you know. You'll have to meet everyone naked as a baby."

"A dirty one at that. How undignified."

"Come on." She caught my wrist and tugged. "Water is my specialty, after all."

● ● ●

The large hot bath was doubly comfortable for having a view of the tempest outside. I'm not at ease with communal bathing—I was married for fifty years and never bathed with my wife—but it seemed natural enough after wandering around together naked on an alien planet, swimming in its mud-puddle sea. I hoped I could trust her not to urinate in the tub. (If I mentioned it she would probably turn scientific and tell me that a healthy person's urine is sterile. I know that. But there is a time and a receptacle for everything.)

On Seldene, I knew, an unattached man and woman in this situation would probably have had sex even if they were only casual acquaintances, let alone fellow artists. She was considerate enough not to make any overtures, or perhaps (I thought at the time) not greatly stimulated by the sight of muscular men. In the shower before bathing, she offered to scrub my back, but left it at that. I helped her strip off the body paint from her back. It was a nice back to study, pronounced lumbar dimples, small waist. Under more restrained circumstances, it might have been *I* who made an overture. But one does not ask a woman when refusal would be awkward.

Talking while we bathed, I learned that some of her people, when they become wealthy enough to retire, choose to work on their art full time, but they're considered eccentric, even outcasts, egotists. White Hill expected one of them to be chosen for the contest, and wasn't even going to apply. But the Earthling judge saw one of her installations and tracked her down.

She also talked about her practical work in dealing with personality disorders and cognitive defects. There was some distress in her voice when she described that to me. Plugging into hurt minds, sharing their pain or blankness for hours. I didn't feel I knew her well enough to bring up the aspect that most interested me, a kind of ontological prurience: what is it like to actually *be* another person; how much of her, or him, do you take away? If you do it often enough, how can you know which parts of you are the original you?

And she would be plugged into more than one person at once, at times, the theory being that people with similar disorders could help each other, swarming around in the therapy room of her brain. She would fade into the background, more or less unable to interfere, and later analyze how they had interacted.

She had had one particularly unsettling experience, where through a planetwide network she had interconnected more than a hundred congenitally retarded people. She said it was like a painless death. By the time half of them had plugged in, she had felt herself fade and wink out. Then she was reborn with the suddenness of a slap. She had been dead for about ten hours.

But only connected for seven. It had taken technicians three hours to pry her out of a persistent catatonia. With more people, or a longer period, she might have been lost forever. There was no lasting harm, but the experiment was never repeated.

It was worth it, she said, for the patients' inchoate happiness afterward. It was like a regular person being given supernatural powers for half a day—powers so far beyond human experience that there was no way to talk about them, but the memory of it was worth the frustration.

After we got out of the tub, she showed me to our wardrobe room: hundreds of white robes, identical except for size. We dressed and made tea and sat upstairs, watching the storm rage. It hardly looked like an inhabitable planet outside. The lightning had intensified so that it crackled incessantly, a jagged insane dance in every direction. The rain had frozen to white gravel somehow. I asked the building, and it said that the stuff was called *granizo* or, in English, hail. For a while it fell too fast to melt, accumulating in white piles that turned translucent.

Staring at the desolation, White Hill said something that I thought was uncharacteristically modest. "This is too big and terrible a thing. I feel like an interloper. They've lived through centuries of this, and now they want *us* to explain it to them?"

I didn't have to remind her of what the contest committee had said, that their own arts had become stylized, stunned into a grieving conformity. "Maybe not to *explain*—maybe they're assuming we'll fail, but hope to find a new direction from our failures. That's what that oldest woman, Norita, implied."

White Hill shook her head. "Wasn't she a ray of sunshine? I think they dragged her out of the grave as a way of keeping us all outside the dome."

"Well, she was quite effective on me. I could have spent a few days investigating Amazonia, but not with her as a native guide." Norita was about as close as anyone could get to being an actual native. She was the last survivor of the Five Families, the couple of dozen Earthlings who, among those who were offworld at the time of the nanoplague, were willing to come back after robots constructed the isolation domes.

In terms of social hierarchy, she was the most powerful person on Earth, at least on the actual planet. The class system was complex and nearly opaque to outsiders, but being a descendant of the Five Families was a prerequisite for the highest class. Money or political power would not get you in, although most of the other social classes seemed associated with wealth or the lack of it. Not that there were any actual poor people on Earth; the basic birth dole was equivalent to an upper-middle-class income on Petros.

The nearly instantaneous destruction of ten billion people did not destroy their fortunes. Most of the Earth's significant wealth had been off-planet, anyhow, at the time of the Sterilization. Suddenly it was concentrated into the hands of fewer than two thousand people.

Actually, I couldn't understand why anyone would have come back.

You'd have to be pretty sentimental about your roots to be willing to spend the rest of your life cooped up under a dome, surrounded by instant death. The salaries and amenities offered were substantial, with bonuses for Earthborn workers, but it still doesn't sound like much of a bargain. The ships that brought the Five Families and the other original workers to Earth left loaded down with sterilized artifacts, not to return for exactly one hundred years.

Norita seemed like a familiar type to me, since I come from a culture also rigidly bound by class. "Old money, but not much of it" sums up the situation. She wanted to be admired for the accident of her birth and the dubious blessing of a torpid longevity, rather than any actual accomplishment. I didn't have to travel thirty-three light-years to enjoy that kind of company.

"Did she keep you away from everybody?" White Hill said.

"Interposed herself. No one could act naturally when she was around, and the old dragon was never *not* around. You'd think a person her age would need a little sleep."

" 'She lives on the blood of infants,' we say."

There was a phone chime and White Hill said "Bono" as I said, "Chå." Long habits. Then we said Earth's "Holá" simultaneously.

The old dragon herself appeared. "I'm glad you found shelter." Had she been eavesdropping? No way to tell from her tone or posture. "An administrator has asked permission to visit with you."

What if we said no? White Hill nodded, which means yes on Earth. "Granted," I said.

"Very well. He will be there shortly." She disappeared. I suppose the oldest person on a planet can justify not saying hello or goodbye. Only so much time left, after all.

"A physical visit?" I said to White Hill. "Through this weather?"

She shrugged. "Earthlings."

After a minute there was a *ding* sound in the anteroom and we walked down to see an unexpected door open. What I'd thought was a hall closet was an airlock. He'd evidently come underground.

Young and nervous and moving awkwardly in plastic. He shook our hands in an odd way. Of course we were swimming in deadly poison. "My name is Warm Dawn. Zephyr-Boulder-Brook."

"Are we cousins through Zephyr?" White Hill asked.

He nodded quickly. "An honor, my lady. Both of my parents are Seldenian, my gene-mother from your Galan."

A look passed over her that was pure disbelieving chauvinism: *Why would anybody leave Seldene's forests, farms, and meadows for this ster-*

ile death trap? Of course, she knew the answer. The major import and export, the only crop, on Earth, was money.

"I wanted to help both of you with your planning. Are you going to travel at all, before you start?"

White Hill made a noncommittal gesture. "There are some places for me to see," I said. "The Pyramids, Chicago, Rome. Maybe a dozen places, twice that many days." I looked at her. "Would you care to join me?"

She looked straight at me, wheels turning. "It sounds interesting."

The man took us to a viewscreen in the great room and we spent an hour or so going over routes and making reservations. Travel was normally by underground vehicle, from dome to dome, and if we ventured outside unprotected, we would of course have to go through the purging before we were allowed to continue. Some people need a day or more to recover from that, so we should put that into the schedule, if we didn't want to be hobbled, like him, with plastic.

Most of the places I wanted to see were safely under glass, even some of the Pyramids, which surprised me. Some, like Ankgor Wat, were not only unprotected but difficult of access. I had to arrange for a flyer to cover the thousand kaymetras, and schedule a purge. White Hill said she would wander through Hanoi, instead.

I didn't sleep well that night, waking often from fantastic dreams, the nanobeasts grown large and aggressive. White Hill was in some of the dreams, posturing sexually.

By the next morning the storm had gone away, so we crossed over to Amazonia, and I learned firsthand why one might rather sit in a hotel room with a nice book than go to Angkor Wat, or anywhere that required a purge. The external part of the purging was unpleasant enough, even with pain medication, all the epidermis stripped and regrown. The inside part was beyond description, as the nanophages could be hiding out anywhere. Every opening into the body had to be vacuumed out, including the sense organs. I was not awake for that part, where the robots most gently clean out your eye sockets, but my eyes hurt and my ears rang for days. They warned me to sit down the first time I urinated, which was good advice, since I nearly passed out from the burning pain.

White Hill and I had a quiet supper of restorative gruel together, and then crept off to sleep for half a day. She was full of pep the next morning, and I pretended to be at least sentient, as we wandered through the city making preparations for the trip.

After a couple of hours I protested that she was obviously trying to do in one of her competitors; stop and let an old man sit down for a minute.

We found a bar that specialized in stimulants. She had tea and I had bhan, a murky warm drink served in a large nutshell, coconut. It tasted woody and bitter, but was restorative.

"It's not age," she said. "The purging seems a lot easier, the second time you do it. I could hardly move, all the next day, the first time."

Interesting that she didn't mention that earlier. "Did they tell you it would get easier?"

She nodded, then caught herself and wagged her chin horizontally, Earth-style. "Not a word. I think they enjoy our discomfort."

"Or like to keep us off guard. Keeps them in control." She made the little kissing sound that's Lortian for agreement and reached for a lemon wedge to squeeze into her tea. The world seemed to slow slightly, I guess from whatever was in the bhan, and I found myself cataloguing her body microscopically. A crescent of white scar tissue on the back of a knuckle, fine hair on her forearm, almost white, her shoulders and breasts moving in counterpoised pairs, silk rustling, as she reached forward and back and squeezed the lemon, sharp citrus smell and the tip of her tongue between her thin lips, mouth slightly large. Chameleon hazel eyes, dark green now because of the decorative ivy wall behind her.

"What are you staring at?"

"Sorry, just thinking."

"Thinking." She stared at me in return, measuring. "Your people are good at that."

After we'd bought the travel necessities we had the packages sent to our quarters and wandered aimlessly. The city was comfortable, but had little of interest in terms of architecture or history, oddly dull for a planet's administrative center. There was an obvious social purpose for its blandness—by statute, nobody was *from* Amazonia; nobody could be born there or claim citizenship. Most of the planet's wealth and power came there to work, electronically if not physically, but it went home to some other place.

A certain amount of that wealth was from interstellar commerce, but it was nothing like the old days, before the war. Earth had been a hub, a central authority that could demand its tithe or more from any transaction between planets. In the period between the Sterilization and Earth's token rehabilitation, the other planets made their own arrangements with one another, in pairs and groups. But most of the fortunes that had been born on Earth returned here.

So Amazonia was bland as cheap bread, but there was more wealth under its dome than on any two other planets combined. Big money seeks out the company of its own, for purposes of reproduction.

● △

Two other artists had come in, from Auer and Shwa, and once they were ready, we set out to explore the world by subway. The first stop that was interesting was the Grand Canyon, a natural wonder whose desolate beauty was unaffected by the Sterilization.

We were amused by the guide there, a curious little woman who rattled on about the Great Rift Valley on Mars, a nearby planet where she was born. White Hill had a lightbox, and while the Martian lady droned on we sketched the fantastic colors, necessarily loose and abstract because our fingers were clumsy in clinging plastic.

We toured Chicago, like the Grand Canyon, wrapped in plastic. It was a large city that had been leveled in a local war. It lay in ruins for many years, and then, famously, was rebuilt as a single huge structure from those ruins. There's a childish or drunken ad hoc quality to it, a scarcity of right angles, a crazy-quilt mixture of materials. Areas of stunning imaginative brilliance next to jury-rigged junk. And everywhere bones, the skeletons of ten million people, lying where they fell. I asked what had happened to the bones in the old city outside of Amazonia. The guide said he'd never been there, but he supposed that the sight of them upset the politicians, so they had them cleaned up. "Can you imagine this place without the bones?" he asked. It would be nice if I could.

The other remnants of cities in that country were less interesting, if no less depressing. We flew over the east coast, which was essentially one continuous metropolis for thousands of kaymetras, like our coast from New Haven to Stargate, rendered in sterile ruins.

The first place I visited unprotected was Giza, the Great Pyramids. White Hill decided to come with me, though she had to be wrapped up in a shapeless cloth robe, her face veiled, because of local religious law. It seemed to me ridiculous, a transparent tourism ploy. How many believers in that old religion could have been off-planet when the Earth died? But every female was obliged at the tube exit to go into a big hall and be fitted with a chador robe and veil before a man could be allowed to look at her.

(We wondered whether the purging would be done completely by women. The technicians would certainly see a lot of her uncovered during that excruciation.)

They warned us it was unseasonably hot outside. Almost too hot to breathe, actually, during the day. We accomplished most of our sight-seeing around dusk or dawn, spending most of the day in air-conditioned shelters.

Because of our special status, White Hill and I were allowed to visit the pyramids alone, in the dark of the morning. We climbed up the largest one and watched the sun mount over desert haze. It was a singular time for both of us, edifying but something more.

Coming back down, we were treated to a sandstorm, *khamsin,* which actually might have done the first stage of purging if we had been allowed to take off our clothes. It explained why all the bones lying around looked so much older than the ones in Chicago; they normally had ten or twelve of these sandblasting storms every year. Lately, with the heat wave, the *khamsin* came weekly or even more often.

Raised more than five thousand years ago, the pyramids were the oldest monumental structures on the planet. They actually held as much fascination for White Hill as for me. Thousands of men moved millions of huge blocks of stone, with nothing but muscle and ingenuity. Some of the stones were mined a thousand kaymetras away, and floated up the river on barges.

I could build a similar structure, even larger, for my contest entry, by giving machines the right instructions. It would be a complicated business, but easily done within the two-year deadline. Of course there would be no point to it. That some anonymous engineer had done the same thing within the lifetime of a king, without recourse to machines—I agreed with White Hill: that was an actual marvel.

We spent a couple of days outside, traveling by surface hoppers from monument to monument, but none was as impressive. I suppose I should have realized that, and saved Giza for last.

We met another of the artists at the Sphinx, Lo Tan-Six, from Pao. I had seen his work on both Pao and ThetaKent, and admitted there was something to be admired there. He worked in stone, too, but was more interested in pure geometric forms than I was. I think stone fights form, or imposes its own tensions on the artist's wishes.

I liked him well enough, though, in spite of this and other differences, and we traveled together for a while. He suggested we not go through the purging here, but have our things sent on to Rome, because we'd want to be outside there, too. There was a daily hop from Alexandria to Rome, an airship that had a section reserved for those of us who could eat and breathe nanophages.

As soon as she was inside the coolness of the ship, White Hill shed the chador and veil and stuffed them under the seat. "Breathe," she said, stretching. Her white body suit was a little less revealing than paint.

Her directness and undisguised sexuality made me catch my breath. The tiny crease of punctuation that her vulva made in the body suit would have her jailed on some parts of my planet, not to mention the part of this one we'd just left. The costume was innocent and natural and, I think, completely calculated.

Pao studied her with an interested detachment. He was neuter, an option that was available on Petros, too, but one I've never really understood. He claimed that sex took too much time and energy from his art. I think his lack of gender took something else away from it.

We flew about an hour over the impossibly blue sea. There were a few sterile islands, but otherwise it was as plain as spilled ink. We descended over the ashes of Italy and landed on a pad on one of the hills overlooking the ancient city. The ship mated to an airlock so the normal-DNA people could go down to a tube that would whisk them into Rome. We could call for transportation or walk, and opted for the exercise. It was baking hot here, too, but not as bad as Egypt.

White Hill was polite with Lo, but obviously wished he'd disappear. He and I chattered a little too much about rocks and cements, explosives and lasers. And his asexuality diminished her interest in him—as, perhaps, my polite detachment increased her interest in me. The muralist from Shwa, to complete the spectrum, was after her like a puppy in its first heat, which I think amused her for two days. They'd had a private conversation in Chicago, and he'd kept his distance since, but still admired her from afar. As we walked down toward the Roman gates, he kept a careful twenty paces behind, trying to contemplate things besides White Hill's walk.

Inside the gate we stopped short, stunned in spite of knowing what to expect. It had a formal name, but everybody just called it *Òssi*, the Bones. An order of catholic clergy had spent more than two centuries building, by hand, a wall of bones completely around the city. It was twice the height of a man, varnished dark amber. There were repetitive patterns of femurs and rib cages and stacks of curving spines, and at eye level, a row of skulls, uninterrupted, kaymetra after kaymetra.

This was where we parted. Lo was determined to walk completely around the circle of death, and the other two went with him. White Hill and I could do it in our imagination. I still creaked from climbing the pyramid.

Prior to the ascent of Christianity here, they had huge spectacles, displays of martial skill where many of the participants were killed, for punishment of wrongdoing or just to entertain the masses. The two large amphitheaters where these displays went on were inside the Bones but not under the dome, so we walked around them. The Circus Maximus had a terrible dignity to it, little more than a long depression in the ground with a few eroded monuments left standing. The size and age of it were enough; your mind's eye supplied the rest. The smaller one, the Colosseum, was overdone, with robots in period costumes and ferocious mechanical animals re-creating the old scenes, lots of too-bright blood spurting. Stones and bones would do.

I'd thought about spending another day outside, but the shelter's air-conditioning had failed, and it was literally uninhabitable. So I braced myself and headed for the torture chamber. But as White Hill had said, the purging was more bearable the second time. You know that it's going to end.

Rome inside was interesting, many ages of archeology and history stacked around in no particular order. I enjoyed wandering from place to place with her, building a kind of organization out of the chaos. We were both more interested in inspiration than education, though, so I doubt that the three days we spent there left us with anything like a coherent picture of that tenacious empire and the millennia that followed it.

A long time later she would surprise me by reciting the names of the Roman emperors in order. She'd always had a trick memory, a talent for retaining trivia, ever since she was old enough to read. Growing up different that way must have been a factor in swaying her toward cognitive science.

We saw some ancient cinema and then returned to our quarters to pack for continuing on to Greece, which I was anticipating with pleasure. But it didn't happen. We had a message waiting: ALL MUST RETURN IMMEDIATELY TO AMAZONIA. CONTEST PROFOUNDLY CHANGED.

Lives, it turned out, profoundly changed. The war was back.

Δ

We met in a majestic amphitheater, the twenty-nine artists dwarfed by the size of it, huddled front row center. A few Amazonian officials sat behind a table on the stage, silent. They all looked detached, or stunned, brooding.

We hadn't been told anything except that it was a matter of "dire and immediate importance." We assumed it had to do with the contest, naturally, and were prepared for the worst: it had been called off; we had to go home.

The old crone Norita appeared. "We must confess to carelessness," she said. "The unseasonable warmth in both hemispheres, it isn't something that has happened, ever since the Sterilization. We looked for atmospheric causes here, and found something that seemed to explain it. But we didn't make the connection with what was happening in the other half of the world.

"It's not the atmosphere. It's the Sun. Somehow the Fwndyri have found a way to make its luminosity increase. It's been going on for half a year. If it continues, and we find no way to reverse it, the surface of the planet will be uninhabitable in a few years.

"I'm afraid that most of you are going to be stranded on Earth, at least for the time being. The Council of Worlds has exercised its emergency powers, and commandeered every vessel capable of interstellar transport. Those who have sufficient power or the proper connections will be able to escape. The rest will have to stay with us and face . . . whatever our fate is going to be."

I saw no reason not to be blunt. "Can money do it? How much would a ticket out cost?"

That would have been a gaffe on my planet, but Norita didn't blink. "I know for certain that two hundred million marks is not enough. I also know that some people have bought 'tickets,' as you say, but I don't know how much they paid, or to whom."

If I liquidated everything I owned, I might be able to come up with three hundred million, but I hadn't brought that kind of liquidity with me; just a box of rare jewelry, worth perhaps forty million. Most of my wealth was thirty-three years away, from the point of view of an Earthbound investor. I could sign that over to someone, but by the time they got to Petros, the government or my family might have seized it, and they would have nothing save the prospect of a legal battle in a foreign culture.

Norita introduced Skylha Sygoda, an astrophysicist. He was pale and sweating. "We have analyzed the solar spectrum over the past six months. If I hadn't known that each spectrum was from the same star, I would have said it was a systematic and subtle demonstration of the microstages of stellar evolution in the late main sequence."

"Could you express that in some human language?" someone said.

Sygoda spread his hands. "They've found a way to age the Sun. In the normal course of things, we would expect the Sun to brighten about six percent each billion years. At the current rate, it's more like one percent per year."

"So in a hundred years," White Hill said, "it will be twice as bright?"

"If it continues at this rate. We don't know."

A stocky woman I recognized as !Oona Something, from Jua-nguvi, wrestled with the language: "To how long, then? Before this Earth is uninhabitable?"

"Well, in point of fact, it's uninhabitable now, except for people like you. We could survive inside these domes for a long time, if it were just a matter of the outside getting hotter and hotter. For those of you able to withstand the nanophages, it will probably be too hot within a decade, here; longer near the poles. But the weather is likely to become very violent, too.

"And it may not be a matter of a simple increase in heat. In the case of normal evolution, the Sun would eventually expand, becoming a red giant. It would take many billions of years, but the Earth would not survive. The surface of the Sun would actually extend out to touch us.

"If the Fwndyri were speeding up time somehow, locally, and the Sun were actually *evolving* at this incredible rate, we would suffer that fate in about thirty years. But it would be impossible. They would have to have a way to magically extract the hydrogen from the Sun's core."

"Wait," I said. "You don't know what they're doing now, to make it brighten. I wouldn't say anything's impossible."

"Water Man," Norita said, "if that happens we shall simply die, all of us, at once. There is no need to plan for it. We do need to plan for less extreme exigencies." There was an uncomfortable silence.

"What can we do?" White Hill said. "We artists?"

"There's no reason not to continue with the project, though I think you may wish to do it inside. There's no shortage of space. Are any of you trained in astrophysics, or anything having to do with stellar evolution and the like?" No one was. "You may still have some ideas that will be useful to the specialists. We will keep you informed."

Most of the artists stayed in Amazonia, for the amenities if not to avoid purging, but four of us went back to the outside habitat. Denli om Cord, the composer from Luxor, joined Lo and White Hill and me. We could have used the tunnel airlock, to avoid the midday heat, but Denli hadn't seen the beach, and I suppose we all had an impulse to see the sun with our new knowledge. In this new light, as they say.

White Hill and Denli went swimming while Lo and I poked around the ruins. We had since learned that the destruction here had been methodical, a grim resolve to leave the enemy nothing of value. Both of us were scouting for raw material, of course. After a short while we sat in the hot shade, wishing we had brought water.

We talked about that and about art. Not about the sun dying, or us dying, in a few decades. The women's laughter drifted to us over the rush of the muddy surf. There was a sad hysteria to it.

"Have you had sex with her?" he asked conversationally.

"What a question. No."

He tugged on his lip, staring out over the water. "I try to keep these things straight. It seems to me that you desire her, from the way you look at her, and she seems cordial to you, and is after all from Seldene. My interest is academic, of course."

"You've never done sex? I mean before."

"Of course, as a child." The implication of that was obvious.

"It becomes more complicated with practice."

"I suppose it could. Although Seldenians seem to treat it as casually as . . . conversation." He used the Seldenian word, which is the same as for intercourse.

"White Hill is reasonably sophisticated," I said. "She isn't bound by her culture's freedoms." The two women ran out of the water, arms around each other's waists, laughing. It was an interesting contrast; Denli was almost as large as me, and about as feminine. They saw us and waved toward the path back through the ruins.

We got up to follow them. "I suppose I don't understand your restraint," Lo said. "Is it your own culture? Your age?"

"Not age. Perhaps my culture encourages self-control."

He laughed. "That's an understatement."

"Not that I'm a slave to Petrosian propriety. My work is outlawed in several states, at home."

"You're proud of that."

I shrugged. "It reflects on them, not me." We followed the women down the path, an interesting study in contrasts, one pair nimble and naked except for a film of drying mud, the other pacing evenly in monkish robes. They were already showering when Lo and I entered the cool shelter, momentarily blinded by shade.

We made cool drinks and, after a quick shower, joined them in the communal bath. Lo was not anatomically different from a sexual male, which I found obscurely disturbing. Wouldn't it bother you to be constantly reminded of what you had lost? Renounced, I suppose Lo would say, and accuse me of being parochial about plumbing.

I had made the drinks with guava juice and ron, neither of which we have on Petros. A little too sweet, but pleasant. The alcohol loosened tongues.

Denli regarded me with deep black eyes. "You're rich, Water Man. Are you rich enough to escape?"

"No. If I had brought all my money with me, perhaps."

"Some do," White Hill said. "I did."

"I would too," Lo said, "coming from Seldene. No offense intended."

"Wheels turn," she admitted. "Five or six new governments before I get back. *Would* have gotten back."

We were all silent for a long moment. "It's not real yet," White Hill said, her voice flat. "We're going to die here?"

"We were going to die somewhere," Denli said. "Maybe not so soon."

"And not on Earth," Lo said. "It's like a long preview of Hell." Denli looked at him quizzically. "That's where Christians go when they die. If they were bad."

"They send their bodies to Earth?" We managed not to smile. Actually, most of my people knew as little as hers, about Earth. Seldene and Luxor, though relatively poor, had centuries' more history than Petros, and kept closer ties to the central planet. The Home Planet, they would say. Homey as a blast furnace.

By tacit consensus, we didn't dwell on death any more that day. When artists get together they tend to wax enthusiastic about materials and tools, the mechanical lore of their trades. We talked about the ways we worked at home, the things we were able to bring with us, the improvisations we could effect with Earthling materials. (Critics talk about art, we say; artists talk about brushes.) Three other artists joined us, two sculptors and a weathershaper, and we all wound up in the large sunny studio drawing and painting. White Hill and I found sticks of charcoal and did studies of each other drawing each other.

While we were comparing them she quietly asked, "Do you sleep lightly?"

"I can. What did you have in mind?"

"Oh, looking at the ruins by starlight. The moon goes down about three. I thought we might watch it set together." Her expression was so open as to be enigmatic.

Two more artists had joined us by dinnertime, which proceeded with a kind of forced jollity. A lot of ron was consumed. White Hill cautioned me against overindulgence. They had the same liquor, called "rum," on Seldene, and it had a reputation for going down easily but causing storms. There was no legal distilled liquor on my planet.

I had two drinks of it, and retired when people started singing in various languages. I did sleep lightly, though, and was almost awake when White Hill tapped. I could hear two or three people still up, murmuring in the bath. We slipped out quietly.

It was almost cool. The quarter-phase moon was near the horizon, a dim orange, but it gave us enough light to pick our way down the path. It was warmer in the ruins, the tumbled stone still radiating the day's heat. We walked through to the beach, where it was cooler again. White Hill spread the blanket she had brought and we stretched out and looked up at the stars.

As is always true with a new world, most of the constellations were familiar, with a few bright stars added or subtracted. Neither of our home stars was significant, as dim here as Earth's Sol is from home. She identified the brightest star overhead as AlphaKent; there was a brighter one on the horizon, but neither of us knew what it was.

We compared names of the constellations we recognized. Some of hers were the same as Earth's names, like Scorpio, which we call the Insect. It was about halfway up the sky, prominent, embedded in the galaxy's glow. We both call the brightest star there Antares. The Executioner, which had set perhaps an hour earlier, they call Orion. We had the same meaningless names for its brightest stars, Betelgeuse and Rigel.

"For a sculptor, you know a lot about astronomy," she said. "When I visited your city, there was too much light to see stars at night."

"You can see a few from my place. I'm out at Lake Påchlå, about a hundred kaymetras inland."

"I know. I called you."

"I wasn't home?"

"No; you were supposedly on ThetaKent."

"That's right, you told me. Our paths crossed in space. And you became that burgher's slave wife." I put my hand on her arm. "Sorry I forgot. A lot has gone on. Was he awful?"

She laughed into the darkness. "He offered me a lot to stay."

"I can imagine."

She half turned, one breast soft against my arm, and ran a finger up my leg. "Why tax your imagination?"

I wasn't expecially in the mood, but my body was. The robes rustled off easily, their only virtue.

The moon was down now, and I could see only a dim outline of her in the starlight. It was strange to make love deprived of that sense. You would think the absence of it would amplify the others, but I can't say that it did, except that her heartbeat seemed very strong on the heel of my hand. Her breath was sweet with mint and the smell and taste of her body were agreeable; in fact, there was nothing about her body that I would have cared to change, inside or out, but nevertheless, our progress became difficult after a couple of minutes, and by mute agreement we slowed and stopped. We lay joined together for some time before she spoke.

"The timing is all wrong. I'm sorry." She drew her face across my arm and I felt tears. "I was just trying not to think about things."

"It's all right. The sand doesn't help, either." We had gotten a little bit inside, rubbing.

We talked for a while and then drowsed together. When the sky began to lighten, a hot wind from below the horizon woke us up. We went back to the shelter.

Everyone was asleep. We went to shower off the sand and she was amused to see my interest in her quicken. "Let's take that downstairs," she whispered, and I followed her down to her room.

The memory of the earlier incapability was there, but it was not greatly inhibiting. Being able to see her made the act more familiar, and besides she was very pleasant to see, from whatever angle. I was able to withhold myself only once, and so the interlude was shorter than either of us would have desired.

We slept together on her narrow bed. Or she slept, rather, while I watched the bar of sunlight grow on the opposite wall, and thought about how everything had changed.

They couldn't really say we had thirty years to live, since they had no idea what the enemy was doing. It might be three hundred; it might be less than one—but even with bodyswitch that was always true, as it was in the old days: sooner or later something would go wrong and you would die. That I might die at the same instant as ten thousand other people and a planet full of history—that was interesting. But as the room filled with light and I studied her quiet repose, I found her more interesting than that.

I was old enough to be immune to infatuation. Something deep had been growing since Egypt, maybe before. On top of the pyramid, the rising sun dim in the mist, we had sat with our shoulders touching, watching the ancient forms appear below, and I felt a surge of numinism mixed oddly with content. She looked at me—I could only see her eyes—and we didn't have to say anything about the moment.

And now this. I was sure, without words, that she would share this, too. Whatever "this" was. England's versatile language, like mine and hers, is strangely hobbled by having the one word, love, stand for such a multiplicity of feelings.

Perhaps that lack reveals a truth, that no one love is like any other. There are other truths that you might forget, or ignore, distracted by the growth of love. In Petrosian there is a saying in the palindromic mood that always carries a sardonic, or at least ironic, inflection: "Happiness presages disaster presages happiness." So if you die happy, it means you were happy when you died. Good timing or bad?

Δ ●

!Oona M'vua had a room next to White Hill, and she was glad to switch with me, an operation that took about three minutes but was good for a much longer period of talk among the other artists. Lo was smugly amused, which in my temporary generosity of spirit I forgave.

Once we were adjacent, we found the button that made the wall slide away, and pushed the two beds together under her window. I'm afraid we were antisocial for a couple of days. It had been some time since either of us had had a lover. And I had never had one like her, literally, out of the dozens. She said that was because I had never been involved with a Seldenian, and I tactfully agreed, banishing five perfectly good memories to amnesia.

It's true that Seldenian women, and men as well, are better schooled than those of us from normal planets, in the techniques and subtleties of sexual expression. Part of "wholeness," which I suppose is a weak pun in English. It kept Lo, and not only him, from taking White Hill seriously as an artist: the fact that a Seldenian, to be "whole," must necessarily treat art as an everyday activity, usually subordinate to affairs of the heart, of the body. Or at least on the same level, which is the point.

The reality is that it *is* all one to them. What makes Seldenians so alien is that their need for balance in life dissolves hierarchy: this piece of art is valuable, and so is this orgasm, and so is this crumb of bread. The bread crumb connects to the artwork through the artist's metabolism, which connects to orgasm. Then through a fluid and automatic mixture of logic, metaphor, and rhetoric, the bread crumb links to soil, sunlight, nuclear fusion, the beginning and end of the universe. Any intelligent person can map out chains like that, but to White Hill it was automatic, drilled into her with her first nouns and verbs: *Everything is important. Nothing matters.* Change the world but stay relaxed.

I could never come around to her way of thinking. But then I was married for fifty Petrosian years to a woman who had stranger beliefs. (The marriage as a social contract actually lasted fifty-seven years; at the half-century mark we took a vacation from each other, and I never saw her again.) White Hill's worldview gave her an equanimity I had to envy. But my art needed unbalance and tension the way hers needed harmony and resolution.

By the fourth day most of the artists had joined us in the shelter. Maybe they grew tired of wandering through the bureaucracy. More likely, they were anxious about their competitors' progress.

White Hill was drawing designs on large sheets of buff paper and taping them up on our walls. She worked on her feet, bare feet, pacing from diagram to diagram, changing and rearranging. I worked directly inside a shaping box, an invention White Hill had heard of but had never seen. It's a cube of light a little less than a metra wide. Inside is an image of a scupture—or a rock or a lump of clay—that you can feel as well as see. You can mold it with your hands or work with finer instruments for cutting, scraping, chipping. It records your progress constantly, so it's easy to take chances; you can always run it back to an earlier stage.

I spent a few hours every other day cruising in a flyer with Lo and a couple of other sculptors, looking for native materials. We were severely constrained by the decision to put the Memory Park inside, since everything we used had to be small enough to fit through the airlock and purging rooms. You could work with large pieces, but you would have to slice them up and reassemble them, the individual chunks no bigger than two by two by three metras.

We tried to stay congenial and fair during these expeditions. Ideally, you would spot a piece and we would land by it or hover over it long enough to tag it with your ID; in a day or two the robots would deliver it to your "holding area" outside the shelter. If more than one person wanted the piece, which happened as often as not, a decision had to be made before it was tagged. There was a lot of arguing and trading and Solomon-style splitting, which usually satisfied the requirements of something other than art.

The quality of light was changing for the worse. Earthling planetary engineers were spewing bright dust into the upper atmosphere, to reflect back solar heat. (They modified the nanophage-eating machinery for the purpose. That was also designed to fill the atmosphere full of dust, but at a lower level—and each grain of *that* dust had a tiny chemical brain.) It made the night sky progressively less interesting. I was glad White Hill had chosen to initiate our connection under the stars. It would be some time before we saw them again, if ever.

And it looked like "daylight" was going to be a uniform overcast for the duration of the contest. Without the dynamic of moving sunlight to continually change the appearance of my piece, I had to discard a whole family of first approaches to its design. I was starting to think along the lines of something irrational-looking; something the brain would reject as impossible. The way we mentally veer away from unthinkable things like the Sterilization, and our proximate future.

We had divided into two groups, and jokingly but seriously referred to one another as "originalists" and "realists." We originalists were continuing our projects on the basis of the charter's rules: a memorial to the tragedy and its aftermath, a stark sterile reminder in the midst of life.

The realists took into account new developments, including the fact that there would probably never be any "midst of life" and, possibly, no audience, after thirty years.

I thought that was excessive. There was plenty of pathos in the original assignment. Adding another, impasto, layer of pathos along with irony and the artist's fear of personal death . . . well, we were doing art, not literature. I sincerely hoped their pieces would be fatally muddled by complexity.

If you asked White Hill which group she belonged to, she would of course say, "Both." I had no idea what form her project was going to take; we had agreed early on to surprise one another, and not impede each other with suggestions. I couldn't decipher even one-tenth of her diagrams. I speak Seldenian pretty well, but have never mastered the pictographs beyond the usual travelers' vocabulary. And much of what she was scribbling on the buff sheets of paper was in no language I recognized, an arcane technical symbology.

We talked about other things. Even about the future, as lovers will. Our most probable future was simultaneous death by fire, but it was calming and harmless to make "what if?" plans, in case our hosts somehow were able to find a way around that fate. We did have a choice of many possible futures, if we indeed had more than one. White Hill had never had access to wealth before. She didn't want to live lavishly, but the idea of being able to explore all the planets excited her.

Of course she had never tried living lavishly. I hoped one day to study her reaction to it, which would be strange. Out of the box of valuables I'd brought along, I gave her a necklace, a traditional beginning-love gift on Petros. It was a network of perfect emeralds and rubies laced in gold.

She examined it closely. "How much is this worth?"

"A million marks, more or less." She started to hand it back. "Please keep it. Money has no value here, no meaning."

She was at a loss for words, which was rare enough. "I understand the gesture. But you can't expect me to value this the way you do."

"I wouldn't expect that."

"Suppose I lose it? I might just set it down somewhere."

"I know. I'll still have given it to you."

She nodded and laughed. "All right. You people are strange." She slipped the necklace on, still latched, wiggling it over her ears. The colors glowed warm and cold against her olive skin.

She kissed me, a feather, and rushed out of our room wordlessly. She passed right by a mirror without looking at it.

After a couple of hours I went to find her. Lo said he'd seen her go out the door with a lot of water. At the beach I found her footprints marching straight west to the horizon.

She was gone for two days. I was working outside when she came back, wearing nothing but the necklace. There was another necklace in her hand: she had cut off her right braid and interwoven a complex pattern of gold and silver wire into a closed loop. She slipped it over my head and pecked me on the lips and headed for the shelter. When I started to follow she stopped me with a tired gesture. "Let me sleep, eat, wash." Her voice was a hoarse whisper. "Come to me after dark."

I sat down, leaning back against a good rock, and thought about very little, touching her braid and smelling it. When it was too dark to see my feet, I went in, and she was waiting.

Δ ● ●

I spent a lot of time outside, at least in the early morning and late afternoon, studying my accumulation of rocks and ruins. I had images of every piece in my shaping box's memory, but it was easier to visualize some aspects of the project if I could walk around the elements and touch them.

Inspiration is where you find it. We'd played with an orrery in the museum in Rome, a miniature solar system that had been built of clockwork centuries before the Information Age. There was a wistful, humorous, kind of comfort in its jerky regularity.

My mental processes always turn things inside out. Find the terror and hopelessness in that comfort. I had in mind a massive but delicately balanced assemblage that would be viewed by small groups; their presence would cause it to teeter and turn ponderously. It would seem both fragile and huge (though of course the fragility would be an illusion), like the ecosystem that the Fwndyri so abruptly destroyed.

The assemblage would be mounted in such a way that it would seem always in danger of toppling off its base, but hidden weights would make that impossible. The sound of the rolling weights ought to produce a nice anxiety. Whenever a part tapped the floor, the tap would be amplified into a hollow boom.

If the viewers stood absolutely still, it would swing to a halt. As they left, they would disturb it again. I hoped it would disturb them as well.

The large technical problem was measuring the distribution of mass in each of my motley pieces. That would have been easy at home; I could rent a magnetic resonance densitometer to map their insides. There was no such thing on this planet (so rich in things I had no use for!), so I had to make do with a pair of robots and a knife edge. And then start hollowing the pieces out asymmetrically, so that once set in motion, the assemblage would tend to rotate.

I had a large number of rocks and artifacts to choose from, and was tempted to use no unifying principle at all, other than the unstable balance of the thing. Boulders and pieces of old statues and fossil machinery. The models I made of such a random collection were ambiguous, though. It was hard to tell whether they would look ominous or ludicrous, built to scale. A symbol of helplessness before an implacable enemy? Or a lurching, crashing junkpile? I decided to take a reasonably conservative approach, dignity rather than daring. After all, the audience would be Earthlings and, if the planet survived, tourists with more money than sophistication. Not my usual jury.

I was able to scavenge twenty long bars of shiny black monofiber, which would be the spokes of my irregular wheel. That would give it some unity of composition: make a cross with four similar chunks of granite at the ordinal points, and a larger chunk at the center. Then build up a web inside, monofiber lines linking bits of this and that.

Some of the people were moving their materials inside Amazonia, to work in the area marked off for the park. White Hill and I decided to stay outside. She said her project was portable, at this stage, and mine would be easy to disassemble and move.

After a couple of weeks, only fifteen artists remained with the project, inside Amazonia or out in the shelter. The others had either quit, surrendering to the passive depression that seemed to be Earth's new norm, or, in one case, committed suicide. The two from Wolf and Mijhøven opted for coldsleep, which might be deferred suicide. About one person in three slept through it; one in three came out with some kind of treatable mental disorder. The others went mad and died soon after reawakening, unable or unwilling to live.

Coldsleep wasn't done on Petros, although some Petrosians went to other worlds to indulge in it as a risky kind of time travel. Sleep until whatever's wrong with the world has changed. Some people even did it for financial speculation: buy up objects of art or antiques, and sleep for a century or more while their value increases. Of course their value might not increase significantly, or they might be stolen or coopted by family or government.

But if you can make enough money to buy a ticket to another planet, why not hold off until you had enough to go to a really *distant* one? Let time dilation compress the years. I could make a triangle from Petros to

Skaal to Mijhøven and back, and more than 120 years would pass, while I lived through only three, with no danger to my mind. And I could take my objects of art along with me.

White Hill had worked with coldsleep veterans, or victims. None of them had been motivated by profit, given her planet's institutionalized antimaterialism, so most of them had been suffering from some psychological ill before they slept. It was rare for them to come out of the "treatment" improved, but they did come into a world where people like White Hill could at least attend them in their madness, perhaps guide them out.

I'd been to three times as many worlds as she. But she had been to stranger places.

Δ ● ● ●

The terraformers did their job too well. The days grew cooler and cooler, and some nights snow fell. The snow on the ground persisted into mornings for a while, and then through noon, and finally it began to pile up. Those of us who wanted to work outside had to improvise cold-weather clothing.

I liked working in the cold, although all I did was direct robots. I grew up in a small town south of New Haven, where winter was long and intense. At some level I associated snow and ice with the exciting pleasures that waited for us after school. I was to have my fill of it, though.

It was obvious I had to work fast, faster than I'd originally planned, because of the increasing cold. I wanted to have everything put together and working before I disassembled it and pushed it through the airlock. The robots weren't made for cold weather, unfortunately. They had bad traction on the ice and sometimes their joints would seize up. One of them complained constantly, but of course it was the best worker, too, so I couldn't just turn it off and let it disappear under the drifts, an idea that tempted me.

White Hill often came out for a few minutes to stand and watch me and the robots struggle with the icy heavy boulders, machinery, and statuary. We took walks along the seashore that became shorter as the weather worsened. The last walk was a disaster.

We had just gotten to the beach when a sudden storm came up with a sandblast wind so violent that it blew us off our feet. We crawled back to the partial protection of the ruins and huddled together, the wind screaming so loudly that we had to shout to hear each other. The storm continued to mount and, in our terror, we decided to run for the shelter. White Hill slipped on some ice and suffered a horrible injury, a jagged piece of metal slashing her face diagonally from forehead to chin, blinding her left eye and tearing off part of her nose. Pearly bone showed through, cracked, at eyebrow, cheek, and chin. She rose up to one elbow and fell slack.

I carried her the rest of the way, immensely glad for the physical strength that made it possible. By the time we got inside she was unconscious and my white coat was a scarlet flag of blood.

A plastic-clad doctor came through immediately and did what she could to get White Hill out of immediate danger. But there was a problem with more sophisticated treatment. They couldn't bring the equipment out to our shelter, and White Hill wouldn't survive the stress of purging unless she had had a chance to heal for a while. Besides the facial wound, she had a broken elbow and collarbone and two cracked ribs.

For a week or so she was always in pain or numb. I sat with her, numb myself, her face a terrible puffed caricature of its former beauty, the wound glued up with plaskin the color of putty. Split skin of her eyelid slack over the empty socket.

The mirror wasn't visible from her bed, and she didn't ask for one, but whenever I looked away from her, her working hand came up to touch and catalogue the damage. We both knew how fortunate she was to be alive at all, and especially in an era and situation where the damage could all be repaired, given time and a little luck. But it was still a terrible thing to live with, an awful memory to keep reliving.

When she was more herself, able to talk through her ripped and pasted mouth, it was difficult for me to keep my composure. She had considerable philosophical, I suppose you could say spiritual, resources, but she was so profoundly stunned that she couldn't follow a line of reasoning very far, and usually wound up sobbing in frustration.

Sometimes I cried with her, although Petrosian men don't cry except in response to music. I had been a soldier once and had seen my ration of injury and death, and I always felt the experience had hardened me, to my detriment. But my friends who had been wounded or killed were just friends, and all of us lived then with the certainty that every day could be anybody's last one. To have the woman you love senselessly mutilated by an accident of weather was emotionally more arduous than losing a dozen companions to the steady erosion of war, a different kind of weather.

I asked her whether she wanted to forget our earlier agreement and talk about our projects. She said no; she was still working on hers, in a way, and she still wanted it to be a surprise. I did manage to distract her, playing with the shaping box. We made cartoonish representations of Lo and old Norita, and combined them in impossible sexual geometries. We shared a limited kind of sex ourselves, finally.

The doctor pronounced her well enough to be taken apart, and both of us were scourged and reappeared on the other side. White Hill was already in surgery when I woke up; there had been no reason to revive her before beginning the restorative processes.

I spent two days wandering through the blandness of Amazonia, jungle laced through concrete, quartering the huge place on foot. Most areas seemed catatonic. A few were boisterous with end-of-the-world hysteria. I checked on her progress so often that they eventually assigned a robot to call me up every hour, whether or not there was any change.

On the third day I was allowed to see her, in her sleep. She was pale but seemed completely restored. I watched her for an hour, perhaps more, when her eyes suddenly opened. The new one was blue, not green, for some reason. She didn't focus on me.

"Dreams feed art," she whispered in Petrosian; "and art feeds dreams." She closed her eyes and slept again.

Δ □

She didn't want to go back out. She had lived all her life in the tropics, even the year she spent in bondage, and the idea of returning to the ice that had slashed her was more than repugnant. Inside Amazonia it was always summer, now, the authorities trying to keep everyone happy with heat and light and jungle flowers.

I went back out to gather her things. Ten large sheets of buff paper I unstuck from our walls and stacked and rolled. The necklace, and the satchel of rare coins she had brought from Seldene, all her worldly wealth.

I considered wrapping up my own project, giving the robots instructions for its dismantling and transport, so that I could just go back inside with her and stay. But that would be chancy. I wanted to see the thing work once before I took it apart.

So I went through the purging again, although it wasn't strictly necessary; I could have sent her things through without hand-carrying them. But I wanted to make sure she was on her feet before I left her for several weeks.

She was not on her feet, but she was dancing. When I recovered from the purging, which now took only half a day, I went to her hospital room and they referred me to our new quarters, a three-room dwelling in a place called Plaza de Artistes. There were two beds in the bedroom, one a fancy medical one, but that was worlds better than trying to find privacy in a hospital.

There was a note floating in the air over the bed saying she had gone to a party in the common room. I found her in a gossamer wheelchair, teaching a hand dance to Denli om Cord, while a harpist and flautist from two different worlds tried to settle on a mutual key.

She was in good spirits. Denli remembered an engagement and I wheeled White Hill out onto a balcony that overlooked a lake full of sleeping birds, some perhaps real.

It was hot outside, always hot. There was a mist of perspiration on her face, partly from the light exercise of the dance, I supposed. In the light from below, the mist gave her face a sculpted appearance, unsparing sharpness, and there was no sign left of the surgery.

"I'll be out of the chair tomorrow," she said, "at least ten minutes at a time." She laughed, "*Stop* that!"

"Stop what?"

"Looking at me like that."

I was still staring at her face. "It's just . . . I suppose it's such a relief."

"I know." She rubbed my hand. "They showed me pictures, of before. You looked at that for so many days?"

"I saw you."

She pressed my hand to her face. The new skin was taut but soft, like a baby's. "Take me downstairs?"

Δ Δ

It's hard to describe, especially in light of later developments, disintegrations, but that night of fragile lovemaking marked a permanent change in the way we linked, or at least the way I was linked to her: I've been married twice, long and short, and have been in some kind of love a hundred times. But no woman has ever owned me before.

This is something we do to ourselves. I've had enough women who *tried* to possess me, but always was able to back or circle away, in literal preservation of self. I always felt that life was too long for one woman.

Certainly part of it is that life is not so long anymore. A larger part of it was the run through the screaming storm, her life streaming out of her, and my stewardship, or at least companionship, afterward, during her slow transformation back into health and physical beauty. The core of her had never changed, though, the stubborn serenity that I came to realize, that warm night, had finally infected me as well.

The bed was a firm narrow slab, cooler than the dark air heavy with the scent of Earth flowers. I helped her onto the bed (which instantly conformed to her) but from then on it was she who cared for me, saying that was all she wanted, all she really had strength for. When I tried to reverse that, she reminded me of a holiday palindrome that has sexual overtones in both our languages: Giving is taking is giving.

Δ Δ ●

We spent a couple of weeks as close as two people can be. I was her lover and also her nurse, as she slowly strengthened. When she was able to spend most of her day in normal pursuits, free of the wheelchair or "intelligent" bed (with which we had made a threesome, at times uneasy), she urged me to go back outside and finish up. She was ready to concentrate on her own project, too. Impatient to do art again, a good sign.

I would not have left so soon if I had known what her project involved. But that might not have changed anything.

As soon as I stepped outside, I knew it was going to take longer than planned. I had known from the inside monitors how cold it was going to be, and how many ceemetras of ice had accumulated, but I didn't really *know* how bad it was until I was standing there, looking at my piles of materials locked in opaque glaze. A good thing I'd left the robots inside the shelter, and a good thing I had left a few hand tools outside. The door was buried under two metras of snow and ice. I sculpted myself a passageway, an application of artistic skills I'd never foreseen.

I debated calling White Hill and telling her that I would be longer than expected. We had agreed not to interrupt each other, though, and it was likely she'd started working as soon as I left.

The robots were like a bad comedy team, but I could only be amused by them for an hour or so at a time. It was so cold that the water vapor from my breath froze into an icy sheath on my beard and mustache. Breathing was painful; deep breathing probably dangerous.

So most of the time, I monitored them from inside the shelter. I had the place to myself; everyone else had long since gone into the dome. When I wasn't working I drank too much, something I had not done regularly in centuries.

It was obvious that I wasn't going to make a working model. Delicate balance was impossible in the shifting gale. But the robots and I had our hands full, and other grasping appendages engaged, just dismantling the various pieces and moving them through the lock. It was unexciting but painstaking work. We did all the laser cuts inside the shelter, allowing the rock to come up to room temperature so it didn't spall or shatter. The air-conditioning wasn't quite equal to the challenge, and neither were the cleaning robots, so after a while it was like living in a foundry: everywhere a kind of greasy slickness of rock dust, the air dry and metallic.

So it was with no regret that I followed the last slice into the airlock myself, even looking forward to the scourging if White Hill was on the other side.

She wasn't. A number of other people were missing, too. She left this note behind:

I knew from the day we were called back here what my new piece would have to be, and I knew I had to keep it from you, to spare you sadness. And to save you the frustration of trying to talk me out of it.

As you may know by now, scientists have determined that the Fwndyri indeed have sped up the Sun's evolution somehow. It will continue to warm, until in thirty or forty years there will be an explosion called the "helium flash." The Sun will become a red giant, and the Earth will be incinerated.

There are no starships left, but there is one avenue of escape. A kind of escape.

Parked in high orbit there is a huge interplanetary transport that was used in the terraforming of Mars. It's a couple of centuries older than you, but like yourself it has been excellently preserved. We are going to ride it out to a distance sufficient to survive the Sun's catastrophe, and there remain until the situation improves, or does not.

This is where I enter the picture. For our survival to be meaningful in this thousand-year war, we have to resort to coldsleep. And for a large number of people to survive centuries of coldsleep, they need my jaturnary skills. Alone, in the ice, they would go slowly mad. Connected through the matrix of my mind, they will have a sense of community, and may come out of it intact.

I will be gone, of course. I will be by the time you read this. Not dead, but immersed in service. I could not be revived if this were only a hundred people for a hundred days. This will be a thousand, perhaps for a thousand years.

No one else on Earth can do jaturnary, and there is neither time nor equipment for me to transfer my ability to anyone. Even if there were, I'm not sure I would trust anyone else's skill. So I am gone.

My only loss is losing you. Do I have to elaborate on that?

You can come if you want. In order to use the transport, I had to agree that the survivors be chosen in accordance with the Earth's strict class system—starting with dear Norita, and from that pin-

nacle, on down—but they were willing to make exceptions for all of the visiting artists. You have until mid-Deciembre to decide; the ship leaves Januar first.

If I know you at all, I know you would rather stay behind and die. Perhaps the prospect of living "in" me could move you past your fear of coldsleep; your aversion to jaturnary. *If not, not.*

I love you more than life. But this is more than that. Are we what we are?

W. H.

The last sentence is a palindrome in her language, not mine, that I believe has some significance beyond the obvious.

● ● ☐

I did think about it for some time. Weighing a quick death, or even a slow one, against spending centuries locked frozen in a tiny room with Norita and her ilk. Chattering on at the speed of synapse, and me unable to not listen.

I have always valued quiet, and the eternity of it that I face is no more dreadful than the eternity of quiet that preceded my birth.

If White Hill were to be at the other end of those centuries of torture, I know I could tolerate the excruciation. But she was dead now, at least in the sense that I would never see her again.

Another woman might have tried to give me a false hope, the possibility that in some remote future the process of *jaturnary* would be advanced to the point where her personality could be recovered. But she knew how unlikely that would be even if teams of scientists could be found to work on it, and years could be found for them to work in. It would be like unscrambling an egg.

Maybe I would even do it, though, if there were just some chance that, when I was released from that din of garrulous bondage, there would be something like a real world, a world where I could function as an artist. But I don't think there will even be a world where I can function as a man.

There probably won't be any humanity at all, soon enough. What they did to the Sun they could do to all of our stars, one assumes. They win the war, the Extermination, as my parent called it. Wrong side exterminated.

Of course the Fwndyri might not find White Hill and her charges. Even if they do find them, they might leave them preserved as an object of study.

The prospect of living on eternally under those circumstances, even if there were some growth to compensate for the immobility and the company, holds no appeal.

●□

What I did in the time remaining before mid-Deciembre was write this account. Then I had it translated by a xenolinguist into a form that she said could be decoded by any creature sufficiently similar to humanity to make any sense of the story. Even the Fwndyri, perhaps. They're human enough to want to wipe out a competing species.

I'm looking at the preliminary sheets now, English down the left side and a jumble of dots, squares, and triangles down the right. Both sides would have looked equally strange to me a few years ago.

White Hill's story will be conjoined to a standard book that starts out with basic mathematical principles, in dots and squares and triangles, and moves from that into physics, chemistry, biology. Can you go from biology to the human heart? I have to hope so. If this is read by alien eyes, long after the last human breath is stilled, I hope it's not utter gibberish.

□

So I will take this final sheet down to the translator and then deliver the whole thing to the woman who is going to transfer it to permanent sheets of platinum, which will be put in a prominent place aboard the transport. They could last a million years, or ten million, or more. After the Sun is a cinder, and the ship is a frozen block enclosing a thousand bits of frozen flesh, she will live on in this small way.

So now my work is done. I'm going outside, to the quiet.

Charles Sheffield was born in England and received his doctorate in physics from Cambridge University. After a notable career in space science, particularly in satellite observation of the Earth, he has turned to an energetic career in hard SF. From his first novel, *Sight of Proteus,* he has dealt in large, philosophically deep issues embodied in scientific issues. It was no accident that he published a novel on the "orbital elevator" concept, *The Web Between the Stars,* the same year as Arthur Clarke's *The Fountains of Paradise* was published. In many ways he resembles Clarke in interests and depth.

In "At the Eschaton," Sheffield takes us from the present to the very end of time. His protagonist is a man of Shakespearean scale, obsessive, using space and time as a stage for his grand passion. This view of humans as the focus of their own narratives lies at the core of much ardent science fiction, such as Frank Herbert's *Dune.* To many in the hard-science-fiction community, the only protagonist worthy of us is the universe itself. Its cool laws ignore us. The slight is not overlooked.

AT THE ESCHATON

Charles Sheffield

Time: the Great Healer, the Universal Solvent.

And if time cannot be granted?

When Drake Merlin finally received a clear medical diagnosis after months of specialist hedging and secret terrors and false hopes, Ana had less than five weeks to live. She was already in a final decline. Suddenly, after six marvelous years together and a future that seemed to spread out before them for fifty more, they saw the world collapse to a handful of days.

Drake had known in his heart that there was a big problem. Ana's loss of weight and general lassitude were bad omens. But it was the translucent, waxen sheen to her forehead and the fine blue veins on her temples that had delivered the worst message. When Tom Lambert, a close personal friend as well as Drake's own family doctor, provided the grim biopsy result it was no real surprise.

"An operation?" Ana, as always, was calm and rational.

Tom shook his head. "Too widespread."

"How about chemotherapy?"

"We'll try that, naturally." Tom hesitated. "But I have to tell you,

Ana, the prognosis with what you have is not good. We can treat you, but we can't cure you."

"I guess that's it, then." Ana stood up, already a little unsteady on her feet because of the muscle loss in her legs. "I'm going to bring coffee for all of us. It ought to have perked by now. Cream and sugar, Tom?"

"Uh—yes." Tom looked up at her unhappily. "No, I mean, cream, no sugar. Whatever."

As soon as Ana was safely out of the room he turned to Drake. "She's in denial. That's natural and not at all surprising. It will take a while for her to adjust."

"No." Drake Merlin stood up and went across to the window. The last heavy snow of the winter was melting, and fresh green shoots of spring growth were poking through. "You don't know Ana. She's the ultimate realist. Not like me. I'm the one that's in denial."

"I'm going to prescribe painkillers for Ana. As much as she needs. There's no virtue in pain, and in a case like this I don't worry about addiction. And I'm going to prescribe tranquilizers, too—for both of you." Tom looked toward the kitchen, making sure that Ana was still out of earshot. "At times like this, I feel that medical science is still in the dark ages. You might as well know the truth, there's not one damned thing we can do for her. Forget the chemotherapy. If it buys more than a few weeks for Anastasia I'll be surprised. As a doctor I have to worry about you now, Drake. Don't neglect your own health. And remember I can be here, night or day, whenever either one of you needs me."

Ana was coming back. She paused on the threshold, holding a tray of cups, coffeepot, and cream. She smiled and arched an eyebrow. "Safe for me to come back in?"

Drake looked at her. She was thin and fragile, but she had never been more beautiful. At the idea of living without her his heart dropped within his chest, to lodge like a cold, heavy stone in the pit of his belly. And then, just as quickly, his mood changed to fierce determination.

Ana was his life, without her there was nothing. He could not bear to lose her, he would not lose her. Ever.

When Tom had gone and Ana was in the bedroom, Drake flushed his prescription down the drain. There would be enough opportunity for sorrow later. Now he had work to do and little time to do it. He needed all his faculties, unblurred by drugs. He and Ana had always done their thinking and planning together. It couldn't be like that this time. If Ana knew or guessed what he had in mind, she would veto it. She would make him promise, on her dying body, that he would not do it.

So she must not know, must never even suspect.

It took three frantic weeks to make his plans, sleeping a couple of hours a night, making his long-distance telephone calls when Ana lay in drugged sleep. For a few days after that he and Ana seemed to live in an opiate dreamworld, touching, smiling, savoring each other, drifting.

Except that Drake had taken no drugs and he could not afford to drift. When he was ready for the final step, he called Tom Lambert and asked him to come over to the house.

Tom arrived early in the evening. It was fantastic May weather, with spring flowers leaping to blossom and bursting life everywhere except in the darkened house. Ana was sleeping in the front bedroom. Tom gave her a brief examination, then led Drake into the living room. He shook his head.

"It's going even faster than I thought. At this rate Anastasia will pass into a final coma in the next three or four days. You ought to let me take her to a hospital now. You really don't want to see what's coming. And you need the rest. You don't look as though you've had a wink of sleep yourself for the past month."

"There'll be time enough for sleep. I want her to stay here with me." Drake placed Tom in the window seat and sat himself down opposite, knee to knee. He explained what he had been doing for the past few weeks, what he wanted Tom to do in the next few.

Tom Lambert heard him out without a word. Then he shrugged his shoulders.

"If that's what you want to do, Drake, it's your call." There was a pitying look in his eyes. "I'll help you, of course I will. And Anastasia has nothing at all to lose. But you realize, don't you, that they've never done a successful thaw and revival?"

"On fish, and amphibians—"

"Which means next to nothing. We're talking *humans*. I have to tell you, in my opinion you are wasting your time. Just making the whole thing harder for yourself. What does Ana have to say about the idea?"

"Not much." It was a direct lie. The idea had never been discussed with her. "She's willing, maybe more for my sake than hers. She thinks that it won't work, but she agrees that she has nothing to lose. Look, I'd rather you don't even mention this to her. It's almost like assuming she is already dead. I'll prepare the papers for you to sign. And I'll get Ana's signature."

"Better not wait too long." Tom's face was grim. "If you're going to do it, she has to be able to hold a pen."

o   o   o

Four days later Drake called Tom Lambert again to the house. The doctor went to the bedroom, felt Ana's pulse, and took blood pressure and brain-wave readings.

He emerged stone-faced. "I'm afraid this is it, Drake. I'll be very surprised if she regains consciousness. If you are still set on this thing, it has to be done now. She still has some signs of normal body functions. Another three days and it will be a waste of time."

The two men went together into the bedroom. Drake took a last look at Ana's calm, ravaged face. He told himself that this was not a last farewell. At last he nodded to Tom.

"Any time."

Time, time. A waste of time. To the end of time. Time heals all wounds. Oh, call back yesterday, bid time return.

"Go ahead, Tom. There's no point in waiting."

The physician injected five cc's of Asfanil. Working together, they lifted Ana from the bed and removed her clothes. Drake wheeled in the prepared thermal tank. He laid her gently into it. She was so light, it was as though part of her was already lost to him.

While Tom filled out the death certificate, Drake placed the call to Second Chance. He told them to come at once to the house. He set the tank at three degrees above freezing, as instructed. Tom inserted the catheters and the IVs. The next stages were automatic, controlled by the tank's own programs. Blood was withdrawn through a large hollow needle in the main external iliac artery, cooled a precise amount, and returned to the femoral vein.

In ten minutes Ana's body temperature had dropped thirty degrees. All life signs had vanished. She was now legally dead. By an earlier generation, Drake Merlin and Tom Lambert would have been judged murderers. It was hard for Tom not to feel that way as they sat in the silence of the bedroom, awaiting the arrival of the Second Chance team. Drake's thoughts were fortunately beyond his friend's imaginings.

Drake had a hard time persuading Tom Lambert and the three women who arrived from Second Chance. Not one of them could see a reason for Drake to go over to the Second Chance preparation facility with Ana's body.

Tom thought that Drake just couldn't face the idea that it was all over, and he urged his friend to come on home with him. The preparation team didn't know what to make of it. Drake probably seemed like a ghoul to them, or maybe some sort of necrophiliac. They carefully explained that the procedures were most unpleasant to watch, especially for someone who was personally involved. Wouldn't Drake be much better off leaving everything to their experienced hands, and going to stay with his friend? They would make sure that everything was all right, and if he was worried they would be sure to call him as soon as the work was finished.

Drake couldn't tell them the real reason why he had to see the whole preparation procedure down to the last grisly detail. But by simply refusing to take no for an answer, he at last had his way.

The head of the team became convinced that Drake wanted to come along because he was afraid that some element of the job would be botched. She explained carefully to him on the one-hour drive, sitting opposite him in the rear of the van next to the temperature-controlled casket.

"Most of the Revivables—we much prefer that term to 'cryo-corpses'—are stored at liquid nitrogen temperatures. That's about minus two hundred degrees Celsius. It's almost certainly cold enough. But it's still about seventy-five degrees above absolute zero. Although all measurable biological processes become imperceptible long before that, you can argue that there are plenty of chemical reactions going on. The laws of statistics guarantee that a few atoms will still have enough energy to induce biological changes. And mind and memory are very delicate things. So for people who are worried about that, we make available the deluxe version. That's what you bought. Your wife will be stored at liquid helium temperatures, just a couple of degrees above absolute zero. Super-safe. When it's so cold the chance of change, physical or mental, goes way down."

And the cost, although she did not mention the fact, went way up. But cost was not even a variable to be considered in Drake's perspective. He hung around the preparation room, ignoring all hints that he should wait outside, and he watched closely.

The team were not unsympathetic. They were now convinced that he was simply terrified that a mistake would be made, and they finally allowed him to see everything and answered all his questions. He was careful not to ask anything that sounded too clinical and dispassionate. The main thing he wanted was to *see,* to know at absolute first hand what had been done, and in what sequence.

After the first few minutes there was not much to see, anyway. He knew that all the air cavities within Ana's body had been filled with neutral solution, and her blood replaced with anticrystalloids. But then she went into the seamless pressure chamber. The body was held there at three degrees above freezing, while pressure was raised slowly to five thousand atmospheres. After that was done, the temperature drop started.

"Back in the seventies and eighties, they had no idea of this technique." The team leader was talking to Drake, perhaps with the false idea that she might be able to make him feel more relaxed. "They used to do the freezing at atmospheric pressure. There was a formation of ice crystals within the cells as the temperature dropped, and it was a mess when the thaw was done. No return to consciousness at all."

She smiled reassuringly at Drake, who was not reassured at all. So they didn't know what they were doing in the seventies and eighties. Would they claim, in twenty more years, that people didn't know what they were doing *now*? But there was no alternative to that risk. He couldn't wait for twenty years.

"The modern method is quite different," she went on. "We make use of the fact that ice can exist in many different solid forms. Ice is complicated stuff, much more than most people realize. If you raise the pressure to three thousand atmospheres, then drop the temperature, water will remain liquid to about minus twenty degrees Celsius. And when it finally changes to a solid, it isn't the familiar form of ice—what is usually called Phase I. Instead it turns to something called Phase III. Drop the temperature from there, holding the pressure constant, and at about minus twenty-five degrees it changes to another form, Phase II. And it stays that way as you drop the temperature still farther. If you go to five thousand atmospheres pressure—that's what we are doing here—before you drop the temperature, water freezes at about minus five degrees and adopts still another form, Phase V. The trick to avoiding cell rupture problems at freezing point is to inject anticrystalloids, which help to inhibit crystal formation, then by the right combination of temperatures and pressures work all the way down toward absolute zero, passing into and through Phases V, III, and II.

"That's what we are doing now. But don't expect to see much except dial readings. For obvious reasons, the pressure chamber is made without seams and without observation ports. You don't get pressures of five thousand atmospheres, not even in the deepest ocean gulfs. Fortunately, once you have the temperature down below a hundred degrees absolute, you can reduce the pressure to one atmosphere—otherwise the storage of Revivables would be quite impracticable. As it is, we have three-quarters of a million stacked away in the Second Chance wombs. Every one of them is neatly labeled and waiting for the resurrection. As soon as someone figures out how."

She glanced at Drake, aware that her last comment might have been the wrong thing to say. The official position at Second Chance was that *everyone* was revivable, and in due course everyone would be revived.

Drake nodded without expression. He had researched the whole subject in detail, and nothing that she had said so far was news. In his opinion it would be as hard to revivify the early cryocorpses as it would be to get Tutankhamen's mummy up and moving again. They had been frozen with the wrong procedure, and they were being stored at too high a temperature.

But who was he to make that decision? They had paid their deposits, and they had the right to sit there in the wombs until their rentals ran out. He had started Ana with a forty-year contract, but he thought of that as probably just the beginning.

He had brought with him a copy of Ana's medical records. He added to it a full description of everything that he had seen in the past hour or two, copied the whole document, and made sure that a complete set was included with the file records on Ana. When Ana's body was finally taken away for storage, he went back to the house, fell into bed, and slept like a cryocorpse himself for sixteen hours.

It was time to drop the other shoe.

When Drake was fully awake again, fed and bathed, he called Tom Lambert and asked to see him at his home rather than his office. He accepted a hefty drink that Tom prepared, after one look at him, for "medicinal purposes," and laid out his plans.

After he was finished Tom walked over to his chair, poked the muscles in his shoulders and the back of his neck, pulled down his lower eyelid and stared at the exposed skin, and finally went to sit opposite him.

"You've been under a monstrous strain this past few months," he said quietly.

"Very true. I have." Drake kept his voice just as calm.

"And it would be quite unnatural for your behavior or feelings to be completely normal. In fact, if you seem normal now it's only because you have completely walled in your true feelings. And you certainly don't understand the implications of what you are proposing to me."

Drake shook his head. "This isn't new. It's only new to you. I've been thinking of this since the day we had the first suggestion of a terminal diagnosis."

"Then that was the day you put the lid on your true feelings." Tom Lambert leaned forward. "Look, Drake, Anastasia was a wonderful woman, a unique woman. I won't say I know what you have been through, because I don't, but I have at least some idea of your sense of loss. But you have to ask yourself what Ana would want you to do now.

You can't let the sad past become your obsession. She would tell you that you still have a life of your own, and even without her you have to live it. She would *want* you to live it, because she loved you. Let me make a suggestion. . . ."

While Tom was talking, Drake had found it harder and harder to listen. The room felt dull and airless and he had trouble breathing. Tom Lambert's words came from far off. They didn't seem to say anything. He forced himself to concentrate, to listen harder.

". . . of your work. You are still a young man. Forty to fifty good years ahead of you. And already you have a reputation. You are one of this country's most promising composers and your best works still lie ahead. Ana may have performed your work better than anyone else, but there will be others. They will learn. With your talent you owe it to the rest of us not to cut your career off before it reaches its peak."

"I have no intention of doing so. I will compose again. Later."

"You mean, later after *that?*" Tom was frowning and shaking his head. "Suppose there is no later? Drake, take my advice as both your doctor and your friend. You desperately need to get out of this house, and you need to take a vacation. Go off on a cruise somewhere, take a trip around the world. Expose yourself to some new influences. I know how you must feel now, but you should give it a year and see how you feel *then*. I guarantee you, everything will seem different. You'll want to live again. You'll give up this mad idea."

The breathless feeling was fading. Drake again had control of himself. He waited patiently until Tom Lambert was finished, then nodded agreement.

"I'll do as you say, Tom. I'll get away from here for a while. But if you are wrong—if I come back to you, in, say, eight or ten years, and I ask you again, will you do it? Will you help me? I want you to give me an honest answer, and I want your word on it."

The tension drained visibly from Tom Lambert. He snorted in relief. "Ten years from now? Drake, if you come back to me in eight or ten years and and ask me again, I'll admit I was completely wrong. And I promise you, I'll help you to do what you've asked."

"An absolute promise? I don't want to hear someday that you changed your mind, or didn't mean what you said."

"An absolute promise, sure I'll give you that." Tom laughed. "But I'm not worried that I'll ever be called on it. I'll bet you everything I own that after a year or two have gone by, you'll never mention that promise again." He walked over to the sideboard and poured himself a drink. "I'd like to propose a toast, Drake. Or actually, three toasts. To us, to your future, and to your next and greatest composition."

Drake raised his glass in return. "I can only drink to part of that, Tom. Here's to us, and here's to the future. But I can't drink to my next work, because I don't know when I'll create it. I have lots of things to do—for one thing, you told me to get out of town. I'm going to do that right away. But don't worry, I'll be in touch."

It was a half truth. Drake would not leave until certain other plans were more firmly fixed. But he certainly expected to be in touch with Tom Lambert when the time came.

There were two problems. One was simple and well defined: money. Drake needed enough to make sure that Ana could remain safe within the icy womb for the indefinite future, until she could be safely thawed and her disease could be cured. Then her life would begin again. There were a few things he obviously couldn't guard against, such as a total collapse of the world to barbarism, or the rejection of all present forms of currencies and commodities. Those were risks that Ana—and he— would have to accept.

The other problem was more subtle. According to Tom it might be a long time before a cure was found for Ana's rare and highly malignant disease. As he pointed out, something that killed only a few people a year did not get the attention of common cancers and heart diseases, which killed hundreds of millions.

Suppose that a cure was not discovered for a century, or even for two centuries. What knowledge of present-day society would interest people in the year 2200? What should a man know or a woman be, for the inhabitants of that future Earth to think it worthwhile to revive them? Drake was convinced that even when a foolproof way of resuscitating the Revivables was discovered, most of the unfortunates in the wombs would remain exactly where they were. The contracts with Second Chance provided only for maintenance in a cryonic condition. They did not, and could not, offer a guarantee that an individual would be thawed.

Why thaw anyone at all? Why add another to a crowded world, unless he or she had something special to offer?

Drake imagined himself back in the early nineteenth century. What could he have placed into his brain, then, that would be considered valuable today, two hundred years later? Not politics, or art. Knowledge of them was quite adequate. Certainly not science, or any technology— progress in the last two centuries had been phenomenal.

He had plenty of time to consider the question; time, which had been denied to Ana. It would be foolish to hurry, when he could plan and calculate at his leisure. He had set a goal of ten years, which would still allow forty of the shared fifty that he had looked for and longed for. But he was quite willing to stretch that by a couple of years.

If it did take more time, it would not be because he was distracted with other activities. While he worked and pondered, his only diversion was to estimate the probabilities that everything would work out as he hoped. Always, the odds came out depressingly low.

While he was trying to decide what he needed to learn, he was hard at work on the first problem: making money. He deliberately turned his back on compositions that broke new ground and offered new challenges. Instead he took commissions, wrote commemorative pieces, gave concerts, made recordings, and produced reams of music for good, bad, and indifferent shows and movies. If anyone thought that he was debasing his art and cashing in on his reputation, they were too polite to comment on it. His own attitude was simple: if it was lucrative, it was acceptable.

Occasionally it was also unpleasant, grinding toil. But sometimes, oddly enough, the commercial challenges seemed to bring out the best in him. The finest melody he had ever conceived provided the theme music to a successful television show. And after four years he had an even bigger stroke of luck.

He had written a set of short pieces a couple of years after he and Ana first met, as a kind of musical joke designed especially to appeal to her. They were baroque forms, with baroque period harmonies, but he had added occasional modern harmonic twists, piquancy inserted where it would be most surprising and most appealing.

They had been quite successful, although only among a limited audience. Now, given a commission to provide the incidental music for a series of television dramas on life in eighteenth-century France, and facing an impossible deadline, he returned to cannibalize and adapt his own earlier work. The dramas turned out to be the hit of the decade, with his music credited as a big part of the reason for their success. Suddenly his minuets, bourrées, gavottes, sarabandes, and rondeaux were everywhere. And as they flooded from the audio outlets, the royalties flooded in from every country around the globe.

Drake went on working as hard as ever, but as soon as he could he established a foundation and trust fund. It guaranteed continued care for Ana's cryocorpse for many centuries, no matter what happened to Drake himself.

Freed from a need for money, his work vectors changed direction. Instead of regular composition he became feverishly busy soaking up all that he could learn of the private and personal lives of his musical contemporaries. He interviewed, entertained, courted, and analyzed them, and he wrote about them extensively. But never quite in full. In every piece he was careful to leave a hanging tail—a hint, that said, "there is much more to say and I know what it is; but for the moment I am deliberately leaving it unsaid."

What would the people of the future most want to know about their ancestors? Drake had his own answer. Their fascination would not be with the formal works, the official biographies, the textbook knowledge. They would have more than enough of those. What they would want would be the personal details, the chat, the gossip. They would want the equivalent of Boswell's journals and of Samuel Pepys's diaries. And if there was a way that they could have not only the written legacy, but the recorder himself, to talk to him and ask more questions . . .

It was not work that could be hurried. But finally, after nine long years, Drake was as ready as he would ever be. There was always the temptation to add one more interview, write one more article.

He resisted, and briefly worried a different question. How would he earn a living in the future? It might be only twenty years, but it might be fifty, two hundred, or a thousand. Could Beethoven, suddenly transported to the year 2000, have earned a living as a musician?

More realistically, how would Spohr, or Hummel, or some other of Beethoven's less famous contemporaries have fared? Drake was betting that they, and he, could manage very well as soon as they had picked up the tricks of the time. Better, probably, than the far greater genius, the titan of Bonn. They were more facile, more flexible, more politically astute.

And if he was wrong, and there was no way that he could make a living from his music? Then he would do the twenty-third-century equivalent of washing dishes for a living. That was the least of his worries.

One day he stopped everything, put his affairs in order, and returned home. Without notice he headed for Tom Lambert's house. They had kept in touch, and he knew that Tom had married and was busy raising a family in the same house that he had lived in all his life. But it was still a surprise to walk along that quiet tree-lined street, look over the same untidy privet hedge, and see Tom in the front yard playing baseball with a stranger, an eight-year-old boy who wore a flaming new version of Tom's greying red mop.

"Drake! My God, why didn't you call and tell me you were in town? How do you do it, you're as thin as ever." Tom had lost some of his hair, but added a paunch to make up for it. He ushered Drake into his house and fussed over him like the Prodigal Son, leading the way into the familiar study. While his wife went into the kitchen to kill the fatted calf, he stood and beamed at Drake with pride and pleasure.

"We hear your music everywhere, you know," he said. "It's absolutely wonderful to know that your career is going so well."

Judged by Drake's own standards, it was not. He knew that he had done no first-rate composition in years. But Tom, like most people, was comfortable musically with what he found most familiar. From that point of view, and in terms of commercial success, Drake was riding high.

He itched to get down to business right away, but Tom's three young boys hovered around the study and the living room, curious to see the famous visitor. Then came a family dinner, and liqueurs after it watching the sunset, with Drake in the guest-of-honor seat and Tom and his wife, Mary-Jane, doing most of the talking.

At ten o'clock Mary-Jane disappeared to put the boys to bed. Drake was alone with Tom. At last. He took out the application and handed it to his friend without a word.

As Tom looked at it and realized what it was, all the happiness faded from his face. He shook his head in disbelief.

"I thought you put all this behind you years ago. What started it going again?"

Drake stared at him without speaking, as though he had not understood the question.

"Or maybe it never stopped," Tom went on. "I should have guessed it hours ago. You used to be so full of life, so full of *fun*. Tonight I don't think I saw you smile even once. When did you last take a vacation?"

"You gave me your word, Tom. Your promise."

Lambert studied the other man's thin face. "Never mind a vacation, when did you last take *any* sort of break from work? How long since you relaxed for an evening, or even for an hour? Not tonight, that's for sure."

"I go out all the time, to concerts and to dinner parties."

"You do. And what do you do there? I bet you don't relax. You interview people, and you take notes, and then you produce a stream of articles. You *work*. And you've been working, incessantly, year after year. How long since you've been with a woman?"

Drake shook his head but did not speak.

Tom sighed. "I'm sorry. Forget that I asked that, it was a dumb, insensitive thing to say. But you need to face a fact, Drake, and you shouldn't try to hide from it: she's dead. Do you hear me. *Ana is dead.* Work won't change that. Nothing can bring her back to you. And you can't go on forever with your own emotions chained and harnessed."

"You promised me, Tom. You gave me your solemn word that you would help me."

"Drake!"

"Do you ever make promises to your children?"

"Of course I do."

"Do you keep them?"

"Drake, you can't use that argument, the situations are totally different. You act as though I made you some sort of solemn vow, but it wasn't like that at all."

"Then how was it? Don't bother to answer." Drake took the little recorder out from his inside jacket pocket. "Listen."

The words were thin in tone, but quite clear.

. . . if I come back to you, in, say, eight or ten years, and I ask you again, will you do it? Will you help me? I want you to give me an honest answer, and I want your word on it.

Ten years from now? Drake, if you come back to me in eight or ten years and ask me again, I'll admit I was completely wrong. And I promise you, I'll help you to do what you've asked.

An absolute promise? I don't want to hear someday that you changed your mind, or didn't mean what you said.

An absolute promise, sure I'll give you that. . . . There was the sound of Tom's relieved laugh.

Drake turned off the recorder. "I said, eight to ten years. It has been nine."

"You recorded us, back then at the very beginning? I can't believe you would do that."

"I had to, Tom. Even then, I was convinced that you would change your mind. And I knew that I wouldn't. You have to live up to your agreement. You promised."

"I promised to *help* you, to stop you from doing something crazy to yourself." Tom's face was flushed with intolerable frustration. "For God's sake, Drake, I'm a *doctor*. You can't ask me to help you to kill yourself."

"I'm not asking that."

"You might as well be. No one has ever been revived. Maybe no one ever will be. If they do learn how, Anastasia will be a candidate. She is in the best Second Chance womb, she had the best preparation money could buy. But you, you're different. You're not even sick! Ana was dying before she was frozen. You're healthy, you're productive, you're at the height of your career. And you are asking me to throw all that away, to help you take the long chance that someday, God knows when, you just might be revived. Don't you see, Drake, I can't help you."

"You gave me your promise."

"Stop saying that! I also made an oath as a physician: to do no harm. But you want me to take you from perfect health to a high odds of final death."

"I have to do it, Tom. If you won't help I'll find someone who will. Probably someone less competent and reliable than you."

"*Why* do you have to do it? Give me one good reason."

"You know why, if you think about it." Drake spoke slowly, coaxingly. "For Ana's sake. Unless I go on ahead, they may never choose to wake her. She could be one of the last on their list. You and I know her for what she really is, a unique and marvelous woman. But what will the records show? A singer, still not as famous as she would have been, who died young of a devastating disease. I've had time to prepare, I'm sure that they will wake me. And it's an advantage that I'm in good health now, because there will be no reason to delay my revival on medical grounds. As soon as I am sure that they have a cure for what killed Ana, I can wake her. We'll start over, the two of us."

Tom Lambert's cheeks had gone from fiery red to pale. "We have to talk about this some more, Drake. The whole idea is crazy. Did you really mean what you said, that if I won't help you will go to someone else?"

"Look at me, Tom. Tell me if you think that I mean it."

Lambert looked. He did not speak again; but his hands slowly came up to cover his eyes.

It took four days of solid argument, another five to make final preparations. Drake Merlin and Tom Lambert drove together to Second Chance.

Drake took a long last look out of the window at the windblown trees and the cloudy sky, then climbed slowly into the thermal tank.

Tom injected the Asfanil.

It took only a few seconds before the long fall began, dropping steadily down the longest descent that a human can ever make.

Down, down, down. All the way to two degrees absolute, colder than the coldest hell ever conceived by Dante.

Drake could never be sure. Had he truly dreamed those superconducting dreams, lying there twelve degrees colder than a block of solid hydrogen? Or had he only dreamed that he dreamed them, as he came slowly back through the long thaw?

It made little difference. There was still an eternity of twisted images, a procession of pale and terrifying lights moving against a pitch-dark background. They arrived well ahead of any form of consciousness, and they went on forever.

It was daunting, to undergo such torment, and then learn that he had been one of the lucky ones. The freezing process in his case had apparently gone very smoothly. Some awoke armless and legless. All that he lost during the thaw were a few square centimeters of skin.

The pain of waking was something else. The final stages, from three degrees Celsius to normal body temperature, had to be taken slowly. They occupied a full thirty-six hours. For most of that time Drake was pierced with the agony of waking tissues and returning circulation, unable to move or even to cry out. In the last stages, before full consciousness returned, hearing came back before sight. He could hear speech around him, but not in any tongue that he could recognize.

How far had he traveled? Even before the pain faded, that question filled his mind.

The answer did not come at once. While he was still half-conscious he felt the sting of an injector spray. He at once blanked out again. After another infinite hiatus he came up all the way, opening his eyes to a quiet sunlit room not too different from the Second Chance facility where he had begun the descent.

A man and a woman were watching him, talking softly together. As soon as they saw that he was awake the man pressed a point on a segmented wall panel. The two went on with their work, lining up two complex and incomprehensible pieces of equipment.

The person who came in presently through the white sliding door was dark-haired and oddly androgynous, with a face that seemed both clean-shaven and also smooth and womanly. The newcomer stepped to the side of the bed and stood looking down at Drake with a pleased and almost proprietary air.

"How are you feeling?"

Drake knew then that it was a man. He spoke in English, oddly pronounced. That was reassuring. Drake had suffered two worries as he slipped under. What if he was revived in just a few years' time, when nothing at all could be done to cure Ana? Or what if he surfaced after fifty thousand years, a living fossil, quite unable to communicate his needs to the men and women of the future?

"I feel all right. But weak." Drake thought of trying to sit up, then knew at once that he could not do it. "I am as weak as a baby."

"Naturally. Are you Drake Merlin?"

"I am."

The man nodded in satisfaction. "Excellent. My name is Par Leon. Can you understand me easily?"

"Perfectly easily." Drake's second worry returned. "Why do you ask that question? *When* am I?"

"I ask it because the old languages are not easy, even with augments and much study. For your second question, in your measure we are now in the year 2587 of the prophet Christ."

Almost six centuries. It was longer than Drake had expected. But better long than short. He had entertained awful visions of being forced to do the whole thing over and over, diving down to the bottom of the Pit and then clawing his agonized way back up to thawed life.

"I have waited here through the whole warming and first treatment," Par Leon continued. "Soon I will leave you here for rest, for more treatment, and for first education. But I desired to speak with you at once when you became conscious. It is not rational, but I feared that there might be a mistake in identity—that it might not be Drake Merlin, the Drake Merlin of my curiosity, who was awakened." Par Leon glanced at the equipment standing at the bedside and shook his head. "You are a strong man, Drake Merlin. Uniquely strong. The record shows that you did not once cry out or complain during all the thawing."

There had been other things on Drake's mind. Could Ana be cured? He glanced across at the other two workers, who were still chatting together in an alien tongue. "Language must have changed completely. I can understand you easily, but I cannot understand them at all."

"You mean, understand the doctors?" Par Leon replied with a surprised expression on his lean face. "Of course not. Neither can I. Naturally, they are speaking Medicine."

Drake raised his eyebrows. The look must have survived with its meaning intact across six centuries, because Par Leon at once went on, "I myself speak Music and History—and, of course, Universal. And I learned Old Anglic enough to be able to study your times and to speak with you. But I know no Medicine."

"Medicine is a *language?*" Drake felt that his mind must be slowed by the long sleep and thawing treatment.

"Of course. Like Music, or Chemistry, or Astronautics. But surely this was already true in your own time. Did you not have languages specific to each—what is your word?—discipline?"

"I suppose that we did, but we didn't know it." Par Leon's question explained a great deal. No wonder that Drake had found psychologists, professional educators, social scientists, and computer scientists—to name but a few—quite incomprehensible. The special jargon and odd acronyms signaled the arrival of new proto-languages, emerging forms as alien as Sanskrit or classical Greek. "How do you speak to the doctors?"

"For ordinary things we employ Universal, which all understand. I do not attempt to speak actual Medicine. If I am in that subject-matter area, we keep a computer in the circuit to provide exact concept equivalents between language pairs."

It occurred to Drake that multidisciplinary programs must be hell. But then, they always had been. He was beginning to feel oddly and irrationally euphoric, a combination of drugs and the idea that he might succeed after all in the longest shot of his life.

He made a determined effort to sit up. His head lifted maybe five centimeters from the pillow, then fell back despite everything he could do to hold it up.

"Slowly. Rome—was not built—in a day." Par Leon glowed, clearly delighted at coming up with such a prize example of genuine Old Anglic. "It will be moons before you are fully strong. Two more things I will tell you, then I will allow your treatment to continue.

"First, it was I who arranged for you to be brought here and revived. I am a musicologist, interested in the twentieth and twenty-first centuries, and in particular your own time."

Drake's bet, six hundred years old now, had paid off. He wondered what modern music sounded like. Would he be able to compose it?

"Under our laws," Par Leon went on, "you owe me for the cost of your revival and treatment. This amounts to six years of work from you. You are most fortunate that you were healthy and correctly frozen and maintained, or the time of service would have been much longer. However, I also believe that you will find your indenture with me both pleasant and interesting. I am proposing that you and I, together, write the definitive history of your own musical period."

So the question of earning a living was postponed for at least a few years. Par Leon would surely have to feed Drake Merlin while he was paying off his debt.

"Second, I have good news for you." Par Leon was gazing at Drake expectantly. "When we examined you, our doctors found certain problems—defects, you would say?—with your body and its glandular balance. They hope that they have cured the simpler body malfunctions, and you should now live between one hundred and seventy and two hundred years.

"However, the glandular imbalance represented a more subtle problem. It was likely to manifest itself as some form of madness, some uncontrollable compulsion. The doctors observed this as soon as you were thawed enough to respond to psycho-probes. They made small chemical changes and have, we hope, corrected the difficulty." Par Leon was watching Drake closely. "Please tell me now of your feelings toward the woman, Anastasia."

Drake felt his heart racing. He could hear the blood pounding in his ears, and it was as hard to breathe as if heavy weights sat on his chest. He closed his eyes for a long moment, and thought about Ana until he became calm again.

It was obvious what the other man wanted to hear; and Ana was worth a million lies. Drake looked up at Par Leon and shook his head feebly. "I feel very little for her. No more than a faint sense that something was once there. It is like the scar of an old wound."

"Excellent!" The smile had kept its meaning. "That is most satisfying. The disease that killed the woman was eliminated from the human stock long ago, by careful mating choice—eugenics, as your language puts it. We could certainly reanimate her, but according to our doctors it is still not clear that we would be able to cure her. However, we can see no reason to awaken her at all. Like most in the cryowombs, she is of little or no value to us. Most important of all, an involvement with her might interfere with your work for me."

"So her body is still stored?"

"Of course. We keep all the cryocorpses. Although most are of no present value, who knows what our future needs might be? The cryowombs are like a library of the past, to open whenever it will serve a purpose. Two hundred years from now someone may find a use for her, and her disease perhaps easily cured. Then she, too, may live and work again."

"Is Anastasia stored near here?"

"Of course not!" For the first time, Par Leon appeared to be shocked. "What a waste of space and energy that would imply. The cryowombs are of course maintained on Pluto, where space is cheap, cooling needs are small, and escape velocity is low."

That sentence, more than any other that Par Leon had spoken, wrenched Drake forward in time. What technology was implied, that could casually ship a few million bodies to the edge of the solar system rather than keep them in cold storage on Earth? If, that is, Pluto *was* the edge of the solar system. Six centuries. More than the time from Monteverdi to Shostakovich, from Copernicus to Einstein, from the Columbus discovery of America to the first landing on the Moon. He had come a long, long way.

Par Leon was still gazing at him, now a little suspiciously. "Again you ask about the woman, Anastasia. Why? Are you sure that you are in fact fully cured? If not, another course of treatment is easy to arrange."

Drake cursed his own stupidity and did his best to smile reassuringly. "I feel sure that will not be needed. Already her memory fades. As soon as I am strong enough, I am eager to begin my work with you."

"Wonderful." The smile was back, but Par Leon was wagging his finger in warning. "We will certainly work together, but only *after* you are fully recovered and have had some essential training. First, you must learn to speak Universal and Music and you must have enough background knowledge to live comfortably in this time. It will also be my responsibility to see that you are able to find suitable activity when your work with me is done, and for that you will need skills that today you lack.

"Rest now, Drake Merlin. I will return tomorrow, or the next day. By that time you will already find yourself stronger. And you will be far more knowledgeable."

As Par Leon left, the medical technicians carried forward a transparent helmet with silvered lines inscribed on its upper part. They lowered it carefully onto Drake's head.

He lost consciousness at once, too quickly to be aware of its cool touch.

When he awoke he already had a smattering of Universal and a good but superficial knowledge of solar-system civilization in the twenty-sixth century. Par Leon's confidence that he would pick up new knowledge quickly did not depend on anything so unreliable as old-fashioned learning.

Facts, vocabulary, and rules could be instilled almost instantly using the feedback helmets. Use of language, particularly spoken language, came more slowly because it required physical coordination and practice.

However, a civilization was far more than facts, rules, and languages. In some areas Par Leon proved to be an extreme optimist. In fact, after a couple of weeks Drake decided that certain aspects of the times would be forever beyond him, no matter how long he lived there.

Science was one of them. Modern science, particularly the basic assumptions that underlay modern science, totally eluded his grasp. It was no surprise that he would find science difficult. That had always been the case. In his own time his teachers had accused him of having talent but no interest, dreaming his days away with words and music.

Even so, the general ideas of science ought to be accessible. They were supposed to be no more than common sense, elevated to become a discipline. But he found himself struggling hopelessly—and he *was* struggling, working harder to understand than he had ever done as a young man.

A scientist recruited by Par Leon did her best to help, explaining the difficulty within the less precise vocabulary available in Universal. Drake had already given up any notion of learning Science for himself.

"It is the typical problem of a major paradigm shift." Cass Leemu was a young and attractive brunette, whose own field of specialty Drake had been unable to comprehend even after hours of conversation. It seemed to be no more than pictures, but somehow it yielded quantitative results. "Drake Merlin, is the name of Isaac Newton familiar to you?"

"Of course. Gravity, and the laws of motion."

"Right. Familiar, and easy to comprehend. We agree on that. But did you know that most of his contemporaries found his work quite beyond them? He introduced notions of absolute space and time, which they found implausible. And his work was best understood employing the calculus, which seemed to the scientists of the seventeenth century to be shrouded in the paradoxes of infinitely small quantities. It took two generations to absorb the new worldview, and work with it comfortably. The same thing happened two centuries later, when Maxwell elevated the concept of a *field* to central importance. And again in the twentieth century, when uncertainty and undecidability assumed a dominant position almost simultaneously in the prevailing worldview."

"And you are telling me that it has happened again?"

"It has happened." Cass Leemu smiled ruefully. "Not once, Drake, but three times. Three major viewpoint shifts. Our understanding of Nature differs more from the perspectives of your time than yours differed from the Romans'."

"So I am going to be like Newton's colleagues, unable to comprehend a new foundation."

"I am afraid so. Unless you can master the concept of—" She paused, then smiled again at Drake, this time apologetically. "I am sorry. The word for the idea that now underlies science lacks any adequate paraphrase in Universal. Even the general data banks are silent. But if you really wish to study science, beginning with the absolute basics, I may be able to help you."

"I can't. Not yet." Drake was reluctant to give Cass Leemu an outright no—he might need a sympathetic ear later. "You see, I owe the next six years to Par Leon. He revived me."

"Of course. Six years only? He is being generous."

Cass was unconsciously pointing out to Drake that the brave new world he now lived in contained other elements at least as hard to grasp as science. Slavery did not exist, but six years of absolute service to another was taken for granted. Its ethical basis was never questioned. But Drake could not understand that basis. He comforted himself with the thought that Henry VIII would have been appalled at wars that killed civilians, while worrying not at all about a public hanging, drawing, and quartering. Humanity needed few absolutes, because people could live within and justify almost any imaginable variation.

Drake resigned himself to his situation. He had survived, and Ana was safely frozen in the Pluto cryowombs. Before he could do anything to change her status he would first have to earn his own freedom. He resolved to give Par Leon six good, solid years of dedicated effort toward the other man's great lifetime project: the analysis of musical trends in the late twentieth and early twenty-first centuries.

After the first few weeks of effort Par Leon's shrewdness and insight became apparent. More important than any facts that Drake might provide were the perspectives that he had to offer. And more than just science and ethics had changed.

Again and again, he found Par Leon shaking his head. "It is truly astonishing. Did man-woman relationships really play so large a part in *everything* in your society?"

"You know they did." Drake was learning his way around the data banks. "Your own records show it, the ones that we were examining just two days ago."

"Yes. They do show it, but believing it is difficult. Men and women actually appeared to hate each other in your era. Yet at the same time there was much random mating, mating on *impulse*. I do not mean mere sexual acts, that I can comprehend. But random mating that produces *offspring*, without benefit of genome maps or the most rudimentary genetic information on parents and grandparents . . ."

Drake was about to explain when he realized that he couldn't. It was another six-hundred-year gulf that would not be crossed. To Par Leon, mating was dictated by the selection of desirable gene combinations. No other approach could be justified, or even understood.

In any case, Drake was beginning to have problems of his own. There really was no case to be made for the production of children, without thought for their future or for their physical and mental well-being. It was merely the blind mating urge of the primeval slime, deified to become religious principle and blind dogma.

Drake listened to his own thoughts and realized that he was beginning to view his own epoch with a new perspective. He must control that tendency, or his main value to Par Leon would disappear. For that reason, and one other, he had to remain an outsider in this century.

More and more, Drake realized that he was earning his keep. Par Leon might be the century's foremost expert on the music of Drake's period, but in many ways he knew nothing. He was endlessly fascinated by the smallest details.

"You say you *knew* him?" Par Leon leaned forward, eyebrows raised on his high forehead. "You met Renselm in person?"

"A score of times. I was present at the first performance of Morani's *Concerto concertante*, written especially for Renselm, and I went backstage afterwards. Then we went to dinner, just the three of us. I thought you already read about all this in one of my articles."

"Oh, yes." Par Leon made a dismissive gesture. "I certainly *read* it. But this is different. Tell me about his fingering, his posture at the keyboard, his strange reaction to applause. Tell me what he said to you about Adele Winterberg—she was his mistress at the time, you know." He laughed aloud in delight. "Tell me, if you can remember it, what you all ate for dinner."

Only once or twice did Par Leon express dissatisfaction. And then it was because Drake had been frozen just before some event that especially interested him. Even that he accepted philosophically and with good humor.

It was by no means a one-way transfer of information. From his vantage point six centuries ahead, Par Leon had insights into the musical life of an earlier era that left Drake gasping. For the first time, he understood where certain contemporary musical currents had been heading. Krubak, in his much-ridiculed late works, had been feeling his way toward forms that would not mature until thirty years after Drake had been frozen.

The work went on, ten to twelve hours a day. When work was over, Drake spent every spare minute learning about the society in which he was living.

It was an abstract exercise. He had no wish to be absorbed by or become part of that society, since he had no long-term intention of remaining there. Yet he had to know certain subjects in great detail, far more than Par Leon could tell him. Fortunately, the general data banks permitted near-infinite cross-checking and depth of inquiry.

Drake continued his own explorations, to satisfy his own needs.

The whole solar system had been explored and mapped in detail. Venus was in the first stages of terraforming, the acid witch's-brew of its atmosphere dropping slowly in temperature and pressure. Mars was colonized, not on the surface but within the extensive natural caverns beneath it. There were permanent active stations—many of them "manned" by self-replicating computers and repair devices—on all the satellites of the major planets.

And Pluto?

Drake gave that world his special attention. A small crew of scientists had a research station on Charon, the outsized satellite that made the Pluto/Charon system into a small planetary doublet. But Pluto itself was uninhabited unless one counted the dreaming serried ranks of the cryo-corpses. The cryowombs were too cold for animate humans, hovering as they did down at liquid-helium temperature (Drake's earlier suspicion of liquid nitrogen storage had proved well founded). The vaults were tended, to the extent that they needed any sort of attention, by machines especially designed for extreme cold.

With the idea of money subsumed into some incomprehensible system of electronic credit, it was not clear to Drake that he would ever be able to afford to make the long trip out to Pluto. He forced himself to be patient, putting that question to one side until his time of service was closer to its end.

And still the work went on, hard but not unrewarding. The text that they were producing grew steadily. By the beginning of the fourth year, Drake shared Par Leon's conviction that they were producing a classic. He listened to the suggestion that in fairness the two of them should be given equal credit, and shook his head.

"It was all your idea, not mine. You could have found someone else to do what I have done. But without you to revive me . . ."

And I do not plan to be here long enough to take credit, even if it were to be given to me.

Before the end of the sixth year they were approaching project completion. They had also become close friends, or as close as Drake dared to permit. It was not surprising that Par Leon, a good man by any moral standards that Drake would ever be able to comprehend, was beginning to worry about a different problem.

He began to hint at other possible collaborations. Drake read a deeper concern. What would Drake's future be when the project ended? It had apparently not occurred to Par Leon six years ago, but a revival was not unlike a birth. And like a parent, Par Leon now felt responsibility for the future of his "offspring."

Drake was soon able to reassure him, and more easily than he expected. While they were still putting the finishing touches to their mammoth study of "ancient" music, he had started to compose again. He had learned during the project that musical knowledge of the centuries before his birth had some big gaps in it, and facility in different musical idioms had always come easily to him. He could steal tricks from the giants of the past, dress them in the modern style, and pass it off as innovation. In less than a year he had a burgeoning reputation, which he knew was undeserved, a group of imitators, largely untalented, and—most important—a growing financial credit.

At last he could explore a long-postponed question. He suggested to Par Leon that with the project completed, he would like to take an overdue vacation. If he wanted to have a look around the solar system, would it be easy to do so? And could he afford it?

To his surprise, Par Leon could not begin to answer. He hardly seemed to understand the questions.

"Free to go?" The furry eyebrows rose. "Of course you're free to go. But why on Earth would you *want* to go? You're not an astronomer, or an astronaut. There's absolutely nothing out in space for a musician."

"But there are ships available?—for people, I mean, not just machines."

"Ships? Of course there are ships. Loads of ships, as many as you want. And as for cost, there's no *human* cost to making a ship. Machines do the whole thing, and they fly them, too. Unless you are planning to have a human along as your guide?"

"No. Actually, I would rather go alone."

"Then cost doesn't even come into it. You only consume credit if you demand human time for something. Like now." Par Leon laughed. With the project wrapped up, he was in a near-constant state of euphoria. "I could charge you for this advice, you know. But I won't. Go on, Drake, take your holiday. You've certainly earned it."

"I will. In a few more weeks."

"But if you are crazy enough to go to space, don't ask me to go with you!"

Drake laughed, too. He was careful not to mention the subject again to Par Leon. He didn't want his friend to suspect the true depth of his interest.

In the next couple of weeks he quietly took accelerated courses in cryonics, astronautics, and space systems. He was astonished by what he found. Ships were available in abundance, with drives that could take them close to light speed in just a couple of hours. Drake did not even try to understand the technique of inertia shedding that bypassed what should have been a killing four-thousand-gee acceleration. Instead, he thought of the other changes in the world. If this capability had been around at the end of the twentieth century, it would have been used by millions. Now, few people seemed to care. Although the stars were within easy reach, humanity was not stretching out to enfold them. Civilization seemed stable, static, content to remain within the comfortable limits of the solar system.

At last he could wait no longer. The night before he left he took Par Leon out for a ceremonial dinner. They went to Par's favorite eating place, ate his favorite foods, and drank his favorite wines. It was an unexpected bonus that by coincidence one of Drake's own new compositions was playing in the background.

Par Leon jerked his head toward an invisible speaker. "Real and deserved fame. Music good enough to eat to."

"But not to listen to, eh?" Drake shrugged off the compliment. "Table music is like table wine, usually nothing special. Telemann could compose it as fast as he could write it down."

He felt the glow that comes with good, compatible company. He was going to miss that.

The urge to tell the truth became very great. Surely, if he did confide in Par Leon, the other man would be a willing accomplice?

He stifled the thought before it could fully develop. His plans might lead to danger and destruction. He would not want Par Leon to bear any guilt by association.

He also would not—could not—do anything at all that might lessen the chance of success.

A little knowledge proved to be almost too much. Back on Earth Drake had become blasé, taking for granted the idea of robotic servants who accepted every command without question. He had assumed that it would be equally true on Pluto, and certainly his command to be taken to the deep cryowombs was obeyed at once.

At the entrance to the Pluto lower vault, he paused. The cryotanks were supposedly stored in neat rows, stretching on forever into the darkness ahead. He could see nothing. Illumination in the cryowomb vault was both unnecessary and discouraged, since any energy release might raise the vault temperature from its liquid-helium ambient. He was at the mercy of his robot guide, a drifting blue pyramid who knew the deep vault's geometry through programmed memory.

Encased within his suit, Drake followed the feeble glowworm light in front of him. When it halted by one particular cryotank he had no idea where he was.

"This is the right one?" He crouched low, seeking some identification.

"It is the one."

"I cannot see. Lift it carefully, and lead me back to the surface and my ship."

He sensed a moment of hesitation, and then the cryotank was lifting in the low gravity. Two seconds more, and the robot's pale gleam was moving again through the vault. Twenty minutes more, and Drake was supervising the careful placement of Ana's cryotank in the aft storage compartment of his ship.

He had already told the robot guide to leave and was beginning to relax when the ship's communication panel lit with a busy constellation of red and yellow warning lights.

"The removal of the cryotank from the wombs, and its placement aboard this ship, is unauthorized," said a quiet voice. "It must be returned at once."

Drake cursed his own stupidity. It had never occurred to him that the actions of the robot guides might be reported automatically to some central data bank. Screening for anomalies apparently took place in close to real time.

Rather than replying, he locked the outside ports and prepared at once for departure from Pluto's frozen surface.

"The removal of any cryotank from the Pluto vaults is forbidden without proper authorization," repeated the voice. "Do not attempt to leave Pluto. It will not be permitted."

Drake ignored the warning, dropped into the pilot's seat, and gave the order for instant takeoff. Unless there was some way that the ship's controls could be overridden from outside, he would take his chances.

The Pluto approach corridor had been deserted on his arrival. Now it seemed filled with ships. His control board indicated at least thirty of them in the space ahead. Where had they all come from?

There was no time to worry that question. They were converging, moving to intersect the course that he had set for the solar-system perimeter. It was obvious that somehow they knew his flight plan.

"DO NOT ATTEMPT TO PROCEED." The command was louder and more peremptory. "RETURN AT ONCE TO PLUTO."

Drake set the ship to maximum acceleration and kept going, driving toward the heart of the converging cluster of ships. Already he was moving at forty kilometers a second. Impact at this speed would leave nothing but fragments of melted metal and plastic.

Collision and destruction were no more than a split second away when at the last moment the other ships sheered off. The center of the cluster became open. Drake flew on through. He decided that the interceptors must be inhibited from harming humans. He aimed wide of another group of ships that had appeared far ahead, and fled for the edge of the solar system. As soon as the sky seemed clear he set a course for Canopus.

And at last he was able to breathe. If he had been judged murderer in an earlier generation for what he and Tom Lambert had done to Ana, he was now thief or worse in this one. Who cared? He and Ana were together again, which was all that mattered. Although pursuit was still possible, he could see no signs of it. And he would be hard to catch. The ship was accelerating monstrously. Soon it would crowd light speed, moving at just 125 meters per second slower than a traveling wave front. It could reach within a meter a second of light speed if necessary.

Unless he saw signs of pursuit, their present rate of progress was just about right. Time dilation was a powerful factor, making three years pass on Earth for every day of shipboard time. The trip out to Canopus and back would be a little more than two months for him, and two hundred years back on Earth.

And for Ana?

She was still trapped outside of time, in her personal fermata, a temporal hiatus without end where duration and interval did not exist.

He felt a sudden urge to gaze upon her face within the sealed cyrotank. Instead he moved forward to peer ahead to the distant star he had chosen as their destination. Even from a distance of one hundred light-years, by some miracle of the ship's imaging system Canopus was already revealed as a tiny bright disk.

He leaned back and did his best to relax, turning his attention to the ship. It could support him and his life-system needs, apparently indefinitely. Its speed and maneuverability never ceased to amaze him. And yet it was in many ways less surprising than the civilization that had made it. To produce such a miracle of performance and potential . . . then allow it to go unused; that was the most incomprehensible mystery of all.

Was it the temporal dislocation produced by time dilation that was psychologically unacceptable? To leave, and upon your return find your friends in the cryowombs or perhaps dead?

Drake noticed that the ship's external mass indicator showed more than 140,000 tons, up from its rest mass of 130 tons. To an outside observer, he himself would seem to mass eighty-eight tons and be foreshortened to a length of less than two millimeters. The shields hid the view ahead of the ship, but he knew that the picture he was seeing on his screen had been subjected to extreme image motion compensation. An unshielded view would reveal the universal three-degree background radiation, Doppler-shifted up to visible wavelengths. Far behind, hard X-ray sources were faded to pale red stars.

And still the ship was nowhere close to its performance limits. He felt that they could fly on forever, to the end of the universe if necessary. He closed his eyes and heard a broad, calm melody, the music of the stars themselves, stirring within his brain. He allowed it to fill his mind.

In the quiet space between the stars there were no distractions. He had already started to compose again—real music, not potboilers or derivative works. The ship's flight was fully automatic. In her safe little room aft, Ana lay peacefully in the cryotank. Drake allowed the new composition to grow within him. He felt optimistic that two more proper-time months would be enough. In the two hundred years that would pass on Earth until they returned, physicians would surely have found a safe and certain cure. If not, he could easily head out again and repeat the cycle.

And if Earth finally failed them?

He could go elsewhere, on to the stars in search of other solutions. The ship was completely self-sustaining, with ample power for many subjective lifetimes of travel.

But Drake hoped that one trip would be enough. It was one of his ambitions on his return to locate the cryocorpse of his friend Par Leon, and return a favor.

He was strangely, sublimely happy.

Drake's original plan had been for a gravitational swing-by, a maneuver that would take the ship through a tight hyperbolic trajectory close to Canopus and then hurtle away again the way they had come.

But perhaps he had been enjoying creative solitude too much, or maybe he felt a simple curiosity to see what worlds might circle another sun. For whatever reason, he chose to decelerate during the last couple of weeks and put the ship into a bound orbit about four hundred million kilometers away from Canopus.

There were planets, as he had hoped, four gas giants each the size of Jupiter. Closer in he located a round dozen of smaller worlds. But he had ignored or forgotten the infernal power of Canopus itself. It was a fearsome sight, more than a thousand times as luminous as the Sun and spouting green flares of gas millions of kilometers long. The inner planets were mere blackened cinders, airless and waterless, charred by the furnace heat of the star. The outer gas giants were all atmosphere, except for a small compressed solid core where the pressure was many thousands of tons per square inch. He saw no chance of life there.

But he stayed and looked. In two days of fascinated observation, his eyes turned again and again to the fusion fire of the star itself. He wondered. Had any other human been here, when the ships were new? Had any *intelligence* been here, human or nonhuman? Or were his the first sentient eyes to dwell on the dark twisted striations—not sunspots, but sun*scars*—that gouged the boiling surface of Canopus?

At last Drake could stand it no longer. Like a lost soul flying from Hell-gate he turned and ran. He needed the infinite silence of space, and after that the comforting shelter of the solar system. If another trip out were necessary with Ana, he knew that it would have to be to a smaller and less turbulent star.

He settled back into the shipboard routine of daily composition. But now all harmony, mental and musical, had been banished. What he saw, over and over, was a vision of Hell. He was circling endlessly in tight orbit around Canopus. Flaming gas prominences, bright jets of green and white and blue, danced a witch's sabbat in his mind. He could not eat, drink, or sleep. The urge to see Ana, to seek peace in her face, grew within him.

Finally he could stand it no longer. He went aft, and lifted the sealed cover.

She lay quietly in the tank, pale and peaceful as a Snow Goddess with pearly eyes and skin of milky crystal. He took one quick look, afraid to open the tank more than a crack in case it interfered with the cooling system, then rapidly sealed the lid again. The one moment was enough. He was able to control himself again and think of other things. . . .

To ponder how fortunate he had been. He had never dreamed of light-speed ships and time dilation when he had made his plans so long ago. At best he had envisioned a chancy succession of freezings and thawings, farther and farther off in time, until at last Ana might safely be revived and cured. He had imagined the multiple uncertainty of waking, not sure where Ana might be, not even sure if she still lay within a cryo-womb.

Instead of such an uncertain quest, he had Ana here with him. He could safeguard her himself and protect her from risks.

The journey home was if anything even more tranquil than the voyage out. He scanned all the ship's communication channels, electromagnetic and neutrino, wondering what might await him back in the solar system, and found nothing but silence. Two centuries was a long time; enough for some totally new communication technology to have taken over. Two centuries was also—a frightening prospect—time enough for humanity to have in some way destroyed itself.

Finally the long journey was ending, in a steady deceleration past the Dry Tortugas, on to the outer borders of the Oort Cloud, into and through the Kuiper Belt. There was still no sign of human presence, not even the scouts who had performed the original outer-system survey. By the time they came to the barren outcroppings of Pluto the ship was crawling along at a mere ten-thousandth of its top speed, and Drake was becoming worried.

He headed for the inner planets. With no idea how Earth or the rest of the solar system had changed in two hundred years he could not guess at his welcome. Must he be slow and careful, or could he be rapid and confident?

That question was answered as the ship passed the Asteroid Belt, floating high above the ecliptic. A navigation and guidance beam locked on to them, overrode the ship's internal controls, and steered it steadily in to a landing on the Moon.

The spaceport was new, massive silver columns set in a regular triangular array. Ships, if they were ships, formed dark, windowless tetrahedra at the center of each triangle. Spaceflight, if nothing else, had changed in two centuries.

A small wheeled guide met Drake at the ship's lock. Its body was a one-foot sphere, with above it a thin upright cylinder topped by a whiskbroom of flexible metal fibers. The broom head dipped toward Drake in greeting, and the machine led him to an oval opening at the base of a silver column. Feeling ready for anything, Drake went through. Although there had been no sign of a lock, his suit monitor suddenly showed breathable air and a comfortable temperature outside it. He removed the suit as his wheeled guide instructed and followed it along a short corridor to another interior chamber.

One man was waiting there, a tall dignified figure with the distant eyes of a prophet. Drake had somehow expected more: a reception committee, or perhaps a show of weapons. But the man merely nodded and said at once in Universal, "Welcome again to Earth-space, Drake Merlin."

Drake realized that he had been wrong. He was prepared for most things, but not to be recognized, and *named*.

Then he realized that he should not be surprised. The ship's identity would have been revealed back in the Asteroid Belt during its first handshake with the navigation and guidance beam. The data banks would show the ship's history, and record its disappearance from the solar system.

Drake wondered what else the files might say about the ship's run from Pluto. "Since you know my name, perhaps you also know my history. If you do, then you realize that I am seeking your help."

It seemed strange that he had been greeted in a familiar language.

Par Leon had been able to speak to him on his revivification, but only because of long preparation for Drake's arrival and extensive studies of that historical period.

Had language become static, totally fixed over several centuries? Or was the robed figure in front of him simply giving a formal greeting, a single sentence that he had learned of Universal?

But the man was nodding, and speaking again. "My name is Trismon Sorel. I do know a little of your history as it has come down to us from long ago, although the early record is seriously incomplete. Also, one version holds that centuries ago you lost control of your ship and were carried off unwilling to the far depths of space. Another version suggests that your removal of a cryocorpse from the old Pluto wombs and the immediately subsequent departure of your ship are linked events—that your disappearance at close to light speed, however bewildering, was intentional. I await your elucidation. However, we should first proceed to another environment, where we will find conversation easier."

There were small pauses in his speech, slight hesitations in places where it was not natural to break the pattern of words. As Drake was led out of the room and down a spiral flight of metallic stairs, he decided that Universal must be a learned language for Trismon Sorel, just as Old Anglic had been for Par Leon. But to learn so *quickly*, in just the couple of days since the return of the ship to the inner system—that was a staggering feat. In spite of Sorel's normal appearance, his grasp of Universal suggested some huge advance in human mental powers.

Sorel entered a room furnished with a desk and comfortable-looking chairs and settled into one of them. He gestured to the little wheeled servant, and as it moved forward with refreshments he gazed at Drake with steady, knowing eyes.

"Speak, Drake Merlin. Tell your story."

Drake nodded and sat down opposite Trismon Sorel. He felt a rising tension. In a few more minutes he would learn if his long quest was finally over.

"My departure from the solar system was intentional." He had to swallow hard before he could speak clearly. "Intentional, and done for a good reason. But I cannot begin there. I must begin long ago, more than eight hundred years ago. At that time, the cryocorpse who now lies safe within the ship was my wife. Then we learned that she was suffering from an incurable disease. . . ."

As Drake told his story he forced himself to relive scenes that he had suppressed over the centuries. If Ana was to be helped, Trismon Sorel had to know *everything:* Ana's symptoms, her illness, the manner of her death and her freezing.

Sorel listened intently. He raised his hand when Drake spoke of the awful hours at the Second Chance cryonics facility.

"One moment. Do you say that the original medical records are now stored with the cryocorpse?"

"Everything is there. Inside the cryotank."

"Then before we proceed further let me summon the necessary experts, in both medicine and old languages. I can say at once that we are able to cure all known diseases, of the present or of the past. However, we will need to examine the records and the cryocorpse itself." He sat, eyes distant, for three or four seconds.

Two waves of emotion swept through Drake. He felt wild joy—Ana would be cured at last—and then an almost superstitious awe. Trismon Sorel's advanced mental powers seemed to include telepathy. "You are speaking to them directly, by transmitting your thoughts?"

Sorel looked puzzled, and again there was a brief pause before he smiled. "Not in the way that you are perhaps thinking. I can do no more than you yourself will be able to accomplish in a few days' time. You will share thoughts with others. You will have instant access to all information in the data banks. You will be able to calculate faster and better than the computer of the ship that brought you here. Look."

He turned his head and raised the hair above his temple. A faint, thin scar was covered by the hairline.

"That marks where the implant sits. It is normally installed in early infancy. It is tiny, smaller and thinner than a fingernail, and it serves multiple purposes: as a body-function monitor, as slave computer, and as transmitter and receiver, so that commands, requests, data, and programs can be sent to or received from data banks or other individuals. I sent a request to bring medical experts to your ship via the Copernicus network. I am able to speak to you now in real time, although your language is new to me, because I am employing the language translation modules within the Tycho network."

Some transfer of information was still person-to-person. Sorel read Drake's misgivings from his facial expression. "Do not worry about this. First, in your case as in all cryowomb revivals, the implant will be totally optional. Before you make a decision you will have ample opportunity to observe its use in others. But I can assure you that if you do proceed, you will find it hard within a few months to believe that you were ever able to function without such a service. You will possess total recall; you will be a calculator beyond the most powerful computers of your time; and you will have immediate access to every data bank within the solar system— though naturally, access and transmission time to people and data banks on other planets is considerable. Do you have questions?"

"Only one. I want to know if Ana can be cured."

"I will ask the medical team that question. They are already on board your ship, and they will be performing their assessment. Be patient for a little, while I talk to them."

The grey eyes widened. Their expression again became remote and preoccupied. This time the wait stretched on, to become one minute and then two.

As the silence continued Drake felt a knife of tension twisting inside him. Something was going wrong. But what could possibly go wrong? He comforted himself with Trismon Sorel's earlier assurance: this society was able to cure all known diseases, past or present.

Finally he could stand it no longer. "Are you talking to them? What do they say?"

Sorel's eyes focused again on Drake. "I am talking now to the medical specialists. It is—complicated. Give me one moment more."

The grey eyes were changing. They became gentler and closer. Trismon Sorel nodded, and he appeared to be choosing his next words with great care.

"They ask me to ask you questions. The woman in the cryotank, Anastasia. According to our records she had been constantly maintained in the Pluto cryowomb. Is that correct?"

Drake nodded.

"And when you found her, she was within a cryotank. You did not remove her, but you brought the whole cryotank with you on board the ship?"

"That's right." Drake's mind was filled with foreboding. "I carried the tank to the ship, just as I found it. I did it very carefully. The gravity on Pluto is low, I had no trouble handling it."

Trismon Sorel was frowning. "Then—did you *open* the tank for any reason, after your ship left Pluto?"

"Just once. For a few moments, after we left Canopus." Drake saw again before him Ana's peaceful face, her pearly eyes and milky skin. "I looked for only a second or two. I was careful to seal the cryotank afterwards. . . ."

It was pointless to try to explain *why* he had done it, to say that he had been unable *not* to do it. Trismon Sorel was regarding him sorrowfully, across an eight-hundred-year gulf. His face was Tom Lambert's, and also Par Leon's. The eyes spoke the same sad message.

"Drake Merlin, a cryotank is not designed for sealing and resealing. Resealing calls for special equipment and special procedures. When a seal is broken, it is assumed that the person will at once be revivified. Do

you understand what I am saying? With an imperfect seal, suitable conditions cannot be maintained within a cryotank."

"Then Ana . . ."

"One moment more. I must consult the data banks." Again the eyes
became unblinking. When they focused again on Drake there was no
doubt in them.

"I have checked all our references," Trismon Sorel said gently. "As
did the medical team. The problem that faced them was quite different
from that of curing a disease. The damage caused to a body, and particularly to a body's brain, when a cryotank is open and revivification is not
performed . . . that is permanent. It cannot be repaired. There can be no
revival. Now, or ever.

"I am sorry, Drake Merlin. Anastasia is dead. Forever dead."

Forever dead. Ana is dead. Trismon Sorel's words echoed those of
Tom Lambert, so long ago. But this time there was the ring of complete
certainty.

For each man kills the thing he loves. Drake knew that he, and not
disease, had killed Ana. Like Orpheus, he had pursued his Eurydice
through a double hell of cryodeath and Canopus. Like Orpheus he had
looked at her; and by looking he had lost her.

With that thought the barriers came down inside his mind. For the
first time he noticed a spicy fragrance in the air, felt a steady dry breeze
blowing past him, and heard the faint concert pitch A-natural of vibrating metal far along the corridor. It was as though his senses were opening again after long centuries of hibernation.

Trismon Sorel was speaking again. "One possibility remains. Anastasia, the woman that you know, cannot be reanimated. However, many
whole cells remain intact within her body. She could be cloned without
difficulty, and growth and education begun anew. But it would be a new
Anastasia. There is no hope of sufficient memory transfer from undam-
aged cells for any inkling of her former existence to pass to her new
body. Your former relationship to her would be known to you, but it
would be irrelevant to her. Should we proceed?"

The temptation was enormous. To see Ana once more standing
before him, blooming and vibrant as he had once known her . . .

She had the right to a healthy new life in this new world, eight hundred years on. He could not deny her that.

"Proceed, if you please. Make a clone of Ana."

She would live again. But it would not be the Ana that he knew and
loved. It would be a quite different person.

Trismon Sorel had assured him that the Ana he had known was gone,

gone forever. He spoke with the authority of eight hundred more years of science and technological progress.

But—

A tiny seed of doubt sprouted deep in Drake's mind. But what would science say in another two hundred years? In a thousand, or ten thousand? Science had come so far. Surely no one, least of all a scientist, believed that it was now at an end and could go no farther.

Trismon Sorel was talking to him, trying to catch his attention. He forced himself to listen.

"Ana cannot be revived and cured," Sorel was saying, "not in the way that you hoped when you took her body from the cryowombs. But we can help *you*."

"Me?"

"Certainly. We can cure you. There is evidence that a cure was attempted more than two hundred years ago, but it clearly failed. We have superior techniques now that will end your obsession. With your consent, of course."

"Do I have a choice?"

"You have an infinite number of choices. The right to self-determination—even self-destruction, if you wish it—is basic." Trismon Sorel leaned forward. "Now I speak personally. I hope that you will agree to a cure, and enjoy your own new life. I have vast sympathy for you. I have searched the whole data bank as we have been speaking, and your suffering seems unique. No quest comparable to yours can be found."

"I have not suffered." Drake had made up his mind. "And I know what I want."

"State it."

"A cloned form for a new Ana, just as you offered."

"It will be done. And for yourself?"

"I want to remain here just long enough to be sure that the cloning can proceed without problems. Then I wish to leave."

"To go?" Trismon Sorel was bewildered. "But go where? We can offer you everything that your heart desires."

"No. You cannot offer me the Anastasia that I know and love. But that is what I want—all I want. Put me back into the cryowombs, with Ana's original body by my side."

"But I told you, the real Ana, the Ana that you knew, is not in that body. Too many brain cells have been destroyed. Ana is gone."

"She is gone. But gone *where*?"

"That is a meaningless question. It is like asking where the wind goes when it is no longer blowing, or where is the odor of a flower after the flower dies."

"It seems a meaningless question today. But it may not always be meaningless. You told me that I have an infinite number of choices. My choice is simple, and I say it again: I want to be placed in the Pluto cryo-wombs. Do I have that right?"

"You do." Trismon Sorel could not conceal his discomfort and disappointment. "I cannot deny it to you. But I beg you to reconsider. You can return to cryosleep for as long as you choose, but when will you be awakened? In one century? In five?"

"I do not know. I want to leave this instruction with my freezing: awaken me when new evidence comes into the data banks that seems relevant to the re-creation of Anastasia's original personality. And not until then."

"I must be honest with you. If you hope to sleep until your Ana can return, I believe that you will sleep forever."

"I will take that risk. It is smaller than risks that I have taken in the past. Can we begin?"

"If you insist." Trismon Sorel held up his hand. Drake was already rising from his seat. "But there is one thing more. While we have been speaking, a group-mind meeting has been in progress involving every human within easy signal range. A conclusion has been reached. Your request will be granted, but with one condition: you must have a companion for your travel into the future, just as each of us has a companion."

"I want no woman in the cryowomb with me, other than my own Ana. And no man, either."

"We would condemn neither living man nor living woman to such a future. Your companion will not reside in the cryobanks. It will be a Servitor, designed for on-demand operation, exactly like my own Servitor," Trismon Sorel gestured to the little wheeled sphere with its metal whisk-broom head, waiting quietly at his side. "So long as you do not call upon its services, it will remain dormant. When you need a companion or an assistant, it will be there to obey your commands."

Sorel stood up. "Come with me now. The preparations are already beginning for the cloning of Ana. While that is proceeding, I will introduce you to the endless virtues of the Servitor class. And you can decide on the appearance and name of your own personal model."

Drake woke quickly and easily, rising at once to full consciousness. That was enough to convince him that something had gone wrong. He had not been taken into cryosleep, but instead was awakening as soon as the Asfanil wore off.

He opened his eyes, expecting to see the cryolab facility and Trismon Sorel's familiar face. Instead he found himself lounging at ease in a deep armchair. A woman with the strong features, raven hair, and dark complexion of a gypsy sat opposite. She was watching him closely. When his eyes opened she nodded but did not speak.

"What happened?" His mouth was dry, but no more than usual after sedation. "Why didn't I go into cryosleep?"

"And what makes you think you didn't?" She arched black eyebrows at him. "Don't you believe in progress? The old barbarism of waking agony is long in the past. Today the thawing is no less pleasant than waking from a natural sleep."

She spoke not in Universal but in perfect English, unaccented and without pauses.

He stared around him. His last waking sight had been of the cryolab, deep within the sterile interior of the Moon. Now he was sitting in a room whose long window faced out over a sandy beach and a restless ocean. It was windy outside. He could hear the gusts moaning around the outside of the building, and see tiny sparks of sunlight reflecting from distant whitecaps.

"How long?"

"I was hoping that we might postpone that question for at least a little while." The woman sighed. "I should have known better. All your records display a remarkable focus of attention. To answer your question, it has been rather a long time—much longer than I suspect you hoped. It is more than twenty-nine thousand years since you last descended into cryosleep."

Long enough for real progress in the reconstruction of his Ana.

Longer, also, than the whole of humanity's previous recorded history. Drake stared around him in disbelief. He had again tried to prepare his mind for anything, for any amount of change. And again he was surprised. The last thing that he expected was *sameness*. But the room he was sitting in would not have been out of place as a twentieth-century living room. The scene outside was a pleasant summer's day, something to be found at thousands of locations on Earth's seacoasts.

"It's not real, is it?" He gestured around him. "All this is an electronic simulation, designed to please me." A worse thought struck him. "In fact, I'm not real, either. I've not been revivified at all. I've been downloaded."

"Not true." The woman frowned reprovingly. "You were certainly revivified, but although the capability exists to do so you have not been downloaded to inorganic storage. You are very real, and you are occupying your own body. However, you are right at least in part. The scene around you was synthesized from your own memories and is being inserted for your convenience into your optic nerve—nonintrusively, I might add. The old indignities of body invasion disgust today's society."

"I don't want a synthesis. I want to know where I really am, with my real surroundings."

"Very well. If you insist."

"I do."

"Then there is one other thing that you should know before you leave derived reality." The woman stared at Drake, her dark eyes serious. "You are real flesh and blood. But I am not. I am a part of the synthesis, and I disappear when it does."

She raised her hand in farewell.

"Wait!" Drake, without moving, found himself standing. "I have to know. Has there been progress in bringing back my Ana?"

"I am afraid that there has not. It is still considered to be an impossible problem."

"But I was supposed to remain in the cryowomb until there was hope of a new approach. Why am I awake?"

"I hear the question." The dark head nodded. "However, it is best answered by another. Goodbye, Drake Merlin."

She was gone. With her went the sunlit room and its pleasant prospect of a windswept ocean. Drake found himself recumbent on an adjustable bed with an array of unfamiliar machinery sitting on both sides of him. The room he was in was small and oddly shaped. Its octagonal walls bulged up to a multifaceted convex ceiling. His body felt close to weightless, as though with a tiny effort he would become airborne and float to rest on that pale-blue upper boundary.

Where was he? And who had wakened him?

Drake stared around the room, expecting to see the familiar wheeled form of a Servitor. And then all questions of his location and condition vanished.

A woman waited in the narrow doorway.

It was Ana.

She was standing exactly as he had seen her a thousand times, head to one side and her mouth quirked into a question. Drake tried to stand up and move toward her, but instead found himself rising straight up and turning end over end.

"Easy now." Ana was somehow at his side, steadying him. "I'm sorry, I ought to have waited until you had become accustomed to a low-gee environment."

"The dark-haired woman—the simulation of the woman—it said there had not been progress—"

"It spoke the truth." Ana had floated them back down, to sit side by side on the bed. "There has been no progress in the problem that interests you."

"But you—you are here, you are alive." A horrible thought struck him: *simulation.* "Aren't you?"

"I certainly am. But it is not the way you think it is." The gentle tone in her voice was infinitely familiar. "Isn't it obvious who I am?"

"You are Ana."

"Yes. But I am not *your* Ana." She took him by the arm, and turned so that they were face-to-face. "I am the Ana to whom you gave life. I am the clone of your wife, the person grown from her cells by Trismon Sorel and his colleagues."

"But the other woman said it had been twenty-nine thousand years—have you been alive for so long?"

"Not continuously. That is not the custom." She laughed, and at the sound Drake felt his heart break. "Like most people, I choose short periods of wakefulness between long ones in hibernation—what you would call cryosleep. Almost everyone is curious to know the future, to meet the future.

"And for twenty-nine thousand years, I have also been curious to meet *you.* Each time I woke, I checked your condition. Each time, before I went again to hibernation, I asked to be awakened should you waken."

"I ought not to be awake now. I was supposed to remain in cryosleep until the restoration of your personality became possible." Except that Drake realized he was delighted to be awake. To be sitting just two feet away from Ana, watching the expressions run across her face—that was infinite bliss.

"I am sorry." She bowed her head. "Forgive me, but that is my fault. I came here to Pluto and countered the instructions given to your Servitor." She frowned. "It says its name is Milton. An odd name for a Servitor."

"Not really." Drake felt a twinge of uneasiness at Ana's comment, which he pushed aside. "Milton is the name that I gave it."

"In any case, I directed that you be reanimated."

"And I'm glad that you did." Drake reached out to embrace her, but she leaned away.

"No. I should have realized that this might happen. Let me try to explain." She stood up and drifted safely out of arm's reach. "You feel that you know me well, and more than well. But I do not know you at all. Although I have gazed at your picture and listened to your voice a thousand times, you are a stranger to me. When I first reached consciousness you were already in the cryowombs. You do not know how much I have longed to see you, to speak to you, to thank you for giving me life. But in the past I always tried to respect what *you* wanted. I knew that you did not want me."

"I have never wanted anyone but you."

"You want Ana—your Ana. I am Ana, too, but a different person. I have my own memories, my own joys and sorrows. You do not share them." She sighed. "Anyway, a few months ago I agreed to do something that I have been asked to do many times: to go away with friends on a long journey. We will fly out to the human colony on Rigel Calorans. I expect to be away for many thousands of Earth years. When I made that decision to leave the solar system for so long, I wondered: When I return, who knows where Drake Merlin might be? I could not bear the thought that I might never, ever, see and know you. So I gave the command to revivify." She gazed at Drake with the clear grey eyes that he had known forever. "I realize now that this was an unforgivable act."

"You are wrong. It is forgiven already."

"It may be forgiven, but it was unforgivable. It was my plan to leave Pluto soon after speaking with you, and proceed to the edge of the Oort where the expedition will assemble. I can no longer do that."

"Stay with me." Drake did not say it, but his mind added the word *forever.*

"I certainly owe that to you." Ana smiled, with a familiar rueful downturn of one side of her mouth. "And now like the self-serving wretch that I am, I will try to justify my own action. There is some level of temporal shock after any hibernation, even if it is no more than a few hundred years. In your case it has been nearly thirty millennia and you were not prepared for it as we are. So it will be my task to lessen the blow of twenty-nine thousand vanished years." She reached out her hand. "Your Servitor is waiting outside. It is most unhappy that a mere irrational human overrode your explicit instructions to it. Come along with me, and listen to my apologies."

Ana's warning of temporal shock at first seemed greatly overstated. The evidence of human presence on Pluto was mostly the cryowombs, and Drake could see little change to them since his mad dash through and away from them, twenty-nine thousand six hundred years earlier.

The evidence that she was right began to appear as they spiraled in toward the Sun. At Ana's suggestion they planned to visit or pass close by each planet. It was Drake's idea to use a small two-person ship, and leave their Servitors behind on Pluto until they returned.

Neptune had developed in a natural way. There were large colonies of humans and machines on the moons, Triton and Nereid, while the planet itself formed the home of hundreds of thousands of Von Neumanns, mining volatiles and collecting the rare heavier elements needed for their own reproduction.

But something monstrous was happening to Uranus.

The major moons of the planet, except for little Miranda nearest to the planet, had vanished. The ship swung into coorbit with Miranda and circled Uranus for two full revolutions. The gas-giant world was marked with a pattern of bright spots, ninety-six of them evenly spaced around the flattened sphere of the planet.

"Nothing yet," Ana said in reply to Drake's question. "In another two thousand years or so, when the preparation work is all done, those will be the main nodes. The stimulated fusion program will begin. Uranus is too small to maintain its own fusion, so there will have to be continuous priming and pumping. They'll move Miranda far out, and do it from there."

She spoke casually, as though the conversion of a major component of the solar system from planet to miniature star was a routine operation.

Drake stared out of the ports and wondered. Uranus was not a promising candidate for life, but it would become far less eligible when hydrogen fusion had turned the whole world to incandescence.

The thought nagged at him: Why do such a thing, within the original home system of mankind? Whenever he thought about the far future he imagined Earth, together with all the original planets of the solar system, preserved as some kind of great museum. Humanity might spread out far across the Galaxy, but the home worlds would always be there. They would remind people of their origins.

The Uranus decision made more sense when they had flown past Saturn and its horde of moons, on toward Jupiter, and descended at last for a feathery landing on one of the Jovian satellites. Drake remembered Europa as an ice world, the fifty-kilometer deeps of its continuous ocean plated over by a kilometer and more of icy plateaus and thick-ribbed pressure ridges. But it was that way no longer. Their little ship landed on a giant iceberg, floating in random currents along a broad river. With the sunlight striking in at a low angle, the long stretch of open water seemed mottled and tawny like the skin of a great snake. It wound its way to the horizon between palisades and battlements of blue crystal. As the berg carrying the ship moved sluggishly along, Drake saw open water leads running off in all directions. He shivered. He could imagine strange creatures, huge and misshapen, writhing along the icy horizon.

Europa in its tide-locked orbit turned steadily about Jupiter. The Sun slowly vanished from the black sky. The sounds of jostling floes became louder, carried to the ship through the water and ice of the dark surface. To Drake's musician's ear the bergs cried out to each other, sharp high-pitched whines and portamento moans in frightening counterpoint against a background of deeper grumbles.

"That's why we need the Uranus fusion project," Ana said cheerfully. "Europa is warmed at the moment by individual plants within the deep ocean, and that leads to patchy melting. It will be a lot better here when Uranus is finished and working. The ice will all go, and we'll have another whole world for development."

She was setting out a meal for the two of them, and she obviously did not share one scrap of Drake's uneasiness. But she must somehow have sensed it, because suddenly she stopped what she was doing and came across to his side.

"Are you all right?"

"I'm fine." It was preposterous to be anything other than fine when he was with Ana again, after such a long separation. But maybe it was *because* he was with her that he could admit fears and doubts. In any case, try as he would he could not stop shivering.

"Here." Ana handed him a drink. "I told you there would be temporal shock, and I was right. It just took a little while to show up. You sip on that, while I order something as close as this crazy autochef can manage to the foods you were raised on. And for tonight I think we'll manage with a little less Europa. I'm going to dim the lights and close the ship screens, and you can sit there and imagine you're safely back on good old Earth."

She could not have known it, but long ago, back in the happy days that Drake would not even allow himself to think about, Ana had done just the same thing for him when he was upset. She was strong when he was weak, obligingly weak when he felt strong.

Drake did as he was told. They ate an easy, leisurely meal, talking about nothing or remaining silent, exactly as the mood struck them. The chef provided a reasonable shot at the foods of Old Earth. Afterward Ana cradled his head against her breast, and he hid himself away in the night of her long brown hair.

It was natural, perhaps inevitable, that they would become lovers that evening. Neither of them realized that Drake, deep inside, thought of it as "lovers *again*."

Physical euphoria carried everything before it, all the way into and through the inner solar system. Lovemaking, as it had always been, was an epiphany for Drake. As an antidote to tempora! shock it could not have been better. Immersed in the familiar touch and smell and taste of Ana's soft perfumed skin, he would have seen Earth and Sun destroyed with equanimity.

It was not quite that bad, although four thousand years earlier the Earth had come close to an environmental runaway.

Recovery had been slow. But when the ship landed on the diminished Antarctic ice cap, mean equatorial temperatures were again below 50° Celsius and land animals were venturing sunward from the lush jungles of the once-temperate zones.

Drake felt a brief desire to visit their old home, heat or no heat, until he learned that it now lay beneath fifteen feet of water. In another ten thousand years, according to Ana, the sea level should have dropped enough for him to pay a visit on dry land. She showed no interest in that particular area, or indeed in any location on Earth. He learned that she had been to Earth three times before and found it rather dull.

They took off for space again and wandered on through the inner system. The ship skimmed low across the broad face of the Sun, to show a surface as raging and demonic as anything that Drake had encountered on his visit to Canopus. With Ana at his side, this time he remained unperturbed.

When she declared that they ought to spiral out again toward Pluto, he agreed. If there had been major temporal shock it now lay in the past. He was feeling wonderful, relaxed and content in mind and body as they cruised out to where his Servitor was patiently (or perhaps impatiently) awaiting his return.

Because his guard was down so completely, the shock when it came was so much harder to take.

"What do you mean, make the most of the last few days here?" Drake had been watching the ship's automatic docking on Charon until Ana's words jerked him to attention. "I thought we could stay in the outer system as long as we like."

"We can. You can." She moved to stand in front of him. "But I can't. I made promises, remember. The people heading for Rigel Calorans are waiting for me, but they won't wait forever. I have to head out and join them."

"But what about *us*?" And when Ana shook her head, he went on, "Look, if you already made promises to them, I completely understand. I wouldn't want you to go back on your word. But I have nothing to hold me close to Sol—nothing but you. I'll come with you, join your group."

"No, Drake, you won't. And you do not understand." She took his hand gently in hers. "I like you a lot, and I will never forget that I owe my life to you. But you can't go with me. Let me put it more brutally: I don't *want* you to go with me. I do not love you as you love your Ana."

"I don't believe it. Everything we've said to each other, everything we've done . . ."

"Everything that *you* have said. We make fine, fond lovers, physically we fit together beautifully, I don't deny it."

"So what's the problem? Ana, we can talk this through, we always have."

"*That's* the problem, right there. I'm not Ana—not *your* Ana. I'm *me*. You and I have never talked through any problems together. Think about it, and you will realize that what I say is true." She released his hand and stepped away. "Drake, this is all my fault. I should never have revivified you. I see you looking at me, and I know you are seeing someone else."

"I don't want anyone else. I want you."

"No. You are blind. You want what you see, what you think I am. There's so much background that you and your Ana shared. I don't have that, but you don't even realize it's missing. Let me give you just one example. You assumed I would know why you call your Servitor *Milton*, so you've never bothered to explain to me. But I don't know."

" 'They also serve who only stand and wait.' An ancient poet, John Milton, wrote that. It was just a sort of joke when I said it, because the Servitor—"

"Drake, I don't know and I don't *want* to know. I want to leave, right now."

"You can't leave. What will I do without you?"

"You will become what you were before I appeared to mess up your life: strong, determined, brave." She came toward him, hesitated, and then at last kissed him quickly on the lips. "Go forward again, Drake. Don't give up. I agree with you, somewhere, sometime, there will be a way for you to find Anastasia. The real Ana. *Your* Ana."

She stepped away and was out of the door before he could do more than reach out a hand in her direction. He took a couple of steps to follow, then slumped into a chair. He was still sitting there, staring blindly at the rugged surface of Charon, when the door opened again.

The little Servitor, Milton, eased quietly into the room. It rolled forward to stand at Drake's side. As though sensing the human's mood, it did not say a word. It knew what would happen next.

There was the same sunlit room as before, the same outlook onto a sandy beach and windswept ocean. But this time ominous rain clouds stood in the middle distance; and in place of the raven-haired gypsy woman, a bald-headed man was sitting in the easy chair opposite.

Drake turned his head back and forth. His neck was feeling slightly stiff. "I'd rather you didn't bother with all this, you know. I much prefer the real thing."

"I think not." The man's English was perfect, accent-free. "There have been changes."

"I expect changes. I *need* changes. My era could do nothing to help Ana. Let's dispense with the simulations."

"That is I'm afraid impossible."

"My body—"

"Is fine. You have not been uploaded to the data banks and your cryocorpse, together with Ana's original body, is still safe in a cryowomb. The womb is no longer held on Pluto, for reasons that will become obvious later. However, your body is unchanged and can easily be revivified. That may not be necessary, since as you see we no longer find it necessary to reanimate you in order to converse. We are maintaining a direct superconducting link with your brain."

"Who are you?"

"That also is not an easy question." The man smiled, an easy and friendly grin that seemed impossible to simulate. "Call me Alman, if you enjoy a mild joke. Let me just say that I am a composite, and to make you feel easier, I will bring another element of that composite directly to this meeting."

The man did not move, but at his side a familiar sphere topped by a metal whisk-broom blinked into existence.

"With apologies." The Servitor nodded its eyeless head toward Drake. "Your instructions to me upon freezing were quite explicit. However, upon multiple reflection we finally judged it necessary to interface with you. I recognize that an argument could be made that you have not in fact been reanimated, and therefore your instructions have not been disobeyed. However, I reject that as a form of special pleading on my own behalf."

"You are Milton? You don't sound at all as you used to."

"I am Milton, and in composition more than Milton. But I am still your Servitor."

"How long?" Drake sat up straight, aware that his real body deep in cryosleep could not move a micrometer. "How long since I went back to the cryowomb?"

There was a perceptible hesitation before Milton answered. "By your standards, it has been a long time. There have been . . . discontinuities . . . in solar-system development."

"You mean a total collapse of human civilization? I worried about that, before I first went into cryosleep."

"There was no collapse in the sense that you imply, with loss of technology. However, on three occasions human development has proceeded in other directions—what we now perceive to have been false directions. During two of those periods, the whole idea of technology lacked meaning."

"How long since I went to the cryowomb? Are you going to tell me, or aren't you? Forget the 'temporal shock' nonsense and tell me. That is a direct command."

"Even without reinforcement from the composite, I am empowered to reject any command contrary to your well-being. However, I will answer. Your body has been within the cryowomb for a period which, in your most familiar units of Earth orbital revolutions, is fourteen million years." The Servitor paused. When Drake did not move, it continued: "Fourteen million years. Which is to say, a period equal to—"

"I know what fourteen million years is." Drake laughed, a harsh humorless bark of disbelief. "I guess I was wrong. I'm not immune to temporal shock at all. I'm *in* temporal shock, right now. Give me a minute or two, Milton, then I'll be fine."

"As long as you need." The Servitor rolled backward a few feet, and the bald-headed man in the armchair continued, "We assume that you refer to subjective minutes. One advantage of a superconducting interface is speed. This meeting is taking place with subjective time lapse equal to less than one thousandth real-time—"

"I need to *know*," Drake interrupted. "I need to know what's happened to the solar system—why you woke me—if there has been progress with Ana's problem." He had a thrilling thought. "Is it possible to interface with her brain, the way you did with mine?"

"Unfortunately, it is not. We made contact, long ago. But too many of her brain cells have been destroyed."

"Let me try for myself." Drake found he was trembling with eagerness. "Put me in touch with her, let me make my own evaluation."

"We judge that would be most unwise." Alman's face was compassionate. "For your sake. Just as it is unwise to expose you to humankind as it exists today. We have no wish to add to your level of uneasiness. If it is any comfort, your strength and mental resilience are extraordinary. We feared that you might retreat to insanity immediately after being contacted. You did not. But contact with the sad, muddied remnant of mind that sits now within Anastasia's body would try your sanity past bearing."

"But has there been other progress? If her brain cannot be repaired—"

"We will come to the question of scientific progress in due course. For the moment, we judge it best for you to begin with the most familiar. Your Servitor will show you around the solar system. Then it will be time for us to talk again."

Drake was not interested in a stupid tour of the solar system. He wanted to know what changes might affect Ana's possible return. He leaned forward, ready to dispute their proposed approach.

And found that he would be given no chance to do so. With one final wave of his hand, Alman vanished.

Although Drake's frozen body remained in the cryowomb, the illusion that he had been reanimated was perfect. He felt that he and Milton were traveling together in a real ship, its motion and progress constrained by the limits of physics and geometry. He experienced real hunger and fatigue. After sixteen hours of subjective wakefulness, he would begin to yawn and feel the need for sleep.

It was the solar system that seemed to lack reality.

They began close to the Sun, where the familiar, steady beacon offered constancy and comfort. A few million years were nothing within the lifetime of a G-class star. It had looked down on Drake's birth, and he expected it would look down unchanged on his death.

But unlike his birth, that death could not take place on Earth. Drake had stared from the ship's ports in awe as they swept out past the hot cinder of Mercury and on to the garden world of Venus, with its blue-white atmosphere, placid seas and sculpted contents. The transformation of that planet was surprising and wonderful. But most of his interest was already focused ahead. Earth. What would the home world have become, after such long habitation and development?

As they drew closer he looked and looked again. The Earth-Moon doublet was growing in the ship's displays, familiar yet oddly wrong. The proportions were right, Earth's disk bulking more than ten times as big as its satellite's; but the colors were strange. The smaller world was an angry red tinged with yellow smears. The larger gleamed white, a dull and almost uniform white, oddly suggestive.

He stared hard at that pale orb, and felt a perspective shift suddenly within his mind.

"That's the Moon! Which means that the *little* one has to be Earth. Is this all just a simulation?"

He hardly expected an answer. Although Milton was at his side, the Servitor had spoken little since the journey began.

This time, however, the response was immediate. "It is no simulation. Although our journey is in derived reality, what you are seeing exactly matches the physical world."

"What happened to the Earth?"

"It is easier to say *why* than *what*. As we told you, three times while you were in cryosleep a strange direction was taken by humanity. In two of those, technology was ignored. In the third, it took a leap which even now we do not understand. The center of that new technology was Earth. One day, without warning, Earth collapsed to a fraction of its old size. Its surface closed. Its mass remained unchanged."

"It collapsed while it was still inhabited? What happened to the people?"

"We do not know, but we believe that in some form they survived. Even after six hundred thousand Earth years, no one has ever managed to penetrate the sphere that you see. It remains impermeable to all forms of matter and radiation. Our best theory is that the sphere is constantly maintained by a single entity within it, a combination of organic and inorganic intelligence.

"Of perhaps greater consequence to the rest of the solar system, at the time of its collapse and closure the Earth was the repository of all major data banks. Their loss had a profound effect on human development—even on human sanity. Everyone was suddenly deprived of a vital group memory and cohesive force. The process of reconstruction began, but it was slow, uncertain, and imperfect. In that era, every person in the cryowombs was revivified to assist in the re-re-creation of old historical records. You alone, because I was armed with your specific instructions, were exempt."

Drake leaned back, his thoughts bitter and far from the Earth that now filled the screens. So all the long shots had paid off after all; even the "useless" ones whom no one had previously thought it worthwhile to revive. Instead of fleeing from Pluto he should simply have placed himself with Ana in the Pluto cryowomb. They would have been awakened together, to live the rest of their lives together.

"Do you wish to go closer, for sentimental reasons?" Milton was at his side, the Servitor's wiry broom of sensors turned toward him. "It is deemed quite safe to do so. There has never been interference with an approaching ship, not even ones that land upon the outer surface of Earth."

"That isn't Earth, no matter what you call it." Drake turned his back on the displays. "Take me away. There's nothing for me here."

Nothing for him, perhaps, anywhere in the whole solar system. That defeatist thought grew stronger as they flew on outward from the Sun. It was not a problem of mere physical change—the rings of Saturn gone into the terraforming of Titan, Uranus like a miniature second sun illuminating the outer planets, Pluto basking in new heat to the point where nitrogen was a liquid on its surface and the cryowomb containing Drake and Ana had been moved to a more convenient and cooler location.

More important than all those were the changes that could not be seen. When Drake first heard the words "fourteen million years" he had at once realized some of the implications. The recent news that everyone else in the cryowombs had been revivified strengthened his understanding that he was now what he had once feared he might become: a living fossil, a creature from the remote past. Even the cryowombs themselves were an anachronism, replaced as a method of hibernation by the far easier and more reliable uploading and downloading of minds to and from electronic storage. Drake owed his own and Ana's continued existence in cryform only to Milton's literal and conscientious mind.

And it *was* a mind. He could no longer think of the Servitor as a simple mechanical aide. Considered alone, Milton possessed powers that rivaled those of any single human from Drake's time; considered as part of a composite, the Servitor far surpassed that.

The familiar constellations had left the sky, replaced by new and anonymous patterns. Fourteen million years was long enough for the slow movement of the "fixed" stars to have changed totally the face of the heavens. On the long flight out to the edge of the Oort Cloud (a dizzying coalescence, now, of a hundred million worldlets and interlocking intelligences) Drake struggled to accept his new reality. He had been told by the composite, of which Milton formed one unit, that the science of today was not merely unknown to him, it was *unknowable*. Although science was not the reason that he had been contacted within the cryowomb, there had indeed been progress in the problem of restoring the original Ana. Unfortunately, that progress was in terms strange to Drake. It had been explained five times by Milton. Still, Drake wondered if his misconceptions exceeded his understanding.

He tried once more, as their simulated journey through the new solar system neared its end and Alman appeared unexpectedly on board the ship.

Drake cornered the bald-headed man in the galley, aware even as he did so how ridiculous his own action must seem. Since everything was in derived reality, Alman could choose to vanish as easily and suddenly as he had arrived.

"Milton says that new developments have made it possible in principle to restore Ana in her original form—not merely her body, but her whole personality."

"No." Alman sighed, a wholly plausible human sigh. "That is not what we said. We said that because of changes in our overall understanding of the universe, it *will be* possible in principle to restore Ana in the future. It is a statement of theoretical interest. It is not possible today."

"Then, *when* will it be possible? And what has changed, to make it possible?"

"It is not easy to explain in a way that you will understand. Or to know where to begin, so as to maximize the probability of your comprehension. Perhaps we should start with a question: Do you know the difference between an open universe and a closed universe?"

"No idea."

"I feared as much. And yet the distinction is easy to define. You know that the more distant galaxies are receding from us?"

"Sure. Even in my time most people knew *that.*"

"Then the definitions become very simple. In an *open* universe, the galaxies will go on receding from each other forever. In a *closed* universe, they will one day reverse their outward motion and begin to approach each other. In a closed universe, the end point for that approach is a final collapse to a point of infinite density, pressure, and temperature. Is that clear?"

"Clear, and totally irrelevant. I'm interested in restoring Ana, not in learning cosmology."

"That is understood. Permit me to proceed. Whether or not the universe is open or closed depends on the overall density of matter within it. If that density is too low, the universe must be open. If it is high enough, past a critical value, the universe must be closed. What I say next will seem very difficult to you, and we are not sure that you can ever understand it fully; but the possibility of restoring Ana—your original Anna—depends on whether the universe is open or closed. Hence it depends on the density of matter, or more strictly speaking on the mass-energy density, of the universe."

"You are quite right, I don't understand. But if I did, so what? Either the universe is open, or it is closed." Drake could not conceal his impatience. Once again he became aware that he did not fit well into the present. He was too focused and direct, an atavism in the more polished and diplomatic society that Alman represented. He did not know what the changed physical form of humanity looked like, but his guess was that nails and teeth had gone. He alone possessed his residual claws and fangs.

"Have patience." Alman effortlessly read Drake's anger and impatience. "If your original training had perhaps been in mathematics and physics, rather than in music . . ." The implied criticism was left hanging in the air, as Alman continued, "Certain other things become possible in a closed universe. Such a universe possesses a single, final end point. And at that *eschaton,* that ultimate stage of confluence of all things, the universe itself contracts toward a single point. All timelike and lightlike curves converge there, and everything meets. This was known to scientists and philosophers, even at the time of your own birth. It was sometimes termed the *Omega Point.* Just before the eschaton is reached, all that has ever been known, all information past or present, becomes accessible. Every item of information about people who died a thousand years ago—or fourteen million years ago—becomes available. At the eschaton, every personality that ever existed could in principle be re-created, in perfect detail."

"Including Ana! I understand, I understand exactly."

But Drake was filled with rage, not exhilaration. "If this was known millions of years ago, why the devil was it never once mentioned to me?"

"Because it seemed totally irrelevant. The potential for such future action exists only if the universe is *closed.* In your time, the observations of mass-energy density provided too low a value, by a factor of ten to twenty. That indicated an open universe. Later, scientists decided on theoretical grounds that the universe ought to sit exactly on the boundary between an open and a closed universe. They sought experimental evidence for the missing matter, and they slowly found it. There was still uncertainty; however, they thought that the universe would expand forever, but more and more slowly. In such a case the Omega Point would never exist.

"But that has at last changed. For reasons that we still do not understand, recent measurements reveal a higher mass-energy density beyond the critical value. That points to a closed universe. The eschaton will exist. One day it must be reached."

"And Ana can then return to me. When? When will it happen?"

"In the far, far future. After a time so long that it makes the interval from your first moment of cryosleep to the present day seem less than the blink of an eye. We recommend that you do not even consider such a forward journey. Still less should you attempt it. But your own wishes are important. We seek to know what you want."

"You're crazy!" Drake glared at Alman in disbelief. "You don't know what I want? Why do you think I was frozen in the first place? I want to be with Ana. I'll wait forever if I have to. I don't care how long I have to stay in the cryowomb."

"We feared such a response. We deem it irrational. However, we sense your resolution and the force of your will."

"Good. Then get out of my mind. Let me sleep in the cryowomb until I can *do* something."

"That is not an option." Alman shook his head. Inexplicably, he vanished and Milton at once appeared in his place.

"Other factors must be considered," said the Servitor. "Your preservation and protection is my prime responsibility. That is why I, with some difficulty, overrode your own command within me and disturbed your cryosleep. The cryowomb will not be adequate for your future needs."

"It did fine so far."

"For an interval of only a few million years, yes. At the temperature of liquid helium all biological processes are imperceptible to normal observation. But random thermal motions still exist. A few atoms occasionally gather enough energy to induce state transitions, and those can lead to biological changes. Small changes, admittedly; but mind and memory are very delicate things." The Servitor paused. "Why are you smiling?"

"You sound just like the head of the Second Chance team, arguing long ago for liquid helium over liquid nitrogen. I thought liquid helium was the coldest you could go in practice."

"By no means. Do you think there has been no scientific progress in nine million years?"

"You still sound familiar. I had the same thought myself, long, long ago. So why not keep the cryowomb at a lower temperature?"

"No matter how cold, there would still be occasional random effects. Alteration could still happen. However, there is another way, and a better way."

"Persuade me." Drake thought he knew what was coming.

"Uploading. The conversion of the complete contents of your brain to electronic storage. Even though such storage is not immune to random statistical effects, those can be eliminated using redundancy and error-checking codes. I will vouch for their efficiency—personally."

"How do you know that you don't change? You could be different than you were yesterday."

"And you may not be the Drake Merlin who went into cryosleep, or the same person who met with Trismon Sorel. I can say only this: uploading represents your best chance of remaining unchanged into the far future. It would be painless, and you would be quite unaware that is was happening."

"I'm not worried by pain. There are worse things in the world than pain. What are you leaving out? You sound uncomfortable."

"Possibly." The Servitor hesitated. "I must inform you of one other factor, which we feel is irrelevant but which may appear relevant to you: it is not feasible to upload the complete Ana. Her full genome is already in electronic storage, so future cloning is trivial. But her brain can offer no more than a random chaos of disconnected elements. Their transference would be pointless."

"If I move, Ana moves as well."

"That is really quite unnecessary. If her personality can ever be restored, the existence of primitive brain residues will not be a factor."

"So you say—now. But I've heard too often that nothing can be done for Ana. Move us both, or neither one of us."

"We hear you."

Milton vanished, but Alman at once popped back into existence in his place. "If you insist, we will agree. But there is one other thing to discuss before uploading begins. Once you have been uploaded, it offers great advantages to become part of a composite—a shared mind, large or small. Will you consent to such a merger?"

The decisions so far had been easy. Now Drake had to think. The pluses were obvious: access to a near-infinite array of facts; a better understanding of the new world he had moved into; probably a better ability to comprehend the arcane but important statements that Alman had made about the eschaton and the far future.

But were there also negatives, so well hidden that the composite represented by Alman was not even aware of them?

Drake could sense one, a subtlety that was hard to define precisely. There was a *softness* to this age, a willingness to bend and compromise and take direction. That sounded like real progress for the human species (if that name still applied). But as part of the composite, he would surely find his own anachronistic claws and fangs vanishing, dissolved by the soft pacifism of the group mind. And what was good for today might prove fatal tomorrow. Might there still be a future when polish and diplomacy were useless, where what was needed to restore Ana was raw resolve and crude energy?

It was a risk too big to take. "I don't want to become part of a composite. I'd like to be uploaded and placed dormant in the database. And I'd like to be activated only if there is significant new information about the Omega Point, useful in Ana's restoration."

He had said what he wanted to say, yet it felt incomplete. He knew that he owed a personal debt: to this epoch, to his faithful Servitor, to the people who had finally offered him a distant hope that he might succeed.

"But if you have problems—tough problems, ones that I might be able to help with—then you have my permission to bring me from dormancy and add me to a composite. I haven't had an idea in fourteen million years, but who knows? Maybe I'll get lucky and think of one."

There are worse things in the world than pain.

It was true. Pain can be channeled and concentrated, marshaled and molded, directed to draw some element of the world into bright particular focus. Harsher pain only leads to tighter focus.

But panic, heart-stilling, gut-twisting panic, has no redeeming value. It dissipates rather than distilling. When blind panic roars and surges, all sensibilities are driven out and all concentration vanishes.

Drake awoke to that knowledge. Terror and horror howled from every direction. He could not learn the cause. He found he was blind to everything, deaf to all but the screaming of minds. He tried to order the chaos around him and structure the questions that must be asked: *What is the source of fear? How long has it been present? How far in the future have I come? Why was I not made aware of the problem earlier, before it became urgent?*

It was impossible. The questions formed, and a hundred billion replies came raging in at once. They said everything and nothing, individual vectors combining to give a null resultant.

Drake made a supreme effort. He ignored the torrent of inputs from the countless billions of minds accessible to his, and looked inward to create his own environment.

A familiar room, windowed and comfortable. A prospect beyond it of a windswept, sunlit ocean.

And in the seat opposite, ready to answer his questions—

He recoiled. Instinctively he had thought of Ana, and she sat waiting. But it was the worst choice of all. In Ana's presence he would dream away the time.

Who?

People flickered into the armchair and were as quickly gone. Alman, Trismon Sorel, Milton, Par Leon, Cass Leemu . . .

Tom Lambert. The figure of the doctor stayed and steadied. He shook his head reprovingly at Drake. "Dumb, very dumb. Not your fault, of course, but the composite's. They should have known better."

"Better than what?" Drake saw that it was Tom at thirty, leaner and younger than the paunchy version of their last meeting.

"Better than to wait until the problem was so urgent, before calling you to consciousness and asking you to deal with a full composite. They should have insisted that you go through practice sessions long ago, as soon as you were uploaded, so you would know how to structure and sort inputs in a hurry when you needed to."

"I managed."

"It's more than they deserved." Tom leaned back, pipe and lighted match in hand. He was still in his tobacco-smoking days, shortly before sinus problems had made him give up smoking completely. "Well, let's get down to business. Some of the questions that you asked are pretty damned hard to answer, you know."

"Like what? I thought they were very basic."

"Well, you asked about time again, how many years it is past your upload into the data banks. You know very well that with people buzzing all over the galaxy, or sitting in really strong gravitational fields, everyone's clock runs at a different rate. They use a completely different technique for describing time now, and if I told you how it worked it wouldn't mean a thing to you. Why don't we just agree that however you measure it, it's been a very long time compared with your previous dormancies."

"Agreed for the moment. I want to come back to it later." *A very long time*—compared with fourteen million years? Drake suspected he would not like the answer, even if it could be put into his old-fashioned terms. "Tell me first about the problem. I asked to be activated if you were close to knowing how to bring Ana back to me, or if you had a big problem. Don't bother telling me which one it is—I already know."

"Sorry about that. But it *is* a problem, the very devil of a problem, nothing to do with Ana. We are beyond desperation. To be honest with you, you are our last hope, and a long shot at that. A *damned* long shot. We need a new thought. Or maybe an old thought." Tom's mouth trembled, and the fingers holding his pipe writhed. On the fringes of his mind Drake heard again the faint cry and yammer of countless terrified minds. He ruthlessly suppressed them, building a gate in his own consciousness that admitted only the calmer components.

"Thanks. That's a lot better." Tom took the pipe from his mouth and laid it down on the broad windowsill. "Might be a good thing if I show you directly, don't you think, and let you see for yourself? You know the old advice: Don't *tell, show.*"

"Go ahead."

"We'll begin with the solar system. Hold onto your hat, Drake. And *hey presto.*" Tom clapped his hands. The inside lights turned off. The scene beyond the picture window changed. Suddenly it was dark outside, with no hint of sea or sky. The room hovered on the edge of a bleak and endless void, lit only by glittering stars.

As Drake stared, the scene outside began to move smoothly to the right, as though the whole room was turning in space. A huge globe came into view. It was bloated and orange-red, its glowing surface mottled with darker spots.

"The Sun?" Drake knew the answer even before he asked the question. If he was within the solar system, this had to be Sol. But Sol transformed by time, from the warm G-2 dwarf star that he had known into a brooding stranger. "What happened to the planets? I don't see them."

"Not enough natural reflected light. But I can highlight them." As Tom spoke, bright sparks appeared to one side of the Sun. "That's Jupiter, and that's Saturn."

"And Earth?"

Tom shook his head. "Sol has advanced along the main sequence to its red-giant phase. It's a hundred times its old size, two thousand times the luminosity. If Earth had remained in its original orbit it would have been incinerated, just like Venus. Mercury was swallowed up completely. Don't worry about Earth, it still exists. But it . . . moved. Far away. No point in looking for it. Sol isn't even visible from Earth's present location. If you like I can show you the Moon, that was left behind."

Far away. How far away? Would a human (if there was still such a thing) see today, looking upward from the surface of that distant Earth?

"I had a dream which was not all a dream." Drake muttered the old words as they welled up in his mind. *"The bright Sun was extinguished, and the stars did wander darkling in the eternal space, rayless, and pathless; and the icy Earth swung blind and blackening in the moonless air."*

"Sorry?" Tom's voice was puzzled. "I don't quite grasp what you're getting at."

"Not my thoughts. Those of a writer dead long before I was born. Don't worry about me. Keep going."

"Right. I wanted to start close to home, give you a local perspective, then move out bit by bit. Here we go again."

Sol was shrinking, as the room that Drake sat in backed away into space and lifted high above the ecliptic. The planets of the outer solar system appeared briefly in the plane below as highlighted points. Neptune was there. Pluto had vanished. Uranus, its fusion fires long stilled, formed an invisible cinder no bigger than a Jovian moon.

And the motion was continuing. In another minute the inner edge of the diffuse globe of the Oort Cloud became visible, billions of separate and faint points of light smeared by distance into a glowing haze. "Every one highlighted for the display, naturally," Tom said casually. "Not much sunlight this far out. And of course we're showing just the inhabited bodies. What you might call the 'old' solar system colonies, before the spread outward really began. Wanted you to see that, but now if you don't mind we're going to pick up the pace a bit. Can't afford to take all day."

The outward movement accelerated, accompanied by Tom Lambert's offhand commentary. The whole Oort Cloud was seen briefly, then shrank rapidly with distance from huge globe to small disk to tiny point of light. Other stars with inhabited planets, or planet-sized free space habitats, appeared as fiery sparks of blue-white. The whole spiral arm came into view. It was filled with occupied worlds. The interarm gaps showed no more than a sparse scattering of points, but across those gulfs the Sagittarius and Perseus arms were as densely populated as the local Orion arm. Finally the whole disk of the Galaxy was visible in the field of view. Blue-white sparks extended from the dense galactic center to its wispy outer fringes.

The display froze at last.

"That's the way it stood," Tom said. "It was like that until just one-tenth of a galactic revolution ago. Development, by organic, inorganic, and composite forms, had been steady and peaceful through twelve complete revolutions of the Galaxy. But not any more. Now I must show you a recent time evolution—in terms familiar to you, I will display what has been happening in the past few hundred millions of Earth years."

There was a tremor in his voice, a new hint of uncounted minds quivering beyond the gate and walls imposed by Drake. The static view outside the picture window slowly began to change.

At first it was no more than a hint of asymmetry in the great pattern of spirals, one side of the Galaxy perhaps showing a shade less full than the other. After a few moments the differences became more pronounced and more specific. A dark sector was appearing on one side of the disk, the blue-white points within it quenched by its touch. Drake thought at first of an eclipse, as though some unimaginably big and dark sphere was occulting the whole galactic plane. Then he realized that the analogy was wrong. The blackness at the edge of the Galaxy was not of constant diameter. It was increasing in size, as though something was moving in to invade the galactic disk and growing constantly as it did so.

"As it is today." The display froze and the lights came on again within the room, as Tom continued, "Except that it has not ended. The change continues, faster than ever."

A great crescent wedge had been carved from the display, cutting out almost a quarter of the whole disk.

"The colonies vanish, without a signal." Tom sounded bewildered. "If all the composites in the vanished zone have indeed been destroyed, billions of sentient beings are dying from moment to moment while we are speaking."

"What have you tried?" Drake had his own idea as to what was happening. It was obvious to anyone from his era.

"We have tried many things. We have sent signals in that direction. There has been no reply. We have sent inorganic probes. We have sent ships bearing individual organic units. We have sent ships carrying full composites. Not one of any type has ever returned."

"Were your ships armed?"

"Armed?" The puzzled reply was that of a society which billions of years ago had found aggressive impulses an impediment to progress. There had never been a need for them in the steady and peaceful spread across the Galaxy.

"Armed with *weapons,* Tom. Able to defend themselves if they were attacked."

Tom Lambert's image flickered and wavered, as though whatever was communicating with Drake had suffered a temporary breakdown. Terror bled in from the host of clamoring minds in the background.

"They had no weapons." Tom was steadying again. "There are no 'weapons.' Even that concept has been relegated to remote third-level storage within the data banks. What are you suggesting?"

"Something very simple. This galaxy is being invaded, by something from outside."

"But what?"

"I have no idea. Whatever it is, intelligent or nonintelligent, it is deadly. Even if it doesn't *mean* to do it, it's doing it anyway. It's killing you. You have to be able to defend yourself against its effects."

"We have no idea how to do that."

"I can tell you." To Drake it was the ultimate irony. That he, a dedicated pacifist in his own time, with a hatred so strong of all things connected with warfare that he would not even compose military music on generous commission, should after uncounted eons emerge as weapons adviser to the whole Galaxy . . .

"I have no idea what science and technology is available to you, and I doubt if I could ever understand it. But I don't need to. I'm going to tell you what weapons *do.* And I'll warn you now, you won't like what you hear any more than I like telling it to you. For a start, let's talk about what self-defense means. After that I'm afraid we'll have to start to get nasty."

o　o　o

It came as a surprise, although it should not have.

Drake was working with beings (with or without their inorganic helpers, he was less and less inclined to label them as "humans") who could turn on and off the light of stars, harness black holes for energy sources, and build space colonies the size of planets. In some way totally mysterious to him they had even managed to bypass the light-speed limit for solid inanimate matter, creating odd space-time singularities known as *caesuras* to send objects at high speed to the most remote regions of the universe.

For the composites, once the necessity had been accepted it was easy to produce devices of bewildering destructive power. The caesura singularities, employed as weapons, had the potential to throw structures completely out of known space-time. Drake saw the method demonstrated on whole uninhabited planets. They vanished without a trace. He did not understand the explanation that the bodies were appearing in some other universe, but he felt a strong foreboding of guilt. Without his guidance, these engines of destruction would not exist.

Once they did, the second and more difficult phase had to begin: someone must be willing to use them. It became more and more clear that he alone could be that someone.

There were other problems. Drake had originally assumed that Tom Lambert's reluctance to discuss the passage of time was a deliberate desire to conceal information. Now he realized that he was dealing with beings who would without hesitation agree to spend fifty thousand years in a dormant and uploaded condition during a slow-speed trip across the Galaxy, often subject to considerable time dilation, then follow it by a period in which their electronic forms operated at a rate millions of times faster than that of organic components. In that environment, absolute time had little relevance to anything.

But the consequence of that loss of time-sense had profound effects on what Drake was beginning to perceive as the "battle to save the Galaxy." A ship, armed with its newly developed weapons, would set off for one of the "danger zones" where colonies were winking out of existence. Whether it succeeded or failed, news might not be returned to the Sol center of operations for more than fifty thousand years. It was also not at all clear what those ships were doing, if and when they encountered the unknown hidden force whom Drake saw as Shiva, the impersonal and ultimate Destroyer. No one had the slightest idea when to run or when to stay, when to defend and when to attack.

Drake chafed at the lack of feedback, even as he resented his own role as military commander. Finally, and reluctantly, he accepted the only logical answer. He must force himself to accept a unique and worrying fate. He would be multiply downloaded, so that Drake Merlin—or *a* Drake Merlin—could be sent out to advise and direct on every ship.

Some of them, he knew with absolute certainty, would "die" when the ship that bore them was annihilated by the Shiva. The other copies of him might learn of that death, but they would know it only abstractly.

Would he then be alive, or would he be dead?

Like many of the questions he had asked himself recently, it seemed to have no meaning. He decided that abundant duplication offered at best a prospect of unasked-for immortality, which for him had little personal appeal.

As the ship came closer Drake Merlin looked out onto a barbecued world, a shrunken planet covered with a crisp black coating. He gave instructions to send those images back toward Sol. Moments after he realized that for some reason the outgoing signals were being inhibited, the ship that was carrying him flamed to incandescent atoms.

Drake Merlin was traveling in the second of two ships, following at a safe distance behind the leader. They were in constant communication. No matter what happened, the trailing ship would return across the Galaxy with full information.

The ship ahead moved peacefully on, heading for a star at the very edge of the danger zone. Without warning, fire blossomed around it. It was gone, without a hint of an outgoing signal to say what had happened.

The second ship turned at once. It was not quick enough. As the same fire moved to engulf them, Drake realized that he had answered at least two questions: Whoever and whatever was invading the Galaxy had to be sentient. And the Shiva were malevolent. There was no other explanation for a trap set to catch more than one ship.

The pity was that no one but he would ever know what he had learned.

It was information of sorts. Where a giant space colony had once floated in free space, the sensors now showed nothing at all. However, the nearest star, no more than a light-hour away, revealed subtle changes in its spectrum. There were more metal absorption lines than had been shown in the old records.

Drake pondered strategy as the lead ship turned cautiously toward the star. He had been downloaded to both ships, and his two electronic versions had worried the problem all the way out from the galactic center. Something new was needed. Ship combinations had been sent out before, without success.

When the first ship was within ten light-minutes of the star, the second one released a tiny pod. It lacked a propulsion system, but contained miniature sensors, an uploaded copy of Drake, and a low-rate transmitter.

He hung silent and motionless in space, and watched the approach to the star of the two ships. The first one vanished in a haze of high-energy particles and radiation. The second turned to flee, but a rolling torus of fire arrowed to it from the place where the other ship had been destroyed.

Drake reached a conclusion: the radio link was an Achilles' heel. The second ship should have been at a safe distance, but after the Shiva had killed the first ship they had been able to follow the tiny pulses of communication between the two.

It was the first meager shred of direct information about the Shiva that anyone had ever obtained. It told him that he had to be ultra-cautious in his own transmission. He began to send data out, warily and slowly, varying the strength and direction of the signal. Thousands of receiving stations, all over the Galaxy, would each receive a disconnected nugget of information. When he was finished someone else would face the task of time-ordering the sequence of weak signals, allowing for light-speed travel times, and collating everything to a single message.

Drake sent the pulses out a thousand times, varying the order of the signal destinations. By the time he was finished three thousand years had passed and he had drifted far from the star where his ships had died.

He had no propulsion system. Even now, he dared not risk a rescue signal.

They also serve who only stand and wait.

He waited. For another one hundred and forty thousand interminable years, he waited. The pod contained minimal computing facilities and no other distractions. There was absolutely nothing for him to do.

At last he gave the internal command to turn off all systems within the pod. And in doing so, erased himself.

If Drake had known what was involved, he wondered if he would ever have begun. He examined the large-scale map, and shuddered at what he saw. The region where human colonies were unaffected now formed no more than a thin crescent on the outer edge of the whole galactic disk. The rest, including the dense center, had been eaten away by the Shiva.

And still he had no idea of their motives. Every attempt at communication with them had failed.

But data about the Shiva had been trickling in over the eons, miserably slowly and in tiny fragments. Their vulnerability was at last becoming clear to him. You did not need to know *why* a flame burned, in order to extinguish it.

If you were also convinced that the flame was alive and intelligent, however, you did need resolve. And the Shiva were certainly intelligent. That presented Drake with a terrible problem. Even as they died, the endless trillions of units and composites working with him shrank from the idea of killing any Shiva. It had to be he, in his uncounted downloaded versions, who must unleash the lightning.

He was also forced to make sacrifices, creating tactical hecatombs that he dared mention to no one. His allies, every one of them, would try to stop him if they ever learned what he was doing. As he baited his traps with whole stellar systems, he knew that when those traps closed he would be a murderer on a scale never seen before in the whole Galaxy. He was incinerating billions, hoping to save trillions.

And he finally forced himself to face another unpleasant reality: if all the Shiva in the Galaxy were destroyed, the task would still not be at an end. It was clear from the manner of the Shiva's appearance on the galactic rim that they had come from *outside*. They could return at any time unless they were tracked down and eradicated at their original source. Before Drake's work was complete, humans and their inorganic allies would need to pursue the Shiva, perhaps all the way to the edge of the universe.

Drake sighed, and gave the command to send out another fifty million ships. Each one carried a new and more sensitive set of detectors for Shiva presence; each one bore the caesura generators, weapons that made the first ones he had used seem like a child's cap gun.

Each one guaranteed that two hundred billion more sentient beings, Shiva or human, would die.

The fight had gone on forever. This was not the end, nor even the beginning of the end; but it might be the end of the beginning.

Drake looked at the display, and saw that for the first time in eons the crescent of human control was no longer shrinking. Considered over a span of hundreds of millions of years, a slow oscillation of the boundary could be detected. The Shiva were advancing in places, but in others they were being pushed back or annihilated, star by bloody star. The idea of human survival—even of human victory—could be entertained as a possibility.

And with that possible success came a new problem, of a completely unexpected kind.

Throughout the endless years of the battle, Drake had remained aloof. He would not allow himself to become part of any composite, organic and inorganic, within the interconnected webs of consciousness. Nor would he share his personal data banks with anyone or anything. His logic was simple and invincible: he alone was willing to make the awful decisions of death and destruction needed to defeat the Shiva. He dared not risk any dilution of that will.

For what seemed like forever, versions of his individual self carrying that lonely resolve had been downloaded and sent out on the warships, to meet their fiery or frigid end at the edge of the Galaxy and beyond.

With the Shiva ascendant it had been a one-way process. But now in some of the spiral arms, humans were beginning to hold their own. As they began their own programs of attack and pursuit into the space between the galaxies, and then on through other galaxies, some of the ships were actually surviving.

And some were coming back. On board each of them was Drake Merlin; each one different, each with his own unique experiences, yet each undeniably Drake.

He had held himself apart from all others. But how could he refuse access to himself?

He could not. Drake at last entered a composite. It was, however, a unique composite in which some version of Drake Merlin formed each component.

At first it was total chaos. His element selves numbered in the endless billions; he had long ago lost count of the number of times he had been downloaded, and the total constantly increased. Parts of him were close by, parts were separated from the rest by millions of light-years; some had been partly destroyed in combat, and had become maimed or incomplete versions of a whole Drake Merlin. All, without exception, were now *different*. Time and events had produced changes in form, perspective, even in self-image. Drake struggled to understand, to assimilate, to integrate, and to maintain or create a single personality among that teeming horde of selves.

Through it all, the battle with the Shiva continued. Humans were at last winning. The need for direct oversight by Drake diminished. As the threat of the Shiva receded and the need for his continuous involvement grew less, Drake became increasingly consumed by introspection. He took less and less interest in any external event, unless it was directly relevant to a substantial fraction of his own components.

However, those components were linked to other composites and to other data banks. They stretched out across the galactic clusters and the great rifts toward the edges of the accessible universe, and they told of an evolving and changing cosmos. The dust clouds had been consumed, the supergiant stars long ago exploded to supernovas or collapsed to black holes. Even main sequence stars like Sol were far along in their lifetimes, reduced from their bloated red-giant stage to tiny white dwarfs no bigger than the original Earth. It made little practical difference to Drake Merlin or the other composites; intelligence had long ago migrated to other dwarf stars, only a tenth of Sol's mass. As available energy was reduced, thought and information collection was forced to operate at a reduced rate; but it went on. The slow-burning small red stars provided only a niggardly dribble of radiation, but their energy supply would be sufficient to permit mentation to continue for at least another hundred billion years.

Except that it would not continue. It came as a shock to Drake when the news drifted into his network that the universe itself had passed a critical point. Remote galaxies, always showing a red shift in the past, now showed a slight blue shift. The microwave background radiation, almost infinitely diluted and cooled by the expansion of the universe, revealed a tiny increase in black body temperature.

The Great Expansion was over. The long fall toward the final singularity of the Big Crunch was beginning.

The news stirred within Drake a strange uneasiness. It brought back memories, so far removed in time that they carried no physical impressions. He had to sift, deep within his own oldest data banks, before he found them. Old information concerning the difference between an open and a closed universe had at last become of significance. As information on that subject flooded in, with it also came a searing guilt.

He had forgotten his own most solemn vow.

It was easy to offer justification for his oversight. He had been preoccupied with a battle for human survival, the greatest war in the history of the universe. There had been no time for any other focus. And after the struggle with the Shiva had reached the point where other composites could begin to handle it, Drake had faced what was in many ways an even more difficult task: the integration of his own diverse and dispersed self to a single personality.

He could offer justifications for forgetting his vow; but he could not accept them. He owed to Ana what he had promised her so long ago: her original personality, as he had known and loved it during the only important years of his life, the short but precious years of their marriage.

Somewhere, somehow, he had lost sight of the prime objective. Now it returned, stronger than ever.

A closed universe. Why had that thought been the key to memories of Ana?

By force of circumstance, many of Drake's components had spent unnumbered millennia studying the technology of weapons developed for the battle against the Shiva. With that study had come an understanding of the science that lay behind the weapons. What had been so obscure to Drake in the distant past now appeared obvious to his extended being.

In a closed universe, a final point of collapse lay at the end of time. The *eschaton*, the *Omega Point*, the space-time *c-boundary*—in his own original era it had been given a variety of names, and its main properties had been defined. From his point of view, two of those properties now were paramount. First, as the universe came close to its final convergence the density of mass-energy would increase dramatically and so would the overall temperature, heading for a singularity of infinite heat and pressure; second, and more important for Drake's purpose, close to the c-boundary all information—everything that ever could be known—would become accessible. Everything that ever could be known; and everything that *had ever been known*.

It was what he had been told, long ago. But now he understood in detail what had before been a vague general concept. If he could survive far enough into the future, and gather and absorb enough information there, a time would come near the end when the accumulation would be sufficient. At that time Ana, the true Ana whom he had known and loved, could by his own efforts be restored to him.

He knew it was infinitely desirable. It even seemed possible in principle. But was it possible in practice?

Drake at this point was far from omniscient. He did not know the answer to his own question. Worse than that, his knowledge of the nature of the c-boundary did not offer any idea as to how to begin.

All he could do was collect information and try to keep intact his myriad components. As time went on that became harder. The universe was shrinking. Contact between far-separated elements was easier, and the need for long-term electronic hibernation lessened—but that merely made more important every difference of component outlook and background. Soon he was scrambling, working nonstop to hold a single point of view and a single goal.

Meanwhile, the collection of information could not stop. Drake slaved on, endlessly collecting, collating, comparing, sorting, and merging, while the sky became brighter and the more distant sources of light glowed steadily bluer. Constantly, he was forced to download more copies of himself to deal with increased volumes of data. The number of his components grew steadily. Contact with some of them, entering from far across the sweep of galaxies, was baffling. He had already been

forced to deal with and try to understand the Shiva as part of his information gathering. Now he found some components of his own self no
less alien. The effort of assimilation became greater and greater.

The cosmos shrank faster, imploding toward the final singularity.
The sky had become one violent actinic glare when Drake became
aware of a new presence, a strangely different voice rising to speak from
among his endless sea of selves.

It emerged from the white noise that formed the edge of Drake's
consciousness and steadily approached his central nexus. And as it
neared it seemed to touch and merge with each one of his components.
Even before direct contact was possible, he sensed who it might be. The
thought spread through all of his extended self and resonated there in
wild surmise.

"Ana!"

"Who else?"

"But where did you come from? Can you be real? I mean, to just
appear . . ."

"We've really got to stop meeting like this, eh? I think I'm real." The
cosmos filled with quiet laughter. "I think therefore I am. I think I'm
me, Drake, I really do. But you know the theory as well as I do; as the
universe converges towards the c-boundary, there's no limit to what you
can know about anything. So it's not beyond question that I am just your
simulation, a construct of your mind. *You* think, therefore *I* am."

"You are not a simulation." Drake suddenly hated his own suggestion that Ana might not be real. "You can't be. Don't you think I would
know it if I was creating a simulation?"

"You might. But maybe other powers come with knowledge. I'll answer your question with another: Is self-deception possible, even for an
omniscient being?"

"I don't know. All I can say is it doesn't *matter*. When you are with
me, nothing else is important."

"All right, let's avoid an argument by agreeing that I'm here and I'm
real. So before I do anything else, let me say thank you. Now I have
another question. How much time do we have?"

She had always been the practical one, the clear-eyed realist, raising
issues that Drake was happy to push under the rug. And as usual she was
asking the right question.

Drake looked beyond himself, to the universe that he had been ignoring. It blazed with energy. The cosmic background had become almost as bright as the stars around which the quadrillions of composites
clustered. And still the pace of collapse was accelerating, rushing giddily
on to the final singularity.

"A few more years of proper time, at most, then we'll hit the c-boundary." He found it impossible to worry. Ana was with him, never again would she leave him.

"Is that all?" The visual construct that she had chosen was frowning. "Just a few years? I mean, it's more than I ever expected, but it's not much of a return on investment for *you,* after all your efforts."

"It's enough. We'll stretch it subjectively. We can run in electronic mode and stay out of hibernation."

"I still don't like it." She was inside his mind, gently feeling her way around. It was the delicious touch of knowing fingers, exploring his most private regions. "A few years isn't nearly enough time to get to know each other again. Don't you think you ought to *do* something about it?"

"Ana, you're talking about the end of the universe." Drake laughed, still delirious with his own happiness. He could feel music welling up inside him, for the first time in eons. "It's the end of everything. The Omega Point. That's all she wrote."

"I remember a different Drake. It was you, wasn't it, who once had a quite different opinion?"

Drake knew it was no question. She was teasing him. Ana was well aware who had thought what. And she must have been happily plundering his data banks of memories for longer than he had been aware of her presence, because he had never spoken aloud the words that she said next. *"Science has come so far. Surely no one believes that it can go no farther.* Remember that?"

"That was when there was time, what seemed like an infinite amount of it. Now there's no time. Not for new science, not for anything but us."

"Once you knew next to nothing, Drake, and you were able to work a miracle. Now that you have all the information in the cosmos available to you, who knows what you'll be able to do. The universe is ending because it's closed, right? So *open it.* The knowledge you need already exists. We just have to look."

Ana picked him up and carried him with her. He found himself cascading through space in all directions at once, while ghostly data banks swirled to him and through him, an accumulation of knowledge unimaginable at any earlier epoch. He recognized within them a million bare possibilities; but they were no more than that.

"We can't avoid the eschaton, Ana. It's there. It's a feature of our universe."

"I thought the eschaton only existed in a closed universe."

"It does. If the mass-energy density had been below the critical value, this universe would be open. But the density is too big."

"So. Reduce it."

"That's impossible." Except that before the thought was complete, Drake had seen the way to do it. The caesuras, created so long ago in the battle with a mortal enemy, sat as scattered and forgotten relics across the whole of space-time. Once they had served to eject the Shiva completely from the universe. They could provide a similar function again, for any amount of mass and energy.

She was inside his mind, and she had caught the idea as it came into being. "Well, Drake. What are you waiting for?"

He could not speak at once. He was engaged on a dizzying involution of calculation, every one of his selves operating at its limit. The answer, when he had it, was not one that he wanted her to hear.

"It's still no, Ana. We can dump enough mass-energy into the caesuras to form an open universe. But we would have to go far beyond that to do any good. We need enough structural bounce-back to avoid a final singularity here."

"So that's what we do. You say the caesuras can handle any amount of energy and mass."

"They can." The dreadful irony of the situation was revealing itself to Drake. "But there's one insoluble problem. Information is equivalent to energy. And I—with all my selves and all my extensions and all my composites—represent enough energy equivalence to make the bounce-back impossible. It's the ultimate catch: Any universe that I am in must be closed."

"You mean with the physical laws that apply in *this* universe. What about other universes, the ones that form the end point for caesura transfer? Look at those, Drake."

He was already looking. There was speculation in the data banks, but no solid information.

"Ana, it's still no. Even if we had all the information possible in this universe, it would not be enough to tell us what lies in other universes. There's no way to find out."

"Not true. There's one very good way. We go and see. Come on."

Suddenly they were hurtling through space, faster and faster. Dangerously fast. Relativistically fast. At this speed, a few subjective minutes brought them months closer to the eschaton. The little time they had together was melting away. Drake coordinated his countless selves. All would have to fly, exactly in unison, into the myriad caesura that gaped black against the cosmic background.

At the edge of the caesura horizon, he slowed and hesitated. Mass and energy was swirling past them into the infinite maws, draining from the universe. But as long as he remained here, the final singularity could not be avoided.

"Second thoughts?" Ana was tugging at him, urging him on toward blackness. "Bit late for those."

"Not second thoughts. I was thinking, it would be just our luck to emerge into some place where the laws of physics are too different to permit life—or be thrown to a universe that's full of the Shiva."

"You worry too much." She was bubbling within his mind, an effervescence that he could never resist. *"Life is a glorious adventure, or it is nothing.* You were the one who first quoted that to me. Have you changed so much?"

"I don't know. I can't bear to lose you again."

"You won't lose me." She was reaching out, enfolding him, confident as he was nervous. "Wherever we go, we go together. You'll have me for as long as there is time. Come on, Drake. You always said you wanted to live dangerously, now's your chance."

They were on the brink of the spiraling funnel, close to the point of no return. Ana was laughing again, like a child in a fairground. "Here we go," she said, "into the Tunnel of Love. And don't forget now, make a wish."

"I already did." It was too late to turn back. Ahead lay total, final darkness. Behind them he imagined the radiance dimming, easing with their departure away from the hellfire of ultimate convergence. The universe they were leaving would become open, facing an infinite future. Not bad, for a man and woman who only wanted each other and had no desire to change anything. "I wished that—"

"Don't tell me, love—or it won't come true!"

"Won't matter if I do tell." They were passing through, heading for the unknown, the last question, birth canal or final extinction. Was it imagination, or did the faintest glimmer of light shine in the vortex ahead?

Drake reached out to embrace Ana, squeezing her as hard as she was holding him. "Won't matter if I do, love. Because it already has."